IMPRESSION

*Poison, murder and kidnap unsettle a
godforsaken Yorkshire town*

RAY CLARK

THE
BOOK
FOLKS

Published by The Book Folks

London, 2020

ISBN 978-1-913516-96-3

www.thebookfolks.com

"This is the sublime and refined point of felicity, called, the possession of being well deceived: the serene peaceful state of being a fool among knaves."

Jonathan Swift

Chapter One

Friday 5th August

The station door burst open with enough force to smash glass.

A couple sitting on the bench in the lobby jumped and glared. A poster on the wall fell to the floor, a potted plant on the window ledge tipped over, and the desk sergeant's wish for an easy, late-summer evening all but disappeared.

A distraught blonde and her male companion covered the distance to the counter within seconds. Her eyes were red, her face streaked with mascara. She was slim and short, with blue eyes and a hooked nose like a female Peter Pan. She wore a blue quilted jacket and faded jeans. One glance and he knew her nerves were shot to pieces. She wrung her hands together continually, twisting the ring around her third finger.

"You have to help me," she pleaded, making a grab for the desk sergeant's hand. "My daughter's missing."

The man with her said nothing. He wore a green overall with a badge bearing the name 'Rudstons', and Wellington boots. His flat cap complimented the image of a farmer. He held a rucksack over one shoulder. From the way he comforted the woman, the sergeant guessed she was his wife.

"What's your name, love?" responded Sergeant Williams.

"My name?" she shouted. "Never mind my name." She stepped back, pointing to the lobby door. "We're wasting time while she's out there."

The man put his left arm around her. "Sally, try and calm down."

"Calm down, Gareth? She's out there. Our baby is lost. She could be anywhere, with anyone, and you want me to calm down." She quickly pointed at the desk sergeant. "And why aren't you doing anything about it?"

Sergeant Williams came round to her side of the counter. "Your husband's right, love. You need to keep calm so you can remember all the details."

"Details?" she repeated, at her wits' end. "What details, for God's sake? I wasn't there."

"What I meant was, try and keep calm so you can answer our questions."

She was about to respond, but Williams held a finger up to cut her off. "Please, if you'll just tell me your name."

The woman hesitated before replying. "Sally Summerby."

When it was clear that she wasn't going to introduce the man with her, the desk sergeant glanced at him.

"Gareth Summerby, her husband."

"And your little girl is missing, you say?"

"Yes. She could be anywhere." The woman's voice started to rise again, hysteria taking over. "Please, you have to help. You have to do something."

Williams knew he needed to take control, otherwise they would have little chance of gaining any useful information. By chance, a WPC whose name he wasn't sure of entered the lobby.

"Is DI Goodman in?" he asked the female officer.

"Yes, Sarge."

"Ask her to come through, please."

The WPC slipped back through the doors without question. Sergeant Williams asked Sally Summerby and her husband to take a seat, even though he doubted she would. Sally was too distraught to do something rational like sit down.

The WPC quickly returned with Goodman, who was immaculately dressed in a tight-fitting, knee-length grey skirt with a dark blue blouse and grey jacket. She was slim, with raven black hair and a smooth complexion. She wore little make-up other than a narrow layer of eye shadow and a touch of rose-coloured lipstick. Williams quickly filled her in on the couple's predicament. Within minutes Goodman had them both in an office, asking another officer to make tea for all of them as the WPC joined them.

"Mrs Summerby. I'm going to ask you a few questions. Please try and stay calm—"

"Calm!" shouted Sally Summerby. "Why the hell is everyone telling me to stay calm? My daughter's missing. She's out there, prey to all kinds of maniacs, and you want me to sit here and drink tea and answer your questions. Why aren't you doing something?"

"We are," replied Goodman. "Believe me. But I need answers to some basic questions. My team will then have the information they need to plan the right course of action to find your daughter."

The WPC spoke up. "Please, Mrs Summerby, we will do everything possible to find your daughter, but you have to help us."

Before Sally Summerby could say anything else, Goodman asked her first question. "Can I have your names?"

"We've already given them to the desk sergeant," replied Sally Summerby.

"I realize that, but please bear with me."

Names were reluctantly given. Sally Summerby had taken to biting her nails and fidgeting in her seat. She was very agitated, as Goodman would have expected. Gareth Summerby wasn't.

"And your daughter's name?"

"Chloe."

"How old is she?"

"Five."

"Is she an only child?"

The mother nodded.

"Where do you live?"

"Esholt," she replied. The rest of the information came out in bullet points. "At the bottom of Main Street, the last house on the left. Near the church hall, opposite the church grounds."

Goodman knew it. Esholt was a small village a few miles south of the A65 into Leeds, with a pub, a church, and a café. The rest of the area was residential, surrounded by farms and outbuildings. She suspected from the overalls that Gareth worked for one of those smallholdings.

"Does she have any disabilities, illnesses we should know about? Receiving medication?"

"No, no, no," cried Sally. She slammed the palm of her hand on the desk in front of them. "Please, do something."

Goodman continued. "When did you last see her?"

Sally turned to Gareth. "You saw her at seven this morning, didn't you?"

He nodded.

"He starts work early. She saw him off at the gate." Her voice trailed off as she started to weep. "You have to find her. She's only five years old. She can't survive out there by herself."

Goodman doubted she *was* by herself. "When did *you* last see her, Mrs Summerby?"

"About twelve-thirty."

"When did you find out she had gone missing?"

"Three o'clock."

Goodman was surprised. She continued to make notes. "Where was Chloe in all that time? Where were you?"

"She'd gone to the local playground with her friend."

"Do they normally go without supervision? Were any other parents or adults there?"

Sally grew defensive – more aggressive. "They go together all the time. And the parents take it in turn to watch. We're not monsters, you know."

"Where were *you*?"

"At home, cleaning."

Goodman was unhappy with her answers. "What's the name of her friend?"

Sally Summerby glanced at Goodman with a blank expression, one she couldn't quite read. But by now she didn't much care. What concerned her was the whereabouts of a five-year-old girl who had been out of her mother's sight for at least two and a half hours, time enough for someone to gain a head start if she *had* been abducted.

"Can you tell me her friend's name, please?"

"Masie Turner." As if she had guessed what was coming next, Sally reeled off all the details. "She's ten years old. Her family live on Station Road, the corner house, at the junction with Main Street." Following a pause, Sally added, "Masie is very trustworthy. She always looks after Chloe."

"Do you know whose turn it was to watch the children?"

Sally's expression changed to one of embarrassment.

"Who was supposed to be looking after them?"

Sally pushed a handkerchief to her nose and continued to cry. She said she wasn't sure.

"Has she been unhappy about anything recently, or acting strangely?"

"She's five years old, what would she be unhappy about?"

The interview continued for another ten minutes, by which time Goodman had ascertained what Chloe had been wearing, her relationship with Sally and Gareth and her friend Masie, and *her* parents. Her questioning also uncovered the fact that there were no relatives in the area, so it was unlikely she had gone to any of those, and that Chloe had never gone missing before.

Goodman listed all the places the Summerbys had so far searched without success. They grew very irritated – almost abusive – when she asked if they had searched their own house. She recommended that someone stay at home all the time, in case Chloe made contact or returned.

With tear-stained eyes, Sally Summerby finally added, "Wherever she is, she has her favourite doll with her. It's called Molly."

"Can you describe the doll?"

Sally Summerby broke down again, sobbing loudly. "I just want her back."

Gareth hugged his wife before reaching for the rucksack under the table. He opened it and produced a small picture, which Goodman took to be Chloe holding the doll that Sally had mentioned. She was quick to spot it only had one arm. Goodman noticed Gareth Summerby had also retrieved something else from the rucksack, but held it in his clenched fist.

"How recent is the photo?"

Goodman hoped Gareth would answer. His input so far had been scant. Instead, Sally replied, "Two weeks ago."

She placed the photo in the folder and turned to Gareth Summerby. "Do you have anything to add to what your wife has said?"

Gareth unclenched his fist, and a crucifix dropped onto the desk in front of them.

"God works in mysterious ways."

Chapter Two

The house in Hume Crescent was late 1940s, council built, with modernized UPVC windows and doors. From what Detective Inspector Stewart Gardener could see of the exterior, it was cream painted and in a reasonable condition, but daylight may well reveal otherwise.

Gardener glanced behind him. A number of adults had gathered – not to mention teenagers – on the opposite side of the street near a playground. A rotund woman of indeterminate age stood beside a pram. She had a toddler on one arm with a mobile in her hand. How she managed to light and smoke a cigarette and hold a conversation, all while cradling the baby, was anyone's guess.

Glancing at his watch, Detective Sergeant Sean Reilly sighed. "Midnight on a council estate in the middle of Batley. Can't wait to see what's in here."

"Tell me about it."

Gardener turned to the PC and flashed his warrant card before signing the scene log and opening the gate. The pair walked up the path. A uniformed PC stood on the path to the right of the front door, which was open. The illuminated porch revealed old-fashioned flower-patterned wallpaper with a faded carpet, chipped skirting and a worn doormat.

Sitting on a wooden dining chair to the left of the front door, wrapped in a blanket, was a woman with grey hair tied up in a bun. She, too, was smoking a cigarette. Despite the fact that it was not cold, she was shaking and mumbling, though Gardener made little sense of what she was saying. She'd obviously been disturbed by what she'd seen. He wouldn't be there otherwise.

"Are you the attending officer?" he asked the PC.

"Yes, sir."

Gardener glanced at the lady wrapped in the blanket. "Did she find the victim?"

"Yes, sir."

"Do you know who she is?"

"Next door neighbour. That's her chair and blanket as well."

"Wouldn't happen to know if she touched anything, would you?" Reilly asked.

"I don't think so. She was well shaken when we topped up. From what I can gather, she went through the living room to the kitchen, and came straight back out again."

"And the victim is definitely dead?" Gardener asked.

The PC nodded. "If you'd seen her, you wouldn't be asking that question."

Both detectives went through the usual procedure of donning scene suits before entering the house.

To the right of the porch, Gardener noticed a staircase leading to the upper floor. A door opened to the left into the living room. As he entered, Gardener detected a stale odour, but not from food; more like whoever had lived there had not cleaned up recently. A two-seater settee, and one chair with a small coffee table, were the only items of furniture. No television, only a radio. The green carpet had seen better days, as had the curtains and most of the furnishings – though they were not dirty – simply old.

"Jesus Christ," exclaimed Reilly. He was standing by the kitchen door. They'd been partners for a number of years. Sean had been trained in Ulster and had pretty much seen everything. His reaction told Gardener the scene in the kitchen must be bad.

Gardener joined him, glancing around the room. It was also barren, furnished with only a cooker, a fridge, a washer, and a small table and chairs. A CD player on the window ledge was lit up and working. He didn't recognize the song; something about someone who lived in a town called Millhaven. Apparently, it was small and mean and cold, but if you were around when the sun went down, the roads turned to gold.

"You recognize this?" he asked Reilly, pointing to the radio.

"No, thank God."

Across the cupboard doors were traces of blood spatter. A pool had formed on the linoleum floor. The table and chairs were overturned. In the centre of the room, the victim was tied to one of them, on her back. She was naked. In her mouth was a blue rose.

Gardener counted a number of wounds, any of which could have been fatal. There was no doubt, however, that the killing blow had been the bayonet, which ran through her and the chair, pinning her to the floor.

Chapter Three

Despite the problems it would cause, Gardener realized the crime scene was simple and straightforward – if there was such a thing. It was self-contained within the house, so its natural boundaries could be used to keep it shut. He needed to call his team, but wanted to speak to his partner first.

The song about Millhaven finished and then started again. The machine was obviously on repeat, which he suspected was deliberate. Someone was trying to tell them something.

"What do you think, Sean?"

"The bayonet's foreign to the scene."

Gardener faced his partner. "I agree. There's not much here in the first place, but that still doesn't fit."

He leaned in closer, studying the corpse. He estimated her age as late twenties, but she'd obviously had a rough life, because emotional scars had taken their toll: bags under her eyes; lines on her face. Her grey eyes were open, registering the fact that she had undergone serious trauma. Through her lips he could see white teeth. She'd been proud enough to keep those clean. She had shoulder-length blonde hair, also clean. Her breasts were pert despite the damage done to them from the wounds. Between her legs she was shaved; he wondered what she did for a living.

He counted eight wounds, mostly deep. If the bayonet was the cause of the cuts he wouldn't like to speculate, but he couldn't see another weapon in the room. She had bled heavily from her neck and body.

He glanced at his partner. "You recognize the bayonet type?"

Reilly lowered himself to his knees and studied it. "No. We'll need an expert from the Special Operations Helpdesk at the NCA."

"A weapons expert in antiques by the look of it."

"If it *is* an antique."

"If it isn't, we could be looking at military or service personnel. Could make life difficult."

Whilst Gardener continued to assess the body, Reilly stood and walked around the room. He opened the fridge.

"Anything?" Gardener asked.

"No. Half a bottle of gin and a piece of cheese… and you'd be hard pressed to eat that."

The Millhaven song stopped and started again. "Do me a favour, Sean. Turn that crap off."

"I'll be doing us both a favour."

Reilly didn't touch the machine, but simply flicked the switch at the wall socket. The silence was heaven sent to them both.

Gardener stood up. "What do you think happened?"

"Crime of passion, maybe. Probably male. If he couldn't have her, no one could?"

"Or a madman," replied Gardener.

"Or both."

"I'm trying not to assume here, Sean, but who would want her? Look at the place. Cheap furniture, and little of it. It's not very clean, doesn't particularly smell nice. There isn't much to actually attract a man, is there? She can't even rely on her looks."

"Takes all sorts."

Reilly opened the kitchen drawers. He pulled out three boxes of condoms.

"These might give us a clue," said Reilly.

Gardener thought for a moment. "If that was her game, she can't have earned very much, judging by what we can see."

"Depends who was controlling her."

"Her pimp keeping all the money?"

"Most of them do."

"An unhappy client then?" Gardener asked.

"Have to be something serious to go this far."

"Maybe she wasn't as careful as she would like people to believe."

"Someone paying extra to ride bareback, you mean?"

Gardener smiled. "Stretching things a bit, maybe. We could be getting ahead of ourselves. It may be nothing like that. We need to lock down the scene and get the team here. We need to interview the old dear outside. She'll certainly know something." He stared at the corpse. "Maybe she shares the house with someone else. The packets may not be hers."

"I'm not sure. Looks to me like she lives alone, but even if she was sharing, I doubt that only one of them would be on the game."

Reilly dropped the boxes back in the drawer and turned back to study the corpse.

Gardener drew out his mobile and was about make the call when Reilly pointed to the floor. "Have a look at this."

The scene suit rustled as Gardener joined his partner. He followed Reilly's pointing finger.

He saw what he thought was a piece of foil underneath her right shoulder. He couldn't see enough to identify exactly what it was, so he dropped to his knees and tried to peer underneath. When that didn't help, Reilly crouched down as well and very gently lifted the body in order for Gardener to grab the item.

The photograph was a girl with blonde hair: a child. She was dressed in a red jumper and white skirt. Her hair was neatly combed. She was very young, and in her right arm she clutched a doll.

Chapter Four

Gardener requested his team, a number of operational support officers, the Home Office Pathologist, and SOCO. He also asked for an undertaker.

He turned his attention back to the photograph. "Do you think it's her daughter?" he asked Reilly.

Reilly glanced at the body. "Could be, but then you'd expect stretch marks. This wee young girl's belly is as smooth as the day she was born."

"There isn't much to suggest a child lives here either. No toys." Gardener turned and stared at the fridge. "No magnets. Kids love them."

"No hand-drawn paintings of matchstick people."

Gardener nodded to the corpse. "No wedding ring."

"Not likely to be, if she's what we think she is."

Gardener left the kitchen and headed for the living room. No TV, DVD, or Sky. He didn't see a laptop, either. None of the machines children liked.

Gardener scanned the room. Besides very little furniture, there were no photos, no personal belongings of any kind.

"What are you after?"

"There's no evidence to suggest even *she* lives here, never mind anyone else. She doesn't even have a magazine rack."

Gardener spotted a small pile of CDs next to the only armchair. He picked them up and leafed through. They were mostly female singers: Toni Braxton, Celine Dion, and Gabrielle. So it was highly unlikely that the CD in the other room was hers.

Reilly went back into the kitchen. "Maybe there's a letter rack in here, or something in the drawers." He drew a blank with his search: no letters, no bills, no documents of any kind to give them a clue as to who she was or how she lived her life.

The sound of vehicles pulling up outside, along with raised voices at the front of the house told them the cavalry had arrived. As they stepped out onto the front porch, Gardener saw his own team of DCs: Colin Sharp, Frank Thornton, and Bob Anderson, with support officers in tow.

Gardener greeted and addressed his men, telling them what he knew – which was very little. He requested each of them to head a small team and start the house-to-house process. He ordered DC Paul Benson to go back to the station, contact HOLMES, and pick a couple of rooms they could use. As they dispersed, George Fitzgerald, the Home Office Pathologist, strolled casually down the path as the SOCOs arrived.

"Why is it always me that gets called out after midnight, and always *you* that calls me?"

"Because you're the best, Fitz."

"And we love you," said Reilly. He turned to Gardener. "You forgot that. You know how sensitive he is."

"I thought that went without saying." Gardener smiled. "We've always shown him the greatest of respect."

"Especially at Christmas," said Reilly.

"That's enough," replied Fitz. "Show me the corpse so I can get back to bed."

"See?" said Gardener. "I told you he was the best, no sooner through the door, and he wants to start work."

The SIO pointed to the kitchen. The crime scene manager, Steve Fenton, led his team in. Gardener briefed them and asked if they would start upstairs while the body was checked and removed. That left Constable Edwards at the front door.

Gardener popped his head around and saw that the lady wrapped in the blanket had stopped mumbling. Perhaps she was ready to make a statement.

"Patrick, can you escort this lady back next door, and I'll be with you in a few minutes? We can brush up your interview technique."

Edwards nodded and did as he was asked.

Gardener entered the kitchen as Fitz was rising from the body, checking a thermometer.

"Pretty straightforward. I suspect the bayonet killed her."

"Don't recognize what type of bayonet, do you?"

"Sorry," said Fitz. "Definitely not my area."

"Do you think it's responsible for the rest of the wounds?"

Fitz leaned in closer. "Hard to say. Can't see the blade, but if it's serrated, I'd say yes. Anyway, there's nothing more I can do here, so let's have her down to the morgue and we can start finding some answers."

"Any idea how long she's been dead?"

"Two, maybe three hours."

Gardener asked for the undertaker to come in. Between the four of them – with Fitz overseeing the operation –

they managed to carefully prize the bayonet free. The blade *was* serrated.

Gardener bagged it for evidence, and the body was lifted.

Reilly pointed to an object that had been underneath the body the whole time.

A syringe.

Chapter Five

Gardener shivered, thrust back in time to another case involving a syringe, christened 'The Christmas Murders'.

He retrieved the object, studied it. Although empty, he noticed the inside was coated in a creamy beige compound. It was nothing he recognized, so he passed it to Fitz. The pathologist couldn't help, so he bagged it, and Gardener asked for it to be tested immediately. Fitz nodded, said he could do no more, and instructed the undertaker to claim the corpse.

Gardener asked Reilly if he would oversee that whilst he went next door to interview the neighbour. He stepped outside and removed the scene suit; people were gathering at the playground to speculate, more than there were before. The single mother had remained, still smoking, still on the phone. Gardener glanced upwards. The sky was clear, the night warm, despite the early hour of the morning. On the path, the dining chair had been moved, and the woman who had happened upon the scene was gone. He nodded to the attending officer as he left.

The interior of the neighbour's house was a complete contrast to the one where the murder had taken place. The grey-haired woman was sitting in an armchair near the fireside in the living room. Patrick Edwards was on the settee: both had a cup of tea. The woman glanced at Gardener and smiled.

The room was clean, and smelled of beeswax and other pleasant scents. The curtains were drawn. The carpet had no flaws that he could see. She had a leather three-piece suite. All her decorative ornaments were polished, as were the mirrors that hung about the room. A large display of photographs showed the woman with a man, which he took to be her husband. She was obviously very house-proud, enough not to have smoked inside.

The TV was switched on with the volume turned low. He didn't recognize the programme.

He took a seat opposite the woman, nodding to Patrick Edwards. "Can you take notes?"

"Would you like a cup of tea, officer?" she asked.

"No, I'm fine, thank you. Nasty business, Mrs…"

"Potts. Beryl Potts. You can say that again. I've never seen anything like it in my life. Only on them TV programmes, you know, *Vera* and *Midsomer Murders*."

Gardener smiled. The less said about those, the better. "How old are you, Mrs Potts?"

"Sixty-eight."

He thought she was doing well for that age. She was smartly dressed in a two-piece olive-green trouser suit, and although she had one or two extra pounds around her midriff, she carried it well.

"Are you married?" he asked, glancing at the photos.

"Widow. Five year now. And I still miss him."

Gardener knew that feeling. It was less than two years since he had lost Sarah. Not a day dawned when he didn't think about her.

"How long have you lived here?"

"About forty years." She finished her tea and placed the cup on a sideboard to the right of her chair.

"So you pretty much know everyone in the neighbourhood?"

"I'll say. Know 'em all. Seen a few come and go."

"And the girl next door?"

"Not as well as I know some of them. She kept to herself mainly, didn't really go in for socializing. Well... depends on what you call 'socializing'."

Gardener made a note to come back to that. "What was her name?"

"Stapleton, Nicola Stapleton."

"Do you know how old she was?"

"No. Late twenties, maybe."

"Any idea what she did for a living?"

"I think we all pretty much know what she did to earn money."

Gardener realized what she meant about 'socializing'. He and Reilly were pretty much spot on. "Go on."

"Far be it from me to cast judgment. I'm sure we've all done things we're not proud of, and I've no wish to see what happened to her happen to anyone. But he who lives by the sword will die by it."

Very fitting, thought Gardener. "Are you intimating she was a prostitute?"

"Very much so. Visitors at all hours. I've seen her take as many as six men a night back there."

Interesting, thought Gardener. If you were that good at the game, you could make a lot of tax-free money. Maybe his partner had been right about the pimp controlling her and keeping it all.

"Did you recognize any of them?"

"One or two."

"Did you see any of those men there tonight?"

"No."

"Okay. We'll need names and addresses. When I've finished interviewing, I'll leave Patrick to collect information from you. When did you last see her alive?"

"This morning, about ten o'clock. She was hanging out some washing, mainly her smalls, and when I say small, I'm not exaggerating. You should have seen them."

Gardener decided he probably shouldn't. "Did you speak to her?"

"No. I saw her through my kitchen window."

"What time did she take the laundry in?"

"Not really sure," said Beryl Potts. "Friend of mine popped round for a cuppa about two o'clock. I don't think it was still on the line then."

"Can you describe how you found her, the events that led up to it?"

The woman relaxed, leaned back in her chair. Her eyes grew vacant. Gardener could tell she was reliving the scene in next-door's kitchen.

"Well. It's Saturday night, see, and I usually go out to the social club a few streets away. It's a good club, one of the few surviving in this area. Always have a turn on, and the bingo. I enjoy a game of bingo, but I go mostly for the company."

"What time did you leave the house?"

"Eight o'clock?"

"See anything unusual, then?"

"No," she shook her head. "I locked my front door, turned right at the end of the path and went off around the corner. But I looked over at her house. Her front door was closed, and I couldn't hear any music. Certainly not that awful row that was playing when I found her."

"There was no car outside her house?"

"No."

"So, you went off to the club for a night out. See any people on the streets you didn't recognize?"

She thought, and she hadn't. She'd met up with her friend around the corner and they'd strolled to the club together, which had taken them about twenty minutes.

"What time did you come back?"

She glanced at her watch, something Gardener often found amusing when he asked a question relating to time.

"Be about eleven thirtyish."

"Was her front door open?"

"Yes, and I could hear that music playing."

"Did you go in straight away?"

"No, I came home first. I went into the kitchen and let my little dog out the back door so she could do her business."

Gardener glanced around, but couldn't see the animal.

"And then?"

"I let her back in ten minutes later and I could still hear the same song, which I thought was a long time for one song to be playing. I noticed her kitchen light was on, but the curtains were drawn."

"Go on," encouraged Gardener.

"Well, I went back out front, see? The song stopped and then started again. I was none too happy about it, so I thought I'd go and have a word. Decent people don't want to be listening to that all hours of the morning."

"Did you see anyone else out front?"

"No. Anyway, I went down her path and knocked on the door and called out her name. I never heard her say anything back, so I knocked again, listened more closely. She still didn't answer. I thought about going home. I mean, you don't want to walk in on anyone doing that sort of thing, do you? Could be rather embarrassing."

Gardener could well imagine, especially for a straight-laced widow of five years. "What made you go inside?"

"Well, the fact that she might not have been... entertaining, so to speak. She could have been hurt. It suddenly crossed my mind that she might have had a fall and lay injured somewhere."

Gardener nodded for her to continue.

"Well, that's when it happened. I decided to go in and see if she needed any help. There's something odd about walking through the house of a dead person, especially when they're in there dead. I can't explain, but I knew the minute I'd walked in that something was wrong... something serious. It's like you're walking through a tunnel. Funny, because I don't actually remember hearing the song after that. All I remember is walking through a room where the walls were closing in, and then I was in the kitchen and it was like looking at her through a telescope. I couldn't see anything else, only her body. She had no clothes on. She wasn't moving. Well, she couldn't, could she? She was pinned to the floor. It was awful, the most awful thing I've ever seen in my life."

"I don't mean to be insensitive," said Gardener, "but was she actually dead at that point? You didn't notice if she was still breathing, or twitching a little?"

"Oh, no, she was definitely dead. Isn't it stupid, because I can actually remember calling out her name? I even asked her if she was all right. Don't know why I expected an answer. I mean, how could she? Poor girl had a bloody great knife sticking out of her chest. How could she speak to me?"

"It was shock, Mrs Potts. You can't answer for, or make sense of, your actions when you're in shock. What did you do then?"

Beryl Potts remained silent, and Gardener was about to ask her again when she finally answered.

"I remember saying to her 'I'll get some help, dear. You wait there.' I mean, where else was she going to go?"

"So you came straight out, didn't touch anything?"

"Oh no, didn't touch anything. Couldn't. I just wanted to leave the room."

"And you phoned the police?"

"Yes, straight away. Came back here."

"What did you do then?"

"I don't remember too much after that. I think I went back round and waited outside the door. When your young men came, I was leaning against the wall... crying." She stared at Gardener. "I don't know why. I mean, I didn't know the girl all that well. Why was I crying?"

"Shock," repeated Gardener.

Beryl Potts didn't answer.

"Can we come back to the scene inside the house? I know you didn't perhaps know her that well, but did you know the house well enough to notice if there were any differences?"

"What do you mean?"

"Was there anything missing?"

"No. I don't think so. Well, you've seen the place. Poor dear didn't have anything, did she? Didn't have anything worth pinching, anyway."

"You didn't see anything out of place? Or, in fact, anything there that shouldn't have been?"

"No."

"How long has she lived next door?"

"About five years. Just after my husband died, God rest his soul."

A long time to have a neighbour and not know more about them, thought Gardener, but he understood enough about people to know that some were like that. They kept to themselves. Beryl Potts was apparently one of them. Her husband dying around the time the girl moved in would certainly make it even more uncomfortable for her to want to learn more.

"Where was she before that? Did you ever find out?"

"No, but she wasn't local. Her accent was southern. London maybe."

Gardener nodded to Edwards; that was a comment he definitely wanted investigating. "Any regular visitors that you know about?"

"Only in the business sense."

"Any family?"

"None that I ever saw."

"Did she have a car?"

"No, but there was someone who came to the house almost on a weekly basis. He had a car."

"Someone you recognize?"

She nodded, before adding. "Only because I saw him every week. Couldn't tell you his name."

"Can you give me a description?"

"I'm not very good at things like that. He was overweight, very heavy: short hair, going grey. Double chin, and not always that well-dressed. Looked a bit scruffy."

For someone who wasn't very good at descriptions, she hadn't made a bad job. He'd had a lot less to go on in the past.

"What about the car?"

"Not really. I've never had a car, never learned to drive. My late husband had one, but I sold it when he passed away."

"Would you know the make, or how old it was?"

"I know it was black, maybe four years old. And I think it was a Ford, but don't ask me what model."

"Registration?"

Beryl Potts shook her head. "No, sorry. Like I said, not very good with that sort of stuff."

Gardener nodded. "Is this your own house, Mrs Potts?"

"Yes. Bought it from the council about thirty-five years ago."

In the boom period, thought Gardener, *when the Conservatives had made it possible for council tenants to own their own house at a knock down price.*

"I can't imagine Nicola Stapleton owned hers. Any idea who did, or was it council property, too?"

She shook her head. "I don't think it belonged to the council anymore. None of them do. Nearly everyone round here bought their house. There are plenty of flats that are council-owned, or private landlord."

Gardener wondered if Nicola Stapleton's pimp owned her house. He could do to find out who did.

"Did she live alone?"

"As far as I know."

Gardener paused slightly, before delivering the all-important question. "Did she have any children?"

"Oh no. I think she was a bit too careful for that. Well, I mean, what kind of a person in her line of business would have children? Put a bit of a dampener on things, wouldn't it?"

Gardener pulled out the photograph of the girl he'd found underneath Nicola Stapleton, carefully wrapped in an evidence bag, and passed it over.

"Do you recognize the girl in this photograph?"

Beryl Potts squinted at it before speaking. "Just a second." She reached into the sideboard, pulled out a pair of glasses, drawing the picture in close as she put them on to study it again. "I think I do."

"Who is it?" asked Gardener.

"Do you mean to tell me you *don't*?"

"I'm afraid not," said Gardener, wondering why she would think he might.

"It's the little girl that went missing from Esholt about two weeks ago."

Chapter Six

Saturday 20th August

It was a little after five in the morning when John Wrigglesworth pulled up to the rear of the shops, switching off the lights and the engine. He was late; not that it mattered, he owned the shop.

He ran his hands through his hair and down his face. He was tired. He had taken over his father's business twenty years ago. Little had changed, including the staff. He was sixty-three years old and despite loving what he did, there were times when he considered selling up and retiring.

He sighed heavily as he jumped out of the car, leaving the decision for another day. He was sure his wife and family would be happy to help him with that one.

With the car locked, he walked around to the front of the block. Glancing up at the sky, he saw that dawn had broken. The rest of the shops were in darkness. He doubted their owners had even woken up yet, let alone thought about opening.

A butcher, however, needed to do a lot more than sell his product before his doors were unlocked.

John heard male voices as he approached the main road. Despite the hour they were laughing and joking, obviously on an early shift like him. Turning the corner, he noticed little traffic other than public transport.

Of the two men he'd heard, both were late fifties, one smoking and coughing. Why people lit those things he would never know. Both men were dressed in flat caps and dark blue overalls, with heavy footwear, suggesting the engineering trade. One carried a hold-all, the other had his slung over a shoulder.

"Aye, aye, here he is," shouted one, sniggering.

"Sweeney Todd's got nowt on you, lad."

John had no idea what they were talking about.

"Aye. I often wondered why your pies were so good."

"Looks like your secret's out this morning, John."

"What the hell are you on about?" asked Wrigglesworth. "Have you been drinking? Just coming home instead of going?"

"They've not even bothered to bag it up."

"As fresh as it gets, I'd say." The pair of them continued jibing as they crossed the road.

John removed his cap, shook his head, and scratched it. He strolled past the other shops to his own. He searched his pockets for his keys, mumbling to himself, wondering what the two clowns were talking about.

As he found his keys, he also found his answer.

Chapter Seven

"Can you remember her name?"

"I think she's called Chloe. I remember she's five years old."

"And you've never seen her at the house next door?"

"No. Never."

"Have you ever seen her in the neighbourhood?"

"No. Only on the television and in the newspapers."

"Was there an appeal on the TV with the parents?"

"Yes."

"Did you recognize either of those? Ever seen either of them around here?"

"No," replied Beryl Potts.

That was the last thing Gardener wanted to hear. He'd hoped for something more enlightening, that the girl had been Nicola Stapleton's next of kin, her daughter living with an estranged ex-husband. Instead, all he had was an ever-growing can of worms. But that was his life.

He needed to call the station. Running a check on Nicola Stapleton was important enough, but now he had a *Missing From Home* connected to his investigation, which would be a separate case for another major incident unit with its own DI. He needed to know who was leading the inquiry, and where. Things could become complicated.

He reached into his pocket for his mobile when he heard a knock at the front door. Colin Sharp walked in. Gardener hadn't realized the front door was still open.

"Think we might have a result, sir."

"Go on."

"Lady across the road, number 51. The house at the end of the block."

"Oh, I know her," said Beryl Potts. "Mrs Comings-and-Goings I call her."

"Andrea Jennings, she's called," continued Sharp. "Anyway, she saw a car parked outside the house next door sometime between ten and eleven. Her and her husband had been watching the news. She came outside for a cig."

"She recognize it?" asked Gardener.

"Yes, it was here almost every week. A black Ford Focus."

"That must be the one I was talking about," said Beryl Potts.

"Registration?" Gardener inquired.

"She noticed it was still there about eleven, before her and her husband went to bed. Anyway, she knew the car well enough, seen it there a few times, so she wasn't too bothered. Registration checks out. It belongs to one Barry Morrison. Apparently him and his brother run a car lot on Leeds Road in Birstall."

"Good work, Colin." Gardener glanced at his watch: five o'clock. "So, if we have a registration, we must have an address. Take one of the lads with you and let's see what Mr Morrison has to say for himself."

"That could be a problem," said Sharp.

"Why?"

"The records indicate he lives next door."

Gardener moved onto the front porch, grabbed his phone, and called the station. He wanted a check running on Nicola Stapleton. What did they know about her? Did she have a record? He also asked for a check on Barry Morrison. Finally, he asked for everything they could raise on the missing girl Chloe from Esholt. He apologized for not having a surname, but he doubted she'd be hard to find, as it had happened in the last two weeks.

When he returned, Beryl Potts was still sitting in her chair.

"Did you know this Barry Morrison?"

"No, not to talk to. Like I said, I've seen him a few times, and we may have nodded or said hello, but that's about it."

"Have you seen him here tonight?"

"No. I would have told you."

"Did it look to you like he lived here?"

"No."

"When was the last time you saw him?"

Beryl Potts scratched her head. "I'm not sure. I think he was here last Sunday. Sometime in the afternoon, maybe three o'clock."

"I would have thought car sales had a better chance of business on a Sunday. More people to look round," said Gardener, more to himself.

"Well, I'm not sure, but I think they had a taxi business from there as well. I've sometimes seen him turn up in a taxi."

"Have you ever used his taxi firm?"

"No. Don't go far enough to need one."

"Had you ever seen him and Nicola together? Could they have been an item?"

"Maybe, but whenever I saw them, they didn't look like a couple. Looked more like business to me. I just took him as one of her regulars."

"What about Barry's brother? Ever seen him, or know him?"

"No. Sorry."

Gardener figured he probably had as much information as he was going to receive for now, so he decided to wrap things up. Still, it was plenty to go on.

"Is there anything else you can add to what you've told me, Mrs Potts?"

"I don't think so."

"Well, if you do remember anything, anything at all, give me a call at the station." He passed his card over. "Once the dust settles, all sorts of things come back to people. Doesn't matter how small or insignificant you think it is, it could be very important to me."

She simply nodded.

"I'm going to leave PC Edwards with you for a few more minutes. I'd like the names and addresses of all the local people you know that Nicola Stapleton entertained."

"Some of them are married. That's not going to look so good, is it?"

"They should have thought of that when they were playing away from home. And you've no need to worry, Mrs Potts, it's confidential."

Gardener's mobile chimed. When he answered, he found it was his DCI, Alan Briggs, on the line.

"Stewart, we've got a major problem. I need you over on Cross Bank Road in Batley. The local butcher's discovered a body on the doorstep of his premises."

"But I'm already on a case at the moment, sir."

"I know you are, but the corpse outside the butcher's is directly connected to your case."

"Why? Who is it?"

"Barry Morrison."

Chapter Eight

They found the block of shops within minutes of leaving Hume Crescent. Traffic had been kind to them. Reilly parked the pool car on a side road between the shops and a set of garages. Both officers jumped out.

Colin Sharp pulled up behind. Gardener barked orders to him and the SOCOs to start cordoning off the area.

"I'm going for a walk around the garages," said Reilly.

"Okay."

They both knew from past experience that murderers often returned to the scene of the crime, or, in some cases, never left. If anyone should be hanging around, the Irishman would find him. Or her.

Gardener sighed. He had no spare scene suit, so he had no choice but to risk contaminating the scene. He approached the shop. The corpse was, as described, propped up in the doorway. Standing to the left of the door was the man Gardener took to be the butcher. He clearly wanted to be anywhere but there. He was rail thin and extremely pale. Gardener doubted seeing the corpse would have done that to him. Being a butcher, he had to be used to seeing and handling death every day.

As a matter of procedure, the SIO felt for a pulse. There was none. He glanced around. Four businesses shared the block with the butcher's: a takeaway, a sports shop, a hairdresser, and a newsagent. Each shop had accommodations above; it was more than likely some of the shopkeepers lived in them. He spotted a CCTV camera on a wall at the end. Surrounding the block in every direction was row upon row of council flats, which would hopefully mean witnesses. It wouldn't be an easy task hunting them down, however.

Reilly arrived on the scene. "All clear."

Gardener turned to the butcher. "Is this how you found him?"

"I'm not sure *I* actually found him."

"What do you mean?"

"I were late for work this morning, first time in years."

"What time do you normally start?"

"Four-thirty."

"And this morning?" Gardener asked.

"It were after five. I parked up round the back, came round the corner, and these two blokes were laughing and joking. Reckoned I had a delivery on my doorstep and made some remark about my pies."

"Did you know them?"

"No. But if they're here at this time every morning, I wouldn't see 'em. I open up at four-thirty, go straight into the back and start cooking, so I've no chance of seeing 'em pass at five."

"Did they wear a uniform you might recognize? Bus driver, British Rail?"

"Boiler suits, boots, and flat caps. I reckon they're in engineering, and there's plenty of firms around here."

Gardener thought he might strike lucky with a press appeal for witnesses. Another option would be to post a wooden top outside the shop every morning for a week at the same time, see if it proved lucrative. Other than that, it was going to be bloody hard legwork covering everywhere within a two-mile radius, which would be about as wide as it needed to be if they were walking to work.

"So, what happened next?" asked Reilly.

"Well, I hadn't a clue what they were talking about, so I marched straight over to the shop. I were hoping the place were still in one piece and hadn't been attacked by vandals."

"You get much of that?" Reilly asked.

"Not really. Couple of times over the last thirty years. Nothing I couldn't handle."

"So that's when you found this fella?"

"Aye."

"And you recognize him as Barry Morrison?" Gardener asked.

"Aye."

"How do you know him?"

"Lives in the flat above the shop," replied Wrigglesworth.

"Pardon?"

"I said he lives in the flat above the shop."

Gardener glanced at his partner. Reilly's expression said he was equally as confused. On the drive over, he'd explained everything Beryl Potts had told him.

So, thought Gardener, the house in Hume Crescent had Barry Morrison as the registered owner, yet here they had a butcher with a flat above his shop that Morrison was supposedly renting and living in. How did that work? What was going on?

"How long has he lived in the flat?"

"At least five years."

Gardener turned his attention to Morrison's corpse. The body was half reclining on the door, half lying on the doorstep. He was naked apart from a pair of trousers and a hat. A jacket and a vest were lying beside him.

Gardener glanced at Wrigglesworth. "This is exactly how you found him? You haven't touched anything?"

"No. I haven't touched him or anything else, not even the bloody door. Had my key in my hand but never managed to get it in the lock."

"John!"

The butcher turned around and Gardener followed his line of vision. Colin Sharp was remonstrating with a woman at the end of the block.

"It's my wife," said Wrigglesworth. "Can I go and see her?"

"Not at the moment, I'm afraid."

A number of squad cars pulled up, and Gardener saw more members of his team jump out, including DCs Paul Benson and Dave Rawson. They had with them a number of operational support officers. Each man stopped and waited on the path for further instructions.

Gardener turned his attention back to Morrison. His hands were crossed over his chest, and his wrists were tightly tied together with a piece of cord. The head, neck, chest, and other parts of the body were swollen. His feet were also tied with the same type of cord. The man was grossly overweight, with a double chin, large eyes, a bulbous nose, and thick lips. He had silver hair cut in a short back and sides, as Beryl Potts had described. To say he'd been propped and left in the doorway wasn't true. He'd been positioned. Someone had taken time, had wanted to make the right impression. Though what that was, he had no idea.

"What do you think, Sean?"

"Hard to say. Part of me thinks gangland execution, but that's only because of how he's been tied up."

"Gangland executions are usually more brutal. They'd either have cut his throat or been equally as savage somewhere else on his torso."

"And probably left him alive so he could sing soprano for the rest of his life."

"But there's nothing, is there?" said Gardener. "His body's swollen, but that could be from any number of things."

Gardener produced a pair of gloves from his pocket before reaching down for the jacket next to Morrison. As he picked it up, he noticed splashes of blood covering the fabric. He passed it to Reilly and asked him to hold it up for him.

The SIO studied the jacket, struggling to imagine the pattern of blood spatter he'd seen back at the house where Nicola Stapleton had been found. It was impossible to tell if they matched. He decided he was clutching at straws, perhaps hoping to find something where there wasn't anything.

"Jacket's a bit heavy, boss. You check out the pockets?"

Another car pulled up at the shops. Gardener noticed a crowd of onlookers had gathered. The scene was obviously better than breakfast TV. Fitz stepped out of the vehicle. That's all they needed, Gardener thought. He and his partner would receive a torrent of abuse, as if it was their fault they now had a double murder on their patch in the same night.

He turned his attention back to the clothing. The jacket had two outside pockets. In one, he found an empty purse. The other contained a knife.

Gardener held it up to the butcher. "You recognize it?"

He shook his head. "No, it's not one of mine."

Gardener wasn't pleased. It was the second blade he'd seen tonight. Nicola Stapleton had been pinned to the floor by a bayonet. Barry Morrison had a knife in his pocket. She had blood spatter in her kitchen, he had it on his jacket. What did it all mean?

One inside pocket had a driver's licence, which confirmed it *was* Barry Morrison. The other pocket had a small rent book. Gardener opened it and sighed deeply.

"What is it?"

He showed the book to his partner. Their problems really were mounting. The name on the rent book informed them it belonged to Nicola Stapleton.

Gardener took the jacket from Reilly and held it out for him. "Take a look. What do you see?"

Reilly peered closely for some time.

"Blood spatter. Do you think it's hers?"

"After finding the rent book, there's no reason to think it isn't."

"Do you think he killed her?"

"Maybe, but who killed him?"

"There is another option. *He* didn't kill her, but he was forced to watch."

"That sounds possible. Whoever killed Nicola Stapleton, and for whatever reason, then brings our friend back home and kills him."

"Where? In his flat?" said Reilly. "There's no evidence to suggest he was killed here."

"You're right, but if he was killed in the flat, why go to the effort of dragging the body all the way down the stairs and leaving him here, outside?"

"Make it public. Maybe there's someone else living close by, and the killer wants to send a message. Maybe he or she wants someone to see this, as an example."

"Could be. How did they kill him?"

Reilly shrugged. "His body's swollen, but it doesn't look like he's taken a beating."

"There's no blood to suggest he was stabbed, either."

"Heart attack?" suggested Reilly.

"Could be, but I don't think so."

Gardener examined the body again, noticing Morrison hadn't been shot or visibly wounded in any way. So where did that leave them?

"Maybe he's been poisoned," offered his sergeant.

"That's the best option at the moment. It's certainly nothing visible," said Gardener.

"I don't think he'll be the last, either," replied Reilly. "These two will be the first. Mark my words."

"I don't doubt you."

Fitz approached the body and glanced down at it.

"You two just don't give in, do you?"

"Come on, Fitz," said Reilly. "You're up now, no point going back to bed."

Fitz smiled at the sarcasm. "What do we know?"

"Nothing much," replied Gardener. He took the elderly pathologist through what the butcher had told him. Fitz leaned into the doorway and dropped to his knees for a closer inspection.

Gardener shouted to Colin Sharp. "I want a tent around the front of this shop as soon as possible." Sharp nodded and reached for his phone.

"A tent?" questioned Wrigglesworth. "You mean I can't open today?"

"I doubt you'll be open for the rest of the week, Mr Wrigglesworth."

The relative silence that followed was suddenly broken by a loud whining noise, as if from a lead guitar. The group glanced upwards. Gardener spotted an open window, and determined the music was playing from inside Morrison's flat.

He sighed loudly. He didn't know the song, but did recognize something important about it. Although it wasn't the Millhaven song he'd heard playing at Nicola Stapleton's house, it was definitely the same singer.

Chapter Nine

John Wrigglesworth unlocked the front door to the flat and let both detectives in. Gardener glanced around.

"How many rooms does it have?"

"Four," replied Wrigglesworth. "Living room, bedroom, kitchen, and bathroom."

"Does he live here alone?"

"As far as I know."

The living room was a standard size, around thirteen-feet square. It was clean and smelled fresh – but that could have been from the open window. A brown cord carpet covered the floor. Gardener saw a pair of two-seater settees, a TV, and a Sky system. One wall housed a fireplace with a mirror above it. Other than that, there was nothing to suggest it was someone's home: no personal items, photos, or ornaments.

The song had stopped playing as they approached the front door, but had now started again. Gardener found the CD player and extracted the CD.

"Nick Cave and the Bad Seeds," he said to Reilly. "Who the hell are they?"

"Someone who doesn't rely on Simon Cowell for a living."

The SIO held up the CD: *Murder Ballads*. "You don't recognize it, then?"

"No," said Reilly. "But the title fits. He's doing a fucking good job of killing the songs."

Gardener glanced in the bedroom: one bed, one wardrobe, one chest of drawers, and one chest at the end of the bed. The bathroom contained only the basics. Judging by what was in the fridge, the kitchen was an alien landscape to Barry Morrison. Gardener glanced inside the waste bin. It wasn't full, but the takeaway cartons were mounting.

Reilly opened up one of the cupboards, which contained half a loaf of bread and two tins of beans. Morrison was no chef. Judging by what he'd seen on the doorstep, the man was dangerously unhealthy. The reason why was here in front of them. He preferred eating out to cooking at home.

"When did you last see him, Mr Wrigglesworth?"

"Yesterday."

"How did he seem?"

"He were never any different. Never had a lot to say. Always seemed as if he wanted to be somewhere else."

"What do you mean by that?"

"He were always distracted. He'd stand and talk, but not for long, and I always had the impression he had more than the conversation on his mind. Regularly checked his watch. Always looking over your shoulder... and his."

"Did he ever mention something bothering him?" Reilly asked.

"No. And I didn't know him well enough to ask."

"Why did you see him yesterday?"

"He came to pay the rent."

"What kind of a tenant was he?" asked Reilly.

"Never had cause for complaint."

"Any problems with the rent?"

"None whatsoever," replied Wrigglesworth. "Regular as clockwork, cash on the nail, every Friday."

"Always cash?" questioned Gardener.

"Always."

Gardener glanced around again. Although there wasn't much, the gear was quality. The TV was 4K – very big: too big for the room. Morrison had a Sky Q box, the CD player a Bose Wave. The twin settees were leather Chesterfields. He walked back into the bedroom and sat on the bed. He jumped up again quickly, watching the quilt move for some time afterwards: a waterbed.

Judging by what he'd seen so far, Gardener decided Barry Morrison was a confusing man who didn't appear to have much on the surface. Judging by the clothes he was found in, he gave the correct impression of someone running a taxi office and car pitch, especially with the current economy. Digging a little deeper, though, it became obvious he had expensive tastes for life. All of his gear had to be paid for. Eating out and takeaway meals also did not come cheaply. The problem was, Gardener realized, even being both a car salesman and a taxi driver wouldn't earn him that much.

"Bit upmarket for a cab driver."

"That's what I was thinking," said Reilly. "But he was more than that. According to what people are saying, he and his brother were partners in a car dealership."

"I think we're going to find there's a lot more to Barry Morrison than meets the eye."

Gardener turned to the butcher. "I noticed some garages across the road. Did Morrison have one of those for his car?"

"No, they all belong to the surrounding flats. He generally parked his car round the back, next to mine."

"But you haven't seen it this morning?"

"No, but I never do see it in the mornings. He works the night shift, so he doesn't normally turn up till around nine, nine-thirty."

"Who collects all the mail for the flat? Does it come into your shop?"

"Yes."

"Whose name is on the letters and bills?"

"His, mostly. Some are addressed to me."

"Who's responsible for the bills?"

"A bit of a split," said Wrigglesworth. "The rates are covered as a premises. There's a meter for electric and gas, and he pays me for them."

"Cash?"

The butcher nodded.

Gardener wandered into the bedroom and opened up the drawers in the chest. Most contained small items of clothing: underwear, socks, and shirts. The bottom drawer had letters and bills. Gardener skimmed through them. He saw receipts for items Morrison had bought, paid for in cash.

"Did he have any friends calling on a regular basis?" Gardener asked.

Wrigglesworth gave him a blank expression. "I couldn't really tell you. I didn't know him that well. I worked days, he worked nights. We didn't cross paths that much. When we did, he never said much, but he were always pleasant. I never had any problems with the rent, or otherwise."

"You never saw him with a woman? Small, blonde, mid-to-late twenties?" Reilly asked.

The butcher shook his head. "No. Like I said, I didn't know him that well."

"How did you two meet?" asked Gardener.

"One of my staff used to live above the shop. Eventually he got married and moved on. I ran an advert in the local paper for a tenant. Morrison turned up. He seemed okay to me, and when I found out he had a car pitch and a taxi business with his brother, I thought he sounded professional enough."

"You ever meet his brother?"

"Aye. Bought a couple of cars from him over the years."

"What's he like?" Reilly asked.

"The complete opposite to him downstairs. Slim, works out at the gym by the look of him. Came in the shop regular and bought meat and the like. No rubbish, mind, always the best stuff."

Gardener placed the bills and the letters back in the drawer. Before the day was out the flat would be stripped by SOCO and everything would be given a closer inspection at the station. Something about Barry Morrison did not add up. In fact, something about the whole sordid business didn't add up, thought Gardener.

"Okay, Mr Wrigglesworth, that's all for now. Would you wait outside the flat for a few minutes? I need to talk to my sergeant."

The butcher did as he was asked.

"What do you think?"

Reilly shook his head. "He wasn't killed here."

"No. Too clean."

Gardener glanced around again. "It doesn't make sense. He owns the house that Nicola Stapleton lives in. Yet he chooses to live here in a small flat above a shop. Why?"

"He's hiding something."

"He's her pimp?"

"Maybe, with more like her on the books."

"So maybe it's not a client who killed her. Maybe he did."

"Maybe he *was* a client, and it all went wrong, so he finished her off."

"I wonder why?" asked Gardener. "Perhaps she gave him something."

"Even so, if *he* killed *her*, who killed *him*?"

"And how?"

"Look at all this stuff. None of it's cheap. You don't get stuff like this unless you have plenty of money, or you load up the plastic."

"I don't think it's on plastic, Sean. There's a stack of receipts in that drawer, and the ones I saw were marked as cash sales. The butcher says he paid for everything in cash, so how is this man making his money?"

"Drugs?" suggested Reilly.

"Could answer for the syringe under Nicola Stapleton. So where does the photograph of the five-year-old girl fit in?"

"Trafficking?"

Gardener sighed. "Well, whatever he's doing, it pays well. We both know that to earn that kind of money, it's probably illegal, which covers one if not all of the things we've mentioned."

"Have they both crossed somebody? The prostitute can't have killed him, because the timing's wrong. Which means he could have killed her, and then someone got to him."

"Or someone else killed them both. Judging by the blood on his jacket downstairs, I'd lay odds that he was made to watch, and then taken somewhere else and killed before being brought back here."

"The footage from the CCTV camera at the end of the shops might tell us something."

"And where's his car?" Gardener asked. "Has someone used Morrison's car to do all of this?"

"The brother?"

"Possible," replied Gardener. "Couldn't be anyone else better placed."

"Which could mean a problem with the business."

Gardener nodded. "Unless the brother's straight, and he's found out what this one's into."

Reilly shook his head. "I'm not so sure about that. Blood ties are usually pretty strong."

"The butcher reckoned the brother was the complete opposite. Could be that he's straight-laced and doesn't approve. Maybe it was something that threatened to bring the business down around their ears."

"There's only one way to find out," replied Reilly.

A knock at the door interrupted their conversation. Colin Sharp popped his head around the door.

"Sir?"

Gardener glanced at him.

"Barry Morrison's Ford Focus has suddenly appeared."

"Where and when?"

"Not sure when, the engine's cold. But it's back where it should be – his car lot."

Chapter Ten

Reilly brought the pool car to a halt. Gardener jumped out. Despite it still being early morning, an August sun had risen, and the temperature was already threatening to hit new records.

Gardener had no idea how to fully judge the success of a car pitch, but it was well-presented, with around sixty cars all washed and polished and ready for inspection. Most of the vehicles were family saloons, priced budget to mid-range. In a compound at the back sat another twenty or so cars.

An office constructed of glass and steel stood at one end. There were signs advertising 'We buy cars for cash', as well as a variety of warranty and finance deals available to attract the punters. He noticed two salesmen watching him, probably wondering whether or not he was there to buy. They obviously weren't confident, because neither left the office.

To his right, tucked away in the corner, was a portacabin. Removing his warrant card, Gardener set off in that direction. Reilly followed.

Inside was pretty much like any other office: small, stuffy, and untidy. He saw a desk with a computer and a printer. Strewn across the top were a number of files. Near the window was a filing cabinet. On top of that was the most important thing to any cabby: tea-making facilities. A couple of chairs were lined against the wall, next to another cabinet. A radio on top was tuned to a local station playing classic gold hits.

"Help you two gentlemen?" asked the man sitting in front of the computer.

"DI Gardener and DS Reilly. We'd like to ask you a few questions about Barry Morrison."

"Have you found him?"

"And you are?"

"Prosser, Sid Prosser."

Prosser was overweight, with a face the colour of a ripe cherry and a big purple nose, which suggested he enjoyed a drink or two. Or more. He had a small amount of hair at the sides of his head. He wore jeans and a check lumberjack shirt.

"What do you do here, Mr Prosser?"

"Driver."

"Night shift only?"

"Aye. Look here. Have you found Barry, or what? I've a few choice words to say to him, abandoning his post like he did."

Reilly sat down. "Have you been here all night?"

"Aye, I have."

"What time did you start?"

"Sometime around seven o'clock. Normally it's eight, but I were a bit bored last night, so I came in early."

"Was Barry here?"

"He was."

"What time did *he* start?"

"He doesn't have a start time. You don't when you're the boss, do you?" Prosser reached over the desk for a cup, draining the last of whatever was in it.

"You lads like a drink?"

"No thanks," replied Gardener.

"Mind if I make a fresh one?"

"Be my guest. So, let's get back to last night. Barry was here before you."

"Aye. But he always is. The man's a workaholic."

"It's his business," said Reilly. "You'd expect him to put the hours in."

"There's work, and there's work." Prosser picked up the boiling kettle and threw a tea bag into his cup before filling it with water. "And then there's Barry."

"What do you mean?" Gardener asked.

"Twelve hours a day, seven days a week, fifty-two weeks of the year. He's never away from the place. He works all hours."

Prosser added milk and sugar to his tea before sitting back down in his chair.

"Does he *ever* take a holiday?" asked Reilly.

"I've never known it, and I've been here at least ten years." Prosser added, "He likes his money, does our Barry."

"Can't get much time to spend it."

"Couldn't tell you, but it doesn't look that way. I keep telling him, you can't take it with you. Get some of it spent, take some time off. Go and enjoy yourself."

"Let's get back to last night, Mr Prosser. You started an hour early. How did Barry seem to you?"

"Fine. He was manning the controls, sending one or two of the drivers to various drops. I made him a cuppa. I would have stayed and talked, but he had a run for me."

"Where to?"

"Leeds/Bradford airport. A young couple going on honeymoon. They had to be there by eight. So I got straight off."

"So he was his usual self? You didn't notice anything bothering him?"

"He was fine. He had a takeaway menu in front of him."

"From where?" asked Reilly.

Prosser glanced out of the window and pointed. "Across the road, The Flying Dragon."

The radio on the desk in front of Prosser interrupted Gardener's next question. He quickly directed the driver to another pick up.

"Did he use The Flying Dragon regularly?"

"Every night. He used to place his order around seven and walk across to collect it around nine."

"Is that what happened last night?"

"I expect so. After the airport run, he sent me into Baildon to pick up a couple who were having a night out at that Russian place, Caffe Natta, in Shipley."

"Then what?" Reilly asked.

"That's where it got a bit strange."

"How strange?"

"Most of the drivers had seen him, or they'd at least heard his voice. We never heard anything after ten o'clock. One driver said he'd had no jobs, and he hadn't been able to contact Barry after nine."

"I'll need a list of all the drivers and the jobs they were on last night."

Prosser was about to pour another mouthful of tea down his throat, but stopped.

"Here, I don't like this." He stood up. "Has something happened to Barry?"

"What time did you come back to the office last night?"

The driver hesitated. "Do I need a lawyer?"

"Why? What have you done?" Reilly asked.

"I've done nowt."

"Then you don't."

"But what's with all these questions?"

"You're helping us with our inquiries." Gardener repeated his question.

"I'm not sure. After the Russian restaurant I collected a bloke from Elland Road, and then another couple from the First Direct Arena. It might have been around eleven."

"Do you have CCTV?"

"Aye."

"Good," replied Gardener. "That will show us what time you came back, so don't worry too much. Was Barry here then?"

"No. But he'd been here, that much was evident."

"Go on," encouraged Gardener.

"A half-smoked cigarette was left in that ashtray." Prosser pointed. It was still there.

"That one?"

Prosser nodded. Gardener bagged it.

"And a cold cup of coffee, half full. But I've washed the cup since. The most worrying thing was the remains of his Chinese takeaway. It was left on the desk. A bad sign, that. Barry never left food."

"Where's the takeaway?"

"In that bin." Prosser nodded again, towards a waste basket next to the desk. Reilly checked and bagged it.

"What you doing all this for? Why are you taking stuff?"

"Did you notice at any point that Barry's car was missing?"

"Yes, sometime around ten. I went outside to stretch my legs."

"What did you do then?"

"Came back in here and ran the place by myself. We still had jobs needed doing, and we were a driver short."

"Did you try to contact Barry?"

"All night. Tried to put calls through to his car, but there was no response."

"What about his mobile?" Reilly asked.

"Aye. Tried that dozens of times. No answer."

Gardener thought about that. Barry Morrison did not have a mobile phone on his person or in his clothes when they had found him.

"I'll need his number before we go. Did you call his brother?"

"Aye, called Billy most of the night as well. I thought there must be some family problem."

"What? You couldn't raise him, either?"

"No. But to be honest, he is on holiday. Him and his wife and children are on a long weekend break in the Lake District. He doesn't like to be disturbed when he's on holiday. Well, let's put it this way, his wife insists he turn off his mobile so it doesn't spoil their holiday."

"So you haven't managed to get through to him yet?"

"Not on his mobile."

"Have you tried the hotel?" Reilly asked.

"Not sure where he's staying."

"We have to find him," said Gardener. "Is it likely to be on the computer somewhere?"

Prosser glanced at the screen. "Maybe, but I'm not very good with these things."

Gardener nodded to his partner. "Sean, you have a root around, see if you can locate him." Then he led the driver outside. "Where's the car now?"

"Over here." Prosser directed Gardener to the end of the lot, behind a range of conifers, to the black Ford Focus.

"What time did you notice it was back?"

"About seven this morning, just before I phoned you lot."

"Was the engine warm?"

"I never thought to check."

"Have you checked inside the car, touched it at all?"

"No."

Gardener glanced through the driver's window, careful not to touch anything. The keys were still in the ignition.

"Don't suppose you have any traffic cones, do you?"

Prosser nodded and led him to a small workshop behind the portacabin. There were half a dozen. Gardener and the driver took three each, and walked back to the car. As it was backed up to the wall surrounding the lot, Gardener placed the cones around the front. He then pulled out his mobile and called the station for a breakdown truck.

"I'm impounding the car, Mr Prosser. We'll have a truck here shortly."

Prosser's expression was grave. "Something has happened to him, hasn't it? Is he dead?"

"I would like to speak to his brother first. But tell me, you say Barry was a workaholic. Did he have many friends?"

"Not really. He was a bit of a loner. He'd sometimes go out with the other drivers for a drink, but not often."

"Female friends? A girlfriend, maybe?"

"In all the time I've worked here I never saw him with a woman."

"How did he get on with his brother?"

"Fine. They were like chalk and cheese, mind. Barry couldn't even spell the word exercise, but Billy's down the gym two or three nights a week. They live totally different lives, but they were brothers. They loved each other, and they both loved the business."

"Is business good?"

"We're not breaking any records, but them two have good business heads on their shoulders. A lot of places round here have gone to the wall in the last year, but not us. They used the profit to reinvest in the business, and they always keep something back for a rainy day."

"So they got on okay? Never disagreed or argued?"

"Do you have a brother, Mr Gardener?"

"No."

"I do. Sometimes you get on, other times you argue like cat and dog, but you always love each other no matter what. Sometimes Billy and Barry would argue, mostly over stupid stuff, sometimes over business ideas. But they always patched it up, and they always came out the other side of the argument talking to each other. And where the business was concerned, they always reached an agreement that would benefit the place. I know you lot always look at family first if there's a problem, but if anything has happened to Barry, you'll be barking up the wrong tree with Billy."

"Pleased to hear it," said Gardener. He entered the portacabin to find his partner replacing the receiver of the office phone. "Any luck?"

"Billy'll be back here around two o'clock."

"So will we."

Chapter Eleven

"That'll be £34.61 please, sir."

"Pardon?"

"£34.61."

"I make it £32.21."

"I'm sorry?" said the cashier, whose name badge informed the customer she was called Rachel.

"I think you'll find the amount is £32.21," replied Vincent.

Rachel glanced at the queue forming behind him.

"No point looking at them, they can't help us."

It was Saturday morning – the busiest day of the week – and Morrisons in Guiseley was fit to bursting. Piped music mingled with announcements over the speaker system about the day's special BOGOF offer. Vincent ignored them. They wouldn't force him to spend more money than he wanted.

"Sorry," said Rachel, "but I think you're mistaken."

"One of us is."

The man behind Vincent joined in the conversation. "Look, mate, why don't you just pay the girl, and we can all be off? Some of us have work to do."

"Why should I pay her when she's wrong?"

"It isn't her," said the woman behind the man. "She hasn't added it up. The tills these days are electronic."

"They're calibrated and tested once a week," said Rachel. "They can't be wrong."

"Oh come on, Vincent," shouted someone at the back of the queue. "Do we have to have this performance every week?"

Vincent ignored the last comment, noticing other customers now avoiding the line he was in.

He turned back to the cashier. "Young lady, I am not moving until this is sorted. I don't care if we stand here till five o'clock, or the store closes. A mistake has been made with my shopping, and I want it checked out."

The customers behind him started placing their shopping back into their trolleys so they could move on.

Rachel stood her ground. "There's nothing to check out. All the items have gone through, the barcode has been checked, and the amount comes to £34.61."

Vincent started removing each item from the shopping basket. Glancing behind him, he noticed only one couple in the queue. Other shoppers in other queues were casting suspicious expressions his way.

Vincent didn't care. Right was right. Wrong was no man's right. Life was pretty much black and white. There were no shades of grey – fifty or otherwise – as far as he was concerned.

He was no idiot when it came to mathematics. He could add up faster and more accurately than any machine, having spent a lifetime with horses and bookmakers. No one pulled the wool over his eyes.

With all the shopping back on to the conveyor, he stared at Rachel. "I suggest we go through that receipt item by item, and we find out which one is incorrectly priced."

Rachel's expression grew grim. She couldn't have been more than twenty years of age: blonde, slim, wore a little too much make up. To her credit, she had been polite, and still was. He agreed it probably wasn't her fault.

"I'm sorry, sir, but you' re holding everyone up."

"As I've said, we'll stay here as long as it takes."

The couple behind Vincent moved to another checkout. A voice to Vincent's right joined in the conversation.

"Morning, Mr Baines. What seems to be the problem, as if I didn't know?"

Eric Johnstone, the supermarket manager had made his appearance. He was big and lumpy and his face was bland: his grey suit summed him up perfectly.

"It's this gentleman, sir," said Rachel. "He seems to think we're charging him too much."

"I don't think it, I know it," replied Vincent.

There were more announcements over the speaker system about cheap bargains. He half-expected the voice to boom out "Would the man in aisle six please pay the bill and fuck off?"

Johnstone asked Rachel to tear off the till receipt and pass it over.

"Are we ready then, Mr Baines?"

"I think you'll find I'm right."

Johnstone said nothing. His expression informed everyone who cared to watch that it was a regular occurrence, and he was used to it.

Having gone through the list, the offending item was identified as a thick piece of rump steak – which Vincent was going to have for his tea – with a yellow ticket on it. Instead of the reduced price, it had gone through at full price, which was exactly £2.40 dearer than it should have been.

With a satisfied smile, Vincent paid his bill, repacked the items, and replaced them in his basket. He chose to say no more about it, and even thanked Rachel for her patience and her time.

On leaving the superstore, his attention was suddenly diverted when two women walked by, discussing what sounded like a double murder in Batley, both bodies having been discovered during the night.

Chapter Twelve

Sitting on a low wall in the furthest corner of the car park gave him a bird's eye view of everything. Beside him was a copy of the *Sun*, opened at the crossword page, with a pen laid across the top. He was comfortably dressed in a grey quilted jacket, black jeans, and a flat cap.

His current position in life was not so good, but on reflection, it never had been. His clothes were stolen, as was the money in his pocket. He had nowhere he could call home save a small room in a hostel three or four miles away, and even there he had to take great care.

He observed a number of people enter the supermarket. As they did, the man he was waiting for came out. He was a little over six feet tall, thin as a rake. His hair was silver and clustered, like a knot of wire wool balls. His long, pointed nose came out of the shop before him. He still wore clothes that were so far out of fashion they were back in again; today was a brown pin-stripe suit.

Raymond Allen smiled as he observed Vincent Baines leave the store: some people never changed.

Chapter Thirteen

Chris Rydell glanced around the surgery with a feeling of trepidation. The room was clinically clean, and full of expensive medical equipment at the forefront of modern technology.

His gaze came to rest on the specialist sitting opposite. Mr Trent studied his notes. Chris noticed the personal file on him had grown much thicker a lot quicker than he'd anticipated. Trent was mid-fifties, tall, dark, and slim, with white teeth, and a glass eye. He lowered the document, glancing up at his patient.

"I'm really sorry, Mr Rydell, but the treatment doesn't appear to be working as well as I'd hoped."

Chris had expected the news. He wasn't stupid. He'd had to live with the condition for long enough.

"I had hoped the latest drug would have stabilized the deterioration of your liver."

So that's what it had come to. His liver had finally called it a day.

Chris stared at the ceiling, sighing. Everything had been explained to him during previous meetings: new drugs were available, one or two of them still in the experimental stages. If he agreed and signed the proper forms, everyone would be happy for him to enter into trials. He was unsure.

Chris allowed his mind to wander to six months previous. The reason for his first visit was flu-like symptoms: a slight fever, shivering. That had grown more serious with periods of confusion and drowsiness, which had affected his working life, resulting in a couple of dangerous near misses on the road. That he couldn't have.

Chris had been sixteen when he took up warehouse duties for a parcel courier company. He kept the warehouse tidy, helped sort through the collections, and loaded the vans for the deliveries; often asking for the delivery manifest to load up the van in reverse, to make life easier for the driver.

When he was old enough, the company had put him through his test. He'd finally started driving and delivering. With a new contract for the medical board, Chris delivered drugs and medicines to the local chemists and hospitals, but it wasn't enough to keep the company afloat. Several cutbacks were made, staff and vehicles to start with. Eventually, they went under; everyone lost their jobs.

Chris's father had persuaded him to go and talk to the man responsible for the medical contracts – to strike while the iron was hot. Chris had enough money to buy a new motorcycle, and as a gesture of goodwill, the people that worked for his father constructed a trailer for the back of his bike.

Chris visited the man with the contracts, persuading him that he would do the job for a fraction of the price the original parcel company had negotiated. He pointed out that he had the experience, because it was him who had made all the deliveries, so he knew the ropes and the locations. He was given a trial.

Within five years, his business had grown, and he'd invested the profits in his little empire by purchasing new bikes and phones, attributing each of them to the different contracts he was picking up. They kept him busy six nights a week. Now, his success was under threat again.

A knock at the door broke his train of thought.

Trent glanced up as the receptionist came through with another bunch of files. "I'm so sorry to bother you, Mr Trent, but you did ask for the results of the latest blood test as soon as possible."

"Thank you, Mrs Pendelbury."

"You're welcome." She smiled at Chris on the way out.

Trent read the results before turning his attention to his patient. "There really is no easy way to say this, Mr Rydell, but you're entering a phase of complete liver failure."

Trent paused. "There is something else we can try–"

Chris cut him off. "Is there any point?"

"There's always a point, Mr Rydell. I wouldn't be doing my job if I didn't explore every avenue."

"Let's put it another way, shall we? Is it going to cure me?"

Trent stared at Chris, taking his time to answer. "Some drugs work better than others. Everyone's immune system operates differently."

Politician's answer, thought Chris. *I ask a direct question, and he gives me anything but a straight response.*

"I don't need to hear all that. What I want to know is, will your latest drug cure me?"

"I can't say, but–"

Chris leaned forward. "I'm sure you can, but you just don't want to."

He reached down to a rucksack on the floor, removed five bottles, each containing different pills. He placed them all on the desk, making sure each one of them was symmetrically placed next to the other.

"Those haven't worked. And those were all the latest stuff. Now, I'll ask you again. Is your next alternative going to cure me?"

"There's no reason to think it will be any less efficient than the ones I've already prescribed."

"Well it couldn't be, could it?"

"We have to try, Mr Rydell."

"And if I don't want to?"

"I really would advise against that."

"Like I said, what if I don't?"

"I'm sure you don't need me to tell you what would happen. You may live six months to a year longer with the drug, or indefinitely if it works."

"And how long if I don't?"

Trent sighed. "I'm sorry, I can't answer that."

"Give it a go."

Trent sat back. "At best… maybe a month."

"What symptoms can I look forward to now?"

"Very unpleasant ones."

"Humour me."

It was obviously against Trent's better judgment, but he did as Chris asked. "Depending upon how quickly the liver failure develops, you will probably start to itch excessively as bilirubin starts to accumulate in the skin. Bilirubin is a waste product from broken down red blood cells that is normally metabolised in the liver. I can help with that."

"I wouldn't bank on it."

"I can administer cholestyramine, which sequesters bile acids, and we can supply a menthol cream which soothes the itching."

"Wonderful. Carry on."

"As bilirubin accumulates, the whites of your eyes will turn yellow, followed by the skin. Your urine will become dark orange, but your stools will be pale, almost white."

Chris smiled. That would make a change from stools that resembled a Jaffa Cake.

"You really don't want me to go on, do you, Mr Rydell?"

"That's why I'm here. I'm not leaving until you tell me everything."

"I suspect the brain will be affected next, as various toxins accumulate in the blood. It's possible you will suffer seizures, and then pass into a coma, or just become comatose straight away. By this time, you will be in hospital, because you will probably die within a few days. Or maybe hours.

"During all of this, and especially if the process is slow – taking several days or weeks to happen – your legs and abdomen will swell up as fluid comes out of the blood and accumulates in the tissues, because the liver normally makes plasma proteins which help maintain the fluid levels in the blood by an osmotic effect."

Chris managed to work the last bit out for himself. "So this would also affect the brain, adding to the risk of fits, then a coma, and then death."

"You don't have to go down that road, Mr Rydell. I will continue to do everything I can for you."

Chris stood up and offered his hand. "I appreciate everything you *have* done, but we both know that the end of the road has come."

He gave Trent no further time to answer as he confidently strode towards the door.

Chapter Fourteen

Gardener and Reilly were sitting in an interview room in Trafalgar House on Nelson Street in Bradford, waiting to speak to DI Karen Goodman. Sergeant Williams had shown them through. He'd assured them they would only have to wait a few minutes.

During their time waiting for Goodman, the pair of them had tried to assess the events of the morning. If Nicola Stapleton or Barry Morrison had taken Chloe Summerby, where the hell was she? Judging by their lifestyles, neither would want her. Living arrangements were a mystery. He had a house he rented to a prostitute and holed himself up in a pokey flat.

But if Stapleton or Morrison hadn't taken her, who had?

Gardener glanced up as the door opened, revealing a slim lady with black hair and an oval face. She was dressed in a royal blue trouser suit and white blouse. She had a thick folder tucked under her left arm.

"DI Karen Goodman." She extended her right hand. "How can I help you?"

Gardener introduced himself and his partner before returning to his seat. He reached inside his jacket pocket and retrieved the photo of the girl.

"I believe you're investigating a *missing from home* involving the young girl in this picture."

Goodman glanced at it. "Chloe Summerby, yes. Where did you get this?"

"She's come up in our murder investigation."

Goodman ran her hands down her face. "I don't think I'm going to like this."

"She's not the victim," assured Gardener. He briefly related his case and what he had so far discovered.

Goodman opened her file and showed Gardener one of the photos they had of Chloe. She asked if she could keep the one Gardener had.

"I'm afraid not, but I can get you a copy."

Goodman nodded. "Okay."

"When was the girl reported missing?"

"Just over two weeks ago, August fifth."

"What happened?"

"Her mother and father came barging into the station about seven o'clock on the Friday night. The mother, Sally, was pretty distraught. What mother wouldn't be?" Goodman continued with a brief version of the night's events.

"So, what did you do?" asked Gardener.

"It's a tricky one with a missing child. You really have to calm the parents down, ask questions. They hate you for it. Think you're not doing anything. They shout and swear and tell you their baby is out there, could be in all kinds of trouble, and you're doing nothing. Some of them start that before you've even asked for a name."

"I can imagine," said Gardener.

"It's the usual stuff to begin with. Full name, age, description, what she was last seen wearing."

Gardener glanced at the two photographs on the table. In each one her clothes were different, which made him wonder when they were taken. Which of the two was the more recent?

Goodman continued. "It seems she had a good relationship with her parents. There were no brothers or sisters, so they doted on her a bit. She was last seen with a friend."

"What was *her* name?"

"Masie Turner," replied Goodman. "The pair of them went to the playground in Esholt. I asked who was responsible for them at the time Chloe went missing. There was apparently a bit of a misunderstanding between a number of the parents, with each one thinking someone different was supposed to be watching. Turns out no one was."

She passed Gardener a file with both girls' names and their addresses. Reilly took notes.

"You don't think they wanted some time on their own, do you? Made up a small white lie about who was supposed to be in charge?"

"Masie claims not. We've asked her a dozen times. Her story checks out, same every time."

Goodman continued with her summary. "Chloe was pretty healthy. No disabilities, not on any medication. All relatives have been contacted."

"Had she ever gone missing before?" Gardener asked.

"Not according to the parents. She didn't seem unhappy about anything, and she hadn't been acting strangely."

Goodman flipped open her mobile and asked for three coffees to be delivered without even asking Gardener or Reilly if they wanted one. "Then we really went into action. We contacted all the hospitals, local schools, other police stations. We broadcast a description to patrols indicating the area she was last seen. We made sure the mother stayed home twenty-four seven, in case Chloe made contact or returned."

"Has she?"

"No. Not a thing. The area CCTV have all been informed and given a description. Within six hours we made a broadcast on the local radio stations. We also set up a twenty-four-hour TV alert and a major incident unit."

"And you haven't seen or heard anything?" Reilly asked.

"No," said Goodman. "It's as if the girl has completely disappeared."

The door opened and a WPC delivered the three warm drinks. Each officer nodded their appreciation before the conversation resumed.

Gardener didn't want to ask the question, but he'd lay odds it had run through Goodman's mind more than once. "Do you think she may be dead?"

"I'd be lying if I said I hadn't thought about it, but as yet we have no body to confirm that. So we have to keep looking."

"Somebody must have seen her," said Gardener.

"I agree, but either *we* haven't found *them*, or they don't watch TV, listen to the radio, or read a newspaper."

"Nobody could be that brain dead," offered Reilly.

"You wouldn't think so," said Goodman.

Gardener felt slightly guilty. He hadn't heard or read anything about it, either, which had surprised Beryl Potts when he'd interviewed her about Nicola Stapleton. He dug out the crime scene photo of the prostitute and asked Goodman if she recognized her.

"No. Can't say she's come up in our investigation. What's her name?"

"Nicola Stapleton."

Goodman shook her head.

"So she's definitely not a relative?"

"Not as far as we're concerned," said Goodman. "Take it someone had a grudge against her."

"You could say that."

"And you say the photo of Chloe Summerby was underneath her?"

"Yes. So now we know Nicola Stapleton has nothing to do with your investigation, someone has obviously put it there for a reason."

Gardener then passed over a photo they had found of Barry Morrison, which had been given to him by Sid Prosser. "This man ring any bells? His name's Barry Morrison, runs a car lot and taxi firm in Birstall."

Once again, Goodman said she didn't.

Gardener figured as much. A gut feeling on the drive over here had told him they could well be wasting their time.

"Well, thank you, Detective Inspector. We're going to need a single point of contact from each team for the incident room meetings."

"Yes. Leave me your mobile number and we'll get something sorted straight away. I'll arrange a meeting for tonight and let you know the details."

"In that case, can we have your officer in Leeds in an hour?"

Goodman nodded, and said it shouldn't be a problem

Before leaving, Gardener asked another question. "I take it you didn't suspect the parents? No foul play?"

"No. The mother's pretty sound," replied Goodman. "Not so sure about the father, though."

"Oh?" questioned Reilly.

"I hate to say this, but he's a bible basher, a bit of a strange character. He never said a word when they came into the station. He put his arms around his wife a few times, but he never said anything. Before finishing the interview, I asked him if he had anything to add, and he simply said 'God works in mysterious ways'."

Gardener and Reilly glanced at each other.

"That it?" pushed Reilly.

"That's all he said."

"Do you suspect *him*?" asked Gardener.

Goodman sighed and spread her arms wide. "I've certainly had my doubts, but he has a cast-iron alibi. He was at work all day."

"Doesn't mean he isn't involved," said Reilly.

"I know, but we haven't found anything to support the theory... yet."

Chapter Fifteen

Following a light snack back at the police station, Gardener glanced around the incident room, pleased with Benson's efforts. The ANACAPA charts and the phones were in place. The HOLMES team were next door.

Murder was never a good thing, but Gardener always cherished the start of an investigation: the fresh challenge, recruiting a team that would become an extension of his own family.

He loaded the charts with the various crime scene photos: a range of shots featuring Nicola Stapleton and her kitchen. She and Barry Morrison covered most of one board.

On the second board he placed the photo of Chloe Summerby. He had a bad feeling about her. It was very difficult in today's world of social media to disappear off the face of the Earth without someone knowing something. Who had her? Where was she? Why was she connected to a murder investigation?

He glanced at his watch. The door opened, his team filtered in, chattering. Most were carrying files. Each man took a seat. The Operational Support Officers were still out gathering evidence. Reilly slinked in last, chewing an apple.

Before he closed the door, DCI Alan Briggs slipped in, accompanied by an officer Gardener had never seen before, which he took to be the SPOC. Briggs introduced her as Sarah Gates. The lady was mid-forties with a tanned complexion and red hair cut fashionably in a bob. She wore a navy skirt, with a crème blouse and a blue leather jacket. Gardener started immediately following the introduction, determined to cover as much ground as he could.

"Thanks for coming back, lads," continued Gardener, detailing the discovery of the victim in Hume Crescent, and concentrating on the weapon used to kill her. "It's very unlikely that a prostitute would keep a bayonet in the house."

"Depends on the punters, I suppose." The comment came from Frank Thornton, a six-foot rake of an officer with thinning grey hair. His frame reminded Gardener of a

POW. He was divorced and Gardener doubted that he overindulged in the kitchen.

"They can't be that bad," replied Reilly. "Not even in Batley."

Gardener smiled, before continuing. "It's not a common choice of weapon. We've requested a weapons expert in antiques from the National Crime Agency to come and give us a professional opinion. These guys can do great things with ageing metals and tracing origins. But while we're waiting for him, does anyone know anything about bayonets? Recognize it at all?"

"My old man has a First World War bayonet hanging from the wall in his man cave," Dave Rawson said.

Reilly laughed at the statement. "A man cave? What the hell is a man cave?"

Dave Rawson had the build of a rugby centre forward, with short black hair, and a beard and moustache, neatly trimmed. Gardener really liked his positive mental attitude to the job: whatever task he was given, he would do. Good or bad, it was all work to him.

Rawson smiled. "I'm not really sure. I've never been allowed in." That remark brought an even bigger laugh, which embarrassed the behemoth of a man.

"How do you know he has one, then?" asked Bob Anderson.

"He told me. Used to tell me as a kid that if I didn't behave, I'd get to see it, no question."

"Does he know much about weapons?" Gardener asked.

"I don't think so. I don't even know where he got it. You want me to go and ask him if he can identify ours?"

"It's worth a stab."

The room erupted with laughter, and Gardener realized what he had said. "Okay, okay, let's get back to business."

"Any sign of a struggle? Forced entry?" asked DCI Briggs.

"Forced entry, no," replied Gardener. "I suspect it was a client she simply let in." Gardener turned and pointed to the photos. "As you can see from these, there was definitely a struggle. Table and chairs all overturned."

"Neighbours hear anything?"

"She lives in an end house, so there's only one. A widow named Beryl Potts. She was out from eight till sometime around eleven."

"So, we're relying on the witness statements," said Briggs. "Still, should be enough of them, looks like a council estate."

Gardener nodded. "The prostitute's name is Nicola Stapleton. She lived on her own, and according to the woman next door, the only visitors she had were her clients. She did, however, have one regular visitor by the name of Barry Morrison. No one yet knows what the relationship between the two was, but I will come back to him shortly.

"Seems unlikely that Stapleton had any family, or if she did, she didn't talk about them. She had a southern accent, so I think that's worth pursuing. I know you're already into the house-to-house inquiries. I want you to continue with that, gather what you can. Somebody on that estate will know something about her. Maybe more than one. Perhaps each one knows a little bit of something different, which might lead us to a bigger picture."

Gardener turned, updating the board with his assignments, so Reilly took over. "Woman next door reckons a number of married men in the area have been making nocturnal visits. We have names and addresses for you to follow up. We'll be unpopular, but if we add a bit of pressure, we might be surprised by what we find."

Gardener continued. "A couple of things worry me. First is the number of wounds. When people tend to kill with a knife – or other bladed weapon – it's either one fatal wound, or the killer goes mad and hacks the victim into pieces. We counted eight."

"You think he or she was playing with her?" asked Thornton.

"Torturing for the fun of it?" added Reilly. "It's possible. Maybe they tied her to a chair and went into some big explanation of why they were doing it. Stabbed her every time they felt like it."

"Or maybe when she displeased them. Or answered a question wrong," Gardener countered. "Anyway, it's all supposition at the moment, but there's enough to feed it into HOLMES, see if anything similar is out there. The other thing is the blue rose in her mouth."

"That struck me, too," said Colin Sharp. "I didn't know you could get blue roses."

"I didn't," said Gardener. "So that's another point worth following up. Can you get blue roses? Is it something the killer had to make specifically for a reason? If so, how did they do it? What did they use? If not, where did they get it? You can see where I'm going with this."

Gardener pointed to the syringe. "One last item, that I think may play a very important part of the investigation, was found underneath Stapleton's body. We don't know yet what was in it, but I've asked Fitz to analyse it and feed back the results."

"Was she a diabetic?" asked Rawson.

Gardener knew Rawson was. "I don't think so, Dave, but Fitz will tell us more."

"Probably drugs," Bob Anderson pointed out. "You know what prostitutes are like. Granted, a lot of them do it to make ends meet. They don't want to. But to the rest of them it's all about the money. The more outrageous you are, the more money you get. Maybe the syringe and the bayonet were all part of what she was into."

Bob Anderson was a solid, dependable officer who could always rely on in a crisis. His frame was bulky, and he was balding, some hair at the sides turning silver. He was married with a son and daughter, who had produced two children each, making him a proud grandfather.

"You're probably right, Bob," said Gardener. "After all, it is the oldest profession in the world. But I doubt very much it was the case with Nicola Stapleton. The carpets, the curtains, most of the furniture come to that, had seen better days. I wouldn't say they were dirty, just old. The fridge in the kitchen was near empty apart from a bottle of gin and some cheese. Looked to me like she was living in abject poverty."

"Did she meet the wrong bloke, then?" suggested Thornton. "He wants something special, a bit of bondage, maybe? She doesn't agree, so he nails her to the floor."

"Bit extreme. Why leave the bayonet? Surely he knows it could condemn him."

"Maybe he's not bothered," said Reilly. "Anybody using a bayonet in such a manner is probably a psycho anyway."

"Might account for the CD that was repeating itself," added Gardener.

"What CD?" Colin Sharp asked. Detective Constable Colin Sharp was a very dedicated professional with a dark complexion, a deep resonant voice, and premature balding. He lived in Horsforth with his wife Jenny. Gardener thought Sharp was an excellent investigator, very thorough, with an unrelenting passion for digging into someone's past. Any task he was given generally yielded excellent results.

"Something called *Murder Ballads*. Some of the most God-awful music I've ever heard. Anyone recognize it?"

"Who's the artist?" Thornton asked.

"Nick Cave and The Bad Seeds, they call themselves."

"I recognize that name," claimed Dave Rawson. "Aussie band. I went out with a woman once. A goth, lived near Whitby."

"The hell were you doing seeing someone up there?" Reilly asked.

"They're all used to him over here, he has to go further afield now." The comment brought a few cheers and jibes.

"Fuck off," shouted Rawson. "I'm trying to help here. Anyway, if you'll all shut your cakeholes, she used to listen to him all the time. Want me to look into it, boss?"

"Please. Go down and the see the exhibits officer. Sign it out, copy it, and then reseal it in a different exhibit bag number. Just record what you've done and why. Pay particular attention to a song about a town called Millhaven. That's the one that kept playing at the scene."

Gardener pointed to the board and the photos again.

"I just want to say a bit more about the syringe. I'm curious about what was on the inside. It was coated in a creamy, beige-looking compound. Seemed quite thick to me. Not what I would have said was your average drug."

"You think there's something new on the market?" asked DC Colin Sharp.

"I hope not," said Gardener.

"I'm surprised you managed to see that much in a syringe," said Rawson. "Normally nothing left."

"That's what worries us," said Reilly.

"I don't think we need to concentrate too much on the contents, at least until we find out what it is. Just keep your eyes and ears open. My main concern is the victim. Who was she? Where does she come from? Who were her clients?"

"Finding her punters might be a major problem," said Anderson.

"She must have a mobile," offered Sharp. "Surely that would tell us something?"

"We haven't found one yet. In fact, we found very little at her house, but I have a couple of officers going through the place, bagging everything up. Hopefully by the next incident room meeting we will be able to tell you more. What I'd like you guys to do is get back out into the field and collect and collate all the information from the Operational Support Officers. Bring it back here, load it into HOLMES, and let's see what happens."

Gardener let the dust settle before his next statement. Very rarely did he have a double murder in the same night to contend with. He could only ever remember it happening twice in his entire career, and both occasions were an absolute nightmare.

"Which brings me to victim number two."

Chapter Sixteen

"Barry Morrison was a fifty-two-year-old taxi driver and part car lot owner from Birstall." Though the team knew some of the details, Gardener relayed it again for the sake of the SPOC: when, where and how they found Morrison; and the information the butcher had provided – that Morrison rented the flat above the shop, was a model tenant and paid the rent using cash, every week without fail.

"What was the flat like?"

"Not a lot in there, but what we saw was very expensive. Most of his stuff was top of the range, and I found some receipts indicating everything was paid for in cash."

"Cab drivers don't earn that much."

"No, but we still need to speak to his brother. He was obviously more than a cab driver and, according to one of the drivers we spoke to at the lot, they were not breaking records. Kept their heads above water. However, the same driver mentioned that Barry Morrison was a workaholic."

"You think he might have been running some illegal little sideline that could have paid for that lot?" Briggs asked Gardener.

"Probably. Just a case of finding out what."

Eager to return to the scene, Gardener pointed to the photos on the board. "As you can see, we found his body half reclining on the door, half lying on the doorstep. He was naked apart from a pair of trousers and a hat. A coat and vest were left on the doorstep next to him, and we're pretty sure they were his."

"Any idea who or what killed him?" asked Thornton.

"No, not yet. There's very little bruising, and despite the fact that it looks like a possible gangland execution, I'm ruling it out. I've sent his jacket for forensic testing, because when Sean and I had a closer look at it, we could see blood spatter patterns."

"So, he was killed somewhere else and dropped there later," said Anderson.

"Yes. There's definitely no evidence to suggest that he was killed where he lay – or that he was killed in his flat. There are CCTV cameras at the end of the block. We're just waiting for them to roll in. But there are a few things with Barry Morrison's murder that really concern me.

"Look closely at the photo. You can see his hands were crossed over his chest, and his wrists were tightly tied together with a piece of cord. His feet were also tied with cord. The head, neck, chest, and other parts of the body were found to be very swollen, but there were relatively few marks anywhere."

"A bit like a ritual killing," said Anderson.

"Maybe. That's an action for you guys. See if you can find anything where the victim's hands and feet have been tied in the same way."

"Maybe he was poisoned."

"It's possible," replied Gardener. "Fitz has the body down in the morgue, we're hoping for his report pretty quickly." He turned back to the board. "In his pockets were an empty purse, a knife, a driver's licence, and a rent book… which had Nicola Stapleton's name on it."

"The prostitute?"

"Yes."

"Do you think *he* killed her?" Briggs asked. "Maybe his illegal sideline involved her. Something went wrong, they had an argument, he lost his rag. Seems strange him having a knife in his pocket and blood spatter patterns on his jacket."

"It crossed our minds. Forensics are testing the knife. We're putting two and two together, but hopefully Fitz will be able to tell us the blood groups of both him and Nicola Stapleton. If we're lucky, we might find the blood on his jacket matches her group."

Sharp spoke up. "But if he killed the prostitute, who killed him?"

"Good question, Colin. That's what Sean and I have been wondering. We're going to speak to his brother Billy. He's been away on a weekend break with his family. He's on his way back now.

"But the reason we don't think Morrison killed Stapleton is because he turned up for work as usual last night about eight o'clock. However, there was a noticeable radio silence from around nine o'clock. One of the drivers – a man called Sid Prosser – popped back around eleven. There was evidence that Barry had been there, because he found a half-smoked cigarette left in an ashtray and a half-full cup of cold coffee on his desk. The partial remains of Barry's Chinese takeaway were also left on the desk, which was a bad sign. Barry never left food. He usually went across the road to The Flying Dragon, so that's another place to visit. There was no sign of forced entry. Barry's car was missing. Sid Prosser continued to run the operation himself, whilst trying to locate Barry."

"I take it he didn't speak to him," asked Briggs.

"No."

"When was the car brought back to the pitch?" Sharp asked.

"About seven this morning," added Reilly.

"So, it's possible somebody killed them both and used Barry's car to ferry them around."

"Yes. I've had the car impounded for further testing."

"Do they have CCTV at the car lot?"

"Yes, we've collected all the tapes, but we simply haven't had the chance to check them yet."

"I reckon somebody defo did 'em both," Patrick Edwards spoke up.

"That's what we think, because there is yet another connection that ties up both scenes. One of the windows in Morrison's flat was open. Within minutes of us finding him, a CD player started cranking some more of that Nick Cave stuff."

"Same song?" inquired Rawson.

"No."

"There was definitely a third party involved here," said Briggs.

"Did we find a mobile with Morrison?"

"No," said Gardener. "And we couldn't find one for Stapleton. So someone really is trying to cover their tracks. It's all the usual stuff to begin with until we build a picture: forensics, witness searches, passive data. We need the CCTV evidence. I have two more officers at Morrison's flat collecting everything they can lay their hands on. Once it's all back here, I need someone to go through it all, start joining the dots. I also want someone doing the rounds of the factories to see if they can find the two men who found the body."

"What was the address on the rent book that Morrison had?" asked Anderson.

"The house the prostitute was staying in on Hume Crescent," said Gardener.

"So he owns the house, then?"

"It would appear so. I logged a call with the council this morning to check their records of when and whom it was sold to. They confirmed it was an ex-council property."

"How long had Morrison lived in the flat above the butcher's?"

"About five years."

Gardener glanced at the ANACAPA chart, and then at his team.

"This case will be a nightmare. It's only the second time I've run a double murder investigation, and the last one was no picnic. Once we've cleared the grass from under our feet with the evidence gathering, I think we'll end up in a TIE strategy."

"What's a TIE strategy?" asked Patrick Edwards.

"Trace, Interview, and Eliminate. They're a bit difficult to explain, Patrick. I'm not insulting you when I say I'll try and keep it simple. Imagine the population of the world. You know your killer is among this group of people, but you want to narrow the search down a bit. So you need to come up with a set of parameters, which still may contain a number of individuals, any one of which might be your killer. You can have more than one group – in fact, you normally have several.

"So, if we start with the prostitute, you'd have a group of her clients. You'd have another group of people known to have visited her flat. You'd probably also have a group of known registered sex offenders, or RSOs, linked to the area – and so on. Our hope would be that the killer would be among one of these groups of people somewhere. It's like having lots of different bags of stones, and in one is a gold nugget.

"I'll set action teams off in tracing these groups of people. So, as an example, Action Team One would have 'go find everyone who has been to her flat in the past two months'. The team would draw up a list, then go and interview each individual to account for their movements during the relevant time of the murder, and usually a few hours either side. When someone says, 'I was with my wife during this time', the action team will go and confirm this information with his wife. So effectively, we'll take one stone out of the bag, tracing, interviewing, and then eliminating each one in turn.

"For the ones we can't eliminate, they stay in the bag until everyone else is out. Hopefully we'd be left with only a few stones in the bottom, which need a closer looking at. Our *persons of interest.* In amongst these may be our killer."

Gardener studied the team. He knew how much work was already involved, but sadly, he wasn't finished.

"I'm afraid we have one more very serious connection to the murders."

Chapter Seventeen

Gardener pointed to the photo of the girl on the second ANACAPA chart, before introducing Sarah Gates.

"Sarah works for the West Yorkshire Police at Trafalgar House, on Nelson Street in Bradford. They're investigating the abduction of Chloe Summerby, headed by DI Karen Goodman. Sarah is our *single point of contact*, because Chloe now has a connection to our double murder."

Gardener nodded to Gates for her to take over from there.

Gates stood and cleared her throat. Sensing something serious was coming, Gardener's team took notes. "Chloe Summerby is a healthy five-year-old girl. Her only recent ailment had been chicken pox. She is talkative and intelligent, well liked, has a number of friends, attended and loved the school in the village. Like most girls of five, she has a stack of dolls that she would play with, but her favourite had only one arm. It went missing with her. She likes picture books, and educational games on the family computer."

"When did she go missing?" Sharp asked.

"A little over two weeks ago."

"From where?" asked Bob Anderson.

"Chloe and her parents – Sally and Gareth Summerby – live in the village of Esholt, a few miles from the A65 at the bottom of Main Street, the last house on the left opposite the church. The village is small, rural, with a pub, a church, a café, a playground, and a post office. The rest of the area is residential, or surrounded by farms and outbuildings. In other words, everyone knows everyone else.

"On the morning of her disappearance, she waved her father off to work at seven o'clock. He's a farmhand on one of the nearby farms. Her mother allowed her to go to the playground on Church Lane at ten o'clock with her ten-year-old friend, Masie Turner.

"Masie and her family live on Station Road, in the corner house, which is located at the junction with Main Street. They both came back, had some dinner, and then Sally told them both to make sure Chloe returned from the playground by three o'clock so that they could go to the nearest ASDA store for a weekly shop. The girl did not return. She was never seen again."

"What about her friend Masie?" asked Sharp.

"Masie said she and Chloe left the playground at about two-thirty. When they reached the crossroads in the village, Masie watched Chloe walk down the lane towards her home, before going into her own house.

"Sally realized she'd become so engrossed in her housework, that she hadn't noticed it had gone three o'clock and the girls still hadn't come back. She went out to look for them. They were not where they said they would be. She called on Masie's mother before finally jumping in the car and touring the village and the outlying lanes, eventually calling the police. A search of nearby barns and outbuildings was set up almost immediately, all to no avail. Chloe Summerby has not been seen since."

"Wasn't anyone watching them, supervising?"

"There should have been," replied Gates. "I think there was a breakdown in communication. When we questioned the adults in the village, no one claims to have been watching them, but each adult was clearly under the impression that one of them should have been."

"I take it you've asked all the usual questions?" asked Thornton. "No one suspicious hanging around the village? A place as small as that, as you say, everybody knows everyone's business."

"No one saw anything. No one saw her taken. No one's seen any suspicious people, or strangers hanging around."

"And no one's seen Chloe," added Reilly.

"What connection does she have to our investigation?" Briggs asked Gardener.

Gardener pointed to the board. "That photograph was found underneath Nicola Stapleton's body. Her neighbour, Beryl Potts, said she had never seen the girl at the house, or in the neighbourhood. She only knew who Chloe was because it had been in all the newspapers. Goodman also ran a campaign on the TV."

Sarah Gates had a number of A4 envelopes with her. She began handing them out as she continued. "I've prepared notes for all of you to save a bit of time. The main points of the case are all in these envelopes. There's one for each of you."

"Is Chloe Summerby related to either of our victims?"

"No," said Gates. "Not as far as we know."

"Have we asked her mother?"

"DI Goodman called her immediately after your officers came to Bradford. Sally Summerby has never heard of Nicola Stapleton, or Barry Morrison."

Chapter Eighteen

Billy Morrison was standing by the desk in the portacabin. He wore a white tee shirt with slim fitting jeans and a pair of *Reebok* trainers. He was trim, carried no extra weight. He had a full head of jet-black hair, blue eyes, and his smooth complexion spoke of a healthy diet.

His expression, however, was haunted, and Gardener had seen it before. He'd be expecting bad news, but still hoping his brother may have been picked up on a minor charge, perhaps be home in a few hours.

Following introductions, Gardener asked Morrison to take a seat.

"That bad, is it?" he said, trying to make light of it.

"Please," said Gardener, also sitting. Reilly stood near the window, glancing out at the pitch.

"We were called to an incident at five o'clock this morning, Mr Morrison," said Gardener. "The butcher's shop on Cross Bank Road."

"John Wrigglesworth's, I know him well. Our Barry lives above it."

"Yes, we know."

Billy Morrison suddenly decided to straighten his stationery, before asking, "You lads want a cuppa?"

"No, thank you."

He collected all the mugs and put them near the tea-making facilities. "Neither do I, to be honest." He turned to face Gardener. "I think you better tell me what our Barry's been up to."

"I'm sorry," said Gardener. He truly was. He hated delivering bad news to anyone, especially if a relative had died. "We were called to the shop because the butcher had found a body in his doorway. We got there as soon as we could. It would have made no difference. I'm afraid your brother Barry had been dead for quite some time."

"Dead?"

Gardener knew Morrison had heard correctly, but it would be some time before it sank in.

"Yes. I'm so sorry. The Home Office pathologist estimated his time of death at sometime between midnight and two o'clock."

Morrison glanced down at his hands and started to rub them together. "Are you sure it was him?"

"He was positively identified by Mr Wrigglesworth."

Reilly turned away from the window, studying Billy Morrison.

Gardener wasn't sure if he would speak again, so he asked, "Would you like us to call someone for you? Or maybe you'd like to see a family liaison officer?"

"No. I'm okay."

"What about your wife? Should we contact her?"

Morrison stared at the ceiling for some time, tears forming in his eyes. Gardener could tell he was struggling to remain composed.

"It's never easy to tell someone they've lost a close family member," said Gardener. "I realize it's a difficult time, but I really do need to ask you some questions."

Morrison still stared at the ceiling and mouthed the words 'Stupid bloody fool' through gritted teeth. Gardener wasn't sure to whom he was referring, but he doubted it would be a senior ranking police officer. Reilly pulled out a pad and pen.

Morrison turned his gaze to the window, and eventually started talking. "Stupid bloody fool. I told him. I kept on telling him, not to work too hard."

He glanced at Gardener. "I always thought he'd work himself to death, you know. He never stopped. He'd be in here at about six o'clock. He'd work right through his shift, and when I came in around eight, he'd still be here, just wanting to finish one more job. Whether that be filing, or keeping records straight, or doing an airport run.

"I always reckoned that when he left here, he never bothered sleeping. He'd just carry on working somewhere else. He was a bit obsessed with money, even when he was a lad. He was always after making a bob or two, always up to some scheme or other. He never used to sit still. When we were teenagers, most of us were out chasing girls. Not our Barry. As far as he was concerned, there was always money to be made."

"Were you partners?"

"Yes, different roles. I run the pitch. He ran the cab business. I have a couple of lads working for me. He had five."

Gardener was pleased Morrison was opening up. He had to make the best of it, because he had no idea when the shock would hit. "And how is business?"

"Oh, you know, up and down. We're scraping a living, not breaking records. Last few years have been tough. An uncertain Brexit and the price of fuel means we sell less cars by day, and less cab rides by night. People are either not going out as much, or they're choosing to walk home. You only have to read the news to see pubs are closing every day."

"But you're not in any financial trouble?"

"Oh, God no," said Morrison. "We make sure of that..." He stopped mid-sentence and composed himself.

"No. No financial trouble. We were partners, and we both ran the business economically. We didn't waste money, or spend it unnecessarily. We always put plenty away in the good times. You see, neither of us like letting people go. It's tough enough out there so we always made sure there was money in the account to pay the drivers and the salesmen. We could both miss a wage or two if necessary."

"So Barry had no money worries?"

"None that I know of."

Gardener wondered how much they would discover that Billy didn't know about Barry.

"Did he ever seem distracted to you, bothered about anything?"

"Our Barry? No. He was just a bloody workaholic. He would live, eat, and breathe work. He was always the same, happiest when he was working. Never took holidays. Don't get me wrong, I've seen him in a mood. Mainly when he was younger, when he had little or no money. When we were setting this place up, it was hard work, I can tell you."

Gardener pictured the flat, and the luxuries in it. He also thought about the receipts, but he still couldn't figure out why Barry had chosen to live *there* and not the house that he owned. Or what his connection with the prostitute could be.

"Did he do anything else apart from work here?"

"Like I said earlier, I always thought he might. But to be honest, I doubt it, not the hours he put in here."

"How long has he lived in the flat above the butcher?"

Morrison breathed in, back out again. "About five years, I think."

"Where was he before that?"

"He was in a bit of a shithole in Beeston. Terraced property, full of druggies, always getting burgled. I wanted him out of there. So I made him come and stay with us for a while. Three, maybe four months, but he couldn't settle. Kept saying he wanted his own place."

"Did he have many friends visit while he was staying with you?"

"No. Always been a bit of a loner, our Barry."

"Any friends visit here, the cab office?"

"No, most of the friends I know about actually work here."

The telephone rang, but Morrison ignored it.

"I would like a list of everyone who works for you. Names and addresses."

"Why? You reckon it might be one of them?"

"Procedure, Mr Morrison. We have to eliminate everyone from our inquiries. I will also need a list of all the jobs the drivers were on last night."

"Sid Prosser can sort that for you. Where's our Barry's car gone?"

"We have it."

"You have it? Why?"

"It's part of the ongoing investigation. How much has Sid Prosser told you?"

"Not a lot."

"Did he tell you that Barry's car was missing from around eleven last night and didn't return until seven this morning?" asked Reilly.

"He said something about it. Apparently, our Barry had been out of contact since around ten o'clock. Sid reckons someone might have pinched Barry's car, and Barry went out looking for him. Have you got our CCTV tapes?"

"Yes," said Gardener. "They're being analysed as we speak."

"So, what happened to him? You haven't said yet."

Gardener ignored the question. Reilly stepped in.

"Did he have a girlfriend?"

"Barry? You must be joking."

"Nobody? You don't reckon he could have had someone and you not know about it?"

Morrison thought about the question, and Gardener could tell from his expression there were things that didn't add up.

"It's always possible, but I doubt it. Our Barry was a man of routine. Money was the love of his life, though God knows how he ever managed to find the time to spend it."

"You ran the company with him," said Gardener. "You must know what his salary was."

"Why do you ask?"

"Because we searched his flat, and he had some very expensive equipment in there, including a waterbed."

"A what? A waterbed? What the hell would he want with one of them?"

"Apart from the obvious," said Reilly. "I gather they're very good for enhancing other aspects of your life."

"By other things I take it you mean women. You're barking up the wrong tree, mate. If our Barry had a waterbed, it was because he had a damn good night's sleep in it. I've never seen him with a woman... or a man, in case that's what you're thinking."

"There was also a big state-of-the-art TV, hi-fi equipment, and a number of other receipts for expensive items, all paid for in cash."

"Like I said, he didn't really have any money worries. He was a partner in the business and drawing a good wage, and I suspect that flat didn't cost him much, so maybe he saved his money and spent it wisely."

"The butcher said he paid the rent every week on the nail, also in cash."

"Maybe he did. He was never a big lover of the banks, our Barry."

"I don't like to ask the question, Mr Morrison, but do you check the business account regularly? Is it possible that large sums of money have gone missing that you can't account for?"

"I never check them, but all it takes is one phone call. We have a man in Leeds who looks after the accounts for us. His name's Frank Fisher."

"And no doubt he would have told you if something was amiss. I appreciate you'll have a lot to do, but can you call him and let us know the outcome?"

"You still haven't said what happened to him, yet."

Gardener noticed that Billy Morrison was becoming agitated, and he knew that he was going to have to tell him the truth, but he wanted to continue building a picture.

Reilly stepped in again. "Did he ever mention the name Nicola Stapleton?"

Billy turned to face Reilly. "Who?"

"Nicola Stapleton," repeated the Irishman.

"Never heard of her."

"What about a house in Hume Crescent, Batley?"

"What are you two not telling me?"

"You didn't know a woman called Nicola Stapleton who lived in a house in Hume Crescent in Batley?"

"I've just told you. Why the hell would I?"

"Your brother owned the house."

Billy Morrison stared hard at Reilly. "Owned? Our Barry never owned no house in Batley. Are you trying to tell me he was shacked up with some bird on the quiet, and he never told me?"

"We don't know," said Gardener. "That's why we're asking."

Billy Morrison immediately checked his computer. Gardener suspected the cab company had regulars, and that he was searching for addresses.

"She's not on the system. Who is this woman?"

"According to her neighbours, she was a prostitute."

"A prostitute? Well, there you are then. Every bloke has needs. Our Barry obviously pays this woman for what he wants…" Morrison stopped to think for a moment before continuing. "Wait a minute. You said, according to her neighbours, she was a prostitute. So you haven't spoken to her? She isn't dead as well, is she?"

"I'm afraid so," replied Gardener. "We were called out to investigate her death at midnight. Before that was brought to a satisfactory conclusion, we were called out to your brother. During the course of the investigation we have found a link. His car was regularly seen round there, at least once a week. We've since discovered that he owned the property."

Billy Morrison was shocked.

"What the bloody hell's going on?"

"That's what we're trying to find out. And I appreciate it's a tough time for you, but if you want us to catch your brother's killer, we have to keep asking questions."

"Well I keep asking you lot one, but you never answer me. What the bloody hell happened to our Barry? I have a right to know."

"We're not sure yet."

"What do you mean, you're not sure? Was he shot, stabbed, beaten up, what?"

"When we found him, his body was leaning against the door, half lying on the doorstep. He was naked apart from a pair of trousers and a hat. We found a coat and vest left on the doorstep, which we believe were his."

"Naked?" repeated Billy Morrison. "Five o'clock in the morning and our Barry's on his own doorstep, naked. Had he been drinking?"

"No," said Reilly. "We certainly couldn't smell any booze on him."

"And he wasn't beaten up?"

"Not from what we could see."

"So how did he die?"

"We'll have to wait for the Home Office pathologist to tell us that. But here is what we do know. Barry was at work last night from around seven o'clock. There was no contact with him from ten o'clock when Sid Prosser popped back and found the place empty. A cigarette was left in the ashtray, and food on the counter. Barry's car was seen at the house in Hume Crescent between the hours of ten and twelve. The only time your bother was seen was early evening when Prosser spoke to him, and five o'clock this morning when he was discovered."

"You ever have any trouble with punters?" Reilly asked.

"Depends what you call trouble."

"Fare dodging, drunks throwing up in the cabs, cars being vandalized?"

"It's a taxi business. We certainly have our fair share of the first two. We've always told the drivers if you have somebody dodging a fare, jumping out on you and making a run for it, let 'em go. We had a couple of incidents years ago where drivers gave chase and ended up being stabbed.

One died. We told them all, 'don't bother, it's not worth your life and it will never come out of your wages.' Drunks throwing up? Well, most of our clients are repeat business, and the once or twice it's happened, they've been pretty reasonable and paid for the mess to be professionally cleaned."

"No cars vandalized then?"

"No."

"It's a pretty good pitch," said Gardener. "You've never had the competition trying to buy you out?"

"No. Nobody's ever bothered that way. There's still enough business to go round."

A banging sound at the entrance to the portacabin diverted the officers' attention. Gardener turned to see a powerfully built man a little over six feet tall, with thinning black hair and blue eyes. He was dressed in faded jeans and a black tee shirt. He nodded and spoke to Billy Morrison, then made his way to the filing cabinet to sort out a drink. Gardener glanced at Morrison for an explanation.

"This is Alan Sargent. He's one of our latest recruits, a driver."

Gardener nodded. "How long have you been with the company, Mr Sargent?"

"Only three or four weeks."

"It was our Barry who brought him in. He alternates between nights and days." Morrison turned to Sargent. "This is the police."

"Everything okay?"

"No. Our Barry's..."

Gardener realized Billy Morrison had never said the words before and didn't think he would be able to say them now. He intervened. "I'm sorry, Mr Sargent, Barry died this morning."

"Oh Christ." Sargent put the mug back on the filing cabinet. "Are you alright, Billy? Is there anything I can do?"

Morrison didn't answer.

Gardener decided to bring the interview to an end. He had everything he needed for the moment. The search of Barry's flat and the results of the post-mortem should give them something more to go on. If and when he needed, he could call back and see Billy Morrison.

Gardener asked Alan Sargent for his details and said they would probably pay *him* a visit in the near future. He also asked for the accountant's details. As they were leaving, Gardener turned and glanced at Billy Morrison again. He retrieved a photograph from his pocket.

"Do you recognize this girl?"

He took it, studied it. Gardener noticed his eyes were red rimmed, his lips pressed firmly together.

"No, who is she?" he asked.

"Just a thought."

Morrison stood up but wavered. Alan Sargent caught him.

"I'll be okay." He faced Gardener. "What does she have to do with all this?"

"We don't know... yet."

Chapter Nineteen

As mid-afternoon approached, both detectives entered the village of Esholt, home to the ITV soap *Emmerdale* for many years. They drove up Chapel Lane and on to Main Street, passing The Woolpack Inn on the way. Gardener noticed a real rarity in the modern day: outside the post office on the right was a public call box. They followed the road to the dead end. A small house nestled on the left, opposite the church ground.

A short, slim, blonde-haired woman, whom Gardener took to be Sally Summerby, opened the front door.

He held out his warrant card. "DI Gardener and DS Reilly, West Yorkshire Major Incident Team."

"Not seen you two before. Sacked the other lot, have they?" She opened the door wider so they could step into a living room decorated in a very olde-worlde style, with ceiling beams, rustic striped wallpaper, and old-fashioned gas mantle wall lights. Despite her problems, Gardener thought the room was clean and smelled fresh. He noticed all the windows were open.

She continued mumbling. "Not surprised the way they carry on. Couldn't catch a cold, them lot."

"I'm sure they're doing everything they can, Mrs Summerby."

"Then how come you two are here? Take it you still haven't found my daughter." She sat down without offering a seat. "I keep telling them, she could be anywhere by now. She might not even be in the country."

"It's very unlikely. Did your daughter have her passport with her when she went missing?"

Sally Summerby glanced at Gardener as if he'd lost his mind. "She didn't even *have* a passport."

"Then she couldn't have left the country."

"That makes it better, does it?" She suddenly changed moods. "Are you going to sit down, or what? If you have something to tell me about my daughter, then at least sit down. Unless it isn't going to take long. And I can't see how it would, because you clearly haven't found her…"

The sentence went unfinished because Sally Summerby burst into tears. She reached for a tissue, which she had conveniently placed up her sleeve.

"I'm sorry… I bet you two think I'm a right cow. The place looks a mess. I do, and all I do is shout at you when you walk through the door."

"It's okay," said Gardener. "We understand." He waited till she'd composed herself. "I think you may have misheard us when we introduced ourselves. I said we were part of the West Yorkshire Major Incident team."

"Which means what?"

Sally Summerby blew her nose and wiped her tears away with her hands. In a softer voice, she asked, "What's happened?"

Gardener nodded in Reilly's direction. "My partner and I were called out to an incident in Batley in the early hours, midnight to be precise."

"What does this have to do with my daughter?"

"Does the name Nicola Stapleton mean anything to you?"

"That Goodman woman asked me the same question earlier. I told her no. I've never heard of the woman."

Gardener passed over the best photo he had of the prostitute. Thanks to Photoshop and the wonders of modern technology, he couldn't actually tell she was dead. "Do you recognize her?"

Sally glanced at it, but immediately shook her head. "No, I've never seen her before in my life. What does she have to do with my daughter?"

Before Gardener had a chance to answer, Sally Summerby flew off the handle again. "Are you trying to tell me she has Chloe but you still don't know where she is?"

"We hope not," said Reilly.

Sally Summerby stood up very quickly. "I want to know. Just give me five minutes with her. I'll kill her! I'd kill anyone who put my daughter at risk."

"You won't need to," said Gardener. "Someone else already has. That was why we were called out. She was found dead in her house."

"Dead?" she repeated. "Who killed her?"

"That's what we're trying to find out."

"Where's your husband, Mrs Summerby?" Reilly asked.

"He's at work, one of the farms in the village."

"Is there any chance we could talk to him?"

"I doubt it. It's their busiest time of the year, they're harvesting. He could be anywhere."

"It's no problem, we can always arrange another visit."

"What do you want with Gareth?"

"We need to ask him some questions," said Reilly.

"About this woman? Why would my husband know her?"

"How long have you been married?" Gardener asked.

"Seven years."

"Had you known him long before that?"

"A couple of years, maybe. We met a bit later in life, which means we're a bit older than most to have a five-year-old daughter."

So there may be something in Gareth Summerby's past that his wife doesn't know about, thought Gardener.

She continued. "I can't see why my husband would have any involvement with this woman. He's a very good husband and an excellent father. He's a God-loving Christian who lives his life by the book, as do all born-again Christians, and I have no problem with it."

"Born again?" questioned Reilly.

"Pardon?"

"You said, born-again Christian?"

"Christian, born-again Christian, what's the difference?"

"Quite a lot, if you speak to a real one. You see, the real practicing Christians see the born-again converts as part-timers – people who are not really taking the Lord and the good book seriously."

"Well, my Gareth isn't one of them. He goes to church every Sunday and prays every morning and night, especially for the safe return of our daughter."

"What did he mean by his comment that 'God works in mysterious ways' on the night you reported Chloe missing?"

"Simply that. Everything happens for a reason, despite the fact that we can't see it."

"And what are your thoughts on it?" asked Reilly. "Are you a Christian, a believer in God?"

"My religious views are my own, Sergeant."

"So you're not a Christian."

"What this has to do with my daughter, I've no idea, but if you must know, I'm an atheist."

"Are you now? Bet that causes some friction."

"Not at all. My husband is a very forgiving person who accepts my beliefs."

Reilly nodded and left it at that.

"Does the name Barry Morrison mean anything to you?" Gardener asked.

"Pardon?"

"Barry Morrison?"

"No, nothing."

Gardener felt she answered too quickly. He didn't believe her answer. "You've never heard of him, either?"

"I've already told you. Look, if you're investigating her murder, why are you in my house asking about Chloe and people I've never even heard of?"

"Because we found this photograph underneath the body of Nicola Stapleton."

Gardener passed it over. Sally Summerby studied the photo. Her eyes filled up. "Oh my God."

"Do you recognize the photo?"

She shook her head to indicate she didn't.

"Or the clothes she's wearing?" asked Reilly.

"No." She handed the photo back to Gardener.

"If you don't recognize it, maybe it's been taken since she was abducted."

"No," replied Sally. "I don't recognize the photo because that isn't my daughter."

Chapter Twenty

Margaret Pendlebury glanced at her watch. It was late afternoon, and the clinic was all but empty. Dr Trent was consulting with his final patient. With her workload finished it was time for afternoon tea and biscuits: custard creams, her favourite. She'd brought a packet in with her on the way to work.

She was in the kitchen when she heard Trent's door open and close, followed by the footsteps of his patient leaving. She glanced at the file sitting beside her on the kitchen worktop. Since she had taken the call with disturbing news earlier in the day, Margaret had been unable to concentrate on anything. She needed to speak to the doctor. She placed everything on the tray and took it through to his room.

Trent glanced up and smiled. "Mrs Pendlebury. What would I do without you?"

"Well, it isn't just you who likes a biscuit or two."

She patted her stomach, feeling a little guilty. Until a number of years ago she'd been slim, but an under-active thyroid gland had increased her weight: when her figure had gone south, so had her husband.

"Well, don't they say a little of what you fancy does you good?"

"In that case, surely a lot of what you fancy must mean you're in heaven."

Trent arched his brow. "Not for long."

"A moment on the lips, a lifetime on the hips. Isn't that what they say?"

"Don't be so hard on yourself, Mrs Pendlebury. None of us can control a thyroid gland."

She smiled and sat down. Trent glanced at the file she'd brought in. "I thought we'd finished with patients for today."

"We have."

"Is that one for tomorrow?" he asked, sipping his tea.

"No. I'm afraid this patient won't be coming to see us anymore."

He placed his cup on the desk. "Why not?"

"I'm not one for gossip as you know, but I was speaking to a friend of mine earlier, and I'm really rather concerned about something."

"Go on," he encouraged.

"It seems that one of our patients has been brutally murdered."

"Excuse me?"

The secretary opened the file so Trent could see exactly whom she was talking about. He picked it up. "Nicola Stapleton? Murdered?"

"Yes. The police were called to her house at midnight."

"How do you know?"

"My friend, Angela Freeman, is a district nurse. One of her patients is a woman called Beryl Potts, lives next door to Ms Stapleton in Batley."

"What happened?"

Margaret Pendlebury had her hands clasped around her cup, as if she was cold. "By all accounts, it was Beryl Potts who found her. She was tied to a chair, and she was naked. She been stabbed a number of times, and she also had a bayonet run straight through her that had pinned her to the floor."

"Good grief," said Trent.

"Puts us in an awkward situation, wouldn't you say?"

"Why?"

"Think about it. If she was naked and tied to a chair, what had she been subjected to? Whoever did this may have had unprotected sex with her. I think the time for patient confidentiality has gone out of the window."

"I see what you mean," said Trent, glancing at the file. "If Nicola Stapleton's killer had unprotected sex with her, they could be in serious trouble."

Chapter Twenty-one

Sitting on the swing seat, Chris Rydell glanced out across the fields, reflecting on the day he'd had: pretty rough by anyone's standards. Staring out at the fields helped him to think, to come to terms with his situation.

Home was a converted barn on the side of the Leeds-Liverpool canal, about two miles outside of Rodley. The lower section of the building allowed for secure parking for his bikes. The upper section was divided into living accommodation, featuring three bedrooms, a bathroom, a living area, and a kitchen.

To the rear of the property, all open fields. The canal ran along the front. It was a pretty sought-after residence, especially during the summer. Many people who walked their dogs along the towpath while watching the boats pass by had often made him an offer.

A noise from the TV in the living room distracted his thoughts. At the moment, he had a houseguest. In the short term they were fine, and his wouldn't be staying long.

He thought of his family again: father, mother, and sister, all gone. He had no fear of dying. If what they said was true about the afterlife, he would meet up with them all again. He owed his father so much.

Chris had started his working life at an early age. When he was little more than eight years old, his first employment had been in a filling station. The garage belonged to a friend of his father's who happened to mention over a drink one night in the pub that he needed a Saturday person for a bit of cleaning. Chris had been suggested because he'd been helping his father at his yard. By the time he was ten years old he had progressed to working in the shop a little, checking and marking stock after deliveries, before helping to serve on the pumps.

He felt a sudden pain in his stomach, but it soon passed. He had no idea if it was a symptom of his condition. He thought once again about Trent's offer to try yet more drugs. What was the point? The ones he'd tried had not worked. It was doubtful anything else would.

Chris finished his water and chucked the plastic bottle in the blue bin as he passed. Upstairs in his study, he checked his computer manifest and the deliveries for the evening ahead. Saturday night was usually quiet. He picked up the blue phone and set it aside. That would go with the blue bike. Blue were Medicare's colours, and that was the company he worked for on a weekend.

He printed off the manifest in the order he chose to do the drops. He always worked to a circular route and was pretty much in the same place at the same time every week. There were those who reckoned they could set their clock by him, which was how he liked things.

Chris had a very methodical mind, planning everything to the last detail: he always knew where he was going to be, and when. A different bike and a different phone for each client, contracting for each company on set days. His bikes had a specially adapted frame to hold all five phones, with a Bluetooth connection fitted inside his crash helmet should an emergency arise.

Glancing at his watch, he realized he would have to leave soon. He turned and left the study and made his way to the kitchen, to prepare a drink for his houseguest before leaving.

The room was spotless, clinically clean: a place for everything, and everything in its place. Chris could not abide mess. Life had to be like that. You had to be in control.

Pity he wasn't now.

Chapter Twenty-two

Earlier in the day, Raymond Allen had shadowed Vincent – the man who considered himself a detective. He couldn't find a date, thought Allen.

He'd followed him into Oldham's chemist on Guiseley Road. Vincent and the owner, John, were big pals. Thick as thieves, following an incident a few years back. Although Allen had to be careful, he'd managed to stay close without being seen. Vincent was rattling on about a double murder in Batley, reckoned he was going to use his influence to find out what was going on.

That was a laugh. The police wouldn't listen to him. He'd failed at almost everything in life, which Allen found interesting considering Vincent's family tree: every one of them had been in the newspaper game, starting with a distant relative by the name of Edward Baines, who'd bought and turned *The Leeds Mercury* into something special. All Vincent had managed was a second-rate daily blog on an obscure racing website.

Allen and Vincent had history: a spell in the Rampton high security psychiatric hospital had been the result for Allen. He'd spent his time well, studying true crime and medicine.

Vincent's conversation with Oldham had given Allen an idea. He'd taken a bus to Batley, and Hume Crescent. The scene tape separated the house from the crowd of onlookers, but they were there in numbers.

Speculation was rife. The occupant had been stripped naked, tied to a chair, raped at least a dozen times, savagely beaten up – there was blood all over the house. It would take a specialist team months to clean it up. She'd been stabbed a dozen times and pinned to the floor, reports varied from a kitchen knife to a spear.

From there, he'd visited the second murder scene, which was the same as the first but no one knew anything for certain. The story doing the rounds was the body in the doorway had been poisoned.

Allen had returned to the Morrisons store in Guiseley, where he'd kept an eye on Oldham's shop, and the windows of Vincent's flat above. Little or no activity had been seen. Didn't surprise Allen. He'd be sat listening to Johnny Cash and poking his nose into the murders.

Allen jumped off the wall, grabbed his carrier bag, and crossed the main road, heading toward the local library.

Inside, he counted only four people and two members of staff, one of which he asked about Internet access. Eventually Allen sat down and placed the carrier on the chair next to him, removing a thin paperback publication entitled *Foul Deeds & Suspicious Deaths In Leeds*. The library was open till seven o'clock, so he had plenty of time.

For half an hour he sat quietly, studying three cases: one committed in 1865, one in 1881, and one that really cornered his attention involving a man called Samuel Birchall in June of 1866.

Chapter Twenty-three

Following the bombshell that Sally Summerby had dropped about the girl in the photo not being Chloe, Gardener's world had nearly collapsed.

"Who the hell is it?" Gardener had asked, back in the car.

"I've no idea," replied Reilly. "But I wouldn't like to be in Goodman's shoes when she finds out."

"Doesn't really bode well for us, either. I thought things were looking up when we had a name."

Reilly glanced at the photo again. "She must be the spitting image of Chloe. It fooled Goodman."

"Not Sally Summerby, though."

"It was never going to. Mothers know their children."

"Which brings us back to the question, who do we have here?"

"We have to go and see Goodman, tell her the news."

"We also need to see if any of our lads have uncovered anything in Stapleton's past. This wee girl could still be a relative of hers."

"Or Morrison's."

"His brother would have said something. If Barry had a daughter, that would have been one of the first things he'd have thought about, what was going to happen to her?"

Gardener glanced at his partner. "So, either he doesn't know, which would surprise me…"

"Or he's involved, and he's covering," suggested his partner.

"Covering what, though?"

"Let's say she *was* Stapleton's daughter, and the woman had carried very well. Maybe Morrison was the father. They have a massive row about how he's treating her, which ends up with abduction and murder."

"Doesn't quite fit for me, Sean. Stapleton wouldn't have wanted a five-year-old ruining her trade."

"Wouldn't be the first time. I've heard of prostitutes who have kids and still carry on working. Some of them dope the kids with a mild sedative so they stay in bed all night."

Gardener thought about it. "Always possible, but then I think Beryl Potts would have known. And if Nicola Stapleton had let Barry Morrison take their daughter while she plied her trade, surely his brother Billy would have known."

"Questionable," said Reilly. "He didn't know about the house."

Gardener sighed, lapsing into silence. Reilly started the car and moved off.

The pair of them visited Goodman, broke the news, left a copy of the photo with her, and asked if the SPOC could be kept in place until they all had more information. Goodman wanted to continue talking, but Gardener informed her they had another appointment.

They were now parked in the mortuary car park, following a call from Fitz.

"I suppose we'd best go and see what Dr Jekyll wants."

"You've got the wrong half of the duo there, so you have."

Both men laughed and left the car. Gardener checked his watch. It was after six, which wouldn't please the old man. They found the elderly pathologist sitting behind his desk, with a coffee. He had a midi hi-fi on the shelf behind him, currently playing a CD from an opera.

Fitz glanced up at them. "Where the hell have you two been?"

"See," said Reilly, "didn't I say you had the wrong half?"

Gardener smiled.

"Wrong half of what?" Fitz asked, standing up.

Reilly strolled behind the desk and placed his arm around his shoulder.

"We've been working our fingers to the bone. We haven't had a break all day, and we've been so desperate to get here and have a cup of that wonderful coffee from that perfect machine of yours. You wouldn't believe how desperate we are."

Fitz mellowed and managed a smile. So did Gardener; the Irishman was a brilliant tactician, capable of defusing any situation. The opera CD finished, and Fitz immediately pressed play again.

"So, what wonderful flavour do you have for us today?"

"It's funny you should ask. Take a seat." The old man wandered around to the machine and poured two cups. "My wife and I were on holiday recently, and we had a trip to Ulverston. Found a little shop specializing in different flavoured coffees: pecan nut pie flavour. Try it, I guarantee you'll want another cup."

Both men did. Even Gardener passed comment.

"Christ, you want to steady on, boss," said Reilly. "You'll be turning into me."

"God help us," said Fitz.

"I hope not," said Gardener.

"There's gratitude for you."

Gardener addressed Fitz. "So, what do you have for us?"

Fitz consulted his files. "Nicola Stapleton. To be perfectly honest, she isn't in too bad a shape. A bit undernourished. She was probably eating the right foods, but by the look of her, not enough. She was in her early twenties. No signs of childbirth. From what I could see, all the stab wounds bar one were definitely pre-mortem."

"She was alive while it happened?" Reilly asked.

"Yes. They'd be no point tying her to a chair, otherwise. From the angle of the cut and the pattern of the bleeding – not to mention the spatter pattern – the killer had plenty of time to do what he wanted."

"Any sign of sexual interference?" Gardener asked.

"No," replied Fitz. "The fatal wound was definitely the bayonet. It went all the way through, severing an artery, before pinning her to the ground. Cause of death was a haemorrhage."

"Would it have taken long for her to die?" Gardener asked. "What I mean is, are we looking for an expert in weaponry, someone who knows how to administer pain and keep someone alive long enough to really feel it?"

"I don't think so, but you can never tell. On the whole the cuts don't look like a professional job."

"Did you recognize the bayonet?" Reilly asked.

"Afraid not. Not my area of expertise. My best guess is World War II, or pre-war but not by much."

Gardener made a mental note. They had an expert back at the station examining it.

"No doubt that the bayonet killed her," said Fitz. "But she has another very interesting problem."

"Which is?"

"Her liver was abnormal, especially for a girl her age."

"How abnormal?"

"There was some scarring. Not a lot, but enough for me to take notice. I'm not sure what's caused it, so I've sent a biopsy for an antibody screen."

"Best guess," said Reilly.

Fitz leaned back, removed his half-lens spectacles, and rubbed the bridge of his nose. Gardener felt guilty, because he realized the old man had probably been working the same amount of time he and Reilly had. That was no mean feat for someone his age.

"My first thought was haemochromatosis."

Reilly threw his pad and pen on the desk. "I can't even pronounce that fucking word, never mind spell it." He glanced at Gardener. "Does he ever speak English?"

"Would you understand him if he did?"

Fitz laughed. "What the hell is with you two today? I'm gonna tell Briggs you're picking on me."

"Like that's going to help."

"Any more of that beautiful coffee, Fitz?"

"Help yourself." Fitz continued with his explanation. "It's a genetic disorder. The body starts to absorb excessive amounts of iron from the diet, which is then deposited in various organs. Mainly the liver, but the pancreas usually gets a high dose, as well as the heart, endocrine glands, and joints.

"The liver generally only stores a small amount of iron, which is an essential source for new red blood cells. Imperative for overall good health. When large amounts of iron are stored in the liver, the result is an enlarged or damaged liver. Deposits of iron can occur in other organs and joints, causing serious tissue damage."

"You said, 'first thought'," Gardener pointed out. "Are you concerned it might be something else?"

"The other possibility is non-alcoholic steatohepatitis. It's known as the silent liver disease. It resembles alcoholic liver disease, but occurs in people who drink little or no alcohol. The major feature in NASH is fat in the liver, along with inflammation and damage. Most people with NASH feel fine. Don't even know they have a liver problem. Nevertheless, it can be severe and can lead to cirrhosis, in which the liver is permanently damaged and scarred and no longer able to work properly. The only means of proving a diagnosis of NASH and separating it from simple fatty liver is a biopsy."

"Presumably, if there are few or no symptoms, it could take a while to show."

"It can take years, even decades," said Fitz. "The process can stop and, in some cases, reverse on its own without specific therapy. Or it gets worse, causing scarring. Or fibrosis can accumulate in the liver. As fibrosis worsens, cirrhosis develops; the liver becomes seriously scarred, very hard, and unable to function normally. Not every person with NASH develops cirrhosis, but once serious scarring or cirrhosis is present, few treatments can halt the progression."

"You don't sound too comfortable with that one either," said Gardener.

"No, not really," replied Fitz. "Under normal circumstances, a person with cirrhosis experiences fluid retention, muscle wasting, bleeding from the intestines, and liver failure. She doesn't have any of that. It's possible that she may have one of the hepatitis strains such as A, B, or C, although NASH is more common. Many patients with NASH have elevated blood lipids, such as cholesterol and triglycerides, and many have diabetes or prediabetes."

"Did she have diabetes?" Gardener asked, remembering the syringe, hoping to hit on something he could investigate.

"No, but not every patient with diabetes has NASH. They have normal blood cholesterol and lipids. NASH can occur without any apparent risk factor, even in children.

"We're not quite sure what causes NASH, but there are several possible candidates. Insulin resistance, for one, but she wasn't diabetic, so it wouldn't be that. Release of toxic inflammatory proteins by fat cells, known as cytokines, is another."

"Not likely to be that either," said Reilly. "She was thinner than a whippet."

"Which is why I've sent for an antibody screen. The third option is oxidative stress, the deterioration of cells inside the liver."

"What about treatment?"

"Currently, there is none. But we can't be certain what it is yet. However, there are some very good clinics, especially the private one on Bond Street."

"I doubt she could afford a private clinic," said Gardener.

"Even if she was a patient, she might not have been paying," offered Reilly, making notes. "If she wasn't, and it is hepatitis, and she was a prostitute, it's possible she's passed it on to a boat load of other people."

"Almost certainly, if she wasn't using protection."

Gardener thought of the condom packets found in her house, but it was still worth following up.

"We have to give it a try," Gardener said to Reilly. "She may have been getting treatment somewhere."

"In which case she would have medical records," offered Reilly. "That could really help, if we can find them."

"Anything else?"

"Nothing more I can tell you about her. It's the man you found slumped in the doorway at five o'clock this morning that presents a bigger mystery."

Chapter Twenty-four

Gardener's stomach lurched. Perhaps he *should* have another coffee.

He returned to his seat. "Go on, then, let's have it."

"His heart was in a state of fatty degeneration, and the liver was also diseased through increased fat. He definitely had NASH. The gall bladder was full of small calculi. The contents of his stomach contained about two fluid ounces of digested food. The only thing I recognized was fat and starch."

"That's Chinese out of the window for me," said Reilly.

Fitz consulted his notes. "He was approximately fifty years of age. Most of the major organs were intact, but as I've said, he had NASH, so he wasn't without his problems."

"Cause of death?" asked Gardener.

"Oh, I certainly know what caused it. I had the blood spatter on his jacket analysed. Same blood group as Nicola Stapleton, so you can definitely place him in the room at the time of her murder. He died in very unusual circumstances. Barry Morrison had something called 'blocked superior vena-cava syndrome'."

Reilly sighed. "Here he goes again."

"You've got me with that one, Fitz," said Gardener.

"It's the big vein that drains blood from the upper body to the heart. His was blocked. The blood accumulated in the upper body causing it to swell. The faster it is blocked, the worse the symptoms. It is usually caused by cancer."

"But not in this case," said Reilly.

"No." Fitz shook his head. "You remember the syringe found underneath Nicola Stapleton? The best I can tell from the remains was hot sealing wax which was injected into the vein, making it look like something else, until I did my job."

"Sealing wax?" asked Gardener.

"I've sent some of it away for analysis. As soon as we get the results back, I may be able to narrow it down."

"Doesn't that stuff harden once it's been melted and left?" Reilly asked.

"It does," replied Fitz. "But it's like everything else these days, it's moved on with technology. Beeswax was the most common ingredient years ago. Then they introduced different colours, made it with different formulas, so in all honesty I have no idea what's in today's wax."

"Maybe the analysis will show us what's been used to keep it moist. Like Sean says, that stuff usually hardens pretty quickly."

"There was definitely no evidence in the house that the killer had heated it up there," said Reilly. "And judging by the timescale I doubt he or she would have had the time to clean up so well. Whoever it is will be quite a pain in the arse to catch."

"The method is specific," said Gardener. "There wouldn't be too many people who know how to do that."

"A job for HOLMES."

"We might have to go deeper than that," said Gardener. "Use the specialist search engines."

Gardener addressed Fitz. "Do you think either of these two were responsible for killing the other?"

"To be honest, no. But I don't think there's any doubt they were both in the same room."

Gardener's head was spinning. Two murders, very few clues, no suspects. They also had an unidentified child with no idea how central to the investigation she may be.

"Someone must have seen something," said Reilly.

"Even if no human saw the killer, the CCTV outside the shops must have picked something up."

"How the hell could they transport two people around in a car, kill one in the house with the other present, then move him somewhere else to kill him without being seen?"

"Maybe we can pick up something on ANPR."

Gardener took a pen and a piece of paper from the desk. "So, what have we got? Barry Morrison was radio silent from nine o'clock. His car was seen outside of Nicola Stapleton's house from around ten. Our killer must have taken Morrison between eight-thirty and nine. So where was Stapleton at that point?"

"She must have been at the house. I can't imagine a killer lugging the two of them all over town."

"No," said Gardener. "Too risky. So let's say he or she silenced Stapleton around seven. That in itself is a risk, because Beryl Potts was at home. And I think she would have seen him or her. So how did he or she get there?"

"Maybe they're local, within walking distance."

"The other advantage to being local is they can move around without drawing attention to themselves," said Gardener. "Here's what I think happened. The killer must have had Nicola Stapleton around seven. At which point, she'd have been tied up and gagged."

"Then the killer goes to the cab office," offered Reilly. "Life gets a bit easier there because he or she can take Morrison's car back."

"They're back at the house for ten and gone again by eleven-thirty."

"That gives them plenty of time to do whatever they want," said Reilly.

"And it doesn't matter too much about noise, because it's an end house with only one neighbour."

"Who was out. And I'll lay odds our suspect knew this. They've done their homework. All of this was too well planned. Sounds like it went without a hitch."

"We need to ask Beryl Potts if she can remember exactly what time she last saw Nicola Stapleton alive."

"So where did they take Morrison between eleven-thirty and four o'clock the next morning?"

"It certainly wasn't his flat," said Gardener.

"And they couldn't take him back to the cab office."

"Before you two get too involved," Fitz intervened, "I haven't finished."

"There's more?"

"Yes. Food wasn't the only thing I found amongst the contents of Barry Morrison's stomach."

Gardener and Reilly glanced at each other whilst Fitz reached into a drawer. He pulled out an evidence bag and dropped it on the desk.

"What's that?" asked Reilly.

"A key."

"I can see it's a key, but it's not an ordinary one, is it?"

Gardener leaned in closer, studying the silver object, which was an inch and a half in length, with five oblong cuts in the side. The head was an inch wide, shaped like a three-leaf clover.

"No. I'm pretty sure it's the key to a safe deposit box, the type held in a bank."

"And that was in his stomach?"

"Yes, amongst the food."

Gardener thought about the body when they'd found it. There were no cuts or lacerations, so it hadn't been placed.

"He was made to swallow it?"

"Almost certainly," said Fitz. "It wasn't easy, but I did manage to find traces of Vaseline."

"The killer's playing games with us," said Reilly. "Another one who wants us to run all over the place solving cryptic puzzles."

"But what?" Gardener asked. "Why do you make a man swallow the key to a safe deposit box? What's in there that they want us to see?"

"People store all sorts of things in them," said Fitz. "Gemstones, precious metals, currency, marketable securities. Important documents such as a will, property deeds, birth certificates."

"Could be anywhere," said Reilly.

"I don't know much about safe deposit boxes," said Gardener. "Are they specific to certain banks?"

"I couldn't tell you," replied Fitz. "But a good locksmith probably could."

Reilly made a note, and Gardener realized they were going to be working all night. They had collected so much information that needed discussing in the incident room, and that wasn't counting what his officers had found out. He glanced at his watch, shocked to find it approaching eight o'clock.

"Well, gentlemen," said Fitz, "I'll send you my report as soon as possible, but I don't think there's a great deal more I can tell you."

The two officers stood up and thanked Fitz for his time. They turned to leave, but the sound of the pathologist's voice halted them.

"For what it's worth, there's something niggling me about this case."

"What?" Gardener asked.

"I don't know. I can't put my finger on it yet... but I will."

Gardener thought about his comment. Fitz was probably the best in the country, having devoted more than thirty years to anatomic pathology. He was a walking encyclopaedia on crime, had an eidetic memory. If it had happened somewhere else in time, Fitz knew. Gardener trusted him implicitly. If he had a hunch about something, Gardener would follow it.

"You've come across it before?"

"Possibly."

Chapter Twenty-five

Vincent took the final mouthful of his favourite meal: rump steak – medium to well done – with lashings of chips. You couldn't have steak without chips, as far as Vincent was concerned. He swilled it down with a can of lager he'd found in the fridge, cursing himself for having forgotten to buy some in the superstore earlier in the day. Not that it was a major problem, the place was open till ten.

Vincent had everything he needed living where he did. Morrisons was across the road, the library two doors down. A computer shop shared the block with a Barnardo's charity shop, a tandoori restaurant, a butcher, and Coral bookmakers – he could waste many an hour in that place.

Walking into the kitchen, he threw his plate and cutlery in the sink with all the others from the rest of the week. He glanced around, scratching his head. The place was a tip, as ever. He could never find anything he wanted, and often turned rooms upside down, without bothering to tidy up afterwards. There were more important things to do than clean.

He strolled back into the living room. As if proving a point, it took five minutes to find the CD he wanted: a Johnny Cash album titled *Man in Black*. Vincent liked country music; in particular, he loved Cash.

He fired up his computer. It was time to compose a blog for what he'd discovered during the day. Which, in all honesty, wasn't much.

What terrible times they were living in. It was coming to something when you weren't safe in your own house.

He'd been to Cross Bank Road earlier. He'd flashed an old press card. People opened up to him. General opinion claimed a middle-aged male had died, but no one knew for certain. Amongst other options, he'd apparently been poisoned. Vincent had come across one or two of those in his time. One person had claimed the man had been brutally stabbed to death. Another idiot said he'd been set on fire. That was when Vincent had called it a day.

By the middle of the afternoon he was in Hume Crescent. A woman had been killed during the night. She'd been found naked, stabbed. A bayonet had definitely been mentioned.

Vincent's head was full of thoughts. He needed another beer. He checked the fridge, hoping he'd made a mistake. One might be lurking in a darkened corner that he hadn't seen earlier. No luck.

In the other room his computer pinged, informing him he had mail. To hell with that; he wanted another drink. He needed to compose his blog and have it on the site by midnight. Then he might pop over and see the police tomorrow, offer his help.

He left the flat, tore down the fire escape, and headed for Morrisons to pick up a four-pack. A simple job, one would think. Not so, these days. It took him ten minutes due to the Saturday night crowds.

Back in the flat, he rummaged around the kitchen for a clean glass. He searched the cupboards in vain. He finally chose a discoloured one from the sink. He was the last one to use it anyway.

Back in the living room he re-started the CD. He didn't like to miss anything from the giant of country music. Having hit the random button, the first track was somewhere in the middle of the disc, but it was his favourite, and he knew every word.

The title track: *Man in Black*.

Sitting at his desk, he took a mouthful of lager, some Belgian stuff he'd picked up. He'd never tried it before, but it was okay.

He opened the desk drawer and found a Kit-Kat to go with it. Could have been there ages, but he wasn't bothered about dates. People were too particular these days.

Seventeen emails sat in his inbox. One stood out, which he found very creepy. Vincent shuddered.

It was actually from The Man in Black. Couldn't be old Johnny Cash himself. He'd gone to The Grand Ole Opry in the sky. Maybe it was some country and western fan club offering him life membership. He opened it.

What he saw was the last thing he'd expected, and certainly had nothing to do with Johnny Cash.

Vincent's stomach lurched as he read the content. He had no idea who'd sent it, but they knew him – very well, judging by the detail.

The email carried two attachments. Vincent opened the first to find a figure in silhouette, resembling the American wrestler The Undertaker, wearing a long dark cloak and a black top hat. On the face he could only see the eyes. The second email was a close up of those eyes. They were veined and bloodshot, and Vincent felt that they were actually staring at him, as though somehow the figure was alive, in control.

Underneath the slogan read: *the man in black is watching*.

The drink and the Kit-Kat all but forgotten, Vincent returned to the text in the main body of the email:

> *If you cross the man in black, there are consequences: a price to be paid. If you need any further proof, check out what happened in Batley.*
> *You crossed me once, Vincent.*

I'm going to give you a fighting chance to see if you can work out who I am, what I'm doing, and when your time is up. To quote your favourite saying, one piece at a time, and you'll have everything you need.

Clue No:1 The sum of the year adds up to 20. Three people were involved: a sixty-year-old widow, an eighteen-year-old mill-hand and a nineteen-year-old cloth finisher. Seems like you couldn't trust women even then. Someone didn't because she ended up with a blade through her. Sergeant English solved it. Can you?

Clue No:2 The sum of the year adds up to 18. A man found dead in a shop doorway. The mystery went unsolved. That would never do for you, would it?

Clue No:3 is the key to your destiny, Vincent, or perhaps I should say demise. The sum of the year adds up to 21 and involves an engine driver with the Midland Railway Company. Do you know what happened?

Anyway, you're the detective: see if you can work things out.

How good is your memory? Do the names Edwin and Elizabeth Lascelles ring any bells?

I'm watching Vincent. You'll never know when, or where, but I'll always be there. As I was today, listening to you talking to John Oldham.

You'll have to work fast, because I'm enjoying some new-found freedom. I fancy I might do another two before I come for you.

The Man in Black

Vincent sat completely motionless, staring at the computer screen, breathing only because it was automatic. The fact that someone knew a whole lot more about the crime scenes in Batley than he did, and had been following him during the day, left him feeling nauseous.

It could only mean one thing: the killer was taunting him.

Chapter Twenty-six

Gardener's team filed into the incident room one by one. Their expressions and postures told him all he needed to know: they had worked hard, and they were tired. So was he. Glancing at his watch, it was a little past nine in the evening. That made it a straight twenty-one hours on duty without a real break.

He sipped from his bottled water. The rest of them had coffees; some even carried snacks.

Briggs came in last, with Sarah Gates. She was in better shape than the others, but Gardener doubted very much she'd been in the field for the same length of time.

Briggs closed the door and came to the front with Gardener. As they glanced at the ANACAPA chart, Gardener studied the updates that had been added throughout the day. Hopefully, some of the mysteries had been solved.

"How have you got on?" Briggs asked Gardener.

"We've found out quite a lot, sir."

Gardener knew the pressure he was under. A normal single murder – if you could call murder normal – occurring in one night would be bad enough, but a double murder made life difficult. If the killer struck again, Gardener hoped he wouldn't choose another two victims. A niggling feeling at the back of his mind, however, told him otherwise.

"Well, that's something," said Briggs. "At least we might be a little nearer catching the killer."

"Maybe," said Gardener. "But there's a bigger shock in store for us regarding Chloe Summerby."

Briggs' chest sunk. "Oh God, she's not dead, is she?"

"Not that I know of, but you'd better sit in till the end, there's a lot to get through."

"Okay, bring it to order, then. I don't fancy still being here at midnight."

"You're not the only one," said Gardener.

Briggs glanced around. "Where's your sidekick?"

"He was here a minute ago."

The door opened and the Irishman walked in with a tray of doughnuts. "Gregg's, round the corner," he said, raising a thumb.

"At this time of night?" asked Gardener.

"If you know the right people. Friend of mine bakes them. These were going in the bin."

"They're not fresh?" questioned Sharp.

"What the hell do you want at nine o'clock at night?"

The team dug in anyway. Within seconds the tray was empty, leaving Gardener without one. But he didn't much care.

"Okay, I'm sure none of you want to stay any later than necessary, so let's get started. We'll go through today's actions, mark them up on the board, and then we'll see what we need to do tomorrow."

Each man nodded, relishing the coffee and doughnuts – fresh or not.

Gardener beckoned Patrick Edwards. He gave him a pen and asked him to update the charts as they went along. He then addressed DCI Briggs. "I believe you have something to say on the bayonet, sir."

Briggs nodded, and Gardener took a seat.

"The National Crime Agency expert identified it as a No. 7 Mk. I/L Knife Bayonet. It was basically part knife bayonet and part socket bayonet, because it could mount to the Lee Enfield and the Mk. V Sten submachine gun. The intention was to utilize the clip point blade and serve a dual role as a fighting knife."

"So, we're looking for a military nut?" asked Thornton.

Briggs didn't answer, returning eagerly to his notes. Gardener knew he'd never been happy taking centre stage.

"The grip scales are made of a resin-impregnated cloth composite, called Paxolin, and have deep finger grooves to allow use as a fighting knife. Other examples with black grips would be those produced by BSA, the Royal Ordnance Factory at Poole, and the one at Newport."

"Sounds to me like there were millions of these things," said Bob Anderson. "What chance do we have of finding out where ours came from?"

"Not as many as you think, Bob. There were one hundred and seventy-six thousand produced in the World War Two years."

"Well that narrows things down. Makes me feel a whole lot better."

"Well if you'll just hold your horses, sunshine, I'll make you delirious in a second."

"I'm a bit tired for that, if you don't mind, sir."

Even Briggs had to laugh. Late and tired, a bit of grave humour often helped.

"The design was perfected by Wilkinson Sword. They made 1,000 bayonets in 1944. Mass production was carried out by four manufacturers from 1945 to 1948: Birmingham Small Arms made 25,000; The Royal Ordnance Factory at Poole, 30,000; and The Royal Ordnance Factory, Newport, 100,000."

"That'll be ours, then."

"No, ours was made by Elkington & Co. of Birmingham. Our expert reckoned most had their own markings. BSA, for example, used 'M-74B'. Ours had the marking 'M-78'. Elkington made 20,000 and are one of the most important names in English silver."

"Any prints?" asked Gardener.

Briggs shook his head. "Not on the bayonet, no. We have identified the footprints in the kitchen, which belong to Nicola Stapleton and Barry Morrison."

Gardener realized that was all the man had to say on the bayonet. But it was something. He stood up and let Briggs have a seat.

"Bayonet actions for tomorrow, then. Someone get on to Elkington in Birmingham, see if they keep records that far back. Can they identify this bayonet, and see if there's a trail from when it was sold? I doubt it very much."

"There's a good chance it was bought second-hand somewhere."

"I was coming to that, junk shops, second-hand shops, antique dealers. Maybe try the local markets. I know some of the antique dealers hang out there. One or two have stalls."

"Where's David Dickinson when you need him?"

"What about Army & Navy stores?" asked Rawson.

"Worth checking," said Gardener. "What do you think, Sean?"

Reilly was the only one with any experience in the field. Having spent a lot of time in the RUC, he'd seen all manner of things.

"Go with it. Probably not their style, but you never know. Someone might have taken it in for a valuation recently, tried to sell 'em one."

"Okay," said Gardener. "We all know what we're doing with this one, but I really don't hold out much hope. For all we know, the bayonet could have been in the killer's family for generations, one of those things handed down from father to son."

"Might be easier to find if it is," said Reilly. "If it was only sold once and stayed in the family, we might have a better chance."

"Good point," said Gardener. "If all else fails, widen the search with the Internet."

Once the dust settled, he asked, "What have we found out about Nicola Stapleton?"

Colin Sharp stood up. "She has something in common with the missing five-year-old."

Gardener's heart sunk. He was going to have to tell them the bad news soon. "How so?"

"She's an MFH."

"She's missing from home? Where? When?"

"Nicola Stapleton, whose real name is Stanton, was originally from Ealing Broadway, London. She left home when she was fourteen in 2001. She had a rucksack, and five hundred pounds she'd stolen from her brother's building society account. Not quite sure when and where she arrived in Batley."

"How did you manage to find this out?" Gardener asked. "Especially as her name isn't Stapleton."

"Bob and Frank were the real heroes. When Morrison's flat was turned over, we found her passport."

"Where?" Reilly asked.

"He had a safe," replied Thornton. "Nothing fancy, one of those with the nine square buttons on the front. Took a while to work out the combination, but we eventually found that on his computer."

"Any evidence to suggest he had more girls than Nicola Stapleton on his books? Was he running his own empire of prostitution?"

"Nothing so far," said Anderson.

"Any porn?"

"No," said Thornton, as if he was disappointed.

"What single man doesn't have any porn?" Reilly asked.

"One who has a prostitute on tap," replied Rawson.

"Was there anything else in the safe?" Gardener asked.

"Plenty," replied Bob Anderson. "But we'll come back to that later. I think Colin has more to say on Stapleton."

"He's not the only one," said Reilly.

Sharp continued. "Before she died, she'd been spending time at a homeless shelter, asking if she could help out. Seems she spent a lot of time with the matron in charge, a woman called Brenda Killen. Stapleton dropped hints about being unhappy where she lived. She was desperate to make a better life for herself. Brenda Killen figured she was keeping a lot back.

"Anyway, I found three Stantons living in North London, but only one had a missing daughter called Nicola. Using the passport photo and a whole host of modern technology, her parents confirmed it was her."

"Did they say why she'd run away?"

"Usual stuff: family disagreements. Being a teenager, she was becoming hard to deal with."

"What about the money?"

"They were mad at first, but as time went on, they just wanted her home."

Gardener nodded. He'd heard the story a hundred times. "Did you tell them what had happened?"

"No," said Sharp. "Not yet. They just sounded so hopeful, so pleased that we'd got in touch."

"What did you say?" Reilly asked.

"Just that she was wanted for questioning, but I couldn't go into too much detail."

"They will have to be informed," said Gardener.

"I'll do it when the time comes," offered Briggs. "Right now, I need you lot to stay on the ground and keep up the legwork."

"Good work, Colin. At least we know who she is. Anything else?"

"SOCO are still searching the house. So far the only thing we've managed to find is her passport, which wasn't *in* her house."

Gardener took over, updating the team on what he and Reilly had found out from Fitz about both victims, and that interestingly enough they both may have had something called NASH.

"Are you sure you don't mean 'rash'?" The comment brought a few laughs.

"What the hell is NASH?" asked Bob Anderson.

Gardener briefly explained before finally adding that it could be something more serious, like full-blown hepatitis. "Which is why Sean and I are going to start a search of the clinics. It's possible she knew she had a problem and could have been having treatment, so there may be something of a medical record somewhere."

Gardener glanced at Sharp again. "Did you say SOCO are still searching the house but nothing has come up?"

"Not so far. If she does have anything of any use, it's well hidden."

Gardener thought about it. Something didn't add up. Where was her phone? No woman in her position would be without a mobile. Come to think of it, unless SOCO had turned one up at Morrison's flat, they hadn't found one for him either.

"Colin, I know there isn't much to go on, but can you try making some headway with the mobile phone companies? You have a name and an address. They should be able to give you something. She must have had a phone."

"I can give it a go."

"Have we come across anyone in the witness statements who saw anything? I thought places like that were supposed to be close-knit."

"I doubt it," said Reilly.

The general feedback to Gardener's question was negative. Either people didn't care what was going on anymore, or they were all up to something they shouldn't and were too preoccupied to be watching what others were doing.

"Okay. I think we should be tramping the streets again tomorrow, armed with a photograph. Plenty of people out there will know Nicola Stapleton. It's just a case of finding them. Have we pulled in any of her clients yet?"

"We've spoken very discreetly to the four names and addresses that Mrs Potts gave us," said Paul Benson.

"Any luck?"

"None of them had used her services on that night. It took quite a while for them to admit they'd used her at all, but we brought a little pressure to bear there."

"But no one had been with her on Saturday night?"

"No," said Benson.

"When was the last time any of them had been with her?"

"Two, maybe three weeks ago."

"Did any of them know Stapleton was servicing all of them?"

"Apparently not," replied Benson. "Or at least they weren't admitting it."

Gardener thought otherwise.

Time was moving on, so he went on to Barry Morrison. Because of the blood spatter pattern on the jacket they could place him at the scene, but were still no nearer to working out whether or not he killed her.

"Is NASH what killed him?" asked Anderson.

"No. He had blocked superior vena-cava syndrome."

"Can we have that in English?" asked Frank Thornton.

Gardener smiled and explained what Fitz had told them.

"Jesus. That had to be someone who knows what they're doing," said Colin Sharp. "Let's face it, how many of us could even find a vein in our arm, let alone where Fitz said it was?"

"You're right, Colin. It's very specific."

"Morrison could still have killed Nicola Stapleton. What if he was made to do it?"

"What purpose would it serve?" Gardener asked. "If the killer wanted Morrison to kill Stapleton, it's more than likely they would have something on him and want to use that information."

"So we still think he was made to watch?" Anderson asked.

"Makes more sense. Frighten him half to death."

"Maybe the killer knew them both," said Rawson. "Maybe the pair of them were trying to stitch him or her up over something, and this was their revenge."

"Could be."

"Well, we've certainly uncovered stuff in his flat that would account for that theory," said Sharp.

"Really?" said Gardener. "We'll come back to that. I want to put some actions into place with this one. The sealing wax hasn't been analysed yet. When it has, we'll have more to go on, but one of you can make a start. Find out all you can about sealing wax. Is there different stuff on the market? Does one brand set faster than another? How easy is it to apply? Can it be used in a syringe? How hard would it be to do what's been done to Barry Morrison?

"Someone should speak to the National Injuries Database. It was started back in the 1980s at Guy's Hospital, and used as a reference guide for doctors who hadn't seen injuries of a certain kind before. It's a good indicator of how common or uncommon an injury is, where it's been seen before, and who has used it as a method to kill. We may strike lucky."

"There's a good chance we won't," said Anderson. "I've never heard of that before."

"That's why we need to widen the field. Inquire at the local libraries, the bookshops, etcetera. See if anyone borrowed − or bought − medical books containing such information. One of you should contact the NCA's Cyber Crime Team. They might be able to tell us who's searched online for these specific forms of killing."

"Have a look at using a browser called Tor," said Colin Sharp. "It allows you to change your IP address, and then you can do a 'Deep Net' search. Normal search engines like Google only search a small percentage − about 10% − of what is actually out there, because only about 10% of the Internet is indexed. If you conduct a deep net search you'll get a lot of information that other search engines don't even know exists."

"Excellent, Colin, that's a little job for you," Gardener continued. "Sealing wax wasn't the only thing inside Barry's body. Someone definitely killed him."

"What else was there?" asked Briggs.

"Fitz found this." Gardener held the bag up for everyone to see.

"What is it?"

"A key. Possibly a safe deposit key."

"Where was that?" asked Rawson. "Wasn't up his arse, for God's sake, was it?"

"It was in his stomach," continued Gardener. "Fitz thinks he was made to swallow it, because he found minute traces of Vaseline."

"Christ," said Sharp. "Someone really had it in for him."

"Do we know which bank it's from?"

"No," replied Gardener. "But a good locksmith might tell us. So, we want one here tomorrow, and then a couple of you trying to locate which companies use that type of lock on their boxes. I don't need to tell you that this is important. Whatever is in that deposit box may move this investigation by leaps and bounds."

"Then again," said Briggs, "it might be another puzzle in a long line."

"Maybe you're right, but either way we need to know. Even if it is another puzzle to solve, it might stop someone else from being killed."

"Only if we solve it in time."

Gardener addressed Sharp. "Colin, you said something about Barry Morrison's flat and the stuff you'd found?"

"The main things were drugs and money."

"I knew it," said Reilly. "This is all about drugs."

"Much?"

"Not much in the way of drugs, but plenty of bundles of cash, hidden all over the place."

"Any idea what type of drugs?" asked Reilly.

"Not yet. It's all in the exhibits room."

"How much money are we talking?"

"A lot," said Sharp.

"That explains his lifestyle," said Gardener. "For that, he would certainly need a mobile. Anyone found that yet?"

Most of the team shook their heads.

"Okay. Someone make a start on the drugs tomorrow. Tell me how much we have, what it is, and the street value. Find out who else deals the stuff, and if there are any connections to Barry Morrison. Sean and I will go back and see Billy Morrison, see if he knows anything about this."

"You'd better search his house and car lot as well," said Briggs. "In fact, shut the place down until we're finished with this whole thing."

Gardener nodded his approval. "Colin, can you also try and trace phone details for Barry Morrison while you're looking for Nicola Stapleton's?"

Sharp nodded, writing it all down.

"Talking of the car lot," said Gardener. "Have we interviewed all the drivers?"

The officers said they had. Each driver had confirmed Billy's words: a workaholic, never socialized. Never seen with a woman. Distracted when he was talking to people. Fidgeted a lot. The only driver who could not comment was Alan Sargent, because he hadn't been with the company long enough, but it was Barry who gave him the job and kept him pretty busy.

"Do you think he was running the drugs operation from the lot?" Anderson asked Gardener.

"Wouldn't surprise me. Sean said something earlier. He was in that cab office all night by himself, no one would see what he got up to."

"The CCTV tapes might tell us something."

"That's a point," said Gardener. "Have we seen those tapes yet?"

"No," said Briggs. He rose from his chair. "In fact, I'll go and set fire to someone's arse right now. We should have had them back."

Gardener glanced at the charts, realizing that one or two subjects were outstanding. Most notably, Chloe Summerby.

"Dave. Anything on the *Murder Ballads* CD?"

"Not a lot to go on, but I did find a link. Seems a bit tenuous, but the way this bloke is operating, nothing would surprise me."

"Go on."

"The only connection I have at the moment is the rose."

"Oh Christ, the blue rose." Gardener had momentarily forgotten.

"It was the ninth studio album by Nick Cave and The Bad Seeds, released in 1996 on Mute Records. The album consists of new and traditional murder ballads, songs that relay the details and the consequences of crimes of passion."

"Well now, that's what we were thinking about the prostitute," said Reilly. "Crime of passion."

"Apparently, it's the band's biggest commercial success to date."

"Who is it again?" asked Frank Thornton.

"Nick Cave and The Bad Seeds."

"I've never heard of them," said Thornton.

"Neither have I," said his partner, Bob Anderson.

"Not surprised," said Rawson. "Don't think you two have got past Mozart yet, have you?"

"Cheeky bastard," mumbled Anderson. "At least they made music in my day."

Rawson continued without rising. "The song you guys heard in the prostitute's kitchen was called *The Curse of Millhaven*. Apparently, it's about a mad woman called Loretta. She has green eyes and yellow hair. In the song, she describes the deaths of the people who live in

Millhaven. She points out how all God's creatures have to die.

"There's a failed stabbing of a woman called Mrs Colgate, which reveals that Lottie is in fact the killer. Millhaven itself is a fictional town created by the author Peter Straub. You'll like this next bit: the book's about the 'Blue Rose Murders'. The song also has the largest number of deaths in a recording, there's at least twenty-three murders."

"So the blue rose must be the key here," said Sharp.

"Anybody ever seen a blue rose?" Reilly asked.

Gardener knew that Thornton was a keen horticultural man. "Frank?"

"No. It doesn't really exist. From what I know, it's usually a white rose that's been dyed. The Australians and the Japanese came up with the idea."

"Did you check out the florists?" Gardener asked.

"Yes," said Rawson. "Same story. None of the shops I spoke to sell them."

"So where's he getting them?" asked Anderson.

"Maybe he's growing them," offered Reilly.

"Can we get someone on to that?" asked Gardener. "See if anyone imports them, or dyes them here locally? See if it's possible to actually grow them."

The team made notes.

"What about the second song, Dave, the one at Morrison's place?"

"That's the tenuous link. It's called *Where the Wild Roses Grow*, a popular duet with Australian singer Kylie Minogue. It was a hit single and received two ARIA Awards in 1996. It was inspired by a traditional song called *The Willow Garden*. Basically, it's a classic tale of a man courting a woman and killing her while they are out together."

"Anyone have any thoughts on that?" Gardener asked.

"Seems to suggest that Barry Morrison and Nicola Stapleton were an item," offered Paul Benson.

"All the evidence suggests otherwise," said Gardener. "Looks to me like he was controlling her. Her rented her a house, and he rented out her body."

"Seems a bit odd to me," said Rawson. "If she was in the house and he only called once a week, why didn't she just leave?"

"That's what we'd like to know," said Reilly.

"Had to be something important, the hold he had over her."

"Must be," said Gardener. "That's why we need to keep digging. Obviously, if he had her passport, she couldn't leave the country."

"Something bad must have happened at home," said Sharp. "She stole five hundred pounds from her brother, but that was years ago. Why couldn't she just go back home? You don't need your passport to travel round the UK."

"That's another question we're going to have to ask the parents," said Gardener. "They deserve to know she's died, whatever happened back home years ago."

"I wouldn't like to think my daughter went missing from home years ago and no one contacted me about her death," said Reilly.

"That brings me on to Chloe Summerby, the other MFH connected to the case."

At that moment, Briggs came back in with the CCTV footage from the shops. He sat down, waiting for Gardener to continue.

"Sean and I went to see Sally Summerby today, the child's mother. She dealt a real bombshell."

Gardener pointed to the photo on the ANACAPA chart. "Whoever the girl in this photo is, she is not Chloe Summerby."

"What?"

The question came from more than one of the team. The only person who did not react was the SPOC, Sarah

Gates. Gardener suspected that Goodman had already briefed her.

"We went to see if she knew either of the victims. She claims not."

After a short silence, Briggs said, "But you think otherwise."

"I certainly think she was telling the truth about Nicola Stapleton."

"Yes," said Reilly. "When she thought her daughter was with Stapleton, she was ready to rip her head off."

"So, what happened when you mentioned Barry Morrison?"

"She brushed it away too quickly," replied Gardener. "However small, I think there's some connection there. So that's another task for us. Check out the Summerbys and see if there's something in the past that connects them with Morrison."

"So, what about the girl in the photo. Who is she?"

"We don't know," said Gardener. "All we do know is that Sally Summerby emphatically denied that it was her daughter."

"So, are we still looking for her as well?" asked Sharp.

"I think we have to keep the single point of contact at both incident rooms until we know a lot more. Technically speaking, it would be Goodman's investigation if she turns out to be missing too, not ours... at least until we find a body."

He let the team digest the information before moving to conclude the meeting. It had been a long, arduous day, and everyone needed a break, a meal, and a decent night's sleep. He knew, however, that one more important bit of evidence needed probing. He glanced at Briggs.

"The tapes reveal anything?"

"Certainly do," said Briggs, approaching the media system.

The mood in the room suddenly lightened.

Briggs slipped in the tape and fast-forwarded until the appropriate moment.

"I wouldn't get your hopes up."

The picture was grainy, but they could still see.

The road and the pavement outside the block of shops on Cross Bank Road was deserted. Barry Morrison's black Ford Focus suddenly pulled up outside the butcher's, literally, because it stopped on the pavement.

Morrison's prone body was forced out of the passenger door. He didn't land how he was found, but Gardener knew he was dead from the way he hit the ground, and the fact that no movement followed.

The driver's door opened. A figure exited and casually walked around the vehicle, took his time positioning the body. He then reached into the car and pulled out the items of clothing, dumping them on the doorstep as well.

"This bloke's not stupid, is he?"

The mysterious figure then walked back round the car, jumped in, and drove off.

"No wonder there's no trace of the man," said Reilly.

The whole team sat staring at the footage, shocked from the realization they'd had their first sighting of the killer, and it wouldn't make a blind bit of difference.

Their suspect had been wearing a police scene suit, protective boots, and a hood.

Chapter Twenty-seven

It was close to midnight. Vincent had scoured his flat for every true crime book he had, which was no mean feat. If the killer thought he was going to outwit him, he could think again.

Publications were strewn as far as the eye could see: *A History Of British Serial Killing; Crime Scene – The Ultimate Guide To Forensic Science; Settings For Slaughter; Heroes, Victims & Villains of Leeds,* to name but a few. He'd gone through them thoroughly but he hadn't found anything to support the clues.

The killer was taunting him, so he had to be known to Vincent. He'd pointed out that crossing the Man in Black carried consequences. Vincent had obviously done so – as had the people in Batley and Birstall. Now they were dead. Which meant he would be on the list at some point.

It was up to him to discover the identity of the Man in Black, and what his clues meant. Seemed like the killer figured he could.

But why would the killer want him to know who he was? He'd dropped two names into the puzzle that were bound to attract his attention.

Vincent leaned back in his chair, glancing over the aged newspaper article.

The Yorkshire Post 1982

A Wakefield man has admitted handling a stolen 18th-century jug, taken from the tack room of a Yorkshire riding stables. A 22-year-old local man, also helping the police with their investigation, was released without further action.

The bronze jug, decorated with coats-of-arms and inscribed with the words "My Darling Wife, Elizabeth", is believed to be one of only three similar jugs in the UK. Its estimated worth is about £500,000. It was stolen from an old barn that was being cleaned and renovated for the world-renowned Rushworths of Rothwell, belonging to Mickey Rushworth.

West Yorkshire Police recovered the jug on 16 May at Leyburn Auction Rooms, shortly after it had been sold to a mystery telephone buyer. Experts believe it had been commissioned for Elizabeth Lascelles, wife of the first Baron of Harewood, Edwin Lascelles, who died in 1795.

Steven Cooper, 39, from Stanley in Wakefield, formerly of Thirsk in North Yorkshire, pleaded guilty to handling stolen goods at Leeds Crown Court. He will be sentenced on 15 July.

The recovered jug has now been returned to Harewood House but has not yet gone back on display.

Vincent recalled the events of 1982.

Despite his interest in writing, the love of Vincent's life was horses.

His thirst for turning detective, however, came when he solved his first case at Rushworth's – his place of employment. It became known, and written about by Vincent himself, as "The Mystery of the Missing Jug". He sold the story to *The Yorkshire Post* for a tidy profit, before turning it into a short story under the pseudonym Victor Briggs and selling that as well.

Steven Cooper had unearthed the jug in an old barn due to be renovated and turned into a tack room. Cooper claimed it was worthless. It went missing. On a whim, Vincent scoured the antique dealers until he found one in Harrogate, auctioning the jug.

The auction went ahead but Cooper ended up in prison as a result of Vincent's interference.

He shuddered at the thought, rising from his chair. Entering the kitchen, he took the final beer from the fridge. The cryptic clues were beginning to make his head itch. The possibility that he had crossed someone could have happened at any time. For the life of him, though, he failed to see how he could have any connection to the two people killed in Batley, whose names were Morrison and Stapleton. He'd never met either. Especially the woman.

Whatever had happened in Batley had happened before, according to The Man in Black. But when? The sum of the years added up to 20, 18, and 21. How was he supposed to work that out? It could be any combination.

He threw some more beer down his neck, thinking about his own case in 1982. The numbers 1, 9, 8, and 2 added up to twenty, and although they involved three people, it was a different set of people with different ages.

The only clue that Vincent felt really affected him was the third, the one involving the engine driver for the Midland Railway Company. He suspected that was important, because as the email inferred, it was the key to his destiny… or his demise.

So he would concentrate on that one. Once he solved it, he would take the fight straight to the killer's door. If the man wanted to play games, Vincent would take him on.

Then it hit Vincent like a brick in the face. It had to be the man who'd pled guilty to handling stolen goods at the Leeds Crown Court back in 1982.

Steven Cooper must have returned for revenge. But why wait till now?

It was a far cry from stealing to killing, but who knew what kind of a life of crime he'd been led into.

Vincent would have to tell the police.

He reached for his keyboard. Perhaps he should tell the world first.

Chapter Twenty-eight

The clock chimed, and eight bells followed. Gardener glanced up. He'd been in the garage two hours, having risen at five. He stood up, wiped his hands on a rag, and finished off what was left of the bottled water, listening to Maria McKee singing *Show Me Heaven*.

He strolled back to the bike, a 1959 T120 Triumph Bonneville. When he'd started the project some time back, the bike was wrecked: bald tyres, rusty exhaust, a rat-chewed seat. Badges were missing, the fuel tank worn down to bare metal, no front number plate, and a dangling smashed headlamp. It was, however, the last thing Sarah had bought him before she died.

Despite being in bits and strewn all over the place, most of it had been lovingly restored and now eagerly awaited reconstruction. Gardener picked up the King and Queen seat his father had bought him recently, trying to imagine what kind of an experience the finished product would be to ride.

Until that time, he would do what he always came in the garage to do whilst working on the bike.

He would think: about the large can of worms that had been opened with the double murder and everyone who had a connection, however tenuous – Nicola Stapleton, Barry Morrison, Chloe Summerby, her parents, and Billy Morrison. Thinking clearly through that lot would be a real task.

The connecting door between the kitchen and the garage opened, and his father came in with a hot cup of tea. The smell of grilling bacon followed.

"How's it going?" asked his father, glancing admiringly at the pieces of the bike.

"Getting there."

Malcolm sipped his own tea. "What time was it last night?"

"Close to eleven o'clock. No one was up."

"I was awake, but I figured after the hours you'd worked, you'd want a little time to yourself."

"Thank you. I wasn't really in any mood for conversation."

"Did you have anything to eat?"

"No. Wasn't in the mood for that, either. Had a shower and went straight to bed," said Gardener.

"It's not good for you."

"Neither is eating at midnight and then going to bed."

"Point taken. I worry about you, that's all."

The telephone in the kitchen rang. Gardener answered it.

The desk sergeant at the station bade him good morning, and then went on to deliver his message.

"I've had a call from a Vincent Baines."

"Who's he?" Gardener asked.

"Someone who claims to know the identity of the killer."

Chapter Twenty-nine

Robert Quarry, Frank Fisher's social worker, made the tea and took it into the living room. He opened a couple of windows.

Fisher was sitting in his wheelchair in the corner. The place was a tip. Not that Robert expected a disabled man *could* do much cleaning, but he'd never quite seen it as bad. A stale odour prevailed, a mixture of old food and someone who hadn't had a shower in a long time. Cardboard boxes littered the carpet. Why Fisher had them, he didn't know. How he managed to wheel his way around was a mystery to Quarry. Frank's desk was a mess: papers were strewn all over it, sweet wrappers littering the surface. Files lay open, no doubt their contents mixed up. Had he been working too hard?

Time and again he'd tried his best to organize help and support, but Fisher was independent and stubborn, flatly refusing any offers. In fact, he became quite abusive when approached about it.

"Come on, Frank, let's have a cup of tea and you can tell me all about it."

"What's the point?" came the sullen reply. "All you'll do is sit there and listen to me drone on, then you'll consult my doctor and he'll prescribe tablets. I won't take them, and you'll come back and the whole sorry fucking process will carry on repeating itself until I'm dead. Why not cut out all the crap and let me just get on with dying?"

"You know I can't do that."

Fisher grabbed his cup and took a sip of the drink.

"No, you can't, can you? It's your job. I forgot about that."

"You know it's more than that, Frank. You've come a long way since you left hospital."

Quarry thought about the man in front of him: a carpenter by trade, self-employed, sharing business premises with a builder. The pair worked hand-in-hand, often winning contracts based on the help the other could supply. But a serious accident at work had left Fisher disabled, living in sheltered accommodation in Richmond Hill on Sussex Street in Leeds.

Fisher slammed his cup on a coffee table in front of him, tea spilling over the edge on to the surface.

"And all for nothing. I'll never get out of this chair, will I?"

Quarry thought he had a point, but not a good enough reason to give up altogether. They'd been here before and lived to tell the tale. Fisher's accident hadn't been the only thing to affect his future. At the time, he'd had been happily married to his wife Anna for twenty years. The happiness had only run one way.

Fisher was a pretty typical Yorkshireman who enjoyed a pint with his mates down the pub. Weekends were spent at the local social club, where he could sink a few more pints, and then have fish and chips on the way home. He usually took two weeks' holiday a year, always the same two weeks, always the same seaside resort of Whitby.

Anna had wanted more. She'd constantly nagged him to broaden his horizons. But it had been good enough for his parents, so it was good enough for him. At the time, Anna was a self-employed accountant. Finally realizing she couldn't shift him, she'd moved herself instead.

Fisher had had no idea she'd been having an affair with another local businessman, Phillip Elmore. It had been going on for two years. Eventually, with enough money for a deposit on a flat, she was preparing to leave Frank when the accident occurred.

Working late one Friday evening some shelving units he had been working under collapsed, unleashing several bags of concrete. Frank ended up with both legs and an arm broken and a punctured lung. He'd also suffered damage to his spleen.

Operations were needed. The spleen had been removed altogether, the legs patched up, and the lung was left to repair itself. Eventually he was informed of the spinal injuries, and the fact he would never walk again. His doctors also brought up the possibility he may need to use a nebulizer for breathing, much like an asthmatic.

The news alone had been bad enough, but his world collapsed completely when Anna had told him she was leaving him.

Fisher had been devastated, requiring months of therapy. Despite being wheelchair bound, he'd eventually returned to work at the insistence of the builder who he had previously worked with, where he could oversee the accounts and the day-to-day contracts. The builder had insisted on paying for everything to cover the courses Frank would need to qualify properly, including his transport costs. Everywhere Fisher went, he did so in a taxi on an exclusive contract with a local company.

"You shouldn't think like that, Frank," said Quarry. "You have so many things to live for."

"Name one."

"You still have your life. Your job."

"Not enough," shouted Fisher, almost leaping out of his wheelchair. "I haven't got her, have I?"

Quarry was unnerved by Fisher's outburst. His patient was heading for one of his depressions, and to Quarry, it was the worst he had seen. There had to be something more to it.

Fisher was probably going to need more therapy, to see if he could unearth the root of the problem. In Quarry's opinion, there was more to it than his wife leaving him. That had happened three years back now. In that time he'd seen Fisher try so hard to put his life back together.

"Frank, we need to try and move on here. I think we've both known for a long time that Anna is never coming back. I thought you were getting over it."

"'Getting over it!' Up until a few years back I had everything. I had a good job. I was healthy. I could walk. I had a wife, a life. How the hell do you expect me to get over everything that's happened and carry on like nothing has? You want to try stepping into my shoes for a week or two, see if *you* can get over it."

Fisher was returning to the state of mind he'd been in when he'd left the hospital. In spite of the help from his friends, he'd fallen into a deep depression, and had tried to take his own life in the office. He'd been found in time by one of the apprentices. From that point on, they had watched him very closely.

A friend had persuaded Fisher to sue for compensation. Quarry had never been sure who that friend was. Fisher would have none of it at first, but eventually decided to do so because he was informed that the builder would not lose out. He would be insured for such things.

But the builder wasn't insured. The policy had lapsed, the money used for something else. So when Fisher won his compensation claim, he took all the money the builder had.

Fisher sat in his wheelchair, shaking.

"What is it, Frank? What are you not telling me?"

Time stood still for Quarry. He stood up and crossed the room despite the smell growing much worse the closer he got to Fisher.

"Frank, you've come a long way. You've gained your self-respect. You have a good job now, accounting for a number of local firms. You have a lot of friends who come and spend time with you. You have a lot more to live for than you think. Please, tell me what's wrong."

Fisher raised his head, and there were tears in his eyes.

"Everything. Everything's wrong. My whole fucking life is a mistake. Marrying my wife was. The accident was. And if that wasn't bad enough, I then decided to listen to my fucking friend, and I sued the builder I worked with. And that was a mistake."

"Why, Frank? It was an act of negligence that nearly cost you your life."

Quarry could see he would have a devil of a job calming Frank Fisher down, the rage within him was so evident.

"Because the builder was my friend. I should never have done it. I should never have listened to someone else."

"Who, Frank? Who did you listen to that you now think was a bad idea?"

"He had to stick his oar in, didn't he? And I listened to him, and that was a mistake."

"Who, Frank? Please, tell me."

Fisher glared at Quarry with such an intense hatred that he feared for his life.

"Barry fucking Morrison."

"Barry Morrison? What's he got to do with all this?"

"He was my friend… and I listened to him."

"You mean he was the one who advised you to sue the builder?"

Quarry was pleased. Fisher had opened up.

Fisher nodded. "Which was a mistake, because Morrison's dead as well, now."

Chapter Thirty

Following a quick early morning call, Reilly collected Gardener in a pool car. They were now sitting in an interview room with a table and three chairs, and a mirror on one wall.

Sitting opposite the two detectives, with a coffee and a plate of ginger biscuits, was the man who had phoned the station claiming he knew the identity of the killer of Nicola Stapleton and Barry Morrison.

Gardener had a pen and pad in front of him. Reilly also sat nursing a coffee, and an apple turnover, claiming it was the nearest he could find to one of five a day.

"Mr Baines," said Gardener, "I believe you have some information for us."

Gardener was struggling to take the man seriously. His dress sense was dated. He hadn't shaved for some time, and although he didn't actually smell, his odour was not exactly fresh. He was as thin as a rake, and Gardener wondered when he'd last eaten. What credentials did he have for making his claim? Was he simply a glory seeker who would expect some money for food? Or a fix?

"I certainly do, and I want you to take me seriously."

"We take everyone seriously," said Reilly.

"How old are you, Mr Baines?"

"I'm not sure what that has to do with anything, but since you ask, I'm fifty-five."

"And you live where?"

"A flat above Oldham's chemist, on Otley Road in Guiseley."

Gardener knew it. Pretty respectable area, affluent, thriving with small businesses. The big supermarkets were there as well.

"What do you do?" Reilly asked.

"Do?" repeated Vincent, with a surprised expression.

Gardener suspected he was desperate to part with his information, but the SIO wanted some background on the man to assess him, to work out whether or not he *was* worth listening to.

"Yes. For a living?"

"Oh, I see. A bit of all sorts, really."

"Does that mean you don't do anything specific, draw a cheque from the social security, and then lounge around all day?"

Gardener smiled. His partner had a way with words. Didn't like to beat around the bush.

"I most certainly do not," Vincent was outraged. "I-I-I work for myself. I have n-no need to work because of a very lucrative spell with the horses a short time ago."

Interesting comment, thought Gardener. *They had a gambler on their hands.*

"How did you manage that?" Reilly asked.

"Do you know anything about horses, Sergeant?"

"I know I've lost a stack of money over the years."

"Then you don't know the right people."

"Maybe I will after today."

Vincent smiled. "Let's see how seriously you take me then, shall we?"

Gardener laughed. "Now that wouldn't be a bribe, would it, Mr Baines?"

Vincent scowled in Gardener's direction. "I'm not in the habit of bribing people, Detective Gardener."

"Tell us about this lucrative incident," Reilly asked.

"Do you know the Steven Barrows stables in Lambourn?"

"No. But that place rings a bell for some reason, and I can't for the life of me think why."

"I happened to be in the Lambourn stables in Berkshire when I overheard a conversation between a stable boy named Conor Murphy and trainer Nicky Henderson. They were talking about a race at Cheltenham."

"This should be right up your street, Sean," said Gardener. "They even have names that you'll be familiar with."

"Nothing wrong with good honest Irish names."

"Excuse me, are you going to let me finish?"

"Sorry," said Gardener, not so sure it would really go anywhere, but the man did have a right to be heard.

"Conor Murphy had decided to put an accumulator bet on five of those horses. He placed £50 and won £1,000,000. He should have won three times that amount, but Bet365, which took his punt, only had a maximum of one million. Murphy wasn't complaining."

"I do remember that," said Reilly. "I would have liked a slice of that. So where do you come in?"

"I wasn't complaining either, but I've always been frugal. I placed a five-pound bet and picked up a little over

£100,000, enough to set me up for a good while and do something I had long wanted to do."

"Which is what?" asked Gardener.

"Travel to every UK racecourse, and solve mysteries. You see, I am a private detective."

Gardener had heard enough. He decided to cut to the chase. "You rang the station this morning claiming to know the killer of the two people in Batley yesterday."

"That's correct." Vincent finished his coffee and biscuits.

"Can you give me his name, a description maybe?"

"His name is Steve Cooper." Vincent then took them through the mystery of the missing jug, whilst Gardener made notes.

"How do you know its Steven Cooper? You haven't seen him since 1982."

"Who else would know the details of my case from all those years ago?"

"Could be anybody," said Reilly. "Maybe one of your stable friends has decided to have a laugh with you."

"This is not a laughing matter," said Vincent.

"Was this case common knowledge?" Gardener asked.

"It was all over the newspapers at the time."

"As you've said, it's more than thirty years ago. Why would Steven Cooper wait all this time to exact his revenge?"

"I have no idea. Criminals work in mysterious ways."

"According to you, he's killed two people in Batley. Did you know either of them?"

"Nicola Stapleton and Barry Morrison?" replied Vincent. "No."

"You had no connection to either of them at all?"

"None whatsoever."

"So why are you claiming that Steven Cooper has killed them, and is intending to kill you?"

Vincent withdrew a piece of paper from his pocket. "This email."

Gardener took it and read it through. He had to admit the clues were interesting enough and suggested that someone appeared to know a bit about historical crimes – if they were referring to true incidents. It still didn't prove anything, other than the fact that Vincent had crossed someone in the past and that person was very probably winding him up, considering he was Guiseley's answer to Hercule Poirot.

He passed the email to his partner and then glanced at Vincent. "And this is all you have?"

"Isn't it enough?"

"Not really. It certainly doesn't prove he's the killer."

"He's telling us what happened to the people in Batley is going to happen to me."

"No he isn't," replied Gardener. "To be perfectly honest, he's asking you to solve a puzzle, which is a long way from saying he killed the people in Batley. Just look at the opening sentence: 'If you cross the man in black there are consequences, a price to be paid. If you need any further proof, check out what happened in Batley'. Nowhere does it say he actually committed the crime."

Vincent took the email that Reilly handed back to him, reading through what Gardener had pointed out. "But he's threatening to kill me, and he says he's following me."

"You were in the chemist yesterday, talking to the owner, John Oldham?"

"Yes."

"Did you recognize anyone that resembled Steven Cooper?"

Vincent thought about the answer. "Not really."

"Not really," repeated Reilly. "You either did or you didn't. How old was Steve Cooper back in 1982?"

"I have no idea. Maybe late twenties, early thirties."

"Which would now make him late sixties or early seventies. Did you see anyone in the chemist near to that age?"

After a pause, he sheepishly replied he hadn't.

"And knowing what we know about the crime scenes in Batley, Mr Baines, I doubt very much a man of that age could have carried them out with such precision."

Gardener also knew from the CCTV footage that the man they wanted was nowhere near the age Steven Cooper would be.

"So you're not going to take this threat to my life seriously?"

"Not with the little that you have to go on, no. But if it makes you feel any better, we will check the details of the case and the records on Steven Cooper and find out what happened to him after the trial, and any subsequent prison sentence."

Vincent picked up his email and left the room with an unhappy expression.

Reilly turned to Gardener. "No mention of a photo there."

He knew that piece of information had not been released to the press.

"Precisely," said Gardener.

Chapter Thirty-one

Chris Rydell glanced out the kitchen window, across the fields. It was warm and clear, and he could see for miles. The colours were startling: blue, red, yellow, and green. When and if anything happened, he would really miss the place.

All within the house was peaceful. His houseguest had not yet risen. After he'd made a coffee, he opened the cupboard and brought down a fresh packet of biscuits: fig rolls. He didn't mind them. They were supposed to be good for you. Not that it mattered now.

He counted thirteen fig biscuits in the packet. Seeing as he was the only one in the kitchen, he took three, and placed the rest in the biscuit tin.

He collected his snack and strolled into his study, reflecting on his night's work. Things had been pretty easy, only eight drops within the LS postcode. Once all the medical supplies had been checked and his trailer loaded, he'd started around ten. He was finished for two, back home for three.

He'd spent a further hour in the study, where some local news had caught his attention. He was in bed at four, and up at seven. For many years now, he'd needed little more than three hours' sleep a night. That disturbed him because it was an odd number, but he couldn't do anything about it: he had a thing about numbers.

In the study he placed the tea and biscuits on the desk, logged on, and re-read the article that had caught his attention in the early hours. It had concerned the murders of the two local people in Batley. True crime was a topic he'd been interested in since he was a teenager. Over the years he'd been fascinated to learn about people, and what made them tick.

Most of the stories concerning the Batley murders contained little or no information. The material presented was littered with questions, ending with the usual statement that the police were continuing with their investigations. Not that he could help them because he hadn't worked that postcode on the night in question.

Before switching off, however, he'd spotted a blog by a local man called Vincent Baines, who claimed he knew the identity of the killer. The email pointed to incidents in the past, suggesting that what had happened in Batley within the last twenty-four hours had also happened at some point in history.

Rydell realized that the blogger was a private detective because he then published one of his own successes, something about a missing jug. He'd pasted the clues he'd been sent, for the world – and presumably the killer – to see, before informing everyone that he would be visiting the police to let them know what was going on.

He read and reread the information and found it fascinating. A series of numbers adding to a year that would then tell Baines, or whoever else was reading, what had happened previously. If of course you were clever enough to come up with the answer in the first place.

He was hooked. So, what were they? And who had put them together? Furthermore, why had he sent them to the detective-cum-blogger?

Rydell stood up and faced his bookcase, removing at least four titles that had been written about true crime in the area of Leeds.

About to turn round, he felt a spasm in his stomach like nothing he'd ever experienced before. As if someone had pierced his intestines with a white-hot knife, then started twisting the blade around to create maximum pain.

He dropped the books as his knees buckled. He hit the floor with a loud thud. Two of the four books hit the wall and slid down. The other two landed outside the study.

He writhed in agony as the pain continued, reaching from front to back. What had started in his stomach quickly moved to his lungs, and then upwards into his shoulder blades, making it difficult for him to breathe.

He brought his knees up to his chin, wrapping his arms as tightly around his body as he could. His breathing grew more erratic. He was sweating, he felt nauseous, and if it carried on much longer, he figured he might lose control of his bowels.

The pain didn't last, however. As quickly as it came, it subsided, allowing him to relax a little. Eventually he was able to stretch out and lie flat on his back. His breathing returned to normal.

He was still on his back on the floor when his houseguest came into view.

"Are you okay, Uncle Chris?"

Rydell glanced up. Not wishing to cause undue concern, he smiled. "Yes, I'm fine. I just tripped and dropped all my books."

His houseguest laughed. "You silly billy."

Chapter Thirty-two

"Do you recognize this?"

"What is it?"

"A key."

"I can see that. What type of a key?"

"A safe deposit box key," said Gardener, moving the exhibits bag closer to Billy Morrison.

"No, never seen it before in my life. Never had a safe deposit box in this family. In fact, this family has never had anything worth putting in one. Where did you find it?"

Gardener and Reilly were sitting in the kitchen of Billy Morrison's detached cottage on Gomersall Road, approximately three miles from the business. Neither detective had been surprised to find that Billy was not at work.

"Was it our Barry's?"

"We're not sure," said Gardener. "It was certainly in his possession when it was found."

"Are you serious? Our Barry couldn't stand banks. He always said they were willing enough to take what you had, but give nothing back."

No need to tell Gardener that.

The kitchen was large and spacious, the walls and floor tiled. The room led into a conservatory. They were all sitting at the table. Gardener figured Billy's wife was a baker, because an electric mixer stood on one of the worktops, along with a plateful of scones on a wire rack next to it.

Billy had made both men a drink. He was dressed in jeans and a tee shirt, and wore carpet slippers. He hadn't shaved since yesterday, but that was no crime. His complexion was pale, his expression gaunt. Gardener wondered if he'd slept at all last night.

"Anyway, where did you find it? His flat?"

"No."

"So how do you know it's Barry's?"

"We don't," said Gardener. "We had hoped you'd recognize it and save us some time and trouble."

"So, if it wasn't in his flat, where was it? His car?"

"His stomach," said Reilly, straight to the point, as ever.

"Where?" said Billy, blinking excessively.

"I'm afraid it was in his stomach," said Gardener.

"His stomach?" repeated Billy, as if he'd either misheard, or refused to believe them.

"Yes. We think he'd been made to swallow it, which is why we're not sure it's his. We really would like to find the box it opens."

Billy remained silent, his brain probably struggling to accept what the detectives were telling him.

"Who would do a thing like that?" he finally said.

"Somebody who had a grudge, maybe trying to teach him a lesson," said Reilly. "We asked you yesterday if you'd had any trouble with the business. Can you still not bring anything to mind?"

"Even if we had, I can't imagine anyone would go so far as to kill our Barry like this. Like I said, the odd fare dodger. Sometimes people would ring us up and when we got there it turned out to be a hoax. No one at that address either wanted a taxi, or ordered one. A lot of it was mischief stuff, nothing serious."

"You never know," said Gardener. "It can start out as mischief, but soon escalate into something much bigger. For example, you go to one of these addresses and no one wants a cab. Let's say the driver is tired and decides to kick off, it ends in a major argument. Before you know it, the person who started the joke then has a grudge against the company and decides to get revenge."

"Revenge is one thing. Killing someone's going a bit far."

"We know that," said Reilly. "That's why we're here. So, can you think of anything that might have led us to this?"

Billy shook his head and put his hands to his mouth. Gardener could see he was struggling to hold it together.

"Is this how he died?" he finally asked. "Someone made him eat a key and it ripped the lining of his stomach?"

No one had touched their drink since the conversation had started.

"No," said Gardener. "Sadly, it was something much more serious than that."

Billy Morrison's expression would have halted electricity. "More serious how?"

"He died of something known as blocked superior vena-cava syndrome, which is the big vein that drains blood from the upper body to the heart."

"What? This key caused that?"

Gardener suspected Billy was clutching at straws because the truth was too hard to take.

He leaned forward. "Is your wife in?"

"No. What's she got to do with anything?"

"I was checking to see if you needed someone with you, Mr Morrison. What we're telling you isn't very nice. I just wanted to make sure someone was here to offer support. We can call for an officer."

"No, she's out. And I don't need an officer. However bad this is, I need the truth. I need to know what happened to my brother."

"I'm just trying to make it easier," replied Gardener. "To answer your question, no, the key did not block the vein."

"So, what did?"

"Sealing wax."

Billy Morrison stood up and walked over to the conservatory window, staring through it. Gardener left him alone to work his head around the information. He returned quicker than Gardener had suspected he would.

"He had sealing wax in his vein? How did it get there?"

"A syringe. The problem is, we found the syringe at the first crime scene, underneath the body of the prostitute, Nicola Stapleton."

"What? She did it?"

"We don't think so. But we know Barry was at that scene, the house in Hume Crescent."

"How do you know?"

"Because the blood on his jacket belonged to the prostitute."

"You think *he* killed *her*?"

"Again, we don't know. We're trying to build up a clear picture of what happened. But if it's any consolation, we don't think he did."

Reilly leaned forward. "Billy... son... we think he was made to watch her die. Not so much a warning, because there'd be no point warning someone before you killed them. We think it was done deliberately to place him at the scene to confuse us – send us off the scent, so to speak. Which is why we need to ask again, are you sure you knew nothing about Nicola Stapleton and your brother, and the house in Hume Crescent?"

"No," shouted Billy. "I told you yesterday. I thought about nothing else last night. Everything you told me yesterday, it's like we're talking about a different person.

Like it's not my brother, just somebody who looks like him. As if he'd been taken away and somebody else was living his life."

The room grew silent before Gardener spoke again.

"From what we've discovered, there was definitely a strong connection between them, but we don't think they were having a relationship. Certainly not a man and wife relationship."

"So, what was it, then?"

"We think he was controlling her. That he was her pimp."

Billy's jaw dropped. "No way. Not our Barry. Not a pimp. You've definitely got something wrong there."

"We found her passport in his flat," said Reilly.

"There you go again. You're talking about someone else, not our Barry. You're making out he was a fucking criminal, as if he was leading a double life and I didn't know him."

"That's about the size of it."

"No. No way, I'm not having it," said Billy Morrison.

"Then how do you explain her passport in his safe, the house in Hume Crescent, and the fact that he was paying her weekly visits?"

"Well there must have been something between them. Like you said yesterday, she was a prostitute. A man has needs. He was probably paying her for sex. Maybe they went on holidays together, that's why he had her passport."

"You said yesterday he never takes holidays."

"Well you know what I mean," said Billy. "Weekends away, that sort of thing."

"When was the last weekend he took off?" Reilly asked.

That question took Billy by surprise. A pause followed before he admitted, "I can't remember."

"That's because he didn't," said Gardener. "You told us he was a workaholic and he never took holidays. Everyone else has said the same thing. Everyone also agreed with another of your statements, that he did not have a woman, was never seen with one. And let's be honest. He had her passport, so why would he keep it in a safe? We never found his in there."

Billy Morrison had no answer. He was too busy ringing his hands together and running them through his hair.

"I know this is hard for you, Mr Morrison. We don't like giving bad news to anyone, but we need your help. We need to find out who killed your brother. We have a number of good reasons for that. Not the least of which is to discover whether or not it's an isolated case, or if your life is in danger."

Gardener's last sentence froze Billy. "Me?"

"Yes, you. Have you considered that they took Barry and not you because you were on holiday? Maybe someone wants both of you. Apart from being a suspect, you're also a potential victim."

"Suspect? I'm a suspect? You think I killed my own brother?"

"It's nothing personal, son. Golden rule of policing, look at family first. Ninety percent of the time, it *is* family."

Billy Morrison's next words were slowly and carefully delivered. "Listen closely to me. I did not kill my brother."

"Pleased to hear it, but we still have to treat you as a possible victim until we can find out more about it."

Gardener sat back and changed topics in order to diffuse the situation. "You also said yesterday that business was okay, but you were not breaking any records."

"That's right. Everybody's the same."

"And you mentioned that you and Barry would go without a wage if necessary, to see that the drivers and the salesmen were paid."

"If we had to."

"Have either of you?"

"No. Haven't had to."

"You have no financial trouble?"

"No."

"I asked you yesterday to check with the accountant if the books were up to date, that no large sums of money had been withdrawn."

"That's right. I left a message on his answering machine, but he hasn't called back yet."

"So you don't know."

"No. But like I said yesterday, if our Barry had been withdrawing large sums of money, I would have known. Frank would have called me. He's as straight as a die, that bloke. Had an accident a few years back, left him disabled. In a wheelchair. But he fought back: he never let it beat him. And he doesn't just do our accounts, he does other people's as well."

"You said Barry liked money."

"I did. He's always liked money. Always worked a bloody sight harder than most people, which is probably why he has a bit put by."

"He had a lot put by."

"Well maybe he did. Like I said, I don't know when he had time to spend it, the hours he put in."

"And he wasn't moonlighting somewhere else?" Reilly asked.

"He didn't have the bloody time. He was always at the lot."

"We found money in his flat, Mr Morrison."

"You probably would. He didn't like banks."

"We haven't had a count yet, but the search of the flat unearthed what looks to be thousands of pounds."

"Thousands?"

"That's how it looks."

"How many thousands?"

"It's all in plastic bags," said Gardener. "It doesn't take a genius to work that there must be at least a hundred thousand."

"What?"

"There was a serious amount of money in his flat, hidden all over the place. Have you any idea where he could have gotten that kind of money?"

Billy Morrison sat gazing at the wall. "Here we are again, talking about someone else. I can't believe what I'm hearing."

"Then you'd better strap yourself into that seat now, son, because that wasn't the only thing we found."

"What, are you're going to tell me the place was loaded to the rafters with drugs?"

No one spoke. Gardener simply stared at Billy Morrison, willing him to explain further. He slumped forward on the table.

"Oh, please don't tell me he was into drugs."

Gardener leaned forward. "We probably found as much in drugs as we did money. Can I ask you once again, do you know anything about what we've told you that will help?"

"No. I've told you I didn't know anything about what he was up to." Billy ran his hands down his face. "How bad is this? Sounds like I didn't even know my own brother."

"You've never seen him take drugs, or sell them?"

"No. I can't say I have, but then again, I've never suspected him, so I haven't been watching."

"You've never noticed him huddled away in a corner speaking to people you didn't know?"

"I've seen him speaking to people we didn't know, that was the nature of the business. But not huddled away in a corner, looking to see who was watching him, no."

"You've never walked in on a phone call that you didn't understand? Thought he might have put the phone down a little too quickly?"

Billy ruffled his hands through his hair. "Not that I can think of."

"Is there any chance he could have been running his drugs operation from the business?"

"Operation? Who do you think he was, Al Capone?"

"He clearly wasn't who you thought he was."

"Jesus Christ," said Billy. "What a fucking mess."

"Did he have a mobile phone?'

"Of course he had one. Haven't you found that? You've found everything else, by the sound of it."

"No. But perhaps you can call it for us."

Billy hesitated, but pulled his phone out of his pocket and rang his dead brother's number. He waited for what seemed an eternity before someone finally answered.

"Who's that?" Billy asked. "Where are you? Okay, I'll speak to you later." Billy put his phone on the table before addressing Gardener.

"That was one of the drivers."

"Which one?"

"New lad, Alan Sargent."

"Why did he have Barry's phone?"

"He didn't. He's at the office. Apparently, our Barry's phone was underneath the portacabin."

Although it was evidence from a crime scene, Gardener wasn't too worried that someone else had handled it. He suspected that they would find Barry's prints and Alan Sargent's, but as he'd already seen, the killer had been wearing a scene suit and gloves, and had left no trace of his existence anywhere else. He rose from the kitchen chair.

"Thank you, Mr Morrison. You're not going to like what I have to say next, but it has to be said nevertheless. I need the name and address of the bank you used for your business. In view of everything that we've found, I will need you to close the business for the foreseeable future so we can make a thorough search. I'll also need you and your family to move into rented accommodation, or in with relatives, because we need to search this place as well."

"You're fucking joking. Shut the business, move everyone out of the house? You still think I'm in on this, don't you? Why don't you arrest me, then?"

"I can't," said Gardener.

"Why not?"

"I don't have enough evidence."

"No, and you know what? You'll never find any, because I'm not guilty."

"I believe you. This is just procedure. I don't make the rules, I only follow them. So, I'd like you to call the car lot and tell them to expect us. There are a couple of officers outside the house. They will remain with you while you make other arrangements."

Billy stepped back. "My wife's gonna love this."

As Gardener moved towards the front door, he turned. "One more question."

"What is it this time? You found underage porn in Barry's flat, and you're gonna ask me if we directed and produced them together?"

"Don't put ideas into my head, Mr Morrison. No, something completely different. Have you ever heard of a man called Steven Cooper?"

"No."

Chapter Thirty-three

"The police?"

"That's what I said. The police."

"At the car lot?" asked Vanessa, glancing up from the ironing board.

"They're all over it like a rash." Sargent pulled a cup down from the cupboard. "You want a coffee?"

"If you're making."

He grabbed another cup and put the kettle on, staring out of the kitchen window.

The Sargents lived in the last house on the left in Morris Grove in Kirkstall. It was basically a two-up, two-down that had seen better days, but Alan Sargent had been out of work for quite some time, having only recently landed the driving job. Now that might be in jeopardy.

They had promised themselves that once they'd sorted out their financial problems, each room would have a makeover. Only the garden stood out, with its water features and rockeries and fishpond, only because he was a landscaper by trade.

The kettle boiled. He made the drinks, placing them on the kitchen table when he'd finished. Vanessa stopped ironing when the drinks were ready.

"What's happened?" she asked.

"I've no idea. Yesterday they were sniffing round asking questions, trying to see what Billy knew about Barry."

"Thick as thieves them two, bet there's plenty he hasn't told them."

"What do you mean?"

"You know what I mean. I never liked that Barry. He had shifty eyes, too close together."

"He's alright, is Barry."

"No he isn't... wasn't, should I say."

"You're turning into your mother, you are."

"Nothing wrong with that. She's got men weighed up."

"Is that why she never has one?"

"She hasn't got one because she doesn't need one." Vanessa helped herself to a couple of bourbons from the biscuit tin. "Anyway, let's get back to the point. Why are the police all over the car lot today if they were only asking questions yesterday?"

"I've told you, I don't know. All I know is we got a phone call to say the police were on their way, and the whole place was being shut down until they'd finished their inquiries."

"Are you telling me the truth, Alan?"

"Why wouldn't I be?"

She banged her cup on the table. "For God's sake we can't afford this. You've been out of work for twelve months, we haven't had a chance to get straight yet."

"Tell me about it. You think I don't know?"

"We've still got mortgage arrears to clear. Look what we had to cut back on. We've cancelled the Sky system. We couldn't go out because we couldn't afford a babysitter. He's been up to no good, that Barry Morrison, you mark my words. And if he's up to no good, you can bet that brother of his will be involved."

"You should write books with your imagination. They're just a couple blokes who have made good. They both work hard, and one of them was good enough to give me a job when no one else would."

"Aye," she said, sipping coffee. "And have you asked yourself why?"

"Because he needed someone."

"He hasn't involved you in anything, has he?"

"Like what?" Sargent fished out another biscuit for himself.

"You tell me. I know what you're like. You don't like to say no. How many times have you come home and told me that you spent most of the night delivering packages and collecting money, that you hadn't seen a passenger?"

"All I've done is drive a bloody taxi for him. He said that night shifts were pretty slow, and they'd picked up a new contract, subletting for a local courier company. I was delivering equipment."

"At night? I'll bet you were. You worked some strange hours, that's all I know."

"That's what taxi drivers do. But I said I'd work all hours so we could get back on our feet quicker. I was sick of being out of work, sick of seeing you and James having to make do."

"I'd rather we made do than you get involved in something illegal."

Sargent sighed. He stood up and pushed his chair under the table.

"Where are you going?" she asked.

"Upstairs. See what I can find to wear tonight."

"You're not still going?"

"What do you mean, not going? Of course I'm going. It's Steve's stag night. I'm the best man. What's he going to think if I'm not there?"

"I'm sure he'll understand, Alan. If you're laid off and can't work, we have no money coming in. I'm not borrowing off my mother again. She kept us afloat last time, but I've got more self-respect than that."

"Vanessa, I can't miss his stag night. He'll never forgive me."

"Of course he will. He'll understand. If sacrifices have to be made, better start now."

Sargent faced her. She was the same height as him, but skinny, with long black hair and a pointed nose. What she lacked physically she more than made up for with her mouth. Vanessa was very feisty, which was why he'd married her, and it was still a quality he loved. Only sometimes...

"Vanessa, it's one night. I've been putting a little aside to cover it."

Her stern expression said it all. There was no arguing with her, so he stormed out of the room. She followed him to the foot of the stairs.

"Don't spend too much money, and don't get legless. If you do, I'd think twice about coming home tonight."

Chapter Thirty-four

Reilly brought the car to a halt, next to another pool car on Cemetery Road.

Gardener jumped out. He glanced around. The view was mostly green fields, with fresh clean air where mills and factories would once have stood. Inside the grounds to his left stood the church, surrounded by headstones and well-kept lawns. In front of him was a large house made from Yorkshire stone with a grey slate roof and old-fashioned, wooden framed windows. Gothic turrets stood either side.

Bob Anderson came out to meet him. His partner Frank Thornton was probably still inside.

"What have you got for us, Bob?"

Reilly came around to join them.

"Evidence that Nicola Stapleton existed outside that hovel called a home. This is a homeless shelter. Run by Brenda Killen."

Gardener remembered Colin Sharp mentioning the name in the incident room the day before.

Anderson pointed to the building. "It's the vicarage, really, but it's big enough to use the rooms to other things. Anyway, the vicar started a homeless shelter a while back, mainly providing food for people less fortunate. Apparently, once they'd finished breakfast this morning and had a tidy round, Brenda Killen was about to make a coffee for herself when one of the volunteers found a box with her name on it."

"Whose?" Reilly asked. "Brenda Killen's?"

Bob Anderson glanced at Reilly as if he'd lost his mind.

"Why don't I like the sound of this?" said Gardener.

"It's nothing bad. You'd better come inside and have a look."

The two men followed Bob Anderson. Through the entrance, they walked past a staircase on the left into a room on the right, which resembled an old schoolroom. The plaster walls were painted magnolia, with the deepest skirting he had ever seen. The windows were all very high up. Posters advertised a variety of ways to obtain help if you needed it.

At the back he saw a counter: behind that was the kitchen, with ovens and pots and pans and cutlery. The shutters were up. Food odours hung in the air, but they were not unpleasant. The radio was tuned to BBC Radio 2. Sitting at a table, both nursing coffees, were Frank Thornton and very obviously Brenda Killen.

Gardener walked over and took a seat. Brenda was late forties to early fifties, with chestnut-coloured hair shaped in a bob. She had brown eyes, and little make up. She was plump and pleasant, wearing a blue and white overall. On the table next to her was a box with her name on it.

She immediately rose. "Thank you for coming. Who's for a coffee?"

"Now that's what I call a grand start," said Reilly. "You wouldn't have a few biscuits to go with that, would you? Or maybe the odd homemade scone?"

Gardener glanced at his partner. "Where the hell do you put it all?"

"A man needs fuel."

"You eat enough to fill a 747," said Thornton.

Gardener asked if he could have water. When they were all seated again, he asked, "Who found the box, Mrs Killen?"

"Jenny Proctor. She only lives round the corner on North Bank Road. Comes in every day to help, bless her."

"Where?"

"In the cupboard under the stairs. She said she was sorting through the cleaning materials when she came across it."

"Was there anything else apart from the box?"

"No. I went to have a look myself."

"Have you checked the contents?"

"Not all of it. I've seen enough to know everything belongs to the woman killed on Friday night, Nicola Stapleton."

"What's in the box?" Reilly asked, having demolished one half of a scone.

"Well I haven't had a good look through, but it's all personal stuff. Diaries, and lots of papers. Some of 'em look like legal papers to me. She'd also left me a letter."

Brenda Killen passed it to Gardener. He took the single sheet of paper from the envelope and read it before passing it to Reilly. It thanked Brenda for being the kindest person Nicola had met in a long time, and that if anything happened to Nicola, Brenda was to keep and read the diaries, and then she would know what to do with them. Had they struck gold at last? Gardener wondered.

"How well did you know Nicola Stapleton?"

"I wouldn't say I did. She's not been coming long, poor lass."

"Why do you say that?"

"You can tell, can't you? I've been at this a long time, and I know a real charity case when I see one. She was clean enough. Her clothes and everything were always clean, but they were old. Not fashionable like girls her age would normally wear if they had the money, which she clearly didn't."

"Did she tell you anything about herself?"

"Not really. I didn't think she was homeless, because she wasn't here for food. No. She came to help. She let slip now and again about where she lived being terrible. I think she had a boyfriend and he was a bit of a pig, by the sound of things. Very controlling. Wouldn't let her out very much, and always wanted to know where she was going and where she'd been."

Still, Gardener could not understand the situation Nicola Stapleton had been in. How had Barry Morrison managed to control her so well? It had to be fear. But why was she so frightened of him? Knowing the means of domination Morrison employed would go a long way to easing Gardener's frustration regarding who the man was and how he operated.

To have that kind of control, he would have to have shadowed her, been with her twenty-four hours a day and never let her out of his sight. According to witnesses he clearly wasn't.

The mystery deepened.

"Did she ever mention her boyfriend's name?"

"Not from what I recall."

"Did she ever tell you she lived in Hume Crescent?"

Brenda Killen shook her head. "No."

"When did she first turn up?" Bob Anderson asked.

"About a week before she was killed, maybe ten days." She put her hands to her mouth. "Do you know I still can't believe it's happened? I never got to know her all that well, but I thought I might in time. I'm usually good like that with people. Have to be in my position."

"And you'd not seen her before that?" Thornton asked.

"No, not even around the town. And let's face it, Batley isn't that big, is it?"

Reilly had finished the scone and was now doing his best to bankrupt the homeless shelter by depleting the supply of biscuits.

"When did you last see her alive?"

"The night before she was killed."

"How did she seem?"

"No different. She turned up around lunchtime, helped out with the afternoon tea and biscuits. In fact, she even helped me prepare the breakfasts for the next morning."

"Did she talk much? Was she preoccupied by anything?"

"Not that I could tell. She disappeared for about ten minutes. When she came back, she said she'd been to the toilet, and then outside for some fresh air. More likely she'd been hiding this." Brenda Killen pointed to the box.

"I reckon her life was that bad that she wanted to reach out to someone, but maybe she was too frightened to tell them everything... whatever that was. Anyway, when Jenny found this, she brought it to me. I didn't open it straight away. I waited till Jenny had gone to make a drink."

Gardener stood up and opened the box. Inside he found a number of books, which turned out to be personal diaries. There were envelopes bearing a name and address in Ealing Broadway: obviously she had written to her parents, but none of them had ever been sent. As Brenda Killen had said, there were other envelopes. At the bottom, underneath everything was a mobile phone, switched off.

Why had she left the contents of the box in a homeless shelter the night before she was killed?

Gardener passed the phone and the diaries to Thornton and Anderson.

"Take these back to the incident room. That phone will hopefully lead us to something."

He glanced through the remaining envelopes that Brenda thought were legal papers. They were not. One contained a medical card. The others were notices, reminders of upcoming doctor's appointments.

She had been a patient of the Bond Street Private Clinic in Leeds, and her doctor's name was Trent.

Chapter Thirty-five

Gardener and Reilly were sitting opposite Peter Trent in his office. His last patient of the day had left fifteen minutes previously. Margaret Pendlebury had offered afternoon coffee but both officers had declined.

"How can I help you?" asked Trent. He was dressed in a dark blue suit with a pale blue shirt and tie.

"We'd like to talk to you about one of your patients."

"Which one?"

"Nicola Stapleton."

"That's a terrible business," said Trent. "I hope you catch whoever is responsible."

"So do we," said Reilly.

"What would you like to know?" asked Trent.

"What you were treating her for?"

Trent picked up the phone and asked his secretary to bring in Stapleton's files.

"I'm a little confused," said Reilly. "We've seen where and how she lived, and I can't imagine she could afford any treatment here."

"It's not all private work, Sergeant. Some of our referrals are from the NHS. GPs will sometimes send people here when the diagnosis and the treatment is out of their field. We specialize."

"Who pays for the treatment?"

"Usually, half from the taxpayer. The rest is paid for by our private investors."

Margaret Pendlebury came through with the file that Trent had requested. She was about to leave, but Trent asked if either detective had any objection to her staying. Neither did. She took a seat at the side of the desk.

After studying the files – no doubt wondering how much to tell them – Trent glanced up.

"She had hepatitis B. It's a very serious disease caused by the hepatitis B virus. Infection with this virus can, and often does, result in scarring of the liver, liver failure, liver cancer, and even death."

"I assume it's transferred in the normal way," suggested Gardener. "Through sex."

"Not always," replied Trent. "Hepatitis B is spread by infected blood and other bodily fluids such as semen, vaginal secretions, saliva, open sores, and breast milk."

That diagnosis would certainly clear things up for Fitz, Gardener thought, though he would no doubt soon find out anyway from the antibody screen.

"How was it diagnosed?"

"She had visited her own GP and asked if she could have a blood test because she'd had unprotected sex with a number of men. I suspect she was making sure she did not have the HIV virus. Hepatitis B was confirmed when the test detected the hepatitis virus and various antibodies against the virus. She was referred to us after the tests, and we took a small biopsy to determine the severity of the disease. I must stress at this point, however, that she was only a carrier."

"What does that mean?" Gardener asked.

"In a lot of cases, hepatitis B causes limited infection. Most people can fight off the infection within months. They then develop an immunity that lasts a lifetime, so it's very unlikely they will ever get the infection again. Regular blood tests show evidence of immunity, but no signs of active infection.

"Some people, however, don't get rid of the infection. If you are infected with hepatitis B for more than six months, you are considered a carrier, even if you have no symptoms. This means that you can transmit the disease to others by having unprotected sex, kissing, or sharing personal items such as toothbrushes or razors. Being a carrier also means that your liver may be more prone to injury."

"But surely if she had it, she wouldn't continue to have unprotected sex with others because the risk of passing it on is great."

"You wouldn't think so, Mr Gardener," said Margaret Pendlebury. "But human beings are fickle, and not everyone thinks the same. Some people are so incensed that they have been infected that they go out and try and infect as many people as they can, a form of revenge if you like. They can't get back to the person who gave it to them because they're never quite sure who it was. So they settle for the next best thing."

Gardener could believe that. He spent his life investigating the darker side of human nature. His mind flashed back to the crime scene. She had been found naked. He'd wondered then if her killer had had unprotected sex with her. He remembered Reilly finding boxes of condoms, but they had yet to find a used one.

"If you are carrying the virus," said Trent, "you should not donate blood, plasma, body organs, tissue, or sperm. Tell your doctor, dentist, and sexual partners that you are a hepatitis B carrier."

"How would you know if you had the disease?"

"There are quite a number of symptoms," replied Trent. "Jaundice, for one, yellowing of the skin or whites of the eyes. A brownish or orange tint to the urine is another, unusually light-coloured stools. You would have unexplained fatigue that persists for weeks or months. More serious complaints are gastrointestinal symptoms such as fever, loss of appetite, nausea and vomiting, or a lot of abdominal pain."

Gardener noticed Margaret Pendlebury suddenly writing something down on a yellow stick-it note.

Even though he suspected he was clutching at straws considering the way she had earned her living, Gardener asked, "In her files, is there a list of her sexual partners?"

Trent glanced through once more. "No, I'm afraid not. We had a number of discussions about that, and I suggested it was her moral duty, if not responsibility, to tell me so we could check other people out."

"She ever tell you what she did for a living?" Reilly asked.

"Not in so many words."

"Did she tell you in any words?"

"It says in her files she was an escort."

"That's the polite version."

"Are you saying she was a prostitute?" Margaret Pendlebury asked.

"All the evidence we've found and the people we've talked to suggest as much."

"Good grief," replied the woman.

Gardener suspected by the way she dressed and spoke and conducted herself, Margaret Pendlebury was a very upright, church-going woman.

"Do you treat other people here, Mr Trent, for the same complaints?"

"As I said, we specialize."

"I will have to see your files so I can cross match."

"Patient confidentiality forbids that, Mr Gardener."

"This is a murder case, which means I have the full power of the law behind me."

"And those patients have a right to their privacy."

"Maybe so," said Gardener. "And I would respect that right, but how would you feel if you found out one of them is a murderer?"

Trent didn't have an answer.

"Maybe we should co-operate, Mr Trent," said Margaret Pendlebury.

"I don't intend to go public with your files," said Gardener. "Every single one of them will be treated in the strictest confidence, but I have a job to do, and I have to explore every avenue. Maybe none of them had a connection to Nicola Stapleton, but I would only need to find one to prevent any further deaths."

Chapter Thirty-six

The second email from The Man in Black was sitting in Vincent's inbox. Since leaving the two detectives – who had refused to take him seriously – he had spent the journey home glancing over his shoulder, and in dark corners where he suspected someone could creep up on him, and staring more intensely at people than he would normally have done.

The rest of the day had been spent sitting in front of his computer, searching for information about the clues he had been given with regards to the murders. As early afternoon had approached, he'd felt it wise to concentrate on the one that affected him personally.

Lunch had been a cold beef sandwich, a sausage roll, and two apple and custard doughnuts, washed down with some more of that Belgian beer from Morrisons. During the evening he had cracked open a bottle of the hard stuff. Two glasses of Glenmorangie later, he was pretty sure he was making real headway:

> *Clue No:3 is the key to your destiny, Vincent, or perhaps I should say demise. The sum of the year adds up to 21 and involves an engine driver with the Midland Railway Company. Do you know what happened?*

He did, and he was far from happy.

The engine driver in question was a man named Samuel Birchall who had worked for the Midland Railway Company. At the tender age of fifty-five he had committed suicide by poisoning himself with opium in 1866, the sum of which added up to 21.

Like Vincent, Birchall had been addicted to horse racing for most of his life and had been described as a man of very dissipated habits.

Someone knew Vincent very well. Was it Steven Cooper? If not, who else could it be?

Vincent reached for his glass of whiskey before opening his second email. The message contained within was shorter, but far more disturbing than the first:

Hello Vincent,

Guess your little trip to the cop shop didn't get you very far. Can't have done, because I'm still at large. So I reckon you gave them duff information.

Let's recap, shall we? The Mystery Of The Missing Jug. My guess is, you went and told them you thought Steven Cooper was responsible. Not such a good move, my friend. All you've done is sent them on a wild goose chase. Don't you think they have enough to do, investigating those two in Batley?

Let me give you some more help, see if you can work out who the man in black really is. Mind you, I would have thought a detective in your class would have been nearer to the truth now.

Anyway, here goes. All these references are from one of your favourite country songs, which also happens to be the snifter of your choice: a nice little Scottish number. Keeping up so far?

Clue No:1 She broke your heart, Vincent. You spent your whole life trying to forget.

Clue No:2 Put the bottle to your head and pull the trigger.

Clue No:3 Is the title of the song.

I'm going now, Vincent, as time is short, for you and for me. I have three more little jobs to take care of, and you're one of them.

Good luck.

As Vincent read through it, he drained his glass, realizing he now had a very big problem. It was no longer funny.

Clue number three, the title of the song was easy: *Whiskey Lullaby* by Brad Paisley. Clue number one was no problem either. A tear formed in Vincent's eye as he recalled Julie, the one and only love of his life.

Julie had been Mickey Rushworth's daughter. They had met at Mickey's stables in Rothwell in their teens. Nothing had developed until Vincent was twenty and he had managed to uncover the jug scam, which could have cost the stable money and jobs. Julie saw Vincent in a different light, and the pair became close, started dating.

Mickey had no problem. Julie had discovered Vincent's true strength when her father Mickey had been unwell for months, and Vincent had persuaded him to go to the doctor for a check-up. Mickey had bowel cancer, and it was far too late to do anything about it.

Julie and Vincent announced their marriage the same day. When they'd told Mickey, he'd wanted a big wedding. His present to them was a quarter share in the stable. Mickey died before the ceremony took place. Further tragedy struck on the morning of the big day when Julie, rushing into the town centre for some very last-minute preparations, was hit and killed instantly by a bus.

It took Vincent years to recover. He did, however, end up with a smaller than planned share in the stable of ten percent. It wouldn't keep him in the lap of luxury, but did generate an income, enough for him to find somewhere else to live because the memories were too painful.

Vincent slammed his empty glass on the desk. He was furious now, and the twitch in his left eye was becoming uncontrollable. He was going to have to try and work out what was going on. The police would have to take him seriously. His life was in danger, as were others. The Man in Black reckoned he had three more jobs to take care of, and Vincent was one of them.

He quickly sobered up, and started to think long and hard about the evasive second clue. You wouldn't put a bottle to your head and pull the trigger. That suggested a gun, and the only thing to come out of a gun was a bullet.

Vincent nearly fell off his chair as he realized what was happening. The clues were there. Scottish snifter, bullet.

They could only mean one thing.

January 14, 1993

The incident involved a winter's night, Rushworth's stables, a champion colt called Bullitt, and three masked gunmen. The result – a stolen horse.

Negotiations were demanded through three horse-racing journalists, one of which was Vincent. Eight phone calls from the kidnappers spread over eight hours, with demands for a ransom from Bullitt's four owners, each with a share worth £250,000.

The syndicate refused to pay the ransom, fearing it would encourage other kidnappings. Talks broke down.

The following Monday, they received a call saying the horse was dead.

The horse, however, was not dead, as Vincent would find out.

Following the trail all the way from West to North Yorkshire, through the town of Redcar, and eventually to North Berwick, led him to a stable run by a Scottish gang, and the infamous Mad Dog MacDonald. Vincent eventually returned home to the local police station in Guiseley, supplying them all the information he had.

He'd watched the raid on the stable in North Berwick the following night on the news. The day after it was in all the newspapers. The horse had been returned safe and sound.

But Vincent wasn't safe: he'd made enemies.

After recalling the story, Vincent felt like death.

Many years after the incident, he remembered reading MacDonald's autobiography. There were clues in the book that led him to think MacDonald had known who was responsible for the horse's return, and Vincent took them as a warning.

He was in very serious trouble if it *was* the deranged Danny MacDonald. He wasn't known as "Loch Ness" for nothing.

He *was* a monster – a real one.

Chapter Thirty-seven

Gardener and his team had been in the incident room for at least twenty minutes and had gained no ground. The bayonet had produced no results. It had not been bought locally. The task was to keep searching. It was boring and soul destroying, but that's how they solved cases.

Two of his team had spoken to the National Injuries Database and the Cyber Crime Team on both crime scenes. As yet, those lines of inquiry had yielded no results. They had found no one who had searched on-line for such a specific form of killing. The libraries and the bookshops had managed to come up with a list of people who had either borrowed or bought books covering anything on the subject. The lists were small, kept mainly to professionals, but at least it was an avenue to pursue.

Trying to find the sealing wax was like searching for a needle in a haystack. Of all the shops that sold it locally, no particular sale had stood out. Dave Rawson was also searching on-line outlets, which made the task doubly difficult.

The locksmith had visited the station. He'd taken impressions of the key. He didn't recognize it at first glance, but said he would report back to them. He was aware of the urgency, but that, too, was another proverbial needle in a haystack.

Paul Benson had remained in the station all day, overseeing the HOLMES team who had yet to come up with anything. There were plenty of murders involving bayonets for the team to trawl through, but the sealing wax was proving much more evasive.

Benson had spent some time having the drugs in Morrison's flat analysed. The bags were full of cocaine, which had an estimated street value of forty thousand pounds. That raised a question: where was Morrison selling it? It was an awful task for someone, not only because they would need to involve the narcotics team, but the fact that so much of it was going on in Leeds, they stood little chance of ever finding out where it was going.

"Did have one stroke of luck, though," said Benson.

"Which was?" Gardener asked.

"Morrison didn't just own the house in Hume Crescent."

"Really?"

"No, records indicate that he had a couple of small flats in the area as well. I got on to the council for addresses and checked the places out earlier. They were rough. Tried knocking on doors, but not many people home. Those I did speak to reckoned the kids who lived there were on benefits. Spent most of the day in bed, and most of the night out. Neighbours weren't surprised they were into drugs."

"Brilliant, Paul. Keep on it. Best thing to do is go back sometime around dawn tomorrow morning, wait for them. Don't let them get back in to sleep, drag them down here if you have to. If it turns out that Morrison was a drug baron and these were his minions, we'll turn the whole lot over to the drugs squad. What about the money?"

"A hundred and twenty-eight thousand."

A few whistles went around the room.

"The bloody hell was he doing with it all?" asked Anderson.

"Nothing," said Reilly.

"He must have had something in mind."

"We might never know what that was, now," said Gardener. "And what really bothers me is, we might never actually get an answer as to what he was doing with Nicola Stapleton. They're *both* dead."

"What about his brother?" Briggs asked.

"We're still no further on there. The business had no financial problems. He still claims he knows nothing about the prostitute or the house in Hume Crescent, and he nearly threw up when we announced that Barry was into drugs."

Briggs turned to Gardener's partner. "What do you think, Reilly? Victim or suspect?"

"I think he's telling the truth, sir. I genuinely don't think he killed his brother, or had anything to do with it. But as the boss man pointed out today, he might be another victim."

"I also asked him to move the family out of the house to stay with relatives so we could make a thorough search of the place."

"Bet that went down well."

"We've closed the business down so we can check for drugs, and whether or not Barry was running things from there. Which reminds me, we also found his phone. Has anyone had a chance to check it out?"

Patrick Edwards nodded. "There's loads of stuff on it. We've got all his contacts, so that's a good start, especially if they're druggies. Might even be the two who live in the flats. Nicola Stapleton's number is used a lot, and there are a few recorded conversations that we need to listen to in more detail."

Gardener continued. "We also found out the name and address of the accountant from Billy Morrison. A man called Frank Fisher, lives on Richmond Hill in sheltered accommodation."

"Sheltered?" asked Briggs.

"Yes, he's disabled." Gardener glanced at Frank Thornton and his partner Bob Anderson. "I'd like you two round there first thing in the morning."

Both men nodded.

"Good work this morning, you lads, by the way. Colin mentioned a homeless shelter yesterday. Frank and Bob went back this morning, and the matron in charge had been left a box by Nicola Stapleton. In the box were her diaries, some letters she'd written to her parents and never sent, and her mobile. Also, we found a medical card for a private clinic in Leeds. Sean and I nipped over there this afternoon."

Briggs intervened. "I took the liberty of phoning her parents this morning. Broke the bad news. They're coming over tomorrow. Any news from the clinic?"

"Yes," said Gardener. "Some of it good. She was a carrier of hepatitis B. Although she didn't give her doctor a list of clients, we have managed to obtain a list of everyone attending the clinic with a similar complaint. I want someone on that tomorrow. Go through the list and see if any name from the clinic cross matches any of the clients on her phone. Whoever killed her may have had unprotected sex with her. Not necessarily on the night he killed her, because Fitz has found no evidence to suggest she was interfered with, but he may be a client."

Gardener was updating the ANACAPA chart as he went along, which was now a mess and resembled a road atlas. He turned back to the group. "Has anyone had a chance to go through *her* phone?"

"Still working on it," said Sharp. "But we have found something interesting. About a month back Morrison phoned her and mentioned a new driver he had by the name of Alan Sargent, and that he was her new point of contact."

"For what?"

"Didn't say."

"Alan Sargent is also mentioned in her last diary," said Paul Benson.

"Does it say why?"

"No. All I noticed on one of the pages was 'new contact', and his name. Never saw anything after that."

Gardener sighed. He would solve the case if it killed him. He asked, "Anyone anything else to add?" He hadn't expected anything. They'd all put in another good day's work, and they were all tired.

"Okay. The two most important actions tomorrow morning are these: Anderson and Thornton, go and see Frank Fisher. I want the company books. Colin, get an address for Alan Sargent and pay him a visit."

Chapter Thirty-eight

The atmosphere in the Vesper Gate on Abbey Road in Kirkstall was pretty ramped up, thought Raymond Allen. Then again, it was ten-thirty. Not that he minded. His initial thoughts had been a quiet drink in a secluded corner of an anonymous bar, where the likelihood of recognition would be scant at best.

However, as beggars can't be choosers, he'd slipped in an hour previously, and had to admit he'd really warmed to the place and the atmosphere. He was enjoying himself. It beat a lonely night at the hostel.

Allen ordered another half of lager, and watched the crowd of men in the corner, growing drunker by the hour. There were ten of them in all, and he'd identified the bridegroom and the best man.

The barmaid served his drink, and he sat on the stool watching the stag party with amusement. They were now involved in a heavy debate about the football match on the big screen.

As far as Allen was concerned, he'd also earned himself a drink that night. He'd had a busy day. The morning had been spent in the Market Place in Shipley, where he'd managed to rob most of the stallholders blind, having ended up with a new outfit to wear that night, and a variety of personal items which had allowed him yet again to alter his appearance. His hair and eyebrows were now a different shade. He wore a pair of tinted glasses, and had started growing a moustache.

Before leaving Shipley he had found a leather wallet outside the police station, of all places, containing over a hundred pounds in cash and credit cards. The cash was a bonus, but he left the cards: they were traceable. He had thought about taking it to the police, but that was far too risky, so he posted it through their letterbox.

During the afternoon he had managed a free meal and dessert in a café. They had not given him the meal voluntarily. He now suspected that some poor soul was paying for it out of their wages. It *had* crossed his mind to pay, as he was cash rich, but then decided better of it.

He had composed and sent Vincent another email, which should by then have had him running around like a headless chicken and posting even more crap on his blog. No doubt he would be over at the police station tomorrow. Checking his watch, he decided it would be his last lager of the night. He needed to be up early in the morning.

At that point, the best man approached the bar. Another hour, thought Allen, and he'd be lucky if he made it to the wedding, let alone home.

"Now then, mate, how's it going?"

Earlier in the evening, the best man's dress sense had maintained an air of dignity, the shirt and tie neatly in place. The tie was now undone and slung over his shoulder. The top three buttons of the shirt stood open, revealing more hairs on his chest than King Kong had.

"I'm okay," said Allen. "You look like you're enjoying yourself."

"Alan Sargent, best man." He held out his hand for Allen to shake.

"Rick Ashworth," replied Allen, taking the hand.

Sargent turned and pointed to the bridegroom. "That man... over there... is my best mate... and the salt of the Earth."

Allen smiled, wondering how many people in the same position had said that over the years. But there was a lot to be said for true friendship.

"Steve Brody," continued Sargent, "has been like a brother to me." There was a long pause before the next sentence. "And he's getting married... to the prettiest girl in the whole... world."

Sargent stopped talking at that point, and started thinking and swaying. He leaned in close. "Apart from my wife, that is. And I love her to tits... no, sorry... to bits." As an afterthought he added, "Mind you... she's got nice tits as well."

"Is she here?"

Sargent bowed his head. "No. We... we... we had a bit of-of-of... an argument." He waved his hand away. "But I'll sort it in the morning."

"Don't you mean the afternoon?" said Allen.

Alan Sargent went deep into thought for a moment, then started laughing uncontrollably. "Hey, you're alright, you are. You don't reckon... I'll be in any fit state in... the morning?" Sargent laughed even louder as he ordered a round of drinks.

"You might not be in the afternoon, either. Let's hope she doesn't shout too loud."

"I never thought... about that," said Sargent. "She *can* shout... my missus."

"Can't they all?" said Allen, which brought more laughter from Sargent.

"You're alright, you. Let me get you... a drink."

Allen declined. "I'd love to, but I have to be up really early in the morning."

"I don't." Sargent laughed again.

After he'd paid for the round he stared more closely at Allen.

"Do you know... I'm sure I recognize you... from somewhere?"

Chapter Thirty-nine

Monday 22nd August, 5:30 a.m.

Gardener glanced around. The sun was shining, the sky blue with little or no cloud, and no breeze to diminish the warmth. The scene before him was peaceful: few cars were passing on the A65. It should have been a moment to treasure.

It wasn't, otherwise he wouldn't be there.

He was standing in the grounds of Kirkstall Abbey, a ruined Cistercian monastery, north-west of Leeds. The building was set in a public park on the north bank of the River Aire, founded circa 1152.

A uniformed constable guarded the entrance. Another was talking to a dog walker who had found something totally alien to the scene.

The dead man was sitting between two trees opposite the Grade I listed building. Behind him, a wall separated the grounds of the abbey from the A65, where a woman was waiting at a bus stop.

Gardener had finished his call to the station to request his team. Walking back to his partner, he stared down at the body. The most disturbing aspect was the fact that he was in a wheelchair.

He vaguely recognized the man as one of Barry Morrison's driver's, Alan Sargent. The dog walker, whose name was Trevor Bannister, was the landlord of a public house further down Abbey Road, called The Vesper Gate. As soon as Gardener had finished with the corpse and had addressed his team, he and Reilly would go and have a word.

Someone had done a real number on Sargent. He had very obviously been beaten to death with a hedge stake that was now lying on the grass behind the chair. He was dressed in a dark-coloured suit with a white shirt but no tie, and covered in blood. His eyes were black and his hands were covered in bruises, probably in an effort to defend himself against the attack.

Gardener suspected a fractured skull, not to mention a broken jaw. His mouth was open, as if protesting. The lower jaw was at an angle to the upper, and a number of teeth had been smashed. He was convinced the dead man hadn't been robbed, because a gold watch was still on his left wrist.

Gardener could hear music, faint and muffled. It came from the inside of Sargent's suit jacket. He didn't know the song, but he knew who was singing. The same voice had been apparent at the two previous crime scenes. He needed Dave Rawson.

Reilly pulled the jacket back to reveal a mini CD player lodged between Sargent's hip and the side of the wheelchair. The sound was a little clearer, but no better. The Irishman carefully extracted the dead man's wallet. Inside were credit cards and money. He pulled back one of the zips, and found a white piece of paper, which he passed over to Gardener.

Unfolding it, the SIO noticed it was a prescription for anti-depressants, which had been prescribed by a Dr Robinson. Gardener wondered if he worked for the private clinic in Bond Street, the very same place they were at yesterday.

"Look at this," said Gardener.

Reilly briefly read it. "No wonder he's on anti-depressants if he's listening to this shit. I'm not surprised he's dead. It's certainly fucking killing me."

"So where does that leave us? Revenge against the car lot? Or is someone picking off clients who attend the Bond Street private clinic?"

"And who's in the frame?" asked Reilly.

"We need to go through the client list and fast, see if we can find a connection there."

"And if we don't?"

"We'll put Billy Morrison back in the firing line. And there's always the Summerbys."

"Somehow I don't have them down as another Fred and Rosemary West."

"That's the problem, isn't it, Sean? You never actually know *who* the hell you're dealing with. Why has their daughter gone missing without a trace?"

"And who's the girl in the photo underneath Nicola Stapleton? Does the killer have both girls? Is it two completely different cases, or is there a connection to our case?"

"Is the girl in the photo underneath Stapleton, Alan Sargent's daughter? And whose wheelchair is it, for God's sake? We saw him on Friday in the portacabin with Billy Morrison. He was walking then."

So much had happened since then. Gardener glanced at the prescription again before calling the desk sergeant at the station. He needed someone to check on the names and addresses of the taxi drivers, in particular Alan Sargent.

He didn't have to wait long for his answer. Gardener broke the connection, replacing his mobile in one of his jacket pockets.

"Morris Grove," said Gardener.

"Where's that?" asked Reilly.

Gardener pointed. "About a mile that way."

"Somebody knew that. Stopped him from getting home. Bet they were both in the pub last night."

A bus drew up on Abbey Road, collected the lone passenger, and moved off, which was perfect timing as Gardener's team started to arrive.

"Dave," shouted Gardener. Rawson came over, rubbing the sleep from his eyes.

"You're an expert on this bloke." Gardener pointed to the CD player. "What song is that, and what's it about?"

Rawson listened for a few minutes before replying. "Sounds like *O'Malley's Bar*. It goes on forever. It's about a man who goes into a bar and kills people who live in the town. Killing people arouses him sexually, but the police catch him eventually. The song runs for over fourteen minutes."

"Fucking won't today," said Reilly, stopping the machine.

Gardener assembled the team to one side, away from the scene. He briefed them before issuing his actions. The outdoor crime scene presented major problems. The weather conditions had obviously been good overnight, and seemed set to stay that way, but he couldn't risk it. A call to the Met Office would provide temperatures, rainfall

– if they expected any – and wind speeds for the next few hours.

Before long, the ruined abbey would be a hive of activity. He needed a decent-sized tent organized so as to stop the rubber-neckers and the press and anyone else within a five-mile radius from taking photos. The curator, or whoever the hell was in charge of the abbey, needed contacting because the place would have to be shut down and sealed off, especially as he needed a PolSA team to do a fingertip search.

He wanted the hedge stake sent for Low Copy Number DNA testing, a super sensitive analysis that would identify DNA from sweat and spit and anyone holding the object. However, Gardener doubted he would find anything there. If the killer was using a scene suit and gloves again, they would be wasting their time.

He also suspected house-to-house inquiries would reveal very little because the grounds were not overlooked by any of the houses nearby, but they still had to do it. Maybe someone else had been in the pub, walking home around the same time, saw something they might have taken as friendly banter between two drunks and disregarded it.

He glanced at his watch. Over an hour had passed. He left his men to organize and carry out his orders before joining his partner again. Gardener glanced at Alan Sargent. "He hasn't been robbed."

"No," said Reilly. "It's personal, we know that now. Something in the past connects all three people, but we haven't found out what it is."

"And how many more will it connect before we do?" Gardener asked. "Let's go and talk to the landlord of the Vesper Gate, see what he has to say."

Gardener approached the man. He asked the constable to go and stand between the corpse and the wall separating the abbey from the road.

He turned to speak to Trevor Bannister, who was late fifties at a guess. Despite being still in the throes of summer, Bannister was dressed in a camel hair coat and trilby, with a pair of dark brown trousers and brown loafers. His eyes were as grey as his moustache. His face bore the years of working in the licencing trade, with enough lines to make a map. Down at his feet was a well-behaved black Labrador, obviously enjoying the fact that his morning stroll was taking much longer than usual. Both detectives introduced themselves.

"Do you normally walk your dog this early, Mr Bannister?"

"Aye, almost the same time every day. Have trouble sleeping, like."

Gardener turned to Sargent's body and pointed. "And this is how you found him, in the chair?"

"Aye. Bit of a shock, I don't mind telling you."

"Do you recognize him?"

"He was in last night, drinking with a stag party. He wasn't in the chair, then."

That really disturbed Gardener. Someone had killed him and dropped him in a wheelchair – why? Was some poor bugger going to wake up in an hour or so, and suddenly find he couldn't make himself mobile today?

"How did he seem?"

"Seem?"

"Yes," said Gardener. "Was he enjoying the atmosphere of the party, or did he look to you like he had something on his mind?"

"Oh. No, nothing on his mind apart from getting drunk and seeing the groom had a good time. He was okay, having a right old drink, he was."

Bannister glanced over at Sargent, who was now surrounded by SOCOs in scene suits.

"To be honest, I thought he were sleeping off a hangover. Buster found him first, ran up to the chair and started sniffing and barking, like. I was on other side o' wall. He'd run off into grounds afore me, like. Always does. We're both getting on a bit, but he has better legs than me. Anyway, I came round and saw this bloke, sitting here. I thought it were odd that he was just sitting here, in the grounds, listening to music. But I've seen some strange stuff in my time. Anyway, I must admit I prodded him and started talking, like, but I didn't think he was gonna answer. That's when I called you lot."

"Did you see anyone else around?" Reilly asked.

"Not that I can recall."

Reilly pointed to the chair. "Apart from the hedge stake, you didn't happen to notice any other weapon?"

"No." Bannister shook his head to confirm his answer.

"What time did he leave the pub?"

"Let me see." Bannister arched his fingers around his face. "Be about midnight, maybe a little later. The stag crowd were the last lot out. A couple of taxis had rolled up, and one or two were getting in. I imagine the others were walking."

Gardener thought about it. The window would have been reasonably tight. Sargent left at twelve. Chances were he would have hung around for half an hour, which would make it twelve-thirty. A walk down here when you're sober could take half an hour, never mind when drunk. He can't have been in the grounds more than four hours at the most.

"How many were in the stag party?" Reilly asked.

"Ten altogether, I think."

"Do you know them all?"

"Most of 'em."

"We'll need to take an official statement from you, but if you can think on, names and addresses of all of them would be useful. So, what happened exactly? You were obviously outside if you noticed taxis rolling up."

"Just that, really. They all staggered outside. I went to lock up and bade them goodnight. Wished them all a safe journey, how ironic is that? I came back in and locked doors. Wife were watching 'em through a window, laughing. She wondered what kind of a head they'd all have this morning."

"Did you see him with anyone in particular?"

"Not that I can think of. He was stood next to the groom, Steve Brody. They were laughing and hugging each other. I never saw what happened after that. So I don't know if he was going home in a taxi, or walking."

"I'd say he was walking," said Reilly, writing down the groom's name. "From what we've found out, he lives in Morris Grove."

"Oh," said Bannister. "Not far, then."

"Do you have CCTV, Mr Bannister?"

"No, never seen the need."

Gardener sighed inwardly. "You didn't see anyone hanging around outside your pub, someone who was not a part of the group?"

"No. Like I said, they were the last out. I wouldn't say it were particularly busy last night. We had a few in, but weekends are not what they used to be. I've seen a time when the place was heaving. But you can't smoke now, and beer's not cheap, so we have to diversify. We have to do meals, and entertainment, Sky Sports and the like."

"Would you say you knew everyone who was in the pub last night? Were they all regulars?"

"I'd say so."

Gardener realized the interview was not progressing positively. He glanced around the grounds of the abbey: no CCTV cameras here either, and none that he could see on Abbey Road. Plenty of speed cameras, but they wouldn't help him. He'd be checking them anyway, although he doubted the killer would have broken any speeding laws. That would have brought unwarranted attention, and he figured their man was a little too calculating to make such a stupid mistake.

"No trouble last night, was there?" Reilly asked.

"No," said Bannister. "We don't get a lot of trouble anyway."

Gardener wasn't sure there was much more he could glean, so he decided to bring the interview to an end. He asked if Bannister would go straight home so that he could send a constable round for a formal statement and collect all the names and addresses he needed.

Bannister called the dog and set off, but turned round very quickly.

"Actually, there was someone in last night I'd never seen before. Didn't take a lot o' notice. He was quiet enough, kept to himself."

"Go on," said Gardener.

"I think he slipped in unnoticed around ten o'clock, sat on a stool, end o' bar, like. Now I come to think of it, he was watching the stag party most o' night. Nowt bad, mind, I think he were just amused."

"Can you describe him?"

"Maybe late thirties. Tinted glasses, moustache. Not too tall, about my size."

"Any hair?"

"Aye, going a bit grey."

"What was he wearing?" Reilly asked.

"Let me think. He had a blue jacket on, sports coat of some description, with a badge or a logo on, but I can't think what it was. He wore a blue shirt under that. Never noticed his trousers 'cause he was sat down most o' time. His jacket was new, not a mark on it."

"Did you speak to him?"

"No, but our barmaid did. She served him wi' his drinks."

"What's her name?"

"Vicky Murphy."

"Oh my God," said Gardener, glancing at his partner. "Another one of your lot."

"Nothing wrong with a good–"

"–honest, Irish name. I know, you keep telling me."

"I think she were quite keen on him, like," said Bannister. "She definitely kept over that side o' bar."

"Why are you telling us this, Mr Bannister?"

"Well, because yon lad there" – Bannister pointed to Alan Sargent – "came to bar to order a round, and they got talking, like. Seemed friendly enough, but I remember Vicky saying afterwards that she overheard them. Anyway, bloke we'd never seen afore said his name."

Bannister made a real point of trying to rack his brains. He'd removed his trilby and began scratching his head. "Rick summat or other. It'll come to me."

Gardener hoped it would.

"That's it," he shouted, startling the dog. "Ashworth was his name. Rick Ashworth. I remember Vicky saying because she said she were going to look him up on Facebook."

Gardener thanked him for his time and glanced at his watch: a little after seven-thirty.

He turned to his partner as they left. "I'm not happy about the wheelchair, Sean. Sargent was not disabled." Gardener stopped walking to answer his mobile as it rang suddenly. "Bob, what can I do for you?"

Gardener said very little else, but listened intently before replying, "We're on our way."

Chapter Forty

John Oldham flew into a panic when he spotted the security door at the rear of the chemist was ajar. Experience told him he had been burgled, and it had to have been either a professional or an inside job: no locks or windows had been broken. He pushed the door all the way open and ran into the yard, glancing in every direction.

"What's up with you?" shouted Vincent, from the top of his metal fire exit stairwell.

Oldham glanced up. Vincent was in his dressing gown, which was nothing new. Some days he was in it all day. He had a coffee in his right hand, and a bagel in the other.

"Did you hear anything odd last night?"

"Odd? What do you mean, odd?"

"Windows being smashed, doors being forced open?" As soon as he'd said it, Oldham felt stupid. Neither of those things had happened anyway.

"No. Why?"

"We've been burgled."

"Oh, Christ." Vincent came down the steps two at a time until he reached John Oldham. "Are you okay?"

"*I* am."

"Is there much missing?"

"I haven't checked."

"Don't you think you ought to?"

"Give us a chance, I've only just got here."

"How did they get in?"

"I'm assuming through this rear door here." Oldham pointed.

Vincent followed the line of his finger, and then glanced at the gate that secured the small backyard to the premises.

"No locks broken."

"I know. That's what worries me."

"You think someone who works here did it?"

"How else could it have happened?" said Oldham. "Anyway, you ring the police and I'll go and check what's missing."

"Do you think you should?"

"I've no choice. Police will want to know what's gone."

"Yes, but he might still be in there."

"I doubt it," said Oldham. "He'll be long gone now."

"You don't know that. And anyway, it's a crime scene. You shouldn't be going in there, you'll contaminate the place."

"Never mind all that, Vincent. It's a bloody chemist. All sorts of dangerous stuff in here. Just get on to the police while I go and see what's gone."

A squad car pulled up outside the chemist within twenty minutes. During that time, John Oldham had made his checks. Most of the drugs and medicines on the shelves had been swept to the floor. None of the bottles had smashed, and the cardboard covers were not damaged. It was almost as if they had been placed on the floor, as opposed to swept.

Oldham didn't think much was missing, but until he had time to go through his register and his computer records, he wouldn't know for certain. The drugs cabinet, however, *had* been broken into, which meant the thieves had known what they were searching for.

Two young constables dressed like Robocop entered the premises. They approached the counter, all flashing lights and alien sounds – conversations going on between God knows who. Vincent crept in through the back door.

The police took down the general details: who owned the shop, who worked for him, and what part Vincent played in it all. Oldham informed them how he'd found the scene, and the fact that there were no signs of a forced entry – the last bit of jargon came courtesy of Vincent.

"Do you know what's been taken, sir?"

"Not had much of a chance to check, yet. Doesn't look to be a lot missing from the shop, but it's the drugs cabinet I'm worried about."

"Would you like to check now, sir, while we're here?"

Oldham drew out his record book. All four present at the scene converged around the cabinet. It took him a further ten minutes consulting his inventory. When he had the answer, he felt weak inside.

"What's wrong?" asked the officer.

"They've stolen the secobarbital."

"Is that dangerous?" asked the officer.

"It's classed as a controlled drug under the 1971 Misuse of Drugs Act. Chemists are required to keep strict records and receipts of supplies. I mean, you lot can inspect the records and the stocks any time you want."

"Anything else?"

Oldham continued until he had checked everything. When he'd finished, he scratched his head. "No. Only the secobarbital."

"Bit strange, isn't it? A thief breaking in and taking only one drug?"

"What would he want it for?" asked the other.

"Any number of things," replied Oldham. "It's mainly a sleeping pill. It's sometimes used short term to treat insomnia, or as a sedative before surgery: similar properties to opium."

Oldham noticed Vincent had paled.

"Still doesn't answer the question, sir. If you knew what you were doing, could you use it to kill someone, for example?"

"Almost certainly," replied Oldham.

"What would it do?" asked the officer. "What sort of effect would it have on the body?"

Oldham thought about it. "Well, in an overdose situation, they would go through the initial stages of euphoria, get extremely excited, before passing into a deep sleep and unconsciousness. The breathing and heart rate would become slower and shallower until they stopped altogether. Death would soon follow."

"So, it's not likely to be a painful death?"

"Not really. Look more like they'd died in their sleep."

Oldham saw that Vincent's expression was now so distant that he may as well have been on another planet.

Chapter Forty-one

By the time Gardener and Reilly arrived in Richmond Hill, a number of vehicles were already parked outside Frank Fisher's house, which didn't bode well, given that one was an ambulance.

Bob Anderson and Frank Thornton were standing by the gate. The SIO had given them the task of interviewing Frank Fisher first thing. They had obviously not had that chance.

"Who found him?" Gardener asked.

"The bloke over there with the two medics," said Anderson. "His name's Robert Quarry. Apparently, he's Fisher's social worker. Came to see him yesterday, was extremely worried about his condition, and decided to book him in to the hospital for some treatment. That's what the ambulance is for. Sadly, they were too late. Fisher had already committed suicide before they got here."

Gardener noted the body language of his two officers: something didn't quite add up. "What are you holding back?"

Thornton leaned in close and whispered, though Gardener wasn't sure who it was he didn't want hearing.

"We don't suspect suicide."

"Why do you say that?" Reilly asked.

"You'll know what we're talking about once you're inside."

"Have you already told *him*?" Gardener nodded towards Quarry.

"No. We'd prefer Fitz to confirm it."

Gardener sighed. They were stretched as it was. Very little headway had been made in gathering evidence for the murder of Barry Morrison and Nicola Stapleton, and now they were facing another two. If he wasn't careful, Briggs would have the circus in town, and he'd start to lose control of his own case.

He phoned the station and requested a number of operational support officers to help with the house-to-house inquiries. From what Gardener could see, it would be no easy task. The area was littered with council houses, not to mention a number of shops and an industrial estate within walking distance. Depending on what time it happened, there could be a number of witnesses. But it would all depend on how long Fisher had been dead. Before cutting the call, Gardener requested Fitz's presence immediately, hoping he could catch the man before he made it to the abbey.

Gardener asked Anderson and Thornton if they would concentrate on setting up a cordon around the house. He had no doubt the scene had already been contaminated, but he wanted to contain as much as he could.

"We'll go and talk to Quarry and the medics. Hopefully, by that time, Fitz will have arrived."

Gardener and Reilly approached, displaying their warrant cards. The two medics were middle-aged, one male, the other female. Both were sipping tea from a flask. Robert Quarry was standing to one side. He was slim with dark hair, cut short. He wore a suit and carried an air of authority. As usual, a number of nearby residents were out on their doorsteps, spectating.

"Can you take me through what happened?" Gardener asked Quarry.

"I'm afraid we were too late."

"For what?"

"I'd made arrangements yesterday for Frank to go into a clinic to receive treatment. These two were coming to collect him."

At the mention of the clinic, Gardener's back bristled.

Reilly beat him to the question. "Which one?"

"The St James hospital."

Gardener was relieved. At least it wasn't the clinic in Bond Street. But Fisher was connected to Billy Morrison's car lot, which didn't put the owner in a good position.

"Why were you visiting him yesterday?"

"A couple of his neighbours were extremely anxious about him."

Robert Quarry went on to explain the problems Frank Fisher had faced over the years: the loss of his livelihood because of the accident; the court case with the builder, which he hadn't wanted to continue with, but had only done so on the advice of a friend. His wife's affair was also mentioned, and the fact that she had left him, and that Fisher had never recovered.

"I spent a couple of hours with him yesterday, and it was obvious he'd had another relapse. Despite what she'd done to him, he would still have taken her back like a shot."

"Some men are like that," said Reilly.

"You mentioned he'd worked for a builder. Can you remember the name?" asked Gardener.

"I've not been his case officer that long. I can only recall his first name. Sean."

"Where was the yard?"

"Rodley."

"Do you know where he lives now?" Reilly asked.

"He went bust pretty much after the court case. I'm afraid he committed suicide as well."

"Why didn't he want to sue the builder, especially if it was negligence?"

"They were partners, and very good friends from what I heard."

"Wasn't the builder insured?"

"Apparently not. He'd let the policy lapse. From what I can gather, he needed the money for something else."

"I see," said Gardener, making a mental note. All the information Robert Quarry was coming out with was worth checking. "And did Frank Fisher know this? Is that why he didn't want to sue?"

"I don't think so," replied Quarry. "As I said, he'd only gone ahead because a friend had pushed him into it."

"A close friend?"

"According to Frank, yes," replied Quarry. "But not anymore."

"What, they fell out after the trial?"

"No, I didn't mean that. I don't think he was blaming the friend for what had happened. He was gutted about his wife, his life, and pretty much everything. The fact that he was trapped in the chair, couldn't go anywhere. One of the reasons Frank was in a really bad place yesterday was because his friend had just been found dead."

"Who was his friend?" Reilly asked.

"Bloke called Barry Morrison. Ran a taxi firm."

"Thought as much," said Reilly.

"Are you two investigating Barry Morrison's death?"

"Yes," said Gardener. "Did Frank Fisher ever mention the name Nicola Stapleton?"

"Not that I can recall. Wasn't she the prostitute who was killed on Friday night?"

"You're well informed."

"It's a small place."

"Did you know her?"

"No."

"Does the name Alan Sargent mean anything?" asked Reilly. "That one ever come up in conversation?"

Quarry's eyes narrowed. Gardener suspected it had, and the man was searching his memory bank.

"I think so. Maybe you guys should dig into the archives of the trial. I'm sure that name was mentioned. What makes you ask?"

"We've just left him."

"Is he okay?"

"Maybe we should examine the scene," said Gardener.

"Of course," said Quarry. "But I'll warn you, it's not pleasant."

"Never is *anything* we have to look at," said Reilly.

They were about to move when Fitz appeared in his silver BMW. Close behind him was another ambulance with the undertakers.

The pathologist approached the two officers. "Morning, gentlemen. You look as if you've been up all night."

"Feels like it," said Gardener.

"How is the case progressing?"

"Slowly," said Reilly.

"What do we have inside?" Fitz nodded towards the house.

Gardener told Fitz what Quarry had told them.

"Have you seen the corpse?"

"No," said Gardener. "We were just about to go in."

"Don't let me stop you. The quicker I see to this one, the quicker I can get over to Kirkstall. Who knows, by the time I've done that one, you might have found some more for me."

"Don't want you sitting idle, do we, Fitz?" said Reilly.

"Carry on lining them up like this, and there's no doubt you'll find I'm one of them."

"Any special requests?" said Gardener.

"Only one," replied Fitz, nodding towards Reilly. "Keep him away from me."

Gardener asked the medics to stay put while the four men suited and booted and set off down the small path towards the open front door. As they drew nearer, he could hear the music. Same singer, different song. That's what Thornton had meant.

The living room proved to be one of the untidiest places Gardener had ever set foot in. The carpet hadn't been vacuumed for some time. All the shelves *he* could see were dusty. There were cardboard boxes all over, some opened, some closed. How could a man in a wheelchair move around such clutter? Sweet wrappers covered a desk, as well as papers and folders. The smell was something else. He spotted a small midi hi-fi system on top of an old-fashioned sideboard. He didn't take too much notice of the song, but the word 'joy' was mentioned more than once.

Quarry led them through the living room to a specially adapted wet room, designed so a disabled person could wheel himself into the shower. The hand basin was much lower than normal, but the toilet was higher to make it an easier transfer from the wheelchair. The floor was non-slip, the walls tiled in a standard shade of council magnolia. The odour in the bathroom was not as bad as the one in the living room because of an open window.

Fisher was dressed in a pair of cotton, flower-patterned pyjamas. Sadly, they were soiled, but Gardener suspected the man was not incontinent. He was kneeling on the floor with his head over the basin, his throat cut from ear to ear. The basin was filled with blood, which had started to congeal.

Fitz moved forward past Gardener and Reilly and placed his medical bag on the floor, immediately removing a thermometer.

Gardener turned to face the social worker, having no desire to watch Fitz take a dead man's temperature to estimate the time of death. He'd seen that once too often.

"How do you think he got in here, Mr Quarry?"

Quarry glanced around uneasily. "He'd have used his wheelchair, of course."

"And where is that do you think?"

Quarry's head moved around like a puppet's. He walked out of the bathroom but returned quickly, anxious, almost beside himself.

"I can't find it. Oh my God, what's happened to his wheelchair?"

"We have a good idea," said Reilly.

Gardener glanced at Fitz. The thermometer was still in position, but Fitz was examining Frank Fisher's head. The scene made for an interesting sight.

The music on the hi-fi stopped and then restarted, which didn't surprise Gardener in the slightest. He wondered whether the tracks at the scenes had been picked out purposely.

"Do you recognize this music?" Gardener asked Quarry.

He shook his head. "No."

"Did you know Frank Fisher well enough to comment on the type of music he listened to?"

"I'd say so, and it wouldn't be this stuff."

"Find me someone who would," commented Reilly.

"He was a sixties fan, easy listening, middle-of-the-road stuff."

"Why do you think he's committed suicide?" asked Gardener.

"Because of how I found him yesterday," said Quarry. "All the signs were there. He was very down. He kept harping on about his wife, the accident, his friend, the builder and Barry Morrison and how everything had been one big mistake, especially his life."

Gardener glanced around the bathroom again. A glass cupboard was mounted on one wall, low enough for a disabled man to open it. He opened one of the doors: the shelves were full of tablets. He rattled the bottles to make sure none were empty. On a window ledge in front of the basin he saw a toothbrush and toothpaste, as well as other items of hygiene.

But the all-important tool was missing.

"Can you see the knife anywhere?" he asked Quarry.

The social worker grew paler. Gardener thought he was going to throw up.

"Oh my God." He brought his hands to his face. "I never noticed. Do you think he's been murdered?"

"And made to look like suicide."

"How do you know?"

Fitz turned to join in the conversation. "Was he right or left-handed?"

196

"Right, I think."

"The officers are right. It was not suicide. He's been cut from left to right. You wouldn't do that if you were right-handed."

Fitz pointed with a pen to prove his point. "The cut is angled upwards, so it had to be someone who was standing over the victim. It's very deep. Someone committing suicide would not cut that deep. An outside force will almost certainly pull the knife into the neck with more force than his victim could."

Quarry leaned back against the door frame.

"Mr Quarry, can you leave us for a few minutes?" Gardener asked. Quarry made no reply. He couldn't find the exit quick enough. Fitz removed the thermometer and made a note of the reading.

"How long would you say he's been dead?"

The pathologist drew in his breath. "You can never say with any accuracy, but my guess would be about nine hours."

"So that puts it at eleven o'clock last night."

"Give or take an hour."

Gardener thought about the time. "What do you think, Sean? Someone kills Fisher about eleven, which would give them time to drive over to Kirkstall in time to grab Sargent."

"But how would they know where Sargent would be, and at what time?"

"They wouldn't, unless they were one of the stag party."

"Fair point. The quicker we get the names and addresses the better, find out if anyone left early."

"We'll also get one of the lads to check the client list on the clinic, see if Fisher has ever been a patient there. It looks more like someone has it in for Billy Morrison and his car lot."

"Or that Billy Morrison has it in for a number of people who work for him."

"Could be. Still can't figure out a motive."

"Maybe he found out his brother was into drugs and prostitution and God knows what, and decided he'd had enough."

"That would only account for his brother. Two more people have been killed since."

"Maybe they were in on it."

"Insurance scam?"

"Possibly," said Reilly. "Or maybe something personal."

"Either way, it doesn't look good for Billy."

"I think I'm about done here, gentlemen," Fitz said as he started to pack up his equipment. "I'll ask the undertakers to come in and take him back to the morgue, if you're okay with that?"

"He's all yours," said Gardener.

"There's something about these four murders that really unsettles me," said Fitz.

"Yeah," said Reilly. "In our case, it's the killer."

"It's the method."

"You think you've come across it before?" Gardener asked.

Fitz nodded and sighed. "Each one that's been killed has struck a chord somewhere. Whatever it is, it's not something that happened recently."

A shuffling noise behind them caught Gardener's attention. Frank Fisher's body had suddenly fallen to one side.

When it hit the floor, all three men were left staring at a photograph: a very young girl with blonde hair, a replica of the one they had found underneath the body of Nicola Stapleton.

Chapter Forty-two

Chris Rydell glanced at his computer screen. It was a little after ten, and he'd been up nearly three hours after having had only two and a half hours' sleep.

He felt okay.

He'd spent the last few minutes in the kitchen preparing his breakfast. He had never been able to eat as soon as he was up and out of bed.

During the last six months however, his diet had changed considerably. Due to the cirrhosis, he'd had to avoid too much fat or too many calories. They caused a fatty liver; some good that would do now.

He also had to be very careful with carbohydrates. Too many could result in diabetes. That was a laugh. Would he actually notice on top of everything else? So his food intake now consisted mainly of chicken, fish, vegetables and salads. Alcohol had to be avoided at all costs. He'd never been a big drinker anyway because of the job. So he stuck mainly to water, or a variety of herbal teas.

Staring into the bowl, he'd prepared a mixture of oats with cranberries, raspberries, and raisins. They'd been infused with white and dark chocolate curls, and he'd also added fresh blueberries. Though why he was bothering was anyone's guess. He'd be dead soon anyway, according to the doctors – well, Trent anyway.

An article on his computer captured his attention. Chris spooned up some granola and started chewing while he was thinking.

Vincent Baines had written another blog about what was happening in his life. It certainly made interesting reading. From what Chris had found out about the man, Vincent considered himself a detective. The latest blog was beginning to prove that there really was some merit in the statement.

Over the last two or three days, Batley and the surrounding areas of West Yorkshire had been rocked by a couple of double murders and Vincent – it would appear – had been taunted by the killer. Whoever had murdered these people had been sending him emails, and questioning his ability to beat the police to identify the culprit.

Rydell took another couple of mouthfuls of his breakfast. Even though he had to eat healthily, he was enjoying it.

He read more of the blog. Seems Vincent had changed his mind about who was popping people off and chasing *him*. He was also convinced that his demise would be based around something that had actually happened in 1866, to an engine driver called Samuel Birchall who lived and worked in Sheffield but visited family in Leeds every two weeks. Ironically, Birchall was also addicted to horse racing.

He placed his empty bowl on the top of the desk and fished out a number of true crime books. How spot on was Vincent?

It took him only a matter of minutes to locate the correct book. Birchall had narrowly escaped being sacked from his job. Rydell suspected that was down to alcohol, from what the book claimed. In June 1866, Birchall was in Leeds for the weekend and had drunk the entire time, commenting to his daughter that he was tired with life and that he meant to do himself some harm.

Before returning to Sheffield, it was obvious he had carried out his threat, as Birchall deteriorated in front of his friends. He had drunk laudanum. His friends had tried to save his life. All the while, Birchall was abusive, shouting and swearing and lashing out, telling them that the doctors could do nothing for him. A stomach pump proved useless, because the poison in his body had done too much damage.

Vincent's blog claimed the killer had threatened to finish him the same way. To top it all, the chemist in

Guiseley had been turned over in the last three hours, and the only thing missing was secobarbital.

Rydell smiled. Something interesting was definitely happening here.

Reading more of the blog, the hairs on the nape of his neck bristled. Vincent went on to state that the double murder that had been committed in Batley was a copy of two more murders that had happened way back in 1865 and 1881.

Rydell delved even further into his books. Another thirty minutes proved that Vincent was not wrong. He had ferreted out the facts. He'd also informed everyone that he was in constant contact with the police.

Rydell wondered how he knew so much – unless he was responsible?

He rose from the desk and took his bowl through to the kitchen. He switched on the kettle and checked the cupboard, deciding on a green tea infused with orange. While he was waiting, he wondered whether he should drop the diet altogether and eat as much fat and crap as he liked. Why not? It wasn't likely it would kill him. What he wouldn't give for a nice juicy Burger King, an Aberdeen Angus with blue cheese.

The kettle boiled, and he dropped a tea bag in the cup and poured in the boiling water. A noise behind distracted him. He turned to see his houseguest, clutching her doll.

His face lit up – as did hers. They were always pleased to see each other. He bent down so he was a little nearer to her height, studying the beautiful blonde curls and blue eyes. Her appearance was always so fresh, and she was always so pleasant. He made sure that she, too, always ate the best of everything.

"Hello. How are you this morning?" he asked.

"I'm good," she replied. "Are you okay?"

"I'm fine, darling."

"You weren't yesterday. You fell and dropped all your books."

"I know. That was rather silly of me. You said so at the time. Remember?"

The girl laughed, revealing small white teeth. She had a beautiful smile; always had, ever since she'd been born.

"Yes. I called you a silly billy."

Rydell laughed. "So you did."

A sudden violent itch on the back of his leg distracted him again, to the point that he almost fell forward, on top of her. The girl moved backwards.

"It's okay, just an itch."

He scratched the area, but it didn't make much difference. He stood up, ignoring the irritation, and checked if she was okay again. "Now, how about some breakfast for you?"

She recovered quickly at the mention of food. "Yes, please."

"What would you like?"

The girl thought about it for a while. He didn't mind; she could take as long as she liked. She was no bother to him. Never had been, despite the fact that he never usually entertained houseguests. She was different.

"I think you'd like a boiled egg with soldiers. Am I right?"

She jumped up and down. "Yes."

"It's always been your favourite."

"Yes."

"Okay," he said. "You go and find your seat at the table, Sam, and I'll bring it through."

She retreated back into the living room, leaving Rydell scratching the back of his leg.

Chapter Forty-three

Gardener glanced at his watch. It was approaching midday, and the whole team was flat out with inquiries relating to the deaths of Frank Fisher and Alan Sargent. They had CCTV to check, witness statements to trawl through. HOLMES had to be updated, as did the ANACAPA chart. The station was like a beehive, fast approaching meltdown.

As much as he hated to pull people from their already overburdened work schedule, there were important actions he needed setting in place before he and Reilly interviewed a very agitated Billy Morrison.

"Frank, Bob, I have another job for you two. I'd like you to go over to the clinic on Bond Street, speak to them about Alan Sargent, and ask if Frank Fisher was ever a patient there."

Both men nodded and indicated they were on to it, once they'd finished a sandwich and a drink.

He glanced around the room, locating Colin Sharp. "Colin, I want everything you can muster on the Morrisons, please."

"Both of them?"

"Yes, but concentrate more on Barry. I suspect he'll have been the more adventurous one. Delve into his past. I don't believe it's possible for a man like him to operate without having upset someone big style. It may be small, it may be hidden, but it'll be there, and you're the best man for the job."

As Gardener headed for the door, he bumped into Paul Benson. "Paul. I have a job for you."

"Yes, sir."

"I want you looking into a court case involving an accountant called Frank Fisher."

"That the bloke we found dead this morning?" Benson asked.

"Fisher, yes. I'm sorry I can't give you more information than that, but we know Fisher was working for a builder when he had an accident, which left him paralysed. Fisher sued the builder. Not sure when it happened, maybe a couple of years ago. Maybe you can find out where it all happened and have a trip over, see if anybody remembers anything."

He turned to face his partner. "Are you ready?"

Reilly nodded. "Let's hope he's calmed down."

Gardener picked up a file and passed his partner a coffee before the pair of them set off down the corridor. As soon as they entered the interview room, Billy Morrison let rip.

"What the bloody hell's going on here?" He stood up. "You drag me down to this place, arrest me for something I didn't do, take my fingerprints, swab inside my mouth, give me this stinking crap to wear, and you leave me here to sweat for an hour. You told me yesterday you didn't believe that I'd done anything. Is this how you treat people who are innocent?"

"We haven't arrested you, we're talking to you under caution."

"Sit down," said Reilly, placing the warm drink on Morrison's side of the table. "Have a coffee."

"You're taking bloody liberties. I might change my mind about that solicitor."

"That's your right, Mr Morrison," said Gardener. "If you'd like to call him, we'll postpone this meeting until he gets here. We don't mind waiting until tonight."

Morrison returned to his seat, still very agitated. "I don't need no solicitor. I'm innocent. I told you that yesterday, and nothing has changed. Only guilty men need solicitors."

Gardener had his hand on the recording equipment. "Are you sure before I switch this on?"

Morrison spun round to face Gardener. "Dead right I'm sure. You ask me any question you like, mate. You won't find a damn thing on me, because there is nothing *to* find."

Gardener set the tapes rolling and took everyone through the preliminaries.

"Alan Sargent."

"What about him?"

"He worked for you."

"You know very well he does. You've seen him more than once. Anyway, he works for our Barry, not me."

"Know much about him?"

"A bit."

"How did he get the job? Did you advertise for a driver?"

"I don't think so. Our Barry organized everything. I think it was a friend of a friend. You might want to speak to Sid Prosser, he knows him. Could have been him that recommended Sargent."

"You know anything about his home life?" asked Reilly.

"Such as?"

"You tell us," replied Reilly. "Did he and his missus get on well? Any financial problems? Did he have health problems?"

"I couldn't tell you," replied Billy, screwing his eyes a little tighter. "I expect they have money problems, he'd been out of work some time. They have a seven-year-old son, so it can't be that easy for them."

Gardener realized Morrison was talking present tense about Sargent. If he knew about the death, he wasn't letting on.

"Did you know that he was being treated for depression?"

"No," said Morrison. "Not exactly a crime, is it? Like I said, the poor bloke's been out of work for some time. Maybe that brought it on."

"It didn't bother you that someone who had a medical condition was driving one of your cabs?"

"One of our Barry's cabs," corrected Billy. "But no, it doesn't bother me. The times that I've seen him, he's been okay. Maybe he has a lid on it. Maybe he's getting better. Maybe our job gives him something to get up for, and if that's the case, then you could say we were helping him."

"Are you aware of any private clinics on Bond Street in Leeds?"

Morrison shook his head. "Can you be more specific? There's nothing wrong with me, or my family. Are you gonna tell me Barry had a problem and he was a patient there?"

"Not that we know of," replied Gardener. "Let's get back to Alan Sargent. Any idea where he worked when he last had a job?"

"I'm not sure," replied Billy. "I think he was a landscape gardener, worked for a place over in Pudsey. Couldn't tell you the name."

"So, if you didn't see much of him, I suspect he worked nights, am I right?" Gardener asked.

"Mostly. He alternates a little bit. I've seen him do day runs once or twice."

"But it was mainly nights?"

"Yes."

"Did you ever see the work sheets, the runs he'd been on?"

"No. Never paid any attention. That was our Barry's job. He looked after the drivers."

"So Barry could have had him doing anything."

"What's that supposed to mean?"

"Well, he could have had him doing local runs, trips out of town, or maybe even airport runs."

"I've told you. I don't know."

"For someone in charge of the business, you don't seem to keep too close an eye on the staff."

"I didn't need to. Me and Barry had different roles, and we looked after different aspects of the business. And if you don't suspect people of doing anything wrong, you don't bother watching them too closely."

"Or he could have had him doing something else entirely," said Reilly. "Something illegal, like running drugs."

Morrison left his seat. "I've told you, I know nothing about the drugs, and I don't believe for one minute that our Barry was running his so-called drugs *operation* – as you lot like to call it – from the car lot."

"He must have run it from somewhere," said Gardener, "considering the amount we found in his flat." He glanced at his partner. "Street value of over forty thousand pounds, wasn't it?"

"Something like that."

"Forty thousand pounds worth of drugs?" Morrison was horrified, judging by his expression.

"Not to mention over a hundred and twenty thousand pounds in money. All cash," said Reilly.

"You two are a double act, aren't you? If you're not, you should be. Our Barry never had that kind of money."

"How do you know?"

"I know him, that's why!"

"I beg to differ, Mr Morrison," said Gardener. "You've told us twice already that you knew nothing about Nicola Stapleton, or the house she lived in that was owned by your brother. And you've also told us more than once that we seem to be talking about someone else, not your brother."

"How do you know all this stuff was his, and not just planted on him?"

"Evidence."

"What evidence?"

"Maybe we should mention the other flats he owned," said Gardener. "They would obviously generate an income. And if, of course, you were right about him not liking banks, all of this money would be tax free, no doubt."

"Other flats? What the hell are you talking about now?"

"Seems your Barry has been a very busy little bee. We have records indicating that not only did he own the house in Hume Crescent, but he had one or two flats in the area as well, which he rented out to undesirables. Wouldn't surprise me if they were all part of his little empire. Maybe he had Alan Sargent roped in on it all."

"Maybe he was blackmailing Sargent," said Reilly.

"Well, why don't you go and ask *him*, instead of hauling me in here?"

"We can't," said Gardener.

"Why? Somebody killed him as well, have they?"

Gardener and Reilly remained silent.

Morrison stood up sharp. "What? Are you two winding me up?"

The two detectives remained tight-lipped. Gardener wanted Billy Morrison to commit himself.

"Are you serious? Alan Sargent is dead? When?"

"We were called out at five o'clock this morning."

"Where?"

"We found him in Kirkstall Abbey, sitting between two trees, opposite the ruin."

Morrison shook his head and ran his hands through his hair. "Oh, Jesus. I can't get me head round all this. How many more?"

Gardener and his partner let the news filter in. Finally, Billy asked, "How did it happen?"

"Someone had stoved his head in with a fence post," said Reilly. "Poor man took a right pasting. He was black and blue."

Morrison leaned back in his chair. Gardener noticed he was trembling.

"Someone must have it in for me."

"We thought that," said Gardener. "But you said you didn't know anything. I do find myself coming back to the comments you made yesterday. For example, we never mentioned drugs, but *you* brought it up. When you called

Barry's phone, Alan Sargent answered. Makes me wonder how innocent you really are."

"Look," shouted Morrison. "I told you yesterday I knew nothing about our Barry and his drugs scam. You lot loaded ten layers of shit on to me, about him having a house and loads of money and a prostitute in tow. There was a lot going on in my head. It was just a wild guess about the drugs, that's all it was. Nothing else. I swear to you I don't know anything about drugs, money, prostitutes, or murders, and I certainly didn't know Alan Sargent was dead."

"Are you seriously expecting us to believe all this was going on behind your back? That your brother was leading a double life, and you knew nothing about it?"

"I don't care what you believe," shouted Morrison. "The one thing I do know is I haven't killed anybody. I didn't kill the prostitute, I didn't kill my brother, and I didn't kill Alan Sargent."

"Or Frank Fisher?"

"No! No! No! I didn't kill…" Morrison stopped mid-sentence. "What did you say?"

"Frank Fisher," repeated Reilly. "You see, when we found Alan Sargent in the grounds of Kirkstall Abbey this morning at five o'clock, you might not have heard us when we said he was sitting between two trees."

Morrison shook his head. "I heard you. I was too busy taking it all in. What do you mean, sitting? On what?"

"In," said Gardener, "not on."

"In what?" Morrison repeated.

"Frank Fisher's wheelchair."

You couldn't have cut the atmosphere with a chainsaw, thought Gardener.

"Are you two having a laugh? His wheelchair?"

"Oh, life's just one big comedy routine for us, son," said Reilly. "We love nothing better than a good old murder mystery which keeps us on our toes and drags us out of bed at all hours. That's if we even manage to get to bed!"

"Frank Fisher's wheelchair? What was he doing in Fisher's wheelchair? Where the fuck was Frank?"

"He was at home, leaning over his basin in the bathroom," said Gardener.

"Leaning over his basin? Has somebody beaten him up as well?"

"No," added Reilly. "They cut his throat."

"No," said Morrison, standing up again. "This isn't happening."

"It is, and it was," said Reilly. "So, within the space of two days, we have four people dead, three of which are connected to you. We found your brother dumped in a shop doorway, one of your drivers beaten to death in a very public place, and your disabled accountant sliced and diced in his bathroom minus his wheelchair that your dead driver just happened to be occupying. Pretty sick, isn't it? Is this all getting a bit too much for you?"

"You're fucking right it's getting too much," shouted Morrison.

Reilly changed topics. "So where were you last night, Billy?"

"Well I wasn't at home, was I? You lot shifted us out."

"That's not the best answer you could have given. We know you weren't at home. What we want to know is where you were? Did you pay a visit to Richmond Hill to silence your disabled accountant who might well have been in on everything?"

"Maybe he was about to blow the lid and take everyone down," said Reilly, "and you thought, I can't have that."

"No, no, no, for God's sake," shouted Morrison. "I've killed no one."

"Then maybe you thought you'd silence Sargent while you were out. Tracked him when he was leaving The Vesper Gate in Kirkstall," continued Reilly. "Noticed he was drunk, thought it was the perfect opportunity to see *him* off as well. All your troubles taken care of."

"Silence him? Why would I want to shut him up?"

"Because he was in on whatever your brother and the prostitute were up to. We found her diaries and her phone. One of the conversations between her and Barry was recorded. Your brother mentioned a new point of contact, a man by the name of Alan Sargent. She kept a record in her diary."

"Anything you want to add, Billy boy?" said Reilly.

"Such as?"

"Do you want to share any thoughts with us about your brother, the prostitute and Alan Sargent? Maybe even Frank Fisher?"

"Maybe he was in on it all as well," said Reilly. "You know, him being an accountant, he could really cook the books, couldn't he?"

"How many times do I have to tell you lot?" shouted Morrison. "If they were up to no good, I knew nothing about it. Seems they were taking me for a right mug. Quite frankly I wish our Barry was here now, I'd bloody well throttle him for what he's done to me."

"Temper, temper, Billy," said Reilly. "You're not convincing us of your innocence with talk like that."

"So come on, Mr Morrison, where were you last night?" Gardener asked.

Morrison sighed heavily. "We were moving in with my wife's sister most of yesterday, thanks to you."

"And she lives in Esholt?"

"Yes."

"And you stayed there last night?"

"Most of it."

"Most? Where were you when you were not at home?"

"I had a walk down to the boozer at the end of the street. Left my wife and her sister to have a chat."

"Does the sister have a husband?"

"No, he died a few years ago."

"What time did you leave them?"

"About nine. I don't know, I never looked too closely at the clock. I was too fucking worried about what was happening to my family and my business."

"Think," said Gardener. "We need to know."

"Maybe it was eight," said Billy. "That bloody soap had just finished, *Coronation Street*. That's a laugh. They want to try living real lives. Like mine, for instance."

"So, you left at eight," said Gardener. "The pub is at the end of the street. You got there when?"

"It took me ten minutes to walk."

"How long did you stay?"

"About two hours."

"See anyone you know?"

"Hardly, I'm not from that neck of the woods, am I?"

"Did you do anything while you were there?" asked Gardener. "Strike up a conversation with anyone?"

"A game of darts, maybe," said Reilly. "Or pool?"

"This is important. We need someone to vouch for you."

"Go and see the bloody barman then. He served me my drinks."

"So, you left around ten o'clock," pressed Gardener.

"Yes. The news had just started on the TV. That good enough for you?"

"So you got home when, ten past ten? Can anyone vouch for that?"

"Yes, my wife and her sister."

"And after that you stayed in all night?"

"Yes. They'd just opened a bottle of wine, so I got another beer out of the fridge."

"What time did you go to bed?"

"Just after midnight. My wife and I went. I think her sister stayed up for a while longer."

Gardener removed a photo from the file in front of him.

"How often do you visit Esholt?"

"Now and again. Maybe go over and have Sunday lunch. Or we take my wife's sister out for the day, but it's not somewhere we'd go and stay over, unless, of course, we're kicked out of our house."

"You're not telling us porkies now, are you, Billy?"

"What do you mean?"

"You've never had any other reason for visiting Esholt?"

"Such as?"

"You tell us."

Morrison laughed. "Oh, I see what you two are getting at. What? You think I'm having an affair with my wife's sister behind her back? You think it runs in the family? Our Barry can't be trusted, so neither can I. Well I'll tell the pair of you now, you're barking up the wrong tree. I don't know anyone in Esholt, and I have no reason to go there other than to visit my wife's sister, with my wife, never on my own."

Gardener slid over the photo of the girl that resembled Chloe Summerby. "Do you recognize the girl in the photo?"

"No."

"You don't know a couple who live in the village by the name of Summerby?"

"No." Morrison stared at the photo more closely. "Wait a minute. Isn't this the girl from the village who went missing? She's called Summerby. The wife and her sister were on about it last night. She's still missing, isn't she? The parents must be going spare."

"You've never seen her before?"

"Only on the news and in the papers." Morrison put the photo down, and an expression crossed his features that could have curdled milk.

"Hey, just a minute. Why are you showing me this?"

"Just asking if you recognize her or if you've seen her before," said Gardener.

"But why?"

"It doesn't really matter, does it? You said you haven't."

"But you could be lying," said Reilly. "We get a lot of that in here. People will say anything to distract us."

Morrison was on his feet again. "Listen you, I'm no scum, and neither is our Barry."

"Barry?" said Gardener. "Who mentioned Barry?"

"We didn't," said Reilly.

"Don't mess me about," shouted Morrison. "You've shown me this for a reason. Either you think I'm up to something more than murder, or you think our Barry or me had something to do with this girl going missing. Well I'm telling you now, you're on the wrong tracks. I'm not into shit like this, and neither is our Barry."

"How do you know?" said Reilly.

"You didn't know he was into drugs," said Gardener. "You didn't know he owned houses, or that he had a prostitute holed up in one against her will."

"Against her will. Have you heard yourselves?"

"Seems you didn't really know your brother that well at all. Let me give you another example, did you know it was your Barry who persuaded Frank Fisher to sue the builder Fisher had worked for?"

"Pardon?"

"You heard," said Reilly. "Face it, your brother was a complete mystery to you. Now you're either telling the truth, or you're the best actor I've ever seen. And I'm telling you now, son, believe me when I say I've seen a few fine actors in my time, so I have."

"So you know for a fact that Barry had nothing to do with the disappearance of the five-year-old?" Gardener persisted.

"He's not like that," shouted Morrison, still on his feet. "He's not a ponce."

"Let's hope that's true," said Gardener, rising to his. "For your sake. Because we found this photo underneath the prostitute when she was killed, and we also found it underneath a dead Frank Fisher, and all of the people mentioned in this interview room today are connected to a murder investigation that involves the girl, and very possibly you.

"And you're the only one left alive at the moment. So when I tell you I am going to get to the bottom of this, you need to believe me, because I will. There will be no stone unturned, Mr Morrison. A lot of people will have sleepless nights before I get to the truth. So when you tell me you are not involved, then you'd better be telling the truth. You'd better hope for your sake that I don't find a single thing on you. Because like I said, you are the only one left alive. You'll go down for the lot, and you know what they do to people in prison who kill children."

Despite everything that had happened in the interview room, Gardener was quite happy that Billy Morrison had been telling the truth. He and his partner had cross-examined literally hundreds of people over the years, and he knew a liar when he saw one.

He turned to his partner.

"Sort out his release papers and see him out, please, Sean."

Chapter Forty-four

Rydell glanced at the clock on the fascia panel of his bike: one-fifteen.

He was in a foul mood. He hated change, anything that interrupted his day. An emergency delivery to Oldham's in Guiseley represented that. Being a Monday, traffic was light. The call had come at eleven-thirty. He'd been at the warehouse around twelve-fifteen, but wasn't loaded up until twelve-forty. Another thirty-five minutes to reach his destination, all of them filled with resentment and terror.

The delivery was small but he still needed the trailer because he had a passenger. He could not leave her on her own in the middle of the day. She was awake, and anything could happen. She was too precious for that. All through the night was different. She always slept soundly and was never awake before he arrived home. There was never any evidence that she had been up during the night.

He parked the bike and retrieved the parcel from the trailer, and asked if she was okay. She was loving every minute of the journey. She had her doll, some sweets, and a drink, and she was quite happy.

He entered Oldham's and was pleasantly surprised. A couple of pensioners waited in a queue for prescriptions. A young woman with a pushchair was eyeing up the perfumes, her baby asleep. The only other person in the shop was a man in his thirties, dressed in a leather jacket and jeans. He wore a pair of tinted glasses and had the beginnings of a moustache and beard. He was vaguely familiar. Oldham was in the corner, talking to none other than the author of all the blogs he'd been reading recently, Vincent Baines.

"Oh, yes, John, I know exactly who it is," said Baines, full of his own importance.

"What? Who robbed my shop?"

"Yes, but more importantly, I know who is responsible for the double murder in Batley a couple of nights back."

"Then why aren't you down the police station?"

"I'm just on my way, but it'll be all hell and no notion right now."

"Not because somebody's pinched some tablets, surely?"

Rydell removed his helmet and lifted his parcel to indicate to Oldham that he had something for him. Oldham nodded.

Baines leaned in closer. So did Rydell. "There's been two more."

The man in the tinted glasses dropped a bag of menthol sweets on the floor. "Sorry," he whispered.

"Two more what?" Oldham asked. "Murders?"

"Yes, not far from here either, one of them."

Oldham offered to take the package from Rydell. The man in the tinted glasses had his back to them, but Rydell reckoned he had an interest in the conversation as well. He wasn't doing much else; he certainly wasn't putting shopping in the basket he held.

Rydell took his time in sorting out the paperwork. He wanted to hear what Baines had to say.

"They found one of them in Kirkstall Abbey, battered to death. Black and blue he was."

"What's the world coming to?"

The pensioners thanked the counter assistant for their prescription and glanced over at Baines before leaving. The young woman with the pushchair had made her choice of perfume and passed it over for payment.

"What about the other one?" Oldham asked Baines.

"Somewhere in Leeds. I don't have much information, but I'm going to see Detective Inspector Gardener now. He's leading the investigation, you know. I went to see him yesterday, offer my help."

The man in the tinted glasses paid for his menthol sweets and headed for the door.

"Are you sure you know who it is?"

"Quite sure. And why he's doing it," said Baines. "He might have the police fooled, but not me. I'm on to him."

Baines headed for the door. The man with the tinted glasses left the shop without holding the door open for Baines. Oldham signed Rydell's delivery note.

Baines left the shop.

Outside, Rydell watched him go.

Chapter Forty-five

Vincent was once again sitting in an interview room. He glanced at his watch. It was approaching three o'clock; he'd been there for thirty minutes. They had supplied him with coffee and biscuits, but he was tired of waiting. He had better things to do.

Having said that, at least he was safe. Out of reach of Loch Ness.

The door opened. Gardener and Reilly came in and took a seat. The DI dropped a manila file on the table.

"We're very busy," said Gardener.

"So am I," replied Vincent. "But I have important information for you."

"Like yesterday, you mean?" said Reilly, taking a sip of his coffee. "What is it this time?"

Gardener took a sip of bottled water. "If you have something important for us, we'd appreciate it," he said. "The last thing I want you doing today is wasting my time. I have enough to do."

Vincent was offended by the senior officer's tone. "Isn't it your job to protect the public?"

"Yes, it is," replied Gardener. "But all of them, not just you."

"Is this how you treat people who are being threatened with their lives?"

"Get to the point, for Christ's sake," said Reilly.

Vincent passed over his own file. "I've received another email."

Gardener read through the email and the notes he'd made, and then passed it all to Reilly. "Where do you think all this is heading, Mr Baines?"

"He's going to kill me. It says so quite clearly in there."

"No it doesn't. He's playing games with you. He's made some reference to an engine driver in 1866 who committed suicide by talking opium."

"Yes, and the chemist where I live had a break-in this morning. The only thing taken was secobarbital, very similar properties to opium."

"Coincidence."

"I didn't think you people believed in coincidences."

"Whether we believe in them or not," replied Gardener, "we're not stupid enough to think they don't exist. Okay, let's play along with your theory. Who is it? And why do you think he wants to kill you?"

"A Scottish gangster called Danny MacDonald."

Vincent went on to relate his tale of the missing racehorse, and then produced the autobiography of the man he'd claimed was on to him, pointing to a passage from the middle of the book.

"So we've gone from Arthur Negus to Braveheart," said Reilly. "Why the hell would a big time Scottish gangster be wasting his time waging a vendetta on small fry like you?"

"Because of what it says in that book, and what I did."

"How long ago did that happen?" Gardener asked.

"Thirty years, maybe."

"And you think a man like Danny MacDonald would have waited until now before coming back for revenge?" Gardener asked.

"You'd have been holding up the M8 motorway long before now, son."

Before Vincent opened his mouth, Gardener continued. "And what does all this have to do with the murders we're investigating?"

Vincent grew angry. "Read the email."

"I have," replied Gardener. "Seems to me the man in here has far more sense than you have. He's playing games with you, and he's admitted absolutely nothing. Look at this paragraph here, the one that mentions Steven Cooper."

Vincent did as he was asked.

"We did a little bit of digging after you left yesterday. Steven Cooper was released from prison in 2002 and took a job at a stable in Ireland. He died in 2006. Now you're in here telling us it's an infamous Scottish gangster called Danny MacDonald. Study the text in the email, Mr Baines. The man writing to you knows a hell of a lot more about you, than you do about him."

"Of course he does, that's why he's threatening my life."

"Well, even if he is, don't you think you ought to look a lot closer to home?"

Vincent could feel the butterflies in his stomach. "What do you mean?"

Gardener withdrew a newspaper from his file and passed it over.

"Read that, and then go and make an official complaint at the front desk, see if they will assign someone to investigate the Pudsey Poisoner for you. We have more important things to do, Mr Baines. If and when you finally turn up dead, then we'll look into the matter, because it will have become a murder investigation. That's where we come in."

Both detectives rose and left the room.

Before doing so, the Irishman turned and faced Vincent. "Don't give up your day job, son. Leave the detective work to the professionals."

Chapter Forty-six

Raymond Allen was in trouble.

After leaving the chemist, he'd made his way to Kirkstall. The abbey had been cordoned off with scene tape. The police were stopping everyone, asking if they had seen anything strange the previous day.

In an effort to try and find out more, he'd evaded them, returning instead to the Vesper Gate. The place was morose, nothing like it had been the night before.

Allen had ordered a drink and questioned a barmaid. The landlord had been down at the police station helping them with their inquiries. The barmaid was pretty sure the man Allen had spent some time with at the bar the previous night was the one who'd been killed. Beaten to death with a hedge stake and dumped in a wheelchair.

Allen was now in the library in Otley. They didn't know him there. He figured he'd outstayed his welcome in the Guiseley library. He had one more email to send to Vincent. It would have to be constructed differently.

His best approach would be to let Vincent know exactly what was going to happen to him, and why. It wouldn't make a great deal of difference, because the self-claimed reporter and private detective still didn't know who he was, or when he would strike.

Even if he did, the man had shown complete incompetence in regard to the clues he'd so far been given. Some detective he was. He hadn't even cottoned on as to who had robbed the chemist in the early hours of the morning. Maybe Vincent should have stuck to backing horses. That's the only thing he'd been any good at.

Allen couldn't stay at the hostel much longer. Once the email was safely on its way, he would have to go back and plan his final assault before bailing out. He would finish what he started, and then disappear for good.

Chapter Forty-seven

"You rang?"

Fitz glanced up from his desk. He ceased writing whatever report he'd been working on, removed his glasses, massaged his eyes and sat back.

"I'm pleased you could make it."

"So am I," said Gardener, glancing at the clock on the wall behind Fitz. Approaching five in the evening meant the case was nearly sixty-five hours old. It felt like sixty-five years. Reilly slipped in beside him and immediately headed for the coffee machine.

Gardener and his partner had been at it for nearly three solid days, investigating, chasing up witness reports, consulting with HOLMES, and chairing meetings, incident room debates, press conferences, and speaking to witnesses. So far they had yet to find anything.

They knew they were dealing with a serial killer, but not an ordinary one. He, or she, followed no pattern. Each victim was killed in a different way so that it appeared to be random, but Gardener knew, in the end, it wouldn't be. That's what was frustrating him. He simply couldn't find the answer.

"So, what do we have in the machine today, Fitz?" Reilly asked.

"I've found something that I think is very important to your case," he said to Gardener.

To Reilly, he said, "Vanilla Chai-spiced coffee."

"Sounds good," said Gardener. "You'd better pour three cups."

The pathologist did as requested before taking a seat behind his desk. Gardener could tell the elderly man was tired. His frame was stooped, his complexion ashen, and the lines on his face definitely deeper. But he could understand why. Fitz worked as many hours as they had.

"Anything on the murders this morning that we might not expect?"

"That's not why I called you. They were pretty straightforward. Frank Fisher had had his throat cut, and bled to death."

"I take it from your findings that he was alive when it happened?" Gardener asked.

"Definitely. Alan Sargent's death was also straightforward. He was savagely beaten and suffered a brain haemorrhage."

"This here stuff you have in that there machine is the business," said Reilly, savouring the sip he had taken.

"Did you listen to anything I just said?"

"Of course, but it was nothing new, was it? Here you are with your college education and all your years of training and letters after your name, and you're not telling me anything I don't know. I could have told you one of them died because his throat was cut, and the other one because he was beaten to death," said Reilly, rising out of his seat. "I think I'll just have another cup. I can't make up my mind whether it's just good or fatally fucking awesome."

"He's a heathen," said Fitz to Gardener.

"You need to tell me?" replied Gardener.

Reilly took his seat again. "So, come on, Fitz, tell us what we really want to hear."

The pathologist consulted his computer. "I think I've found a pattern to your murders. I've been at this all day. It's bugged me since we found Nicola Stapleton. It goes back around a hundred and fifty years."

"Pardon?" said Gardener.

"I've found an incident that took place in Batley in 1865. It concerns a woman called Sarah Brooke. She was a widow, but she lived with her eighteen-year-old daughter called Hannah, who was a millhand."

Gardener cringed inwardly. Fitz was famous for his history lectures; the SIO was sure that most were simply a means of passing the time and showing his greater knowledge. Having said that, Gardener had the greatest of respect for the man, and his lectures had helped them out on more than one occasion.

"Is this leading somewhere?"

"They lived in Hume Street."

"And?"

"Seems that until August 1865, young Hannah was stepping out with a nineteen-year-old cloth finisher by the name of Eli Sykes. A month previous, however, she met a man called James Hurst from Wakefield at a feast in Dewsbury. On the 13th August, they were having tea together at his house. Sometime in the early evening they were at the front door when Sykes walked by. In a fit of jealousy he returned about ten o'clock when Hannah had gone home, informing Hurst that if he couldn't have her, no one could.

"Sykes was a private in the West Yorkshire Volunteer Corps. Now this is the bit I wanted you to hear. On the 19th August, late in the evening – which compares with the date of your first murder – Sykes went to the Brooke house demanding to know if Hannah still wanted a relationship with him. She turned him down and fled into the confines of the house. He followed her and attacked her with the butt end of his gun."

"The butt end?" questioned Reilly. "What was on the other end?"

"A bayonet."

Gardener put his coffee on the desk, realizing where Fitz was heading.

"He eventually drew that bayonet, repeatedly stabbing both mother and daughter. Despite Sarah having multiple wounds, she managed to get to the door and cry for help. A neighbour heard the cry and ran to her aid. The pair found Hannah dead, pinned to the floor with the bayonet."

"Where did you say this took place?" Gardener asked Fitz.

"Hume Street, Batley."

"When?"

"1865."

"Is it likely that Hume Street in 1865 is where Hume Crescent is today?" Reilly asked.

"Exactly." Fitz turned around his computer monitor so it faced both men. "I kept telling you these murders reminded me of something. Anyway, I approached a company called Alan Godfrey Maps. They gave me access to an old ordnance survey map of Batley in 1892. I also got hold of a modern-day map and managed to superimpose one onto the other."

Gardener leaned in closer. Sure enough, when viewed side-by-side and one on top of the other, the locations matched perfectly. Gardener sat back and glanced at Reilly.

"Coincidence?" he asked.

"We don't believe in coincidences."

"That's what I thought."

"There's obviously more, Fitz," said Gardener.

"Yes. I think your man has his roots in true crime. You'd have to have made a real study to operate on this level. You'll need a profiler for this, but in my opinion, he's not your average everyday psychopath. He's working to a plan and, personally, I think he'll stop when he's reached his number."

"Whether we catch him or not," said Reilly.

"We will," said Gardener.

Turning to Fitz, Gardener said, "There's a match for each murder, isn't there?"

"Yes. The second one was known as The Batley Mystery, and actually went unsolved. Happened one morning at the end of May, in 1881. A miner and his son were walking to work down Batley High Street, what you now know as Cross Bank Road. They were heading to The West End Colliery in the town."

"So, if they were miners, it would have been early," said Gardener.

"Four-thirty."

Even the timings were almost exact, thought Gardener.

"The boy thought he had seen a sack on the doorstep of one of the local shops."

"Wouldn't happen to have been a butcher, would it?" Reilly asked.

"It certainly was. Belonged to one Mary Wrigglesworth."

"Are you serious?" asked Gardener.

"Deadly," replied Fitz. "If you'll pardon the pun. Anyway, the father examined the sack. Inside was a body, half-reclining on the door, half-lying on the doorstep."

"This is getting freaky," said Reilly.

"Judging by what you've said, these murders are anything but random," said Gardener.

Fitz nodded. "Your man is very definitely working hard to pattern his killings after these. I'm simply not sure why.

"Police were called. They established that the body in the doorway was one John Critchley, the son of a JP Critchley of Batley Hall, called James. He was wearing only a pair of trousers and a hat. In the doorway were a coat and a vest, which they believed belonged to the man. His hands were crossed over his chest, and his wrists were tied together with a piece of cord, as were his feet."

"As was Barry Morrison," replied Gardener.

"Was it murder?" Reilly asked.

"The police who investigated the scene of the discovery found no evidence that he'd been murdered," continued Fitz. "It does appear, however, that there were some circumstances which led them to believe that he had been the victim of brutal violence."

"Were there any other similarities to Barry Morrison?"

"I haven't found anything specific on the cause of death, but Critchley – like Morrison – also had a swollen head, neck, and chest. But there were relatively few marks on Critchley's body, which led the police to believe the swelling was due to internal problems rather than any violence."

Fitz added, "I realize it's not an exact copy of your case, but the police at the Batley Police station also believed he was murdered somewhere else and dumped on the doorstep. In Critchley's pockets they found an empty purse, a knife, some letters, a number of other papers, and a photograph of Mary Wrigglesworth. There are enough coincidences for me, gentlemen, to start taking this seriously."

Gardener helped himself to a second coffee. "What about the other two, Fisher and Sargent?"

"In September 1864 the public was allowed to watch the first and last double execution at Armley Gaol. James Sargisson and Joseph Myers had each been found guilty of murder. Myers was a saw-grinder from Sheffield, a heavy drinker with an evil temper who had killed his wife.

"James Sargisson was twenty years old and had no police record until he attacked a man called John Cooper in April 1864. Cooper was twenty-seven and worked as a gardener. On his way home to his parents' house in Stone near Rotherham, he stopped off at the pub and sank four glasses of ale. He left around ten o'clock, and the records state that Sargisson, along with his friends, noticed the watch Cooper was wearing and the money he had. Cooper left the pub and was eventually attacked. He suffered repeated blows from a hedge stake. The following morning, he was found by the roadside near to Roche Abbey."

"With exactly the same injuries as Alan Sargent?" Reilly asked.

"As near as," said Fitz. "Fractured skull, broken jaw. His eyes were black, and he was covered in bruises where he'd tried to defend himself. The hedge stake had been left lying next to him."

"The pattern changed slightly," said Gardener, "but only out of necessity."

"Yes," said Fitz. "Geographically speaking, your man wasn't going to Rotherham to commit a crime, nor was he going to take his victim there."

"Must have been very convenient for our man to have his intended victim living so close to Kirkstall Abbey," said Gardener.

"Coincidence?" Reilly asked.

"I didn't think we believed in them," said Gardener.

"You two should be on television," said Fitz.

"We have been," said Reilly. "A few times."

"What about Frank Fisher's murder?" Gardener asked.

"It's a copy of a suicide," said Fitz.

"Which was how it was made to look to us," said Reilly.

"Pretty much down to the last details," replied Fitz. "James Foreman lived on Sussex Street on Richmond Hill in Leeds."

Gardener shook his head. "It's unbelievable."

Fitz continued. "He committed suicide in 1856. He was a fifty-seven-year-old woodcarver and a widower. The similarities in history between him and Fisher are also quite startling. He was a secretary to a friendly society, and a few weeks before his suicide, he became concerned that his accounts for the society were incorrect."

"He was an accountant?" Gardener asked.

"Seems so. Anyway, due to accounting problems, he sank into a deep depression and cut his own throat."

"It's uncanny," said Reilly. "But surely our killer couldn't know this."

"Well, even if he did," replied Gardener, "how could he possibly twist people's lives so that it all happened exactly as it had in the past?"

"He couldn't," said Fitz. "It's simply fate."

"Or it could be—"

"Don't you dare," Gardener threatened his partner. He turned back to Fitz. "Was this suicide guy found exactly the same way as Fisher?"

"Yes. His friends gained access to his bedroom and found him kneeling on the floor with his throat cut, his head above a basin full of blood."

"Where did you find all this, Fitz?"

The pathologist reached into one of his desk drawers and passed a paperback book across the desk to the senior officer. It was a standard, perfect bound 6" x 9" publication entitled *Foul Deeds and Suspicious Deaths in Leeds*.

Gardener leafed through the book, which was only around a hundred and fifty pages. The blurb on the back informed the reader that it covered a few of the most intriguing murder cases to occur over the last two hundred years in Leeds and the surrounding areas. There were four bookmarks indicating the chapters that covered the deaths the pathologist had informed Gardener about.

He had a sudden thought about the visits Vincent had made. He turned to his partner.

"Maybe that lunatic Baines who came to see us isn't as mad as we thought. His first email made reference to numbers, and the date of the first murder adding up to twenty, which 1865 would."

"And not 1982 like he thought," offered Reilly.

"Precisely. And the second one added up to 18."

Reilly glanced at the pathologist. "What was the year the body was found in the doorway?"

"1881."

"There's your 18," said Reilly.

"What if it was the killer who had contacted Baines?"

"I wonder if he knows Baines as well as he makes out."

"Or is he using him as a mouthpiece?"

"Who's Baines?" asked Fitz.

Gardener briefly ran through it.

"Is there any mention of a man called Samuel Birchall in this book, apparently died from an overdose of opium?"

Fitz nodded. "I think it's on the very last page."

Gardener found it in a chapter titled 'Suicides 1849 – 1909'. He quickly read through the four paragraphs, which were exactly as Vincent had mentioned.

"Maybe he's a lot better than we gave him credit for," said Gardener.

"I don't think so, boss. We gave him hard evidence that it could be someone known as the Pudsey Poisoner, a man called Raymond Allen. He hadn't even considered that one."

"No. Is Allen responsible? Nicola Stapleton was found with a syringe underneath her that had been used to inject a compound into Barry Morrison, which was about as lethal as a poison."

"Even so, I still think it would be out of a poisoner's league to have come up with stuff so elaborate."

"You're probably right, Sean, but I think we need someone on Allen. Check out his background, exactly when he was put away, what he was up to inside, and where the hell he is right now."

Gardener glanced at his watch. "Fitz, I really appreciate this. It's given us something else to go at, but we really will have to go. We have an incident room meeting in about half an hour."

"Before you do," replied Fitz, "there is something else in the book which I found very disturbing. Please turn to page 55 and read it now. You might find your whole incident room meeting will be centred around that chapter."

Gardener glanced at Reilly before delving into the book.

It took him nearly twenty minutes to read the thirteen-page chapter. During that time he didn't speak, and he'd held his breath on more than one occasion.

When he'd finished, he placed the book on the desk and his head in his hands.

"Oh, Christ!"

Chapter Forty-eight

The team assembled in the incident room.

On the way back from the pathology laboratory, neither detective had said a word. The implications of what they'd read were too horrendous to even think about, let alone mention.

While he was waiting for his officers to settle, Gardener found his thoughts consumed by Raymond Allen, The Pudsey Poisoner.

One question was uppermost in his mind: had the killer been under their noses all along? Allen had obviously been watching Vincent Baines, which would have given him ample opportunity to observe the police. If Allen was responsible, did he have the missing girl?

Allen definitely knew a lot about Baines. The pair had history, from what Gardener had managed to dig up. The Pudsey Poisoner also had detailed information about the first two crimes.

But surely he only had a score to settle with Baines. Allen had been inside for quite some time. How could he possibly know Nicola Stapleton and Barry Morrison?

Gardener thought about running the name past Billy Morrison, but he decided that he'd given Billy enough grief for now. He had never been convinced of his guilt.

Gardener noticed Briggs walk into the room and close the door. He was usually last, which signalled the start of the meeting.

"Thanks for coming, everyone. I want you all to know I appreciate everything you're doing. I might be the DI, but I'm nothing without my team, and you lot are a credit to myself and Sean."

"Jesus," said Reilly. "Listen here, boss man, I'm not having a whip round, so you'd better get on with it."

Gardener laughed, as did most of the team.

He started with Colin Sharp. "What have you got for us? Anything interesting on the Morrisons?"

Sharp consulted his notes. "I've managed to uncover a collision that Barry Morrison was involved in. It's interesting to say the least."

"Go on," said Gardener.

"The driver of the other vehicle, which happened to be a motorbike, was a courier delivery driver called Rydell."

"Rydell?" said Paul Benson.

"Yes, Chris Rydell. Why, do you know him?"

"Not personally," said Benson, "but that name has cropped up in my investigation."

"Excellent," said Gardener to Benson, "but let me come back to you."

"Not a common name, is it?" asked Reilly. "Do we have an address for Chris Rydell?"

"Yes," said Sharp. "Lives in Rodley."

"That's exactly where his father, Sean Rydell had his yard," said Benson.

"There's a link here," said Gardener. "It's worth checking so I'd like someone on it first thing."

He addressed Sharp again. "When was the collision?"

"A couple of years back."

"What happened? What set you off on this track?"

"With everything that Morrison was involved in, I checked to see if he had a record. I've been at the magistrates' court all afternoon, going through the files. They were trying to prosecute for dangerous driving, failure to identify a driver, and failure to report or stop after an accident."

"Tell me more," said Gardener.

"It happened in December. Weather was cold, bit misty. He'd picked up a passenger from the train station at Horsforth, just after eight in the evening. Pulled out of Station Road without looking, clipped a motorbike that he hadn't seen coming. The bike and the driver ended up in the middle of the road at the nearby dental surgery. Thing is, he just drove off as if nothing had happened.

"Seems there wasn't much damage either to Rydell or the bike. There was one witness, a woman named Margaret Pendlebury, lives on Town Street in Horsforth."

Gardener stopped him. "Where do we know that name from?"

Reilly answered the question. "Isn't she the secretary at the clinic in Bond Street?"

"You're right, Sean." Gardener wrote it on the chart. "I'd like someone to go and see her in the morning. I know it was two years ago, but she may remember something that she's never told anyone."

Gardener turned and addressed Sharp. "Carry on, Colin."

"She saw what happened, ran to his help. She got the number plate of the car. Rydell phoned the police and reported it. Margaret Pendlebury was a key witness."

"Sounds pretty serious, Colin. Did he manage to get off with it?"

"Yes. Claims he was nowhere near Horsforth that night. It was blamed on a driver who quit the job at the end of the week, because he and his family were emigrating to New Zealand."

"How convenient," said Reilly. "But surely this Pendlebury woman must have been a good enough witness to cook his goose."

"Morrison had a witness to prove he wasn't there – his passenger."

"Why do I get the feeling it was his brother?" Gardener asked.

"You'd be wrong," replied Sharp. "His passengers were Chloe Summerby, and her mother Sally."

Reilly glanced at Gardener. "She claimed she didn't know Barry Morrison."

Gardener immediately drew a few link lines on the whiteboard to connect the names. "Why would she say that? What hold did Morrison have on *her*?"

"He couldn't possibly have had that hold after he'd died," added Briggs.

"Depends what it was," said Gardener. "And with all due respect, he has only just died."

A number of thoughts ran through Gardener's mind, but he kept them private for now. He turned to his partner. "We'll talk to her again in the morning."

"I would if I was you," said Sharp. "Sally Summerby was in court. She confirmed that she was in one of Morrison's taxis that night, and it *was* Barry Morrison driving. But they were miles away in Shipley. If she was lying, she did so under oath."

"Why? Who was she protecting?"

"Could only be herself or the taxi driver."

"Or her daughter," suggested Reilly.

"I can't see that," said Gardener. "What could she possibly be protecting her daughter from?"

"I don't know," said Reilly. "I'm working on the fact that there were only three of them in the cab. Her, Morrison, and Chloe, so she had to be protecting one of them."

"You've spoken to this Summerby woman, haven't you, Stewart?" Briggs asked.

"Yes. She said she hadn't heard of Nicola Stapleton or Barry Morrison."

"Looks like she lied at the trial, and she certainly lied to you," said Briggs. "Drag her down the station tomorrow morning, early as you like. Question her under caution."

"We'll make it first thing. Have you found anything else, Colin? Any hint that connects the three of them further?"

"Not yet, sir."

"Keep on it, but well done. That's just the kind of break we needed."

234

Patrick Edwards stepped forward. Gardener wanted a little more from Benson but he figured Edwards must have something further on Morrison.

"Sir, we managed to run the druggies to ground, the ones who lived in Morrison's flats."

"Excellent, did they squeal?"

"After a while. Seems they've had a couple of good days selling the stuff because the money's all been profit, going straight into their pockets and no rent to pay either, now that he's pegged it."

"What was the score there?"

"Barry Morrison let them live there for a small rent because he creamed fifty percent off whatever they made on the drugs. And it was all cash."

"At least we know where his money was coming from. Where are they now?"

"We've let them out for the time being, but told them to report back every day while we look deeper into what was going on."

"Did they know Stapleton?"

"Yes. Morrison was renting her out, and he had her dealing."

"Did they know why?" Reilly asked. "How he managed to keep her there?"

"I got the impression they were all pretty frightened of him. Seems he had something on all of them, maybe even enough to send them all down."

"Any ideas?"

"No."

"Keep on it, Patrick," said Gardener. "Find out everything you can. Let's have a list of their clients, and one of Stapleton's if possible. Which reminds me, have you retrieved any more information from her mobile or her diaries?"

"Sorry, sir, I've been tied up most of the day with the drug dealing scum."

"It's okay, Patrick. Don't apologise, you've only got one pair of hands. Get back on to the diaries and phones tomorrow and see what you can find. In fact, go through all the phones: Morrison, Stapleton, Sargent, and Fisher. There will be a link somewhere."

He glanced at Anderson and Thornton. "Talking of Fisher, did you find out if he'd ever attended the clinic in Bond Street?"

"He didn't," said Anderson. "All his treatment was at the St James hospital. They wouldn't tell us much, patient confidentiality and all that."

"Can we have a warrant tomorrow, seize their files on Fisher?" Gardener asked Briggs.

"I don't see why not. I'll get on to it in the morning."

Gardener nodded, made a note on the board.

A knock on the door had all heads turning in that direction. The desk sergeant popped his head through the gap.

"Just had a call from the locksmith. He's identified that safe deposit key in Morrison's stomach. Said he was coming in, but he's had to attend an emergency. He's hoping it won't be long, but he does want to come and see you."

Gardener nodded. The desk sergeant left.

"Attend an emergency?" said Anderson. "What kind of an emergency would a locksmith have at eight o'clock at night?"

"No idea," said Gardener. "We could always put out a warrant for his arrest. He'd certainly have one then."

A little levity helped brighten the team's spirits.

"Benson? You mentioned Sean Rydell earlier. You were looking into Fisher's accident. Have you found a connection?"

"I know that Sean Rydell was Frank Fisher's business partner. Apparently, Fisher was rendered disabled because of an accident at the yard where they operated. The case went to court, which was probably down to some friendly persuasion from our infamous taxi-driver. Fisher won compensation. Sean Rydell committed suicide.

"I've been at the Crown Court in Leeds most of the afternoon. The woman in the archive office was very helpful. She's going to print out all the notes for tomorrow morning. I'm going back when they open."

"Well done. As soon as you have everything let us know."

They were still unable to connect all the dots, thought Gardener, but things were beginning to fall into place nicely. The news on Sally Summerby definitely helped. He had not trusted her on the very first meeting, but he couldn't let it cloud his thoughts tonight. He still had a lot more ground to cover.

"Dave. Sealing wax?"

"I've found a place in Rugby called The Celtic Shop. They sell all sorts of stuff, including wax gun kits, and they advertise it all on the Net. They have contracts with builders' merchants nationally, some of which are in the LS postcode."

"What's in a wax gun kit?"

"Lots of different coloured wax, a gun, and a number of syringes. Could be just what we're looking for."

"Get on to the company first thing in the morning, see if you can get all the invoices for the last six months. Find out which merchants are stocking it, and then contact them, see if you can narrow it down further."

"Will do, sir."

Gardener made more notes. As he turned back to address the team, another knock on the door interrupted the meeting. The desk sergeant entered and held up some paperwork.

"Sir, we have a couple of witness statements here that make interesting reading. A Brian Rutter who lives on Willow Approach, round the corner from the television studios, reckons he saw a motorbike with a weird shaped trailer on the back, sometime in the early hours of the morning."

"What time, and which way was it going?"

"About two o'clock, heading towards the abbey. Reason he thought it odd was because he'd convinced himself he could see a wheel sticking out the back, and maybe, just maybe, a foot poking out from underneath the canvas. But he'd had a bit to drink, so he couldn't be too sure."

"And the other?"

"Yes. Second one – Alan Wilton of Rothwell – definitely saw the contraption outside the bus stop near the abbey, parked up an hour later around three o'clock. He thought it was odd, but he couldn't see anybody about, and he was in a rush to get home. He'd been away for a week on business in the Czech Republic, and his plane had recently landed. All he wanted to do was get home."

"Okay, something more to go on. I want both of those witnesses contacted tomorrow morning. Visit them, talk to them – see if you can get more. And there are speed cameras and CCTV on those roads, so I want every scrap of footage on this. A motorbike with a weird trailer won't be hard to spot."

He turned to the board once more. "Mess" was not the word he would use. It resembled a minefield where several of them had gone off. Gardener pulled a file off a nearby chair and spread out its contents on the table in front of him.

"These are a couple of emails sent to a private detective by the name of Vincent Baines, reputedly from someone identifying himself as The Man in Black. In these, there appears to be a somewhat mild threat on the detective's life. Personally, I think he's in more danger if he ends up meeting Sean again."

"Aren't we all?" said Thornton.

"Some more than others," added Reilly.

"We're not sure, but we think they come from a man called Raymond Allen."

"I've heard that name before," said Bob Anderson.

"Well, maybe you and Frank could check it out for us. Raymond Allen has earned himself the nickname The Pudsey Poisoner. He escaped from Rampton a few weeks back, and no one has seen him since. From what I can work out, he seems to have it in for Vincent Baines because he feels Baines was responsible for him being sent down.

"The main reason I want him checking out is because in these emails he makes reference to the double murder in Batley, and has left a number of other cryptic clues that put him in the frame."

"How do you mean?" asked Thornton.

"He's claiming that the murders we're investigating are parallel to something that happened way back in time, that history is repeating itself with these crimes. He informed Baines that the number of the year the first crime was committed added up to twenty. Baines was adamant that it was the first case he got caught up in. The year was 1982. Ironic that it should turn out that way, but Baines was wrong. Fitz has confirmed that Nicola Stapleton's crime scene was identical to the murder of a woman named Hannah Brooke in Batley in 1865, which also adds up to twenty. And get this, it appears to have happened in exactly the same place."

"Same house?" Briggs asked.

"I can't say for definite that it was the same house, but it looks like it was. Fitz had sent for a detailed map of Batley in 1865."

"Christ," said Anderson. "Can you actually get such a thing?"

"Not quite. The best he could do was 1892, but everything was still there. Superimposed onto modern-day Batley, you find that Hume Street in 1865 is now Hume Crescent."

"How weird is that? He's obviously trying to frighten Baines because the private dick sent him down. Question is, is he trying to confuse him?" Briggs asked.

"Maybe. He's definitely using Baines as a voice, because Baines has a blog."

"We need a lot more on this bloke Allen," said Briggs. "Did he have cryptic information for the second crime?"

"Yes," said Gardener. "He reckoned that year added up to eighteen."

"And what did Baines have to say about that?"

"He didn't," replied Gardener. "At that time he was too fixated on his 1982 mystery, persuading us that the recent double murder had been committed by a man named Steven Cooper."

"I take it you've checked that out? Why did he suspect Cooper?"

"Long story," said Gardener. "But it has nothing to do with Steven Cooper. He died in 2006."

"But Baines has been back to see us," said Reilly. "Only now he's convinced it's some haggis-eating heathen by the name of Mad Dog Danny MacDonald, because Vincent solved something else that happened in the early 1990s involving MacDonald. He reckons this big Scottish gangster is after putting the record straight."

"What?" said Briggs. "And he's waited thirty years?"

"That's what we said."

"Take it from me, big time gangsters do not wait thirty years to settle scores, and when they do, they don't bother with clues. You're either holding up a motorway bridge, or you're wearing concrete shoes at the bottom of a very deep lake."

"That's why we've told him to stop wasting our time," said Gardener. "However, we can't ignore the clues and the evidence that Fitz has come up with."

Gardener produced a copy of the book he'd taken from the mortuary, *Foul Deeds And Suspicious Deaths In Leeds*. It took him another thirty minutes to bring his squad up to date on what Fitz had told them, pointing out the parallels for each of the four murders.

"The killer is obviously someone who's studied true crime to have copied the scenes exactly," said Thornton.

"But why is he doing it?"

"Well, these people don't have to have much of a reason, do they?" said Anderson. "I mean, he's obviously got a damn good reason in his head for killing four people, but as for how he does it, well that could be anything."

"You're probably right, Bob. Sarah Brooke was a widow, and her daughter Hannah was a millhand; neither were prostitutes. John Critchley was the son of a JP and unemployed. So why he's picking out that particular way of murdering someone is anyone's guess."

"We might never find out," offered Reilly.

"However, all the people he's taking out are connected. There must be an incident in the past that involved all of them."

"Or maybe they've all crossed him at some point," added Reilly.

"It doesn't have to be anything with a psychopath," added Rawson. "He could simply start and stop when he feels like it."

"I'm not so sure he is a psychopath," replied Gardener. "I know what he's done is bad, but maybe he's on a mission. Talking to Fitz, he firmly believes that that's what it is. It's possible his agenda only has so many people, and when he's done, he'll stop. We may find the man has a clean record, never done anything like this in his life."

"There's still the five-year-old girl to consider," said Sharp.

"Or girls," added Anderson.

"Neither of those has turned up anywhere, have they?" Briggs asked. "Is there anything in the book about that?"

Gardener allowed a hush to descend over the room before tackling his final point.

"Oh, Jesus," said Briggs. "There is, isn't there?"

"I'm afraid so," said Gardener. "It happened in 1891. According to the book, five-year-old Barbara Whitham Waterhouse was last seen on Saturday 6th June during the afternoon peering into a shop window in Town Street. She was playing with a friend who was asked by her mother to go and fetch some sandwiches. The two girls collected them before separating. Between the Saturday afternoon and Wednesday 10th June, nothing more was seen or heard of Barbara.

"Her body was found behind the Municipal Buildings in Leeds on that Wednesday evening. *The Yorkshire Post* published the fact the day after the body was found. It appears that her injuries were so horrific that the mother fainted, and the father was unable to bear up."

Colin Sharp broke the haunting silence in the room. "What happened?"

"The murder happened at a time when Jack the Ripper was at large in the East End of London. The Yorkshire newspapers pounced on it. She was wrapped in a shawl, and it was reported that the body had actually been washed after the murder. At some point in the afternoon, one eyewitness report said they had seen a small girl fitting her description in Woodside, perhaps going towards Leeds, and she was accompanied by a man and a woman.

"Apparently there were forty-five different wounds on the body, including cuts and stab wounds. The deepest of which ran from the bottom of the stomach to the chest. It would seem that the murderer had stabbed the little girl in the chest before ripping the body right up to her neck. Her throat was cut, and her legs had almost been hacked away from her body. Judging by the cuts on her fingers, it was evident that she had tried very hard to resist the attack."

Gardener allowed the dust to settle before adding, "I understand all about police budgets, but some things are more important. I want officers behind the municipal buildings every night from now until we catch the lunatic responsible for these four murders."

Chapter Forty-nine

Vincent had been in a state of shock since Gardener and Reilly had shown him the article in the newspaper – for two reasons. First, he could not work out how he had missed that edition of *The Yorkshire Post*. Second, his life was in far more danger than he had realized.

He left the police station, went straight home, locked all the doors, and barricaded himself in. Raymond Allen was a lunatic – a very dangerous lunatic, who knew poisons better than anyone else, including John Oldham.

Vincent became involved when he overheard John Oldham the chemist talking to another staff member about the sickness problems they had been having at the shop, and that they had only started since the apprentice Raymond Allen had joined them.

Vincent confronted Oldham and asked him if he was serious about the comment. His reason for asking was fact that he'd discovered bottles and cartons tucked away in the bottoms of bins and behind them, and he was of the opinion that poisons had to be disposed of properly: that there were set down procedures.

Vincent tracked down Allen's family, where he was shocked to learn the extent of Raymond's experiments. His mother had died in childbirth and from a young age his fascination for poisons and the effect they had on people grew rapidly.

When he was twelve, he had tested poisons on his family, enough to make them violently ill. He'd gathered large amounts of antimony and digitalis by repeatedly buying small amounts, lying about his age and claiming they were being used in science classes at school. Allen's stepmother, Sarah, died from poisoning in 2003.

Allen's sister informed Vincent of the two occasions when Allen himself had become as ill as the rest of the family. Vincent decided that Allen had either forgotten which stuff he had laced, or he had deliberately poisoned himself to make it appear genuine.

As one of Allen's duties was making tea, Vincent asked Oldham to analyse it. The tea had in fact been poisoned and the stock in the shop was incorrect. The police were informed and Allen was arrested, after confessing to the attempted murders of his father, sister, and friend.

Raymond Allen was sentenced and sent to Rampton hospital for the criminally insane.

Since constructing his blockade, he had sat in front of his computer, watching and waiting. He'd eaten nothing apart from a chocolate bar. But he had polished off his entire stock of lagers before starting on the Jack Daniel's.

He was now on his third glass. It was eight forty-five in the evening, and his email inbox had pinged. The Man in Black had sent another.

His message was more direct than any of the previous emails. The friendly tone was missing; gone were the clues.

Vincent filled his empty glass with whiskey again, draining the last drops from the bottle, realising he did not have another to replace it with. He was buggered if he was going across the road to Morrisons.

He read the email:

Hello Vincent.

If you haven't guessed by now you never will. You're not really the detective you thought you were. Seems you've wasted most of your time in a blind panic, hoping the two detectives leading the double murder case will save you.
They won't.
Keep your thoughts on Samuel Birchall.
Keep your eyes open and your ears peeled.
I'm on my way.

The Man in Black

Vincent had been expecting another message, but not one so direct. He had not spent the afternoon idly, and now felt it was time to tell the world what was going on. He was not convinced of Allen's innocence of the double murders, either.

He posted his latest blog, with two photographs to help with identification – though he doubted they would be up to date.

Chapter Fifty

Gardener was still sitting in the incident room at ten o'clock waiting for the locksmith when Sean Reilly opened the door, carrying a bag of sausage rolls. At that point, he realized that he couldn't remember having eaten anything since breakfast. The Irishman also came with tea because he knew Gardener would not entertain coffee from the machine. They both sat and ate.

"Cheers, Sean, you're a lifesaver."

"I'm starving, I know that."

"Where the hell is this locksmith?"

"Maybe you *should* have put a warrant out for his arrest. I'm sure we'd have found him before now."

Gardener laughed. He was seriously flagging now. The investigation was seventy hours old, and they had slogged their guts out for most of them.

"What do you think about Sally Summerby?" he asked Reilly.

"I'm not sure what to think, boss. She's obviously been up to something, decided to play her cards close to her chest. But why?"

"Maybe now that she knows Morrison is dead, she feels it's not worth talking about, whatever it was."

"The secret dies with him, you mean?"

"It hasn't, though, has it? She must have known we'd find a connection eventually."

"So, what is it? Drugs? Money? An affair?"

"I wouldn't have thought so. I'm not a fan of the woman, but she is attractive. Very slim, blonde hair, dresses well. What the hell would she see in Barry Morrison?"

"I doubt the attraction was physical. From what we know of Morrison, he'd give any of the famous despots a run for their money. No, he had something on her, as well as everyone else we've come across."

"And his brother still knows nothing about it."

"So he claims. But he must know something about this collision. It was a company vehicle in company time, and it went to court. He has to know something."

"Which brings us back to the question, is Billy Morrison involved somehow? Or better still, is he our killer?"

"My gut instinct still tells me he's innocent of the actual murders."

"I think so as well. But could anyone be that naive?"

"You probably could be if you had a brother like Barry. From everything we've heard, he has to be the most devious person I've ever come across."

"No wonder he's dead, then."

The desk sergeant opened the incident room door. "The locksmith's here."

"Show him in," said Gardener, moving his food and drink to one side.

The man was dressed in stained grey overalls. He introduced himself as Patrick Lewis, and Gardener estimated his age to be late forties. What was left of his hair was ginger. He wore glasses and was pretty stocky, with a potbelly.

"What do you have for us?"

He extracted a copy of the key from his toolbag, along with notes he'd made.

"A tough one, this. I'd have been here earlier, but I had an emergency."

Gardener wondered if he was going to launch into what had kept him. "I don't mean to be rude, but I've been here since around six this morning. All I need to know now is where I have to go to get the answer to my questions."

"Sorry," said Lewis. "There's a little town over near Harrogate called Bursley Bridge."

Gardener knew it well.

"Place reeks of money," said Lewis. "There's a private bank in the market square called Roland's, next to one of the up-market hotels. Only very wealthy people go to Roland's bank. They like to attract a particular kind of clientele."

"All well and good if you can pick and choose these days," said Reilly.

"That's banks for you," said Gardener.

"Believe me," said Lewis, "the taxpayer does not own this bank. There was never a need to bail these people out."

"So this key fits one of the safe deposit boxes inside that bank, does it?"

"Yes."

"Do you know the manager's name?"

"Giles Middleton."

"Contact number?" said Reilly.

"They won't be open now."

"He means a mobile," said Gardener.

Lewis was reluctant, but Gardener knew he would certainly have the number. The man was obviously a reliable locksmith and had probably dealt with the bank on a regular basis – almost certainly out of hours.

Gardener passed the number to the desk sergeant. "Tell Giles Middleton to meet us there in half an hour. If he doesn't, I will issue a warrant for his arrest, and he won't see daylight for the next ten years."

Gardener thanked the locksmith for his time, and he and Reilly left the building.

True to their word, they were outside the bank thirty minutes later. Middleton wasn't.

Gardener called the station on his mobile. The desk sergeant said that Middleton was on holiday, but his deputy, David Challenger, should be with them by now because he lived in Bursley Bridge.

As Gardener disconnected, a man around thirty years of age came into view. He was dressed in a tee shirt and jeans. The night was warm enough not to wear a jacket. One of the pubs advertised a live band; a number of couples outside were drinking and smoking, listening to the band and singing along; a number of others milled around the square.

As Challenger approached, Gardener and Reilly showed their warrant cards.

"How can I help you?" he asked.

Gardener briefly explained. The doors were unlocked, and they all went inside. The assistant disabled the alarm and walked them through to the vault. Gardener felt that the bank was probably no quieter at night than it was during the day, the only difference being that no phones were ringing. The hum of electrical apparatus was more prominent.

The vault was clinically clean, and Gardener could see a steel door in front of him like he'd never seen before. It if it wasn't bomb proof, he'd be surprised. On a shelf built into a recess was a computer monitor and keyboard with a CCTV camera above it. The monitor screen flickered into life when Challenger moved the mouse.

"Don't think I've ever been in a bank this late," said Reilly.

"You wouldn't be now if Mr Middleton was here."

"Trust me," replied Gardener, "we would."

"Have you any idea what you're looking for?" asked Challenger.

"Other than a safe deposit box, no."

"Do you know whose?"

"I think you need to start with the name Barry Morrison."

Challenger nodded. "Can I have the key?"

Gardener passed it over, and Challenger consulted the computer files.

"Doesn't make sense, does it?" Reilly asked. "Morrison didn't like banks, so why this one?"

"I don't think this is anything to do with Morrison," said Gardener. "Whoever did this to him knew we'd eventually come here. He's made it easier for us. He wants us to find out what's inside the box because it's bound to be something we don't know."

"And he's obviously not bothered if we do."

"In the typical arrangement," said Challenger, "a renter will pay the bank a fee for the use of the box. It can only be opened with *that* key, the bank's own guard key, and the proper signature. Sometimes also a code. Some banks additionally use biometric dual-control security to complement the conventional security procedures. We don't, but I think we can dispense with all the familiarity here, Inspector."

Gardener nodded.

"Here we are," he said. "Barry Morrison. He only opened the account two weeks ago. He's never been in or used it since. We do have some CCTV footage, would you like to see it?"

"Please."

It only took moments to find. The picture was grainy, but not so bad that they couldn't see clearly enough.

The figure that came into view kept his head down all the time, from the opening of the steel door, to the placing of what appeared to Gardener to be a document inside the safe deposit box.

"That's not Barry Morrison," said Reilly.

"No surprise there," said Gardener.

Challenger was shocked. "Well, who is it? There are strict procedures with this sort of thing. Documents and proof of who you are and where you live are needed."

"They can all be forged, son."

Challenger was about to speak again.

"Can you please just open the door for us?" Gardener asked.

The assistant did as he was asked, and then took them through another two doors and into a room with hundreds of boxes. He found the box they needed, unlocked the outer lock and slid it out of the rack, placing it on the table and stepping back as if Gardener was the customer and was due his privacy.

Gardener opened the box, which contained one piece of paper, folded into quarters.

He pulled it out, unfolded it, and read it.

He passed it to his partner to read.

"How interesting," said Reilly.

Chapter Fifty-one

Tuesday 23rd August

"Come in, sit down. Pull up a chair."

"Pardon?" said Gardener.

"Come in, sit down, pull up a chair. Speak the truth when you tell me you care," replied Sally Summerby, rather sullenly. "It was my mother's favourite song in the seventies. *Sister Jane* by New World."

Gardener said nothing. She wasn't here to talk about pop music, and neither were they. Nor would he let her control the conversation, unlike the last time they met. Reilly took a seat.

"Anyway, why the hell am I here? You still don't seem to have found my daughter, but I notice you're moving heaven and earth to find everyone else around here."

She's started, thought Gardener. It *was* only eight o'clock in the morning.

Gardener and his partner had started earlier than that, arriving in Esholt at six-thirty. Gareth Summerby had been picked up shortly after setting off for work. He'd been brought to the station and put in another interview room. Gardener and Reilly then went back and picked up Sally Summerby, so that neither of them knew the other one was here.

"It's my job."

"So whose job is it to return my daughter safely to me?"

"DI Goodman's. But we're not here to talk about that. As you said, we're trying to find killers."

"Which has nothing to do with me."

"Nicola Stapleton," said Gardener, glancing at the file in front of him.

"What about her?"

"You said you'd never heard of her."

"I hadn't," said Sally Summerby with a sigh.

Gardener could tell she was gearing up to have a go, so he let her.

"Let me tell you what I now know. She was killed in Batley on Friday night. You found a picture of a blonde-haired girl who looked like my daughter underneath her. Oh, yes, she was a prostitute. Of course, that's something you forgot to tell me."

"You're on dodgy ground there, young lady," said Reilly.

"Meaning what, exactly?"

"So, you do not know Nicola Stapleton," persisted Gardener. "You've never met her in the course of your life."

She leaned forward. "I've told you enough times. Don't you people ever listen? I am not in the habit of mixing with loose women. I do not know Nicola Stapleton, but I seem to remember asking you lot a question about her and my daughter. Like, did she have her?"

Gardener removed a clean sheet of paper from the file and made a note.

"Does the name Frank Fisher mean anything?"

"What is this? Have you seriously dragged me all the way over here – which, by the way, I think is a breach of my human rights, seeing as I've done nothing wrong – just to ask me about people I've never even heard of?"

"Answer the questions," said Reilly. "Otherwise we'll be here all day. I'm sure you'd rather be somewhere else."

"You lot should be. There's a missing five-year-old girl out there, which you seem to be doing nothing about–"

Gardener cut her off. "Frank Fisher? Do you know a man called Frank Fisher?"

Sally Summerby shook her head and ran her fingers through her hair. "No, I do not know anyone called Frank Fisher."

Gardener made another note.

"Alan Sargent?" said Reilly.

"Who?"

"Alan Sargent. Do you know a man called Alan Sargent?"

Sally Summerby clammed up, crossed her hands, and rested them on the table.

"We can do this another time, if you'd prefer."

"There isn't a time that would suit me," she replied. "But if you're offering, yes, I would prefer to do it another time."

"Why?" Reilly asked. "Do you have somewhere else to go?"

"Anywhere but here would be better. At least I wouldn't be wasting my time."

"Or ours." The two detectives rose from their seats.

"Am I free to go?"

"No," said Gardener. "We're just going to leave you here until you're ready to answer our questions. Like you, we have better things to do."

Sally Summerby stood up as well. "You can't keep me here for no reason."

"We're not. You're here for questioning, and for that we can hold you for a certain amount of time. If you choose not to answer the questions, then you can sit here in silence until such time is up." Gardener and Reilly made for the door.

"Okay, okay, if it gets me out of here quicker, I'll play your stupid games. I've done nothing wrong."

Gardener sat back in his chair. "It's funny how many people have said that recently. But somebody has, and it's our job to find out who. And what you should bear in mind is that the quicker we do, there's every chance we can resolve your daughter's abduction at the same time."

"Are you saying whoever killed these people has my daughter?"

"Okay, let's run through it again. You don't know Nicola Stapleton, or Frank Fisher, or Alan Sargent. Where were you on Sunday night and Monday morning?"

"I was at home."

"And your husband can verify this, can he?"

"Of course, depending on the times. Like I said, they're harvesting, so it's his busiest time of the year. He left for work on Sunday morning about eight, but he was back home at two. We spent the rest of the day together. He left for work on Monday morning at seven."

"You didn't go out on Sunday night?"

"No. I cooked a meal and we stayed in and watched some TV."

"Do you use the pub in the village?"

"Sometimes. We might have a Sunday lunch with his workmates, but we haven't this weekend. Why are you asking me about my movements?"

"We're eliminating you."

"From what?"

"What do you think?" Reilly asked.

Gardener could almost hear the cogs in Sally Summerby's head turning. "Have those two people you've just mentioned been killed?"

"That's what we do," said Reilly. "We investigate people who have been killed and try and find out why, and who did it."

"But I haven't killed anybody. For God's sake, my daughter is missing, and we're beside ourselves most of the time working out where she could be. We spend most of our time at home thinking about her and the hole in our life she's made, and pray for her safe return."

Sally Summerby was close to tears. She removed a tissue from her sleeve, wiping her eyes and nose. "I have not killed any of those people, and I don't know any of them."

"You also claimed you didn't know Barry Morrison," said Reilly.

"Who?"

"Come off it. We only spoke to you on Sunday about him, and you told us you didn't know him."

"Oh, him, that taxi driver."

"We never said he was a taxi driver."

"I'm sure you did."

"I'm sure we didn't," said Gardener. "We simply asked if you knew him, and you said you didn't. Now you claim he's a taxi driver."

"Well, I must have read it in the paper."

"So you're still claiming you didn't know Barry Morrison?" asked Gardener.

"We're just going round in circles here. You two are desperate. Four people have been killed, you have no idea who's done it, and you're clutching at straws trying to pin the blame on anyone. Is this what we pay our taxes for?"

"No," said Gardener. "You pay them so that we can look after you. We can investigate and lock up murderers and keep the streets safe from the likes of you."

"The likes of me? What the hell is that supposed to mean?"

"People who waste our time and don't tell us the truth. People who hinder the investigation, which then takes longer, and possibly gets more people killed."

Sally Summerby leaned forward again, obviously offended by Gardener's tone. "I don't like your attitude. And if you continue to try and bully me, I'll have a solicitor down here so fast you won't know what's hit you."

"I'll give you one more chance to come clean."

Sally Summerby sat back and folded her arms in defence. "Come clean? I think you've lost the plot. You are in so much trouble, Detective Inspector."

"One of us is," said Gardener, removing the square of folded paper he'd taken from the safe deposit box the previous evening. He unfolded it and slid it toward Sally Summerby. She read the page. Her face drained of colour.

"Where did you get this?"

"You recognize it, then?"

"I asked you where you got it?"

"Barry Morrison was killed in Batley on Saturday morning. We found a safe deposit key inside his stomach. Last night we found the bank that held the key, and we had the assistant manager out after ten o'clock, because you pay your taxes, you see, which pays our wages. Anyway, you know the rest. We found that birth certificate in the box, which states that Barry Morrison is the father of your daughter. Would you care to expand on the theory, or are you still claiming you don't know him?"

Sally Summerby broke down, and Gardener figured she would need more than one tissue. He left the room and returned a few minutes later with a box of tissues and three teas.

"Thank you," she said, as he passed them over.

"Are you ready to tell us now?"

"Oh Christ, this is such a mess." She took a sip of tea. "Gareth knows nothing about this. You have to promise me he never will."

"I can't promise any such thing, Mrs Summerby. I'm investigating a murder here, and to be able to do my job, I need the truth." He allowed her a minute to calm down and take more sips of tea.

"Chloe is the result of a taxi fare I couldn't pay."

"Excuse me?" asked Reilly.

"I was out in Leeds one night. It was a hen party for a friend of mine. There were ten of us altogether. We were all over Leeds like a rash. Got completely plastered, like you do. We all decided to go home about three o'clock in the morning. Three of us took a taxi – Barry Morrison's. He dropped my friends off first. They got out without paying. I was so drunk I hadn't realized. When he dropped me in Esholt, the bill was over eighty pounds. I didn't have the money in my purse. Do I need to spell the rest out for you?"

"You didn't have the money on you. Did you not have any money in the house?"

"No. It was nearly Christmas. Gareth only *works* on the farm, he doesn't own it. Money wasn't brilliant. We'd spent most of it on presents for relatives, and food for ourselves."

"Could you not have come to another agreement?" Gardener asked. "He knew where you lived. He could have come back the next day, or you could have gone to the office and paid with a credit card."

"He didn't look the type to give credit. He was undressing all of us with his eyes the minute we got in. For Christ sake, we all had micro skirts on. He probably used his mirror to see as far up the skirts as he could. In fact, he probably didn't need to, we were all as pissed as farts, so we probably had our skirts round out chest anyway."

"Are you saying he raped you?" Reilly asked.

"No."

"You did it willingly?" Gardener asked. "You didn't put up a fight?"

She didn't answer straight away. "Look, I'm not proud of myself."

Gardener remained silent.

"I suggested it," said Sally Summerby.

"It was your idea?"

"I thought it was a one-time fix. I could get him off my back. It was only sex, for God's sake!"

"Only sex?"

"Yes. Only sex. A lot of women use their bodies to get what they want. It's no big deal."

"And you called Nicola Stapleton a loose woman," said Reilly.

She turned on him. "I'm not a prostitute."

"What would you call it, then?"

"I'd never done it before, and I've never done it since."

"So how did you feel when you found out you were pregnant?"

"A bit shocked."

"A bit?"

"Like I said, I'm not proud of myself. I was shocked at first. When I'd calmed down and I thought about it, I realized I could probably turn it to my advantage."

"I think I'm losing the will to live here," said Reilly. "Advantage, how?"

"Me and Gareth had been trying for a baby. Nothing was happening, so we went to the doctors. Took all the tests. There was nothing wrong with either of us, but Gareth had it in his head that it was probably him. He reckoned he hadn't always been a good person, a good Christian, and maybe the Lord was punishing him."

Gardener quickly made a note.

Sally Summerby continued. "The doctor said it was probably stress, and that all he had to do was stop trying so hard and calm down. It would all happen naturally – eventually."

Gardener couldn't believe what he was hearing. "Is that why you lied at Barry Morrison's trial?"

"Pardon?" Sally Summerby paled even further. "How do you know about that?"

"Barry Morrison was involved in a collision with a motorcyclist called Chris Rydell, December two years ago," continued Gardener. "It happened near the station in Horsforth. You and your daughter were his passengers. You lied when it went to court. Would you like to tell us why?"

"Oh my God. You two are a pair of bloodhounds. Do you like ruining people's lives?"

"Most people don't need us. You were in the taxi at Horsforth, but you denied it to the police, and in court. Why? You said that you *were* in a taxi that night, but you were miles away in Shipley."

She finished her tea and used another two tissues. "You don't know what Barry Morrison was like."

"We're finding out," said Reilly.

"He threatened to blackmail me if I didn't lie in court. I was in the taxi because he wanted to see Chloe. I have no idea how he managed to find out about her, but he did. He came to the house once when Gareth was out, and he said he wanted to see her. He'd bought a present for her. If I didn't agree to what he wanted, he said he would tell Gareth.

"We had a massive argument. I'm surprised the whole village didn't hear. Anyway, he said he would come back for us a couple of days later, and he would take us out for a couple of hours. We could have something to eat, he would give her a present, and then he would bring us back home. He said he didn't want any more than that. He simply wanted to see her, see what she was like. He promised he wouldn't bother us again after that."

"And you believed him?"

"What choice did I have? Anyway, he took us for a drive. Chloe loved it. At that time we didn't have a car. We ended up in Horsforth at a small café. He did what he said he would. Treated us to a meal. Gave her a present. It was when he was about to take us home that it had come in a bit foggy. He pulled out of the road, and this bike came from nowhere. We didn't actually hit him, just forced him into another direction."

"Did you stop?"

"No."

"Why not?"

"I wasn't driving, was I?"

"Did your daughter witness anything?"

"No, she was almost asleep. I wanted to get home as quickly as possible. I didn't want Gareth asking too many questions. If we could get back before he came home from work, I could probably smooth it all over. Though God knows why, he doesn't deserve all this, does he?"

"He doesn't deserve a wife like you, you mean?"

Sally Summerby scowled at the comment, but made no reply.

"Talking of your husband," said Reilly. "How is he?"

"He's fine. Why do you ask?"

"How would you say your marriage was?"

"My marriage? It's fine."

"No problems?"

"Every marriage goes through problems."

"You said earlier that money wasn't good where he works. Do you have financial problems?"

"We manage."

"And what does Gareth do... on the farm?"

"He looks after the animals, mainly. The farm has its own slaughterhouse. Gareth is a big believer in doing things humanely, otherwise he wouldn't work there. The animals are bred and slaughtered properly. He even walks them to the place of slaughter, about a mile away from the farm. The meat is better because of how well they're looked after."

"Does *he* slaughter them?"

"Sometimes."

"Don't think I could do that," said Reilly. "Surely it takes a certain kind of person."

"What's his temperament like?" Gardener asked. "It's my guess you'd have to be a bit emotionless to do something like that."

"On the contrary. You have to be someone who loves animals and cares about their welfare to be able to do it properly, without suffering. So, yes, it does take a certain kind of person."

"It's just that we keep coming back to the comment he made to Goodman on the night Chloe went missing: 'God works in mysterious ways'."

"I've already told you about that."

"He seemed very calm about it all."

"He's always been very level-headed."

"Sounds like he was too calm to me," said Reilly. "To be sure, if my daughter had gone missing, I'd have turned Leeds upside down to find her."

"Your husband seemed to take everything in his stride. Maybe he knew."

"Knew what?"

"That he wasn't Chloe's father."

Sally Summerby's eyes grew very wide. "Gareth does not know. He's not the sort of man who could live a lie. He's a Christian, for God's sake. If he found out, I think it would kill him."

"Not necessarily. I thought Christians were supposed to forgive."

"Then again," said Reilly, "maybe he really does live his life by the Good Book, and he's decided it's an eye for an eye."

"What do you mean?" asked Sally Summerby.

"Come on, young lady. You're not that stupid, and neither are we. Maybe your husband found out about your infidelity and decided to take the law into his own hands."

"Even the score with Barry Morrison," added Gardener.

"Are you saying my husband killed the taxi driver?"

"We're looking for motives here," said Gardener, "and he certainly has one."

"So, what motive would he have for killing the other three?"

"We don't know... yet. We haven't got to the bottom of the investigation."

"I can tell you now, Gareth is not your killer."

"How do you know?" Gardener asked. "The man is a *born-again* Christian, which tells me that he is hiding something from his past. Most of them are. How do you know your husband is not the killer?"

She stood up again and slammed her hands on the table. "I just do."

"And you don't think he's capable of abduction either?"

"Abduction? What, you think he's taken my daughter somewhere, held her hostage?"

"Funny you should use the term 'my daughter', and not 'our daughter'."

"You know what I mean."

"No, I don't," replied Gardener. "Do you use the term regularly at home?"

"No." Her reply was defensive and quick. "Oh, I see what you're getting at. You think I keep saying 'my daughter', and he's read something into it. Yes, I may have said 'my daughter', but it's just a figure of speech."

"He may not see it like that. As you said, he may have read something into it. Have you ever noticed a time when he's been different with Chloe? Lost his temper over something puerile? Is he the kind of father that regularly treats his daughter and then stopped, suddenly acted different toward her?"

"Look, I'm telling you, he believes he is Chloe's father because I've given him no reason to think otherwise. He has not abducted our daughter, and he is not your killer."

"Okay," replied Gardener. "Let's assume he isn't. We still need to find someone with a motive, and the only other person in the frame is you."

"Me?"

"Yes, you. You've admitted you couldn't pay your taxi fare, so you let him have sex with you. You then found out you were pregnant. You admitted he wanted to see her once. That ended badly, and you lied in court for him. How do we know that he hasn't been blackmailing you ever since, and you were at the end of your tether and decided to finally put an end to the matter?"

"I didn't kill him."

"How did you manage to keep it all from Gareth?" Gardener asked. "Are you telling me he's never seen the birth certificate?"

Sally Summerby said nothing.

Reilly leaned forward. "What are you hiding now?"

"How could I let him see the certificate? I had to have a false one made."

Reilly sat back and threw his hands in the air.

Gardener realized how deep and devious Sally Summerby was. He could quite well believe she would use her body for what she wanted. He was beginning to question every answer she gave, but still, he had no proof that she had done anything. And he knew very well from the CCTV footage of Morrison's body being dumped that the offender was male. The time was fast approaching when he would have to let her go, pending further inquiries.

"Where did you get that made?" Reilly asked.

"The Internet."

"What did you do with the original?"

"I gave it to Barry Morrison. He asked for proof, so I gave it to him. I told him he could keep it, and I didn't want him bothering us again. I wanted him to leave us alone, to get on with our lives."

Gardener wondered how she slept at night. "Okay, Mrs Summerby, that's all for now."

"Pardon?"

"I said, that's all for now."

"You mean I can go?"

"Don't look so surprised. Someone has killed four people. You certainly had a motive for one of them. So did your husband. If you say that neither of you have done it, then I have to believe you for now and continue with my investigation. But when you're back home this afternoon sitting with a coffee and your feet up, think about this: your daughter is still missing. Somewhere at the bottom of all this, apart from murdering people, someone has your daughter. Now it may be someone who has a grudge against all the people he's killed, or it might be another reason altogether."

Gardener stood up.

Chapter Fifty-two

Gardener was still sitting at the table in the interview room when Reilly returned from seeing Sally Summerby out. He sat down opposite and finished his tea.

"Christ! What a piece of work she is."

"She has to be the most cold-hearted, calculating person I have ever met."

"Do *you* think he knows about the daughter?" Reilly asked.

Gardener shook his head. "I really have no idea, Sean."

"Can you imagine how you'd feel? You bring the child into the world, and for five years you love and care for it, and then you find out it's not yours. Born-again Christian or not, it's bound to tug at your heart strings."

"You really don't like them, do you?"

"No I do not. They're full of shit. They're the ones who have caused the most trouble in their lives, and then they expect God to forgive them and think everything will be fine when they go upstairs. Do they really think that St Peter is just going to open the gate and welcome them in? Even the ones who have committed murder and then claimed they found the good Lord in prison. I don't think so, somehow."

Gardener thought about that. "So, we have one of three options. Either he genuinely doesn't know. Or he's found out and turned the other cheek."

"Or he's found out and flipped. The girl hasn't been kidnapped, but holed up somewhere. Only he knows where. Then he's gone out and disposed of Morrison."

"It's one thing to slaughter animals, but quite another to dispose of a human being. What does he intend to do with Chloe? And where is she?"

"Maybe we need to pay a visit to the farm. Search the place. Talk to the farmer. Find out how the animals are slaughtered."

"What difference does it make how the animals are slaughtered?"

"Well, is it the normal way with the bolt gun, or is it some new humane way that involves chemicals and syringes?"

"I see where you're coming from. But the problem with our theory is that he only has a motive for Morrison, not the other three."

"Not unless there's something in his dark and devious past. Like I said, I've come across these guys before. They've set fire to things: buildings, cars. They terrorize people, give them grief, and then one day it's as if a light has been switched on and they totally change. They can't do enough for you, and they're constantly spouting quotes from the Bible. Maybe he's been really bad, done something he can't forgive himself for and before it went too far, sought out God and tried to convince the Big Man up there that he'll stop all this shit and live a life of respect."

Gardener rose from his seat and picked up his file. "Maybe it's time we went and found out."

The pair of them left the interview room. Before taking the corridor to where they had Gareth Summerby, Gardener said he wanted to check if any news had come in.

Passing the office with the HOLMES people inside, was like walking into The Stock Exchange. Ninety percent of them were on phones, and the rest were logging information into computers, hoping to hit on a cross-match.

Gardener passed by and glanced through the open door to the incident room. Patrick Edwards was standing in front of the ANACAPA chart with a puzzled expression, trying to follow a series of lines that would put the National Grid to shame.

"Everything okay, Patrick?" Gardener asked. The young man was showing a lot of promise, and Gardener liked him. He wasn't frightened of hard work, and if you gave him a task, he stuck to it. Edwards was a young Colin Sharp in the making.

"Depends how you look at it, sir."

"What's wrong?" Reilly asked.

"I've comes across a name in one of Nicola Stapleton's diaries that we've heard before." He turned to face his superior officer. "The one involved in the collision with Barry Morrison."

"Chris Rydell?"

"Yes."

"What's it say?"

"It was a couple of years back now. It was his birthday. His friends had managed to get him out for a drink. They all clubbed together and paid her a fortune – more than she would normally earn – to take him back home and show him a good time."

Gardener and Reilly glanced at each other, before the SIO asked Patrick his next question. "Is that all? Does it say any more?"

"Not that I've come across."

"Patrick, I'd like you to do me a favour." Gardener dug out a card from the clinic and passed it to the young PC.

"That's a private clinic on Bond Street. I'd like you to call the number and speak to Margaret Pendlebury. Ask her if Chris Rydell was ever a patient at the clinic. If he was, check to see if we have his files. Sean and I are going to interview Gareth Summerby. I'd like an answer for when we come out of the interview room."

Chapter Fifty-three

Gareth Summerby was sitting with his arms folded, staring at the wall. He was dressed in a Rudstons green boiler suit and a flat cap. To Gardener's way of thinking, he was the complete opposite of his wife. But they do say opposites attract. An empty coffee cup sat on the table in front of Summerby.

Both officers sat. Gardener placed his file on the table in front of him. "Sorry to keep you, Mr Summerby."

"That's okay. You have a job to do. Have you informed my boss?"

"Yes, we have spoken to him. As far as he's concerned, you're helping us with our inquiries with regards to your missing daughter."

"Which I believe I am."

Gardener said nothing, but decided he may as well start with that. "How is life at home at the moment? It must be tough."

"There's definitely a hole that needs filling."

"I understand what you're going through," said Gardener. "My son was kidnapped about nine months back. Held hostage by some lunatic hell-bent on getting me back for simply doing my job."

"*Do not judge, or you too will be judged,*" replied Summerby. "*For in the same way you judge others, you will be judged, and with the measure you use, it will be measured to you.* Matthew 7:1-3. So, were you doing your job, Mr Gardener, or were you judging unfairly?"

Gardener had absolutely no intention of going down the religious road, but wondered how he would be able to stop Summerby spouting quotes. He would find one for everything. Reilly simply shook his head and smirked.

Summerby noticed it. "Another non-believer. Come Judgement Day you will have to answer for your sins."

"I take comfort in knowing I won't be by myself, sunshine."

"Can we get back to the question?" Gardener asked. "How are you finding life at home at the moment?"

"Our daughter is missing, and we have to carry on as if nothing has happened. So yes, as you pointed out it's hard. It's tough, but I have to go to work every day to continue providing for my family because I know things will return to normal. We will see her again, she will come back, and when she does I want her to know that everything can go back to normal in her world."

"And you and Sally are getting on okay? It must be a strain."

"It is. But I understand her loss, what she's going through. I respect her privacy, and I'm there for her when she wants me. And every evening we sit and pray for the return of our daughter. And God will answer those prayers, because we believe in him."

Gardener was keen to try and steer the man away from his favourite topic. Reilly had been right. They love nothing better than to ram it down your throat.

"And how is work? That must be helping to take your mind off things."

Gareth Summerby smiled, one of those irritating lop-sided grins that Gardener disliked and distrusted.

"I enjoy my work. We're always busy, especially at this time of the year. We harvest; we have to continually mend fences and walls and repair equipment. The animals always need looking after. We have our own slaughter yard. We slaughter our own animals, and we have contracts for other local farmers."

"How are the animals slaughtered?"

"Pigs and sheep and chickens are stunned so they know nothing of what's happening. I'm afraid cattle have to go through the usual – the bolt gun. But at least it's quick."

"Are you responsible for that?"

"Sometimes. We breed them properly, outdoors. They're given the best of everything, and then when it's time, we go for a nice stroll down the lane."

Summerby made it sound wonderful. Perhaps how Gardener would like to go.

"You've mentioned the repair work. Is there a lot?" Reilly asked.

"Yes, there's always something to do."

"You ever use sealing wax?"

"Sealing wax? Don't think so. I've never used it, don't know about the others, but I've never seen any on the farm."

Gardener changed tactics. "You obviously work long hours, do you have much of a social life?"

"We sometimes use the pub in the village."

"What about further afield?"

"We haven't always had a car, but now that we have, if we get the chance, we'll take Chloe to the seaside sometimes."

"Do you and Sally ever have nights out that don't involve the car?"

"Sometimes, but not often."

"Would you use taxis?"

"Yes."

"Any particular company?"

"No idea. Sally always takes care of that. Probably because I work so hard, she's always there looking after our daughter, the home. If we do have holidays and the like, she usually organizes it for us. She's a good wife, asks little. I did okay when I found her."

Gardener knew otherwise. Before long it would have to come out. He needed to know whether or not Summerby had any motive – or if he could break his cool reserve and see a more honest reaction.

"Do you know anyone called Barry Morrison?"

"Only what I read in the papers. I know his name's come up at work recently."

"Why?"

"Because of the way he was found, in a shop doorway early one morning. Sounded pretty gruesome to me. Matthew 7:19; *every tree that does not bear good fruit is cut down and thrown into the fire.*"

"It's funny how you lot judge people and apply the rules to them, but not to yourselves," said Reilly.

"You lot?" questioned Summerby.

"You born-again Christians. Seems to me that what you just said about bad fruit should apply to you, but it never does."

"The apostle Paul in Ephesians 2:1 says, '*and you He made alive, who were dead in trespasses and sins*'. To the Romans he wrote, '*for all have sinned and fall short of the glory of God*'. Romans 3:23. Sinners are spiritually 'dead'; when they receive spiritual life through faith in Christ, the Bible likens it to a rebirth. Only those who are born again have their sins forgiven and have a relationship with God."

"So, what have you done that's so bad?"

"I've done nothing wrong. You'll find nothing on me."

"I imagine you're the first, then," said Reilly. "Can't see why you'd call yourself born again if you haven't done something wrong and gone through the re-birth process after cleansing yourself."

"Like I said, I have done nothing that you two should worry about."

Interesting choice of words, thought Gardener.

"We haven't," he replied, "I'll give you that. You have no criminal record. That doesn't mean you've done nothing wrong. You just haven't been caught yet."

"As I've already said."

"What about sin? Are they all equal?" Reilly asked. "How do you lot judge sin? For example, is adultery a sin?"

"In Matthew 5:21-28, Jesus talks about committing adultery with lust in your heart and committing murder with hatred in your heart. What he was trying to say is that sin is still sin, even if you only want to do the act, without actually committing it. Jesus wants them to realize that God judges a person's thoughts as well as his actions: that our actions are the result of what is in our hearts. Matthew 12:34.

"Some sins are worse than others. In regard to both eternal consequences and salvation, all sins are the same. Every sin will lead to eternal condemnation. There is no sin too big that God cannot forgive it. Jesus died to pay the penalty for our sin: are all sins equal to God? Yes and no. Are all sins equal in severity? No. Are all sins equal in penalty? Yes. Will they all be forgiven? Yes."

Gardener found his comparisons of adultery and murder very interesting. "What about you? Can you forgive a sin?"

"If the need arises. But it isn't me that matters, is it? I've just said, if you commit the sin, you will have God to answer to."

"But surely if a sin is committed against *you*, it's *you* that will initially have to pass judgment."

"And which direction would you choose?" asked Reilly. "Do you become the good Christian and turn a blind eye and let your Lord deal with it? Or do you take the Bible literally, and take an eye for an eye?"

For the first time since they had been speaking to Gareth Summerby, Gardener felt that his attitude was beginning to change. His eyes had narrowed, and his expression had darkened.

"Whatever the sin was, it would not be up to me to judge. The Lord would do my bidding. I would simply pray to him for guidance."

Gardener needed results, and he really could not make up his mind whether or not Gareth Summerby was guilty of anything. He felt the time had come to light the blue touch paper, and sit back and watch what happened. If the man was guilty of abducting Chloe and murdering Barry

Morrison, he needed to know now. He opened his file and passed over the birth certificate.

Gareth Summerby read through the contents, and then glanced at Gardener and smiled. The same sickly smile he had used throughout the interview; the one that said 'whatever you throw at me, I have the Lord on my side, and you cannot touch me'.

"You're barking up the wrong tree, officer. I have not killed Barry Morrison. I have not abducted my daughter. I do not know where she is. I want her home safely, like my wife. And I already know about this."

Chapter Fifty-four

It was approaching mid-day when Gardener and Reilly stepped back into the incident room, shocked by Summerby's revelation.

"What's up with you two?" Briggs asked Gardener.

"We've just been wrong-footed," replied Gardener, placing his file on the table, glancing around the room to take note of who was in. Most of the team was present, judging from what he could see.

"Why?"

"We've interviewed Sally Summerby. Turns out Barry Morrison is Chloe's father."

"Morrison?" shouted Briggs. "How the hell did that happen?"

Gardener briefly took him through the details.

"Which gives her a prime motive, especially if Morrison has been blackmailing her."

"Except for the fact that she has an alibi, and we could quite clearly see that it was a man who dumped him on the butcher's doorstep."

"She could have arranged it. What if they're in it together?"

"Husband and wife, you mean?" Reilly asked.

"Why not?"

"Well, that's the other fly in the ointment," said Gardener. "We've interviewed him, and he claims to know about the birth certificate."

"Do you believe him?"

"I'm not sure what to believe anymore."

"So, if he knows about the certificate, then there's even more reason to suspect that the pair of them have cooked something up."

"But where's the girl?" asked Gardener.

"And what's their motive for killing the other three?"

Gardener could tell Briggs wasn't happy by his expression. What he'd suggested didn't really add up; but then again, neither did anything else.

"Keep digging," said Briggs. "The pressure's on. We have to find an answer soon, before there's two more."

Briggs wasn't telling Gardener anything he didn't know. The DCI left the room, leaving Gardener and Reilly to come up with other ideas.

"The problem we have is the amount of people in the frame. Billy Morrison knows three of them, but he's maintained all along that he doesn't know Nicola Stapleton."

"Sally Summerby knows one of them," said Reilly, "but not the others."

"No proof of that. We need something more on her."

"Gareth Summerby doesn't know any of them, but has the best reason."

"If he's telling us the truth," said Gardener.

"You think he was lying about the birth certificate?"

"It got him out of the room, didn't it?"

Reilly finished his coffee. "Maybe he didn't know anything about Barry Morrison fathering his child, but he's kept a lid on it to us."

"Until he gets home. No one knows how good a marriage is unless they're in it. Maybe he's going home now to deal with her."

"Leaving us to wonder which side of the fence his born-again Christian attitude falls down on."

"Meanwhile, Chloe is still missing." No matter how the case proceeded, there was still the problem of the girl hanging over his head. He might have been searching for a killer, but she was still playing a central part. Her abductor must have something on her parents. But where did the other girl fit in?

Benson came through the door and approached Gardener.

"Got something for you, sir."

Gardener took a seat while Benson had his say.

"Frank Fisher sued the builder, Sean Rydell. Cleaned him out completely. Compensation was about thirty thousand in cash. The business went belly up, and Sean Rydell committed suicide. But here's the big one: Alan Sargent testified in court that it was all Rydell's fault. He claimed that the yard had never been maintained, and was a health and safety nightmare."

"Is that so?" Reilly asked. "How did he know?"

"I went round to see Sargent's widow, Vanessa. Apparently he'd done some odd jobs for the company. They were thinking of expanding, he was about to be offered a full-time position. Obviously, that all went tits up when the business folded. Sargent was given a lifeline by Barry Morrison, which helped with their financial problems."

"Why did Sargent speak up for Fisher in court?"

"She doesn't know. There's only one reason I can think of: Frank Fisher must have been blackmailing Alan Sargent."

"Or convincing him," replied Gardener.

"What do you mean?" asked Benson.

"That Sargent was being offered a payout of the compo," replied Reilly.

"Something doesn't add up," said Gardener. "Maybe Fisher didn't pay up. That court case was over two years ago. The money would have been through well before now, easing their financial situation. According to Billy Morrison, the taxi job was a lifeline for the Sargents."

"So, if anything, Sargent had a reason to kill Fisher."

"But not Morrison or Stapleton."

"And very likely not himself."

"So we're still no further on," said Gardener.

Patrick Edwards nearly pushed the door from its hinges.

"Sir, Chris Rydell is a patient of the clinic. The Pendlebury woman has a copy of his files at the clinic, if we want to send someone over. Seems he was there on Friday. His first visit was six months ago, when he was diagnosed with hepatitis B. On Friday he found out it's developed into full-blown cirrhosis."

"We'll go and see her, Patrick."

Before the young officer left, Gardener called out to him again. "Do we have any news on Raymond Allen, or from the Municipal Buildings in Leeds last night?"

"Nothing from the Municipal Buildings. All was quiet. Colin Sharp has been to see Raymond Allen's family. They haven't heard anything at all since his escape. He reckons they're living in fear that he does turn up. Before he got sent down, he nearly poisoned them all. Father said son was responsible for the death of his mother, and if he never saw him again, it would be too soon. Wasn't suspected at the time, and they couldn't exhume the body for tests because she was killed in a car crash which resulted in a fire. Anyway, Colin asked them about Allen having a driving licence. His father said that Allen had never even learned to drive."

"I'd still like to know where he fits in with everything. It's not impossible for him to have done everything even though he can't drive."

"Unlikely, though. I doubt anyone in Rampton would have taught him."

"Is he our killer, or is he simply using the situation to his advantage to frighten Vincent Baines to death?" Gardener asked.

"Wouldn't take a lot to frighten that idiot," said Reilly. "I'm more concerned with this Chris Rydell character. If his father committed suicide, is he using that as an excuse to gain revenge?"

"Possibly," said Gardener. "He has a means of getting around. He's a motorcycle courier."

"But can we connect him to all of the deceased?"

"Maybe. He's made an appearance in one of Nicola Stapleton's diaries. He was involved in a collision with Barry Morrison."

"Who uses Sally Summerby to lie for him in court," said Reilly.

"That's another connection. Maybe *he* has Chloe," said Benson. "Frank Fisher worked with his father, and sued him, and forced the closure of the business."

"And maybe his father's suicide was all down to the court case," said Gardener.

"And we now know that Sargent testified in court so that Frank Fisher won his case."

"Which leads us to suspect that Alan Sargent also lied in court," said Gardener.

"We need to get to that clinic," said Reilly. "What if Nicola Stapleton was responsible for his liver failure?"

"He could well have started his killing spree off with her and took the others out because of all the connections."

Gardener stood up when Patrick Edwards came running back in. "Sir, CCTV from Kirkstall Road shows a weird shaped trailer on two separate sightings relevant to the times of the murder."

"Weird shaped trailer?"

"Doesn't look like a standard trailer. It looks... well... I don't know. Homemade? It's being pulled along by a motorbike."

Gardener stood up. "I want the registration and the owner as quick as you can. We're going over to the clinic."

Chapter Fifty-five

Raymond Allen was standing at the back of the library in Otley. From his vantage point, he was in the perfect position to keep an eye on the rear entrance of the chemist. There was no access to the shop from Vincent's flat other than the fire escape, so Allen didn't have to worry about what was happening around the front. If Vincent made a move, he would know.

Having sent his final email to the self-proclaimed sleuth the previous night, Allen had then set about gathering his belongings together – which consisted of some stolen clothes and money. Both should last him for a week, at least. He could always steal more. Also in his suitcase were his true crime books, and a little something for Vincent.

Allen had left the hostel under the cover of darkness shortly after midnight. He'd spent two hours in an Internet cafe, because no one had bothered him. During that time, he'd studied and seethed at the blog that Vincent had posted. Not only had he told everyone about Allen's history, he had posted two photographs. He had made it very clear that he thought Allen was responsible for the recent double murders.

Having finally made his way to the library in Otley, behind the building Allen had found a disused garage with the front door missing. It had plenty of cardboard and had served as somewhere to rest until morning came around.

From the garage doorway he'd noticed John Oldham's car arrive at seven to open up for business. Another score needed to be settled with him.

Vincent had appeared on his fire escape in his dressing gown at around nine o'clock. He had a sandwich in one hand, a mug in the other, and a pair of binoculars hanging around his neck. What use he thought they would be, Allen had no idea.

At twelve o'clock he had reappeared, still in his dressing gown. The sandwich had been replaced with a scone, the warm drink by a glass of the hard stuff.

Allen figured that would be his downfall. Alcohol and secobarbital were definitely not a good mix.

Allen glanced at his watch: three o'clock. He was starving, could have done with a drink as well, but couldn't risk going for either. Being seen in public wasn't as important as keeping tabs on Vincent. Not that he thought Sherlock Holmes was going anywhere. He'd no doubt barricaded himself in, keeping a constant eye on the local news and the Internet for any sightings of The Man in Black.

Well, he need not worry on that score.

He would be seeing The Man in Black soon enough.

Chapter Fifty-six

Reilly was driving. Gardener reckoned they were two minutes from their destination.

The meeting at the clinic had been successful. Apparently, Rydell discovered he had contracted hepatitis B around six months ago. Sadly for him it had developed into full-blown cirrhosis, from which there was no cure.

A few days previously, Rydell had refused any treatment whatsoever. Knowing that Nicola Stapleton was a carrier of the virus, the fact that she had written notes about Rydell in her diary, particularly the night his friends had clubbed together and bought her services, was enough of a connection for Gardener to think the worst.

"We're here," said Reilly.

Rydell lived in the detached converted barn that Gardener took to be his father's old place, on the south side of Rodley, running along the canal: the nearest neighbour was across the stretch of water.

Gardener stepped out of the vehicle into the August afternoon heat. The pool car that Dave Rawson had taken for his tour of the builders' merchants stood in the drive.

"What's he doing here?" Reilly asked.

"No idea," said Gardener. "We'll take it as a positive step. If *his* investigation has brought him here, it can only be another nail in Rydell's coffin."

"Judging by what Pendlebury told us, he's going to be needing that soon enough."

Gardener thought about that. Rydell's fate hung in the balance now that he had refused all treatment. No one could say how long he had left to live, but from the way Pendlebury had talked, probably not long enough to serve his sentence should he be arrested, charged, and found guilty.

"Nice piece of property," said Reilly. "Wouldn't mind a place like this myself."

Gardener turned. "You say that everywhere we go."

"Yeah, and most of the houses have been in the hands of the people we've arrested for murder."

"Just shows, it really doesn't pay."

"Not in the long run."

The pair of them walked around the building to a view of long, stretching fields and an abundance of colours, not to mention Dave Rawson staring upwards at an open window.

"Hello, chief."

"Dave. What brings you here?"

"Same reason as you I suspect. Chris Rydell."

"What have you found out?"

Rawson took a long swig of Coke from a can.

"I chased up all the builders' merchants for those sealing wax kits. Why is it always the last place you look? Anyway, seems he got it from a place out Bradford way. He bought it about four weeks ago: booked it to his father's account."

"He still had one?" Reilly asked.

"Apparently. Anyway, the bloke who served him remembered it well, because he said the account had been inactive for ages. He hadn't really known what was going on, whether or not someone had taken over the business and shopped elsewhere, or what. Rydell signed for it, but said very little. I have a copy of the receipt here."

Rawson passed it over for Gardener to read.

"How long have you been here, Dave?"

"About half an hour. There's no one home, and no one's called since I've been here. Keep looking at that open window, though."

Gardener and Reilly glanced upwards.

"You've not tried to access it, then?"

"No. I was going to come back later. Thought if he'd left a window open, he was planning on coming back."

"You'd have thought so."

Reilly disappeared without a word. On his return he was holding an aluminium ladder tall enough to reach the window on the upper level. He placed it up against the wall and started to climb.

"Be careful, Sean. If you find anything up there, it's completely inadmissible. Briggs will have a field day."

"If I find anything, we can always go back to the station and obtain a warrant on the information Margaret Pendlebury gave us."

"I was just thinking the same."

"Thought I could smell burning."

Gardener laughed. "Best let me do it, Sean. I'm the senior officer. If anything goes wrong, I'll be taking the flack anyway."

"You sure?"

Gardener nodded. Reilly and Rawson held the ladder while Gardener climbed upwards.

As he reached the window, he had the good sense to delve into his jacket pocket and produce a pair of gloves. No point placing yourself in the middle of the scene if you were not supposed to be there. From his vantage point at the top of the ladder, he glanced around. The colours of the flowers were incredible.

A thought crossed his mind.

"Sean, what are those flowers over there?" Gardener pointed.

Reilly scurried across the yard and stepped into the field. After a minute, he shouted back to his SIO.

"Roses."

Gardener thought they might be, which reminded him of the song at the second crime scene: *Where The Wild Roses Grow.*

"Any blue ones?" he asked.

"Not that I can see."

Gardener turned back toward the window as his phone chimed. The timing was terrible, and he nearly fell off. He retrieved it and answered.

"Sir? Patrick Edwards."

"What have you got for me, Patrick?"

"Registration on the bike. Definitely belongs to Rydell. Got an address for you."

"Go on," said Gardener, despite already being there.

After Edwards had reeled it off, Gardener told him to put a marker on the PNC against the vehicle number. If an officer found and stopped him, he was to detain Rydell and call the station immediately. He also told Edwards to put the bike on the ANPR database. If Rydell drove through a camera and it pinged on the system, they would know about it.

He disconnected and decided to finish what he was doing as quickly as possible. He did not want Rydell arriving back in the middle of an illegal entry. After forcing the window open as wide as he could, he carefully climbed inside. Once in the room, Gardener placed a pair of paper booties over his shoes.

He was in a study. The room was crammed full of books on shelves. A computer desk stood near the window. Rydell had a desktop PC with two printers, a monitor, and a variety of other equipment, all switched off. The room was spotless and smelled fresh.

Gardener studied some of the books on the shelves. Most of them were about true crime.

"Well, well, well," he said, as he perused one of the shelves, sliding out a copy of *Foul Deeds And Suspicious Deaths In Leeds*. "It's not looking good for you, Mr Rydell. But then again, do you care?"

Aware of time becoming a problem, he inspected the rest of the upper level. It was divided into living quarters. Gardener noticed three bedrooms, a bathroom, a living area, and a kitchen, all of which were immaculately clean.

He delved deeper, wondering if there were any signs that someone else other than Rydell actually lived there: a five-year-old girl, for example.

He found no evidence to support it. Everywhere was far too clean and tidy. A five-year-old would run riot, and Rydell didn't seem the type to want to put up with that.

Which begged another question. If he actually had her, where was she? And if he didn't, where was she?

It was when Gardener entered the third and final bedroom that Rydell's luck ran out.

The room was dark – too dark. Gardener reached in and switched on a light, noticing blackout curtains. He saw a wooden floor with a stool in the middle. Nothing else.

Each of the walls were covered from top to bottom with newspaper clippings, photographs, magazine articles, and a potted history of the four victims: Nicola Stapleton, Barry Morrison, Alan Sargent, and Frank Fisher.

Gardener stepped inside, crept over to the far wall. His phone startled him.

It was the Irishman. "What the hell are you doing in there? Quick look, you said. Have you made yourself tea?"

"Keep your eyes and ears peeled, Sean. I'll be down shortly."

"Have you found something?"

"Enough to ask Briggs for a warrant."

Gardener disconnected and returned his attention to the clippings. Everything had been carefully plotted and detailed on the wall, from a layout of each scene of each crime, to an itinerary of each victim down to the very last detail.

19:00 hrs – Wait for Nicola Stapleton to leave her house, knock her unconscious. Take back inside, gag and tie her to a chair before leaving.
20:30 hrs – Enter the cabin where Morrison works, wearing a scene suit, with paper mask, boots, and gloves. Render Morrison unconscious with a stun gun, gag and tie him up.
20:45 hrs – Park Morrison's car in front of cabin, load him into it. Drive back to Stapleton's place.

22:00 hrs – drag Morrison inside her house so he can witness her brutal demise (bitch to rue the day she crossed me).

22:30 hrs – Load Barry Morrison back into his car. Drive to a safe location, inject Morrison with the sealing wax into vena-cava. Patiently wait while he dies – all the time explaining how uncomfortable it will be, and why I'm doing it.

04:00 hrs – Plant Morrison on doorstep of butcher's shop on Cross Bank Road, Batley before returning his taxi to the lot.

Gardener grew cold at how meticulously it had all been planned, down to the last detail. On another wall he saw the itinerary for Alan Sargent and Frank Fisher's murder. Rydell was extremely clinical, leaving absolutely nothing to chance.

But how could he have known exactly where everyone would be and at what time? People were given to changes of mind at the last minute.

What then?

Obviously they hadn't done. Rydell must have made a very close study of everyone involved to have been able to plan with such accuracy.

Gardener turned to the only wall he couldn't see from the doorway. It was covered with information on his father, including the court cases.

Gardener noticed letters written to his dead father, explaining in detail how he would avenge those who had treated them both so badly, with his plans outlined. More recent letters praised his success. In another, he thanked his father for everything he had done for him, and he hoped that he had done as much in return.

The final letter indicated it would not be long before the two of them met up again.

Another wall contained a tribute to the man they had been listening to at each crime scene, Nick Cave. A large poster advertised the *Murder Ballads* album, covering most of the wall, with a list of the tracks. Against four of them, Rydell had pencilled in the names of the victims and what each song represented about the scene.

Gardener then noticed one more person on the wall.

Five-year-old Chloe Summerby.

Her details chilled him to the bones. It was obvious that Chris Rydell had her. There was no mention of another five-year-old girl.

Still, a mystery remained.

Did he have them both?

And if he did, where were they?

Chapter Fifty-seven

Raymond Allen glanced at his watch: five o'clock.

He was now watching the front of the shop. He knew Vincent wasn't going anywhere, because he'd made a barricade outside the gate that served as a rear entrance to the shop. Some kind builder had left a dozen pallets at the back of another one of the shops.

No one had used the chemist in the time he had been watching. A few minutes previously, the two staff that had been working with John Oldham had left for the day. Late night opening was Thursday, so as far as he could tell, there should be no interruptions.

He glanced around once more. There were relatively few cars in Morrisons. The librarians were closing and locking the building. A walk up and down the block assured him that the rest of the shops were not doing much business, so it was now or never.

He quietly opened the front door to Oldham's chemist and slipped inside.

John Oldham finished his phone call and made his way behind the counter to the pharmacy at the back.

"Be with you in a minute," he said.

That would do nicely for Allen. He turned, switched the sign on the door to 'Closed', and easing the latch, ensured the door was locked. He then pulled the blind down.

He was wearing a thick leather jacket. From the inside he retrieved a long piece of wood that he had managed to prise from one of the pallets – the thickest and biggest he could find. It had to do the job. Also in one of his jacket pockets he had a coiled rope. He'd found that underneath a piece of the cardboard in the garage. He could hear Oldham pottering around, and he definitely knew the rattle of tablets when he heard it.

Allen slowly made his way behind the counter. He sneaked a peek around the corner and couldn't have been more pleased. Old man Oldham had his back to Allen, which allowed him to slip past the counter toward the steel door at the back of the premises. Though the door was closed, it would not pose a problem.

Oldham finished what he was doing and came back into the shop. "I'm so sorry about that," he said, seeing that the store was empty. "Must have gone," he said to himself.

Oldham turned and froze. The expression on the old man's face was priceless, as if he'd seen a ghost. Allen suspected he probably thought he had. The Pudsey Poisoner was probably the last person he thought he'd ever see again.

"Bye, bye, Mr Oldham," said Allen, raising the wood and cracking the old man straight across the face.

He had no time to shout out, simply dropped like a sack of shit, a bruise on his face rising instantly.

Allen wondered if he'd killed Oldham. He hoped he hadn't, because he wanted to have a lot more fun later on. For now, he needed him out of the way as quickly as possible.

Allen dropped the wood and leaned over the old chemist, checking for a pulse. It was weak, but it was there, and he was still breathing. Lifting Oldham by his arms, Allen dragged him back into the prescriptions bay where he found a chair.

Sweating, he pulled Oldham into the chair. The man had gained more than a few pounds since they had last met. Once positioned, he tied him tightly, glancing around for a gag. The most suitable thing he found was a roll of bandage, which he tied and sealed with surgical tape.

Oldham was going nowhere; now for the second part of the plan.

Allen slipped around to the rear security door and pushed it open. He glanced outwards and upwards, toward the fire escape. There was no sign of Vincent.

As he came back into the shop, he dashed over to the telephone and flicked through the contacts on speed dial. Vincent's number was tenth.

He put it on to speakerphone, scooting to the other side of the shop whilst it dialled. With a bit of luck, the distance would be enough to make his voice sound different, enough – hopefully – to fool Sherlock.

Vincent answered.

"Vincent, quick!"

"What's wrong?"

"Come down to the shop. Hurry up, please."

"John? Are you okay?"

Allen ran forward. "Quick, Vincent."

Before he gave Detective Baines the chance to answer, he picked up the phone, throwing it at the wall. The unit separated on impact, and the two halves bounced in different directions.

Allen ran to the back of the shop, down the small passage to the right of the security door. Within seconds he heard Vincent's door open, and the sound of footsteps on the fire escape. If that idiot wasn't careful, he was going to fall and break his neck, and that would really piss Allen off.

Vincent entered the chemist at warp speed, and Allen noticed the idle pig was still in his dressing gown. Vincent shouted for Oldham. Allen quietly followed.

"John, where are you?"

At that point, Vincent noticed the broken phone. He picked it up and turned very quickly.

The sight of Allen stopped him dead in his tracks.

"Hello, Vincent."

Chapter Fifty-eight

An air of excitement prevailed as the team marched into the incident room, despite the time pushing six o'clock in the evening.

The only officer Gardener could not see was Colin Sharp, but he'd be out somewhere, digging up further information that no one else had probably thought about.

Briggs, last in, closed the door behind him.

Gardener was pleased about what he, Reilly and Rawson had found, although it had to be kept under wraps for the time being. He had discussed everything he'd found inside Rydell's place with the two of them; each one agreed that from the evidence already accumulated, it was doubtful that Briggs would oppose a warrant for Rydell's arrest, or a search of the premises.

"Thanks for coming, lads. We have had significant developments over the course of the day, and I'm pleased to say I'm very confident that we have identified a suspect in connection with the murders of Nicola Stapleton, Barry Morrison, Alan Sargent, and Frank Fisher."

The buzz of hushed conversations circled the room.

"Anything on the missing girl?" asked Rawson.

"I wish I could say yes, but I have no proof that the suspect has her. The sooner we have him in custody, the sooner we can start interrogating him."

"Press on then, Stewart," said Briggs, glancing at his watch.

"Sean and I followed a lead on the clinic in Bond Street today, concerning the name Rydell, which had popped up more than once in the investigation.

"Patrick Edwards discovered evidence on the CCTV cameras of a motorbike with a weird shaped trailer in the vicinity of Kirkstall Abbey, between the hours of two and four o'clock on Monday morning. Seems it was the same trailer that the eyewitness had seen with a wheelchair, and possibly a foot, sticking out the bottom. Chris Rydell owns the bike.

"Rydell is also a patient of the clinic in Bond Street. His first visit was six months ago, where he was complaining to his GP of flu-like symptoms that wouldn't shift. He was referred to Bond Street, and was diagnosed as having hepatitis B, which has now developed into full-blown cirrhosis."

Gardener pointed to Nicola Stapleton's name and photograph on the ANACAPA chart. "The first connection starts here. She was employed by a group of his friends to show him a good time one night after he'd got drunk. According to her diary, he wasn't so drunk that she could earn her money without doing anything. Nicola Stapleton gave Chris Rydell hepatitis B."

"Is that the only connection?" Briggs asked.

"To her, yes."

Gardener continued unperturbed, pointing to Barry Morrison's name.

"Two years ago, Barry Morrison forced Chris Rydell off the road in Horsforth. It wasn't a serious incident and no one was hurt, but Rydell had a witness who confirmed the number plate. It was followed up and the car belonged to the taxi firm that the Morrisons run."

"Was Barry Morrison driving?" asked Frank Thornton.

"We reckon he was," said Reilly, "but his star witness, Sally Summerby, swore blind in court that she was in a taxi that night with Morrison, but they were miles away in Shipley."

"So which poor bastard copped for points on his licence?" asked Anderson.

"No one. They blamed it on a driver who was no longer with the company when it was investigated. He'd emigrated to New Zealand."

"So Morrison got off with it?"

"Yes."

"Why did Sally Summerby lie to the court and the police?" Briggs asked.

"Because Barry Morrison is Chloe's natural father."

Gardener realized it was news to his team.

"How the hell did that happen?"

"Long story," said Gardener. "But it involved a huge fare that she couldn't pay."

"Hell's teeth," said Benson. "I think I might change my vocation."

"Not if you end up dead, you won't."

"True," said Benson, laughing.

A knock on the door interrupted the proceedings. The desk sergeant pushed the door open and spoke to Gardener.

"Sir, we've had a ping on the ANPR system. Rydell's machine has been spotted around Guiseley."

"Good," said Gardener. "Get the local traffic division on to it. See if we can pick him up."

"Where did you go after the clinic?" Briggs asked Gardener.

"Rydell's home. Place was empty."

"Have you left an officer there?"

"No, but I'm coming to that."

Gardener pointed to Frank Fisher's name. "Frank Fisher worked for Sean Rydell, the builder, and Chris's father. He had an accident, which left him paralysed. Barry Morrison pressed him to sue for compensation. When it went to court, Alan Sargent testified that the place was unfit to work in, a health and safety deathtrap. Fisher won his case."

"How did Sargent know?" asked Rawson, even though it had all been explained to him outside Rydell's place.

"He did some work for the company."

"So, it's fair to assume that each of these people have crossed Rydell – or his father – and they've paid the price," said Briggs.

"So where does the book come in, that one about *Foul Deeds*?" asked Anderson.

"Not sure, yet," said Gardener. "There may be a very good reason inside the killer's head for using the scenes, or it may be something he's picked at random. We won't know until we've talked to him."

Gardener stared at Briggs. "I'd like a warrant tomorrow – or tonight, if it can be arranged – for his arrest, and also to search his premises." If only Gardener could have mentioned what he'd found inside Rydell's home.

"Shouldn't be a problem. I think we have enough on him for that. Are you absolutely sure that Rydell is your man?"

"I can't see it being anyone else."

"What about this Allen fella?"

"I appreciate he's still someone we need to find, but so far we haven't found any evidence that he actually knows any of the deceased. Seems to me that he's hell-bent on making Vincent's life a misery. Colin Sharp spoke to

Allen's parents earlier today. He cannot drive, and has never applied for or held a licence, which would make it difficult for him to do what's been done. He specializes in poisoning people."

"Okay Stewart, if you're sure. You've been doing this long enough now to follow your nose."

Gardener nodded.

"But what about the girl? Is there any evidence to link her to Rydell?"

"We haven't found any," said Gardener. "And something about that really bothers me. Sally Summerby is still alive. Rydell must know all about her lies in court, so why hasn't he killed her? Or did he feel that taking her daughter away from her would be a greater punishment?"

"It certainly would be," said Thornton. "But if that's the case, does he still intend to kill Chloe? You remember what it said in the book about another five-year-old behind the Municipal Buildings in Leeds."

Gardener glanced at the photo on the chart of the girl that Sally Summerby claimed was not her daughter. Who was she?

"I know this sounds awful," said Briggs, "but until we find the body of either Chloe Summerby, or another five-year-old, there is very little we can do."

Frustrated at the lack of evidence surrounding the girl, Gardener continued.

"I want to put some actions in place for you guys to follow up. Let's start with two officers behind the Municipal Buildings again tonight. We really can't afford to slip up on that one; the press would lynch us."

"Not to mention Joe Public," said Briggs.

Gardener nodded. "I'd like two officers at Rydell's place. He'll have to return at some point. When he does, I want him."

"You've ruled out Billy Morrison, I take it?" Briggs asked.

"Yes. He simply doesn't fit the profile."

"And what about this born-again Christian fella, Sally's husband?"

"Gareth? We interviewed him today. He claims he knows about the birth certificate, about Morrison being Chloe's father. Has done for some time. Seems he's done the Christian thing and turned a blind eye."

"And you believe him?"

"I don't have a lot of choice at the moment. Quite apart from the fact that he has alibis for each murder."

"Okay," said Briggs. "Just making absolutely sure. Because if we pull this bloke in and anything else happens while he's with us, the shit will hit the fan."

"Don't you think I know that, sir?" Gardener was itching to tell Briggs why he was so positive about Rydell. He mentally checked off the two actions he'd given the team, and he really couldn't think of anything else. Markers had been put on PNC and ANPR. The local traffic division all had details of what to watch out for.

"Other than that, I don't think there's a lot more we can do. If you can all make sure that everything you've so far uncovered has either gone into HOLMES, or will go in tonight, I'd greatly appreciate it."

As the team started checking their files, the desk sergeant reappeared again. "Sir, we've got a situation in Guiseley."

"We've caught him?"

"No. We got a phone call a couple of minutes back, from Vincent Baines."

"Here we go," said Reilly. "What the hell does he want?"

"Wherever he is, he's left the line open, and it looks like he's been attacked and threatened with his life. We've heard some of the conversation, but it's muffled. There's been talk of the recent murders and a definite threat made on his life. The phone masts all point to him being in Guiseley. So maybe he's at home."

Gardener glanced at Reilly. It didn't make sense. So far, he had not been able to link Chris Rydell with Vincent Baines.

But what if he was wrong?

The ANPR had already picked up Rydell's vehicle in the area. What if Vincent's blogs had caught the attention of Rydell, and he'd gone there to finish the man off?

"Do you want me to send a couple of officers round to Baines' place?" asked the desk sergeant.

Reilly nodded to Gardener. He knew that nod. The Irishman wanted to take it himself.

"No, it's okay. We'll go and have a look."

"Do you want some back up, Stewart?"

"Sean?"

"I doubt it. Knowing that silly bastard he'll have got drunk, rung the wrong number, and left his phone near a radio with some stupid detective series on."

Gardener glanced at Briggs. "We'll handle it. I'll call for back up if it's heavy."

"If you're sure."

"I'm sure. It's probably like Sean said. The rest of you, stay here and input the data you have into HOLMES."

Gardener and Reilly left the room and crossed the lobby, heading for the pool car in the car park. As they were leaving the building, Colin Sharp was walking in.

"Oh, sir."

"I'm sorry, Colin but we have to nip out."

Sharp was persuasive. "I've found something you might want to hear."

Gardener stopped and listened. Sharp was good, very good. If he thought it important, it would be.

"Go on."

"Chris Rydell. He had a younger sister, by the name of Samantha."

"Had?"

"She disappeared without trace... years ago, in the mid-nineties."

"Disappeared without trace?"

"According to what I've found out, which isn't much because I only came across the information half an hour ago. She was only five years old when she disappeared. She's never been seen since."

"Get in the car," said Gardener.

Chapter Fifty-nine

"See anything?"

Gardener shook his head. The shop windows were cluttered with displays of almost everything a chemist would have. The blind had been drawn down over the door.

Gardener glanced behind him: seven o'clock on a warm Tuesday evening. Morrisons was busy.

He stared up at the window above the shop, where he knew Vincent lived. It was closed, with no sign of life. He realized then that he didn't have a landline number for him.

"Let's go round the back," said Reilly.

"Colin, can you wait at the front of the shop?"

Sharp nodded, and the pair of them walked off towards the library.

It occurred to Gardener that he had not seen any mode of transport that resembled the machine Rydell owned.

"I just can't imagine we're going to find Rydell in here," said Gardener.

"Nor me. There's been nothing to link him with either the chemist or Vincent."

"The only person connected to either of these two is Raymond Allen, and to be perfectly honest, he must be long gone by now."

"If he was ever here in the first place."

The pair of them rounded the corner to an alley between the library and the end shop. Gardener glanced upwards, peering above the wall.

"It must be that one with the fire escape. Looks like the flat door at the top is open."

"Now would you look at that," said Reilly, "some kind soul has left a bunch of pallets outside this gate for us. Make things easier to climb over."

As they did so, Gardener noticed the back door of the chemist was ajar.

On the other side of the gate, a number of large wheeled bins stood to the right. Gardener lowered himself onto one, and then down to the ground.

Observing the yard, he was unhappy about the situation. The shop at the front was locked, but the rear entrance was open, as was the door to the flat above. Something was wrong. People were not known for leaving their doors open around there.

When Reilly was on the ground, Gardener quietly crept to the open door, listening intently. He couldn't hear anything.

"What do you think?" Gardener asked Reilly.

"Should we call for back up?"

"And say what?" responded Gardener. "We might save lives if we act in time."

"Or end our own."

Reilly smiled and said, "Fuck it! Let's go in."

Gardener nodded. He entered first. A clinical smell hung in the air. He saw a passage to his left, with a number of boxes stacked up. He passed a cupboard door on his right, ajar.

Gardener eased it open. It was full of stock – no people.

He moved further in, toward the front of the shop, aware that on his left he saw an opening leading to an upper level, where they made up prescriptions.

He glanced at Reilly, pointing upwards.

Gardener slipped quickly past the opening. Reilly immediately turned left and up the two small steps.

The Irishman shook his head.

Gardener continued into the shop.

The only two people in the place were tied to chairs. One was Vincent; he suspected the other to be the chemist himself, John Oldham. Vincent, for some reason, was still wearing a dressing gown. Oldham had a white smock on. Both appeared to be asleep.

Gardener ran forward, stared at both men. There was no movement.

Reilly checked the remainder of the shop, but it was obvious there was no one else home. He opened the front door and let Colin Sharp in.

Gardener felt both men for a pulse. It was weak, and their breathing was very shallow, but both were still alive. For how much longer, he wouldn't like to say.

"Sean, phone for an ambulance. Colin, can you call the station and request some additional support officers?"

To his right he noticed a countertop, which contained an empty brown bottle. He read the label: secobarbital. The name Samuel Birchall came to mind. The bottle stood on top of a copy of the book *Foul Deeds and Suspicious Deaths in Leeds*. Behind was a pair of disposable gloves.

Had Chris Rydell been here? Had they missed an obvious link?

Raymond Allen? That meant that Vincent *had* been on to something, and they had taken him for an idiot.

Gardener remembered one of the last things he'd said to Vincent: if anything happens to you, that's when we'll be called.

"On their way," said Sharp.

In the open doorway, an old couple had dropped by.

"Are we open, mate?"

"No, sorry, we have an emergency," said Gardener, closing the door.

He heard them grumble from the other side, but he had no idea what they'd said.

"Has Rydell been here, Sean?"

"Judging by the stuff on the counter, you'd say yes."

"Why haven't we found any evidence that links Rydell with Baines or the chemist?"

"Maybe we simply haven't come across it yet. Let's be honest, a lot's happened in four days. Had we been going two weeks, it might have been a different story."

Gardener's phone rang. He answered, found himself talking to the desk sergeant.

"Sir, we've had another ping on the ANPR system."

"Where?"

"Leeds Road, going towards Shipley."

"It's definitely Rydell?"

"One hundred percent."

He cut the connection and told Reilly.

"So it must be him. He's been here, finished these two off, and now he's going somewhere else."

"But why these two?" asked Gardener. "I can't imagine either of them were a threat to him."

The blaring sirens announced the arrival of the ambulance, which pulled up at one side of the shop. A squad car with four officers met them at the other.

Gardener went outside and addressed the medics. He asked his officers to wait whilst they removed the two victims. Time was obviously critical to saving their lives.

He thought about the ping on the ANPR. How could they have been so wrong? What vital evidence linking Rydell to Baines had they missed?

Maybe he could have saved two lives if he'd paid more attention.

"Colin, when you've finished here, can you organize these officers to do a search and a house-to-house?"

Sharp nodded.

"If Rydell has been here, where is he heading now?" he asked Reilly.

"That depends on what he has in store for the girl. It can't be the Municipal Buildings, he's going in the wrong direction."

"Unless he has her stored somewhere else."

He turned to Reilly. "What was Colin on about in the car? He said Rydell had a younger sister that had disappeared without trace."

"Why do I get the feeling that Gareth Summerby fits into this mess somewhere? What if Rydell recently found out what had happened to his sister, Summerby's involved, and that's set him off on a trail of justice?"

It hit Gardener like a sledgehammer.

"Bingo. There are two missing girls but one is a cold case. You reckoned there was something in his past that he was hiding. Samantha Rydell's disappearance must be connected to Gareth Summerby. Rydell's somehow found out and played him at his own game."

"An eye for an eye?" said Reilly. "Like the good book claims?"

"Get in the car."

Chapter Sixty

"In nature there are neither rewards nor punishments – there are consequences." Robert Greene Ingersoll, *Lectures and Essays.*

Reilly drove the pool car slowly down Main Street.

Tuesday, eight in the evening, the village was quiet. A middle-aged couple outside the pub were too busy drinking and talking to notice the police car. A couple of the older residents were watering hanging baskets in their front gardens.

Reilly slowly cruised to the end of the lane, parked up, and switched off the engine. Gardener opened the door and stepped out.

Glancing to his left, Gardener saw Rydell's motorbike and trailer contraption parked in front of the village hall. Peering at the Summerbys' house, he saw little sign of life, but there had to be something going on.

"I'm not sure what's happening in there, Sean, or even if anyone knows we're here, but I don't think we should announce our arrival by knocking on the front door."

"So let's walk round the back. Summer's night like this, quiet village, a lot of people are probably sitting in the back garden enjoying the weather with a drink. Wish I was."

"If it's any consolation, I doubt the Summerbys will be either, but at the very least we may find an open door."

Through the front gate the path took them past a well-maintained garden in full colour. Around the corner they saw that open back door they'd hoped for.

Gardener stopped, listened. He couldn't hear anything: no TV, no music playing, nor any voices, which he found disconcerting. Something to give them a fighting chance would have been preferable.

"I don't like it, Sean. It's too quiet."

"Doesn't mean they're not in there. Rydell might have them hostage upstairs."

"Which means he will have had his eye on the window, so he already knows we're here."

"Now it's a question of what he's using to hold them hostage."

"Not known for firearms, is he?"

"No," replied Reilly. "But he's nothing if not unpredictable."

"I should have read that *Foul Deeds* book cover to cover. Might have helped us with this situation."

"Standing around here talking won't. Let's go and see what's happening."

Gardener entered an old-fashioned style kitchen. Wooden shelves on each wall contained jars: tea, sugar, coffee, and flour, to name but a few. A small table and three chairs were positioned along one wall, and a full spice rack on another. A number of country kitchen prints hung around the room.

"You'll have to speak at some point," said the voice. Gardener recognized it as Gareth Summerby's.

"For God's sake, tell us why you've done this," shouted Sally. "Why have you kidnapped my daughter?"

"*He* knows why I've kidnapped *your* daughter." The last one was a voice they didn't recognize, so it could only be Rydell.

"Why would I know?" asked Summerby.

Gardener decided there were only three people in the room, and no one had pressed the panic button yet. He nodded to Reilly, and the pair edged forward toward the living room.

Gareth Summerby came into view, and the last thing either detective expected to see was a double barrel shotgun, pointing straight at them.

"Come in," he said. "We've been waiting for you. Or should I say, he has."

They had no choice. Though Summerby should have been controlling the show, Gardener didn't think he was.

"Take your phones out of your pockets and throw them in the middle of the room."

Summerby was tucked into the corner of the room, which gave him a bird's-eye view of everything. His wife was standing against the wall, next to the door through which they had entered.

"What the hell are you doing, Gareth? The police are here. They've come to help, and you're holding them at gunpoint?"

"Fat lot of use they've been so far. They've blamed both of us for the killing spree. Treat us like criminals, and it's our daughter that's missing."

Interesting, thought Gardener. *He's using the term 'our' daughter.*

"We have not blamed either of you, Mr Summerby. We were trying to eliminate you from our inquiries."

"So you say. Well, I'm the one in charge now. Not you two. I've got the gun, so we'll do things my way."

"Going back to our youth, are we, son?"

"What's that supposed to mean?"

"You know very well what I'm talking about," challenged Reilly. "You born-again Christians are all alike. You've done something terrible in your life, and suddenly you wake up one day wanting to confess everything to God, hoping he'll forgive you so you can set the record straight and start again. What a crock of shit, son. You will never cleanse your soul as long as you have a hole in your arse. You know it and I know it, so why don't you put that fucking gun down and let us sort this mess out?"

You could always count on the Irishman to speak his mind, despite being at a disadvantage, thought Gardener.

"You don't know what you're talking about."

"I think he does," said Rydell.

Gardener glanced at Rydell. He was early twenties, with black hair in a short back and side fashion. He was very slim, dressed in jeans and a leather jacket with leather boots. His complexion, however, told Gardener he was far from healthy. But they all knew that.

"You know something we don't?" Reilly asked Rydell.

"I know a lot you don't."

Rydell remained seated, as if he didn't have a care in the world. *But then, why would he?* thought Gardener. *He was dying. That's what his medical files had indicated.*

"I suspect you're here because you already know I'm responsible for the double murders over the last four days."

"That much we'd worked out," replied Gardener. "We know about Stapleton, Morrison, Sargent, and Fisher. And we're pretty sure we know why you did that. All of those people crossed you in some form or other."

"Me and my father," said Rydell. "He was a good man. He didn't deserve what happened."

"A lot of good men don't deserve what happens, son," said Reilly. "But there are ways and means of doing things, and there are laws to protect and help people."

"He's right," said Gardener. "You simply can't take the law into your own hands. I know what they did was wrong, but why poison Vincent Baines and the chemist?"

"Poison them?" repeated Rydell. "If they've been poisoned, it had nothing to do with me. My mission didn't include those two. It brought me here to finish what I'd started. Had my illness not been terminal, the outcome may have been different."

For some reason, Gardener believed Rydell. If he said he wasn't responsible for the poisoning of Vincent and the chemist, it had to have been Raymond Allen.

"What?" said Sally Summerby. "You're dying, so you get back at the people who have wronged you? What has my daughter ever done to you?"

"Nothing," said Rydell.

"Then why take her?"

"Like I've said, he knows why." Rydell pointed to Summerby. All eyes went in his direction.

He raised the gun. "Don't you dare blame this on me!"

"Calm down, son. Don't be too hasty."

"He's blaming all this shit on me," shouted Summerby, staring at Reilly. He aimed the gun back at Rydell. "I've never met him before, and I have no idea who he is, and he's trying to tell me it's all my fault."

"You're right," said Rydell. "You haven't met me... until today. But you have met my sister."

Chapter Sixty-one

Time stood still. The whole room became a vacuum, the atmosphere having been sucked out with that one statement.

Gardener glanced at Rydell. His expression was deadly serious.

"What's he talking about, Gareth?" said Sally.

"I've no idea."

Gardener could see that he had. The man was shaking, and the detective was worried that he still held the gun.

"Well, well, well," said Reilly. "Are we finally getting to the truth about you, now?"

"Shut your mouth, Irishman, before I silence you all."

"I doubt that, son," said Reilly. "We're all in different parts of the room, you'll never get all of us."

"So long as I get *him*, that's all that matters to me," said Summerby, levelling the gun at Rydell.

"Do that, and you'll never find *her* daughter."

"What the hell's been going on, Gareth?" demanded Sally. "I want to know. I swear to God if you've put my daughter's life at risk, I'll kill you."

They were all at it now, thought Gardener. It was definitely Sally's daughter.

"I thought as much," said Reilly. "What have you been up to that you want keeping a secret?"

"You're a fine one to talk." Summerby aimed the comment at Sally. "You're as much to blame for this as I am. Sleeping around with your taxi driver friend."

"How dare you?" shouted Sally. She took a couple of steps forward, and Summerby stopped her dead as he swung the gun from Rydell to her.

"Take one more step and so help me God, I'll put you in the ground first."

"Don't tell me the big man's deserted you already," said Reilly, glancing at Gardener. "What did I tell you?"

"Shut it." The gun was now pointing at Reilly.

"Come on, Gareth," said Rydell, "tell us all about the night my sister Samantha went missing."

"I don't know anything about your sister!" shouted Summerby, the gun back on Rydell.

Gardener spotted the lie. Summerby's world was falling apart before his eyes. His God certainly couldn't help him now – or any of them, if he didn't manage to diffuse the situation.

"In that case, I'll finish what I started," said Rydell. He glanced at Gardener. "You want the truth, I'll tell you it. When it's all over, I'll walk peacefully out of here to your car, and you can do what you like with me."

"I wouldn't bank on it," threatened Summerby.

Gardener glanced at him. "Put the gun down. The story is going to come out regardless. There's nothing you can do to stop it."

Summerby said nothing.

Rydell continued. "When I was eight years old, my father found me a job in a filling station. The garage belonged to a friend of his. I stayed there for three years, eventually working in the shop, checking stock, taking deliveries. They even let me work on the pumps now and again. My world imploded when I was eleven.

"I was left alone for fifteen minutes one night, whilst that garage owner cashed up and put the takings in the safe, ready for the bank the following morning. Samantha, my younger sister, was with me." Chris smiled as he relived the moment, tears in his eyes.

"She thought she was helping. She was eating chocolate, mostly. All she was interested in was an old camera that my dad's friend Patrick had given her the previous week. She took it everywhere with her, fascinated by the fact that it could produce pictures that slid out of the bottom.

"There were no customers in the shop, and we hadn't seen anyone for over an hour. It was close to Christmas. The weather was dismal, foggy, cold. My mum and dad were out Christmas shopping. They were coming to get us before the garage closed."

Rydell stopped, as if it was too hard to continue, but Gardener sensed it wasn't that. The man was clearly in pain. He leaned forward and held his stomach, but before anyone could ask him anything, he continued.

"I only went to the toilet. I left Sam alone for five minutes – with her camera. Me and Patrick came back into the shop to find an open front door, an empty cash till, and no Samantha. Oh, and a pump that had delivered what was probably a full tank of fuel for someone.

"I was beside myself. Patrick was panicking. We looked all over the place, outside, around the garage, into the outbuildings. We searched everywhere, every nook and cranny that she might have crept into. But we couldn't find her.

"At the time, we lived in a small hamlet called Jack Hill. The filling station was on the road between Jack Hill and Farnley, a lonely stretch of road that caught traffic returning mostly from Harrogate and Keighley back into Leeds.

"CCTV cameras were in their infancy. The garage didn't have any. There was no one around we could ask. The only conclusion we could make was that Samantha had noticed a car, and instead of shouting for us, she had been her usual friendly self and gone out to talk to the customer."

Once again he lurched forward to the edge of the seat.

"Are you okay?" asked Sally Summerby.

"Leave him," said Summerby. "Let him rot in hell."

"How Christian," commented Reilly.

Sally Summerby glared at her husband with an intense hatred. "What the hell does all this have to do with you?"

"Whatever it is, we want to hear it," said Gardener.

Despite his discomfort, Rydell continued. "My parents suddenly drove in. Fraught with worry, the police were immediately called. House-to-house inquiries revealed nothing. Flyers and posters were all over the place, *Crimewatch* were involved.

"The story went national, but still nothing came to light. It was as if Samantha had simply opened the door, walked out, and was never seen again. Her body was never found. The driver was never caught.

"I never gave up hope of finding Samantha. This is the last picture ever taken of her, the day before she went missing."

Rydell withdrew the photo from his pocket and threw it over to the detectives. They'd seen it twice already.

Sally Summerby stole a glance. "Oh my God. She's the image of my Chloe. That's the girl you thought was my daughter."

She turned to Rydell. "You haven't said how you know this involves him." She pointed at her husband, though she did not glance his way.

"By accident, really. Isn't that the way of things?"

"What do you mean?' said Sally, still staring at the photograph. Then she begged him. "Please say that my daughter is still alive. Please tell me you haven't done anything to her."

Rydell continued as if he hadn't heard her. "I found out about your husband when I was subcontracted to make a delivery to your house about two months ago. There was no one home. A note on the door informed me to leave the parcel in the shed round the back. I checked, but I wasn't happy. It wasn't safe enough.

"As I was leaving, I walked into a box, knocked it to the floor. Imagine my horror when I found myself staring at a camera. Not only that, but probably the last photo Sam had ever taken, all those years ago."

The atmosphere in the room was electric. No one had any choice but to hear the story out.

Gardener glanced at Summerby. His eyes were glazed over. As the story progressed he would probably be less of a threat, but Gardener would still have to find a way to grab the gun and make the situation safe again.

Rydell stared hard at Summerby. "You were very young, but still recognizable. I knew the camera immediately because it had a scratch on the back."

"Don't be stupid," said Summerby. "It could have been any old camera. It was bound to have scratches on if it was that old."

"So where did *you* get it?" Sally asked her husband.

"It was hers," replied Rydell. "I know because I had to look at it every day for a week. The scratch meant that the door was out of alignment and difficult to open. It couldn't have been anyone else's. I knew I had to find out the truth, make you pay. I also decided then that four other people who had crossed me were going to pay as well. I was sick to death of people treating me and my family like shit. What did I have to lose?

"I reckoned the only thing I could do was to adopt a very Christian attitude where you were concerned. An eye for an eye, and all that. I'm sure you'll understand that. I studied you all very closely, and when the opportunity arose, I took Chloe."

Rydell started coughing, and Gardener noticed he was scratching himself a lot. But still he continued. The young man was determined to tell his story.

"I wanted you to suffer so much for what you had done to my family. You destroyed us. I wanted to systematically destroy you, to make you feel for just one second what it was like to lose the most precious thing in your life."

Sally Summerby fell to her knees, weeping openly, staring at Rydell – the photo still in her hand. "Please tell me where my daughter is… please."

Rydell glanced at Sally. "Before I tell you where your daughter is" – he turned to her husband – "maybe you can tell me where my sister is."

Chapter Sixty-two

Gareth Summerby wept openly. Gardener sensed it was the moment he had needed for most of his life. His explanation would be the real cleansing of his soul. Pity it had taken such evasive action.

He then did something totally unexpected, as far as Gardener was concerned. He lowered the gun and stood it to one side, although still close enough should he need it.

"I'm so sorry," said Summerby.

"Gareth?" called Sally. "Is he telling the truth? Did you really have something to do with the disappearance of his sister?"

He brought his hands to his face, as if to hide his shame. "It all got out of hand. I never meant for anything to happen."

"So, what did?" demanded Rydell. He'd slid from the chair to his knees, clearly in pain.

"It was a joyride, a prank that went wrong," said Summerby. "I was a teenager–"

Sally cut him off. "Being a teenager was no excuse for what you've done."

"Hear me out, Sal, please."

She was about to have another go when Gardener raised his hand and stopped her.

Summerby continued, gripping the chair in front of him for support, tears still freely running down his face.

"I'd stolen the car from the ASDA car park in Pudsey, me and Mickey Cross. The store was open late for Christmas shopping. I was well known by local gangs, but I had no record. I'd never been caught.

"We'd been drinking when we pulled into the filling station. We filled up the tank but never really had any intention of paying... till I noticed no one about inside. Mickey wanted fags, and I thought I'd empty the cash register. There wasn't much, probably only the float, but it would do – especially as we had cigs and a full tank of petrol."

Gardener glanced at Rydell, hoping he would make it to the end of the confession. The man needed a hospital, and fast. He decided to risk asking, "Mr Summerby? Can I have my phone? This man is seriously ill."

"No," he replied. "He wanted the story, and he can damn well hear it. He can hear my confession."

"We'd rather have it on tape," said Reilly.

"Not going to happen. This is your only chance."

Rydell nodded to Gardener: let the man continue.

"I was suddenly bathed in light. Made me jump. I had no idea what had caused it. A little girl had appeared from nowhere, taken a photo."

He brought his hands to his face again. "Christ, if I could turn back time–"

"You can't," shouted Rydell. "Never mind all that now, I want to know what you did."

"So do I," said Sally, clearly disgusted.

"Go on," shouted Rydell. "What did you do?"

"I grabbed her and folded her in my arms. Keeping her trussed up with one hand around her mouth, I quickly bundled her and the camera into the car. Took off as fast as we could.

"There was a lot of arguing going on with Mickey. The girl wasn't part of the plan. He was shitting himself. So was I. You have to understand, it wasn't planned."

"I don't care," shouted Rydell, trying to raise himself to his feet, using the chair as a crutch. "Now get on with it, or so help your God, my God, and every other fucker's God, I will kill you."

"Not before I do," said Sally Summerby. "If I don't get my daughter back, there isn't a prison in this land that will keep you safe."

Summerby continued, as asked. "We kept driving, really fast, panicking about what we were going to do with our passenger."

"Couldn't you just take her back?" shouted Reilly. "All you'd done was stolen a car."

"And do time?"

"First offence, son. You'd have gotten away with it."

"I didn't know that, did I?"

"So, what happened?" Rydell reminded him. "Tell me what happened to my sister."

"We finished up at Holme Wood. Took the bend far too fast, rolled the car down an embankment. The car flipped, I don't know how many times. All the windows were smashed. None of us wore a seat belt. I think we were all thrown clear."

"You mean you don't know?" Rydell asked.

"No. When I woke up, I found Samantha–"

"Found?" shouted Rydell, now using the wall for support, having inched a little further forward. "Alive?"

It was some time before Summerby answered. "No."

Rydell was in tears.

"I panicked. I wandered around for half an hour, wondering what to do."

"So come on, don't stop there. What did you do? She hasn't been seen since."

Summerby stared at each of them in turn. "I came across a disused mineshaft. It seemed like the only answer to the problem."

The impact of that statement silenced everyone.

"You didn't?" whispered Sally.

"I didn't know what else to do, Sal. I was fourteen. What was I supposed to have done? I'd killed two people."

"You were supposed to have owned up. I thought you were a born-again Christian."

"Not then."

"Whatever you were, you were not supposed to dump an innocent girl's body down a mineshaft and leave her family distraught for the rest of their lives. What kind of a monster are you?"

"Carry on, son," said Reilly. "What did you do next?"

"After I'd disposed of the body, I set fire to the car."

"Jesus Christ," said Reilly, turning to face the wall. "It started out simple, probably a bet. 'I dare you to pinch a car'." He faced Summerby. "If you'd taken it back, all of this could have been avoided. Instead, it ends in sheer carnage."

"How have you managed to live with that on your conscience, Mr Summerby?" asked Gardener.

"I don't know," he cried. "But it was the one thing that made me stop and think about my life. I finally ended up in a confessional at the local church. That life-changing moment made me realize I was on the road to nowhere, and that if I didn't change, there would be nothing but problems ahead."

"I've got news for you, son, there still is."

Chris Rydell suddenly made the most awful keening sound that Gardener had ever heard. He dropped to his knees and suddenly vomited blood – lots of it. The red liquid splashed all over the carpet, up the wall, even on the curtains.

Summerby pushed the chair out of his way and raced forward to help him. He cradled Rydell in his arms and screamed how sorry he was, begging forgiveness. Sally Summerby picked up both mobile phones and gave them to Gardener.

"For God's sake, call an ambulance. He's going to die."

Reilly knelt down in front of her, Rydell, and Summerby. "Get yourself out of the way, son. I think you've done enough damage."

Whilst on the phone, Gardener pulled Summerby further back. "Stand back, will you?"

He finished his call and knelt down to help his partner. "It's okay, Mr Rydell, the ambulance is on its way."

He'd stopped vomiting blood and was now sitting with his arms around his knees, rocking backwards and forwards, shaking, repeating one word: "Samantha."

A gunshot suddenly reverberated around the small room. Gardener ducked and threw himself to one side. Reilly shielded Rydell.

Gardener glanced around to where the gun had been. Sally Summerby held it close to her chest, her finger still around the trigger.

"An eye for an eye, isn't that what the good book says? Live by the sword, die by the sword. Choose any one you like, that bastard had it coming."

She was staring at her dead husband.

Chapter Sixty-three

Gardener lurched forward and carefully removed the gun from Sally Summerby's grip. He checked to see if it was still loaded, emptied the remaining shell, and threw it on to the floor.

"You just shot your husband," said Gardener. "What the hell were you thinking?"

"He deserved it," said Sally.

Gardener knew from the expression in her eyes that she meant it.

"He killed an innocent five-year-old girl. He put my daughter's life at risk. He deserved to be punished."

"Maybe," replied Gardener. "But his punishment would have been up to the courts to decide."

"Oh, right," she said. "He'd go to prison for three years and be out in one for good behaviour. He'd probably study law while he was in there and come out a fully qualified solicitor. Some sentence that would be. Three square meals a day, gym, sauna, pool table..."

Reilly had left Rydell and was now checking Summerby. He stood up and shook his head: too late.

Summerby had a huge hole in his chest, and the wall he was sitting against had a trail of blood and intestines running down it.

Gardener couldn't believe what had happened. He thought, at worst, he would be walking into a hostage situation, and someone might have been injured.

He turned to Sally Summerby. "Whatever you think about the system, you have no right to take the law into your own hands. *You* could go to prison for this."

"What does it matter? My daughter's dead."

"We don't know that. It hasn't been established. All we know at the moment is she's missing."

She suddenly went and sat by Rydell, her left arm around his shoulder. "I'm so sorry for what happened to you and your family, but please, you have to tell me where you have my daughter." She had tears in her eyes.

Rydell was still rocking, in shock. He glanced up at Sally Summerby.

Through his tears he said, "I never gave up, you know. I never stopped looking for her."

Her expression softened. "I know what you're going through, but you don't want the same to happen to me and Chloe, do you?"

"She meant the world to me," he said. "All these years, I've never given up hope."

Rydell glanced at Summerby's lifeless body. "And all this time, he knew."

The sound of sirens diverted their attention.

Gardener opened the front door as the ambulance drew level. The medics jumped out. A second ambulance pulled up behind, parking on the area in front of the village hall, close to Rydell's contraption.

"In here."

One of them went back outside, returning quickly.

"Grab the chair and a stretcher. We'll need a body bag as well."

Three more police cars sped down the main street, coming to a halt at one side of the first ambulance, careful not to block it in.

The peaceful summer evening had suddenly come alive. Half the village was out of their front doors, spectating. Further down the street, people were standing outside the pub. Most had had the forethought to carry their drink with them.

Briggs approached. "What's happened?"

"Well, we certainly have our man," said Gardener.

"Rydell?"

"And Gareth Summerby," offered Reilly.

"What? They were working together?"

"It's a long story," said Gardener.

"I'd still like to hear it."

315

"You will."

The first set of medics brought Rydell out. He was wrapped in a blanket, strapped to a wheelchair. They rolled him toward the ambulance.

Sally Summerby was frantic, pleading. "Please Chris, please tell me where you have Chloe."

"You mean we still don't know where she is?" Briggs asked.

Gardener ran over to the ambulance, stopped the medics from putting Rydell inside.

"Come on, Mr Rydell. I know you've suffered, probably more than anyone else I know, but please don't make Mrs Summerby face the same fate."

Rydell coughed, a nerve-racking jolt that must have caused intense pain.

"We have to get him to a hospital, sir," said the medic.

"Please, Chris," begged Sally. "I have to know. If you haven't killed her, please don't leave her to die. She's only five years old. She needs me. She's the innocent one in all of this."

"Come on," said Gardener. "Do the right thing and tell her."

Rydell smiled at Gardener.

He then turned and glanced at his motorbike and trailer… and waved.

Sitting inside, waving back, smiling, clutching the one-armed doll, was five-year-old Chloe Summerby.

Epilogue

Friday 26th August

Three days later, Gardener and Reilly were in Holme Wood with a forensic team.

It had all started here eighteen years ago. Who would have believed so much carnage could have been caused by a simple act of stupidity? That simply stealing a car could have caused so much anguish?

Nicola Stapleton, Barry Morrison, Alan Sargent, and Frank Fisher had all died, but were not directly connected to the missing girl. Vincent Baines and John Oldham had died from secobarbital poisoning, but they weren't directly connected either. Gareth Summerby had been blown away; he'd started it, deserved to be punished, but the end was too soon.

Reilly walked up to Gardener. "We've found her."

He simply nodded and glanced up at the sky.

He'd received a call four hours ago to say Chris Rydell had also died. Despite everything he had done, Gardener figured he had suffered more than any of them.

So he'd made a promise to him in the hospital.

He would find Samantha Rydell's remains and make sure they were buried with her brother.

The Yorkshire Press

Friday 26th August

Pudsey Poisoner returns: "old scores settled?"

Three weeks after the Pudsey Poisoner had absconded from the Rampton high security psychiatric hospital in

Nottingham, Raymond Allen casually walked
through the gates and gave himself up.
Following a briefing, the governor of the prison
Malcolm Warner gave a short press release.
When asked what Allen had been up to for three
weeks, he simply replied:
"I had to finish something I'd started."

Acknowledgements

I am always in debt to a number of people when I take up the challenge of a new book – no author writes alone. I would like to thank Iain Ross for many things, and certainly for looking after my website. Andrew Gardener, the author of a number of crime novels, has a keen eye for detail and always keeps me on the right track. Darrin Knight, my real-life Gardener, chases criminals for a living; fortunately for him, none of them are as bad as the ones I write about, but his knowledge of policing is invaluable to me. Bob Armitage is a chemist whose patience for helping me out seems limitless, especially with the kind of things I throw at him. David Johnson, my friend, and personal editor, sorts out my books even before my publisher sees them. And thanks to Peter James, fellow author and friend, who writes novels to such a high standard that it's almost impossible to keep the pace. On a more personal level, Peter has offered so much help and support to me that I am eternally grateful. It's an honour to have such a close friend. Also, huge thanks go to The Book Folks for taking a chance on me.

If you enjoyed this book, please let others know by leaving a quick review on Amazon. Also, if you spot anything untoward in the paperback, get in touch. We strive for the best quality and appreciate reader feedback.

editor@thebookfolks.com

www.thebookfolks.com

BOOK 1 IN THE DI GARDENER CRIME FICTION SERIES

IMPURITY

A thrilling murder mystery full of devilish twists

RAY CLARK

IMPURITY

Book 1 in the DI Gardener crime fiction series

Someone is out for revenge. A grotto worker is murdered in the lead up to Christmas. He won't be the first. Can DI Gardener stop the killer, or is he saving his biggest gift till last?

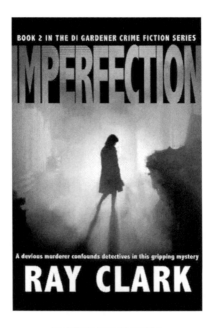

BOOK 2 IN THE DI GARDENER CRIME FICTION SERIES

IMPERFECTION

A devious murderer confounds detectives in this gripping mystery

RAY CLARK

IMPERFECTION

Book 2 in the DI Gardener crime fiction series

When theatre-goers are treated to the gruesome spectacle
of an actor's lifeless body hanging on the stage, DI Stewart
Gardener is called in to investigate. Is the killer still in the
audience? A lockdown is set in motion but it is soon
apparent that the murderer is able to come and go
unnoticed. Identifying and capturing the culprit will mean
establishing the motive for their crimes, but perhaps not
before more victims meet their fate.

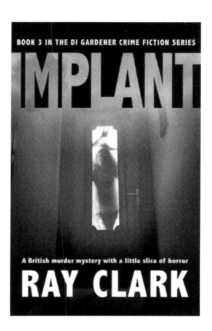

IMPLANT

Book 3 in the DI Gardener crime fiction series

A small Yorkshire town is beset by a series of cruel
murders. The victims are tortured in bizarre ways. The
killer leaves a message with each crime – a playing card
from an obscure board game. DI Gardener launches a
manhunt but it will only be by figuring out the murderer's
motive that they can bring him to justice.

Printed in Great Britain
by Amazon